Praise for *Trial Run*

"*Trial Run* is a fast-paced, mind-bending thriller that has readers questioning everything and anxiously awaiting the next twist."

—RT Book Reviews

"Davis Bunn fans will love his writing as Thomas Locke, delivering this psychological page-turning thriller that you won't be able to put down."

—CBA Retailers + Resources

"This book is a true psychological thriller that cannot be put down once the story begins to unfold."

—Suspense Magazine

"A fast-paced, constantly unfolding mystery with well-developed characters, *Trial Run* promises to begin a strong new series that manages to transcend the bounds of science fiction writing."

—Manhattan Book Review

"*Trial Run* is wonderfully told: a swift, engaging story that shows a large understanding of the human condition, our essential frailty, our drivenness, our need for connection. This is artful writing, full of suspense."

—Jay Parini, *New York Times* bestselling author of *The Last Station*

"A thrilling cocktail of science, technology, and danger elegantly served at breakneck speed. Intoxicating and se̶   ̶ ̶ ̶ddictive as only Thomas Locke can deliver."

—**Tosca Lee**, *New York Time̶*

Books by Thomas Locke

LEGENDS OF THE REALM

Emissary
Merchant of Alyss

FAULT LINES

Fault Lines
Trial Run
Flash Point

RECRUITS

Recruits

FAULT LINES

THOMAS LOCKE

Revell

a division of Baker Publishing Group
Grand Rapids, Michigan

Published by Revell
a division of Baker Publishing Group
P.O. Box 6287, Grand Rapids, MI 49516-6287
www.revellbooks.com

Printed in the United States of America

Library of Congress Cataloging-in-Publication Data
Names: Locke, Thomas, 1952– author.
Title: Fault lines / Thomas Locke.
Description: Grand Rapids, MI : Revell, [2017]
Identifiers: LCCN 2017005876| ISBN 9780800724375 (pbk.) | ISBN 9780800724382 (print on demand)
Subjects: | GSAFD: Christian fiction. | Suspense fiction.
Classification: LCC PS3552.U4718 F38 2017 | DDC 813/.54—dc23
LC record available at https://lccn.loc.gov/2017005876

17 18 19 20 21 22 23   7 6 5 4 3 2 1

In keeping with biblical principles of creation stewardship, Baker Publishing Group advocates the responsible use of our natural resources. As a member of the Green Press Initiative, our company uses recycled paper when possible. The text paper of this book is composed in part of post-consumer waste.

BOOK 1

1

The Satellite Beach community center was not the sort of place to require an armed agent guarding the coffee machine. It was located in a former auto supply warehouse. The four bay doors had been replaced by walls of glass. The view was over a parking lot, a lawn shared with the neighboring church, and the inland waterway. That Monday evening the setting sun turned the bay into a burnished copper shield.

Charlie Hazard stood in what had become his normal station, midway between the coffeemaker and the jukebox. His job was to make sure the local surfers didn't totally freak out the old-timers. There were nights when he would have rather faced incoming fire.

The center was situated three blocks from the home he had inherited from his father. Charlie had been dropping by a couple of nights each week for nineteen months and he still didn't know why. He went off on a job, got it done, came home, and a night or so later he was back. The place suited him. It was safe. Charlie liked safe. And sane.

A lot of his life away from this place wasn't either. Lately he found himself looking forward to coming back. He was comfortable with little triumphs these days—another day staying clean, another night without sweats and fever dreams.

Julio, a Hispanic kid in his late teens, hit the button on the music machine. Immediately the place was invaded by rap. Julio was a local surfer, tall and handsome despite his baggy jeans and prison tats. Charlie had every reason to dislike him and his attitude. But something about Julio hit him at gut level. What was more, Charlie's best friend here was the youth counselor, a retired Orlando detective named Irma Steeg. Irma had a definite soft spot for the kid. So Charlie kept his voice mild as he waved Julio over and said, "Think maybe you could hold off for another hour?"

Julio gave him attitude. "What's your problem, man?"

"See the old people over there by the windows? Forty-five minutes, they'll leave for their nightly meds. Then you can play the track that sounds like a bad day in Baghdad."

Irma settled a hand on Julio's arm, halting his comeback. She asked, "How about something from Ol' Blue Eyes?"

Charlie walked over to the machine and ditched the rap. To the groans of everybody under twenty, Frank Sinatra and his horn section asked Charlie to fly him to the moon.

As Charlie returned to the coffee bar, Irma gave Julio her number-one smile. "Everybody likes Sinatra, right?"

Charlie knew Julio wanted to tell Irma exactly where she could put Sinatra and his entire big band. But Julio had enough street sense to notice the steel behind Irma's smile.

He told the departing kid, "One hour, tops. Then the place is yours."

"Whatever, man. Make yourself some oatmeal, why don't you. Easier to chew, you don't got no teeth."

Charlie said to Irma, "Remind me why you put up with that lip."

"Julio has nothing and nobody. I always had a thing for strays." Irma offered him the same soft-hard smile. "As you should know."

He skipped his retort because an unfamiliar woman chose that moment to walk through the door. When her smile lit up the room, even the kids gave this new arrival thirty seconds of silence.

The strange thing was, the beautiful woman was not actually smiling at anyone or anything in particular. She seemed genuinely ecstatic to simply be here. In a former auto supply warehouse.

Maybe she had a thing for Sinatra.

Then she spotted Charlie, and the smile grew larger still.

Irma said, "Have you been holding back on me, sport?"

Charlie tensed as the woman headed straight for him.

"Apparently so," Irma said.

Charlie guessed the woman's age at early thirties. She had almond eyes tilted at an impossible angle. Dark hair. A body that couldn't be masked by her tan skirt and jacket.

Charlie knew what the woman saw as she approached his end of the counter. His late wife had described him as an old soul trapped in an underwear model's body. Dark hair trimmed short. A single scar that rose from his collar to just below his left ear. Strong features. Watchful grey eyes.

The woman stopped at the counter, stared at him for what seemed like a good year or so, then asked, "Is there somewhere we could have a private word?"

Her accent could only be described as seductive.

Irma slipped from her stool. "I was just leaving." From behind the woman's back she mouthed to Charlie a silent, *Eeeooowwww.*

Charlie asked, "You're here looking for me?"

"I think so."

"You think."

"Yes." She had lips like bruised grapes. Cheekbones from some forgotten tribe. She did not speak so much as gradually tasted each word. "Are you a policeman?"

"Sorry, no."

Her look of defeat was a potent force. "What do you do, please?"

"Where are you from?"

"Italy. Milan. But I live here now."

"Can I ask your name?"

"Gabriella." She smiled. "I should have introduced myself. For-give me."

"No problem." For another smile like that, Charlie would have climbed on the roof and howled at the moon.

"You see, I am very nervous. Please, can you tell me what you do now?"

"I'm afraid that's confidential."

She pressed against the counter. "Your work, is it protection?"

He hesitated, then said, "We call it risk containment."

Her pleasure at his response was as intense as her plea. "Will you come with me?"

"What, now?"

"It is very urgent."

He was out the door and into the fading dusk before it occurred to him. "Do you even know my name?"

"It doesn't matter." She beeped open the door to a brand-new Range Rover, then added, "Yet."

Gabriella took the coastal route south. She gave the road an intense focus. Cape Kennedy's rush hour was over, and traffic was light. In the high season, license plates along the coastal highway were from all over the country. Driving along A1A was like traveling through congealed grits. But this was May, and most of the snowbirds had retreated with the last northern freeze. Even so, Gabriella drove with a two-fisted grip on the wheel and watched the road with unblinking concentration. Charlie suspected it was her way of avoiding a conversation.

Like most guys who had known combat, Charlie had a well-developed awareness for trouble. Surviving the front line meant cul-tivating a second set of eyes, the kind that looked beyond what was visible to civilian senses. He had learned to trust this ability when entering new terrain. Afterward, when the cordite burned the throat and the muscles jerked with the drain-off of adrenaline rush, Charlie saw precisely what had given him that first life-saving alarm.

But when he used that extra sense now and tasted the air, he found no danger whatsoever. So he turned toward the sunset-drenched window and put his memory into rewind. He walked back through what had happened since the woman's appearance in the community center. Taking it slow. Doing what he had been trained to do. What he was best at.

He said, "You were excited the minute you came in."

"Please?"

"You walked in and lit up the room with your smile. Like you had already found exactly what you had been looking for. Even before you spotted me."

Gabriella glanced over but said nothing.

"What, you were supplied with a photo of the center?" As soon as he said the words, he cast them aside. "You sent in somebody else. A spotter. You had gotten word—"

She pulled up to the next stoplight and kept her eyes pointed straight ahead. "We have not been spying on you."

Charlie gave himself a moment to absorb a fraction more of that beautiful face. Her scent was a heady mix of rare flowers and money.

"If you will please just wait, everything will become perfectly clear." Gabriella spoke the words in a carefully rehearsed manner. "Anything I tell you now will not clarify matters at all."

"Whatever you say." Charlie settled back. He had no problem with silence.

Gabriella entered the lonely reaches south of Melbourne Beach and drilled through a thickening dusk. She traversed the miles of empty green marking the Sebastian Inlet State Park, then climbed up and over the bridge linking them to the next island. The coastal route was summertime empty, a lonely asphalt ribbon laid along the narrow strip of land separating the Atlantic from the Indian River. Charlie had been figuring all along they were headed for Vero Beach. The Sebastian Inlet Bridge marked the border between NASA's working stiffs and the serious money farther south.

He heard bikers approaching from behind but paid them little mind. Daytona Bike Week brought in over a quarter of a million bikers from all over the globe. Many liked the area enough to stay. Sunsets along the coastal route were punctuated by multiple deep-throated Harleys. Gabriella's fragrance and her sultry tones made it far too easy to focus upon the car's interior. For a security specialist, this was tantamount to a death wish.

The first biker passed them, riding a chromed-out Harley Softail. Then Charlie's alarm senses were triggered by a second set of headlights. He leaned forward and focused on the biker riding alongside the Range Rover. He was not passing. He was moving into position.

A glint of whirling metal flashed above the biker's head, a scythe cutting into the sunset, wreaking havoc and destruction. The biker swung the chain like he was going to lasso the Range Rover, which in a sense he was. Charlie knew the chain was linked to fishing hooks the size of his fist, intended to catch the tire, the wheel casing, the brake sleeve, the axle, the undercarriage, anything. When he turned around, the biker offered him a death's-head grin.

Charlie leaned over and pressed his hand hard on Gabriella's right knee, jamming the gas pedal to the floor. He heard her gasp and felt her leg fight against him. He forced it down harder. The Range Rover's motor responded with an eight-cylinder bellow and bolted ahead. Charlie heard the biker shout his frustration as he released his chain. It rattled fiercely against the rear tire and wheel well and fender, the hooks scrambling for a hold.

Charlie released Gabriella's knee and yelled, "Brake! Brake!"

To her credit, she responded instantly.

He used his left hand to ram her back in her seat, bracing her for impact, and cocked his arm to take the air bag's first punch. His hand slammed her chest hard enough to push the air from her body. He used his right hand to turn the wheel hard to the left. It meant his body would take the coming blow at a dangerous tilt. But that could not be helped.

The chain caught hold and wrapped up with a fierce, metallic *zing*. He shouted, "Brace for impact!"

Clearly his maneuver was the last thing the biker expected. The standard response would be to move away from the threat and if possible save the car. But Charlie knew the car was finished. He turned the vehicle *toward* the danger.

The Range Rover was a two-ton beast that was not made for a maximum turn angle at high speed. The car's front tires locked just as the chain trapped the rear wheel and snapped home. From inside the car it sounded like a cannon shot and felt almost as powerful. If they had been going straight ahead, the car would have shuddered and jerked to a halt, slamming the driver straight into the steering wheel and the passenger into the dash, because the air bags would not have been inflated by any frontal impact. But Charlie's actions meant the car catapulted into the air, rolling over and blocking the entire road.

The attacking biker slammed into the vehicle's underbelly with a crash that only accelerated their roll. As the Rover flipped onto its roof, Charlie caught sight of the biker in front of them falling into a high-speed skid that shot sparks into the night. The car kept rolling, over the side and finally banging onto the four tires. The Rover bucked through a sideways slip, tilting and almost going over on its side again. Then it bounced back and quivered, and finally stilled.

Charlie was already moving. He kicked out the remaining glass from the side window, squirmed through, and tumbled from the car. He slipped to the asphalt and dropped to all fours, then scrambled forward and scouted past the hood. The remaining two bikers were huddled around their fallen men. Charlie knew he and Gabriella had only seconds before the remaining enemies came looking for revenge.

He could not risk opening the door, so he slipped back through the window, unhinged Gabriella's seat belt, and pulled her forward. She shifted feebly, either to help or hinder, and tried to shape words.

Charlie hissed, "Quiet. For your life, don't speak."

Gabriella's flailing movement stilled somewhat. She tried to look at him but her gaze would not fasten. But there was no bleeding from her nose or ears that Charlie could see in the dim light. All her limbs moved well, so he risked hefting her over the central console and dragging her out the window. He lifted her onto one shoulder and jogged for the dunes.

"Stop, please," she gasped. "If they make us late, we lose."

Charlie took another half-dozen strides before the words fully registered. He settled Gabriella into a sandy defile and squatted down beside her. "Say again."

"Timing is everything." Her voice gathered strength with each word. "We need to arrive in precisely . . ." She examined her bare wrist. "What happened to my watch?"

Charlie had a hundred questions of his own, but there was only time for, "This is for real?"

She shoved the hair from her face. "If we are even two minutes late, we have lost. They did not need to kill us. Just slow us down."

The intense manner in which she had driven them south suddenly made sense. "Who is 'we,' Gabriella?"

The moon reflected her darkly frantic gaze. *"Please."*

Charlie gave the span of two breaths to weighing his options. He was not under contract. This was not his client. He had no idea who his opposition was or why they were after them. Or if the woman was just the target or also part of some larger conspiracy. "They're not out to kill us?"

"I don't . . . No. Probably not. Too messy. If we're late, it's over anyway."

"If *we* are late."

"That is correct. We have to arrive together, and precisely on time."

He checked his phone. Smashed. "Best guess. What is our destination and how much time do you think we have?"

"We are headed for a lab at the Indian River University hospital." She thought hard. "We have ten minutes. Perhaps fifteen."

Charlie pointed her around to the south. "Run down two hundred meters. Stay in the dunes. Then come to the road. I will meet you there."

"But—"

"Go."

Charlie waited until she sprinted away, then ran parallel to the road in the opposite direction. He jerked hard left, bounded over a small dune, and hit asphalt just as the moon slipped behind scattered clouds. One of the bikes was burning fiercely, and the fire silhouetted the three bikers still on their feet. They were standing around a man lying prone on the road. Which indicated that Gabriella had told him the truth, at least about the bikers not being sent to take them out. These men were certainly not hunters. In fact, the way they stood suggested their job was done—running them off the road.

Two of the bikers must have heard him, for they turned and shouted. One of them went for his gun. Charlie came in straight and hard. He chopped the gunner in the throat, striking the soft point just below the voice box, then kicked the second man in his knee, jamming it backward. The last man still on his feet was going for his weapon, but his movements were unsteady and his forehead was bleeding. Charlie grabbed his hand, swung it in the forward motion the man was going for, and kept going, flipping him on top of the second man, trapping them both. He disarmed the gunner and brought the weapon down hard on the third man's forehead. He then swung back to the first man just as he tried to pull a sawed-off 12 gauge from a holster sewed into the right thigh of his pants. Charlie hammered him between the eyes with the pistol, plucked the shotgun from his spasming fingers, then struck him again.

He trotted away, aiming for the one bike that was still running.

He straddled the leather, gunned the motor, then shot the tires of the other bikes with the 12 gauge as he powered past.

Gabriella was there waiting for him on the roadside. He slowed and waited until she was snugged in tight and her arms were clenched to his chest, then blasted into the night.

2

Eight minutes later, they entered the world of five-million-dollar condos and Bentley convertibles and women who looked like Gabriella. Charlie had the road pretty much to himself. The high-society towns rimming Florida's southern coasts started at Vero Beach, continued south to Palm Beach, swung around Miami's Fisher Island, and ended at Naples and Sanibel Island. Such places had very small core populations. In the high season, the traffic was bumper-to-bumper. But most people who could afford life on the Gold Coast wouldn't be seen dead there in the off-season. Charlie had worked for enough wealthy clients to know serious money did strange things to people.

Like sending beautiful Italian assistants north, hunting men with dark edges whose name they did not even know. Or luring them into traps where lost lives became just another term for loose change.

Charlie raced across the first barrier island bridge and into the Indian River University campus. Gabriella directed him past the hospital to a building whose newness shone in the streetlights. The surrounding grounds held an unfinished raw-earth look.

Gabriella waited as Charlie cut the engine and pulled the bike up on its parking stand, then said, "Our new research facility is located here."

"Okay."

"You must have many questions."

"Only one that can't wait." Charlie rose from the saddle so he could face her full on. There were worse things to do with a lonely evening than stare at a beautiful woman. Even one whose dress was torn and whose hair was turned wild by the wind. "Will we face more danger in there?"

"No, Charlie. We will be safe." She must have sensed his unease, for she added, "If I say anything more, it will prejudice your situation."

"My situation?" he asked.

She eased off the saddle, resting a hand on his arm until her legs stabilized. "Come with me."

He followed her down the sidewalk. The university's spring term was over and the campus was silent, empty. Gabriella unlocked the glass doors, waited for him to enter, and locked them inside.

The building's interior smelled of fresh construction and dust. The lobby's main desk was an unfinished skeleton of raw wood. A sign that read "McLaren Teaching Hospital" lay on the flagstone tiles beside a wall glistening with wet paint. The lobby's ceiling panels were stacked by the side wall. Overhead dangled a trunk of electronic and fiber-optic cables thick as his thigh.

Gabriella saw the clock behind the desk and sighed with relief. "We have six minutes. When we meet the others, would you please not tell anyone about what just happened?"

"Sure."

"They know there is danger, but they think it is distant." She waved at the night beyond the front windows. "I want them to feel protected until we have passed the coming test."

Charlie knew she was dancing around whatever he would face

18

upstairs. But for the moment, he took her at her word. "If you don't want anyone to know, we better clean up."

"The restrooms are down the hall. Please hurry."

He entered the men's room and washed his face and finger-combed his hair and straightened his clothes. His knit shirt had a tear on the side, but it wasn't noticeable so long as he kept his arms down. There was nothing he could do about the bloodstain on his jeans.

He returned to find her waiting by the elevator. She did not sparkle, but her hair was neatly tied back and her clothes were as straight and clean as she could make them. He pressed the button and waited for Gabriella to meet his eye. "Tell me your last name."

She tasted several responses, then settled on, "I don't know."

The elevator walls were covered with paint-stained blankets and the floor was protected by thick sheets of plastic. Gabriella used a key to access the top floor. The elevator light had a short and flashed intermittently. She winced as though fearing another assault.

The elevator doors opened to reveal a penthouse lab. The foyer was rimmed by glass-fronted rooms like petals of a mahogany flower. Everything about the place was as polished and rich and pristine as the man seated in the leather-backed chair. There were six others ranged about the room, but Charlie knew the reason they were gathered was this man. He looked fifteen to twenty years older than Gabriella and wore thousand-dollar jeans and a cotton pullover that exposed a perfect tan. He was a silver wolf—a gleaming example of all the health and looks that money could buy.

"Welcome, welcome. Our young man has arrived. Splendid." He was clearly accustomed to charming with his smile. "My wife was correct after all."

Charlie caught Gabriella's tight head shake and knew the guy rising from his special leather chair was not as in control as he thought.

"Byron McLaren." He offered his hand. "And you are?"

"Behind the curve," Charlie said. "Gabriella didn't seem to think my name was all that important."

The guy's grip was practiced, hard, swift. "So she didn't tell you why you were asked to join my little team?"

"No."

"Yet you came anyway."

"I'm here."

"Indeed so." He gave a little laugh that was not shared by anyone else in the room.

Charlie stepped in close enough to get a good look at the guy's pupils. No sign of dilation. No smell of booze. No sense of the man being behind the attack. "This is your hospital?"

"Ah, you noticed the sign downstairs in the lobby. My trust donated quite a substantial sum. The university insisted on naming this building after me. What I really wanted was this research facility. A place where we could delve into the eternal mysteries in sterile comfort."

The others in the room did not share the man's ebullience. Charlie had no reason to doubt his claim.

One of the three other women was Anglo, lean with spiky blonde hair and a T-shirt that read "The evidence is behind your eyes." The other two women were Asian, with features that suggested Laos or Burma or one of the Himalayan kingdoms. Both were very slight, probably weighing in at less than one hundred pounds, and held themselves as though intending to occupy the smallest possible space. One of the men was very dark, Charlie assumed either of African or Caribbean heritage. He seemed to be in his early thirties and reserved, clearly uncomfortable with Charlie's presence. As was the Anglo woman.

The guy farthest from the elevators was another Anglo, tall and handsome and with eyes only for Gabriella. Either they were an item or he very much wanted them to be.

Charlie asked, "What are you researching?"

Byron turned to Gabriella. "You haven't filled him in?"

"I told you I wouldn't. He has already said as much."

"I need to be certain."

"You heard him say. I don't even know his name." Her voice had gone as wooden as her features. "We all agreed it was crucial he came of his own volition."

"All right, Gabriella."

"All I know about him is that he is in the risk containment business." She shot him a quick glance. "And that he is very good at his job."

The skinny guy by the far wall muttered, "Oh wow."

The blonde lady muttered, "Can you *believe* this?"

The dark-skinned guy let out a soft, "*Assombroso. Chocante.*"

The words, Charlie knew, were Portuguese. Which meant the guy was probably Brazilian.

Byron said to Gabriella, "Perhaps he lied."

"Why should he? He doesn't even know why we needed him to come."

"And you found him where?"

"The community center. Exactly as I—" Gabriella clamped down on whatever she had started to say. "I think we should start now."

"Just a moment." Byron turned back to Charlie. "Is there any reason why I shouldn't know your name?"

"Charlie Hazard."

"Excellent. We're making progress. Mr. Hazard, would you like to sit down?"

"I'm good, thanks."

"We are conducting a series of experiments. We want you to participate as a subject."

"That's not true at *all*." Gabriella flashed genuine irritation. She looked to Charlie. "The reason you need to participate is because it is the *only* way you will *ever* understand."

"Yes, all right. Forgive me, Mr. Hazard. My wife is correct." Byron was clearly only comfortable when holding center stage. "Most people secretly yearn to pierce the unseen and hear the unspoken. Wouldn't you agree?"

Gabriella was shaking her head before the guy stopped talking. "Byron, please."

"No, no, I'm not done. Wouldn't you agree, Mr. Hazard, that there is more to reality than what we can detect with our physical senses?"

Beside him, Gabriella crossed her arms and looked at the carpet by her feet. The others held to a respectful silence, their faces careful masks. No question, this guy controlled the company wallet.

Charlie said, "Sure thing."

"But seldom are we brought face-to-face with this alternate reality. Which is why—"

"Byron. This must wait until we are certain." She paced the words out in tight little bursts.

The blonde woman said quietly, "Gabriella is right, Byron."

The handsome guy agreed. "We've gone to a lot of trouble to ensure the subject—"

Gabriella chopped the air. "He is *not* a subject."

"Children, please. No bickering. Mr. Hazard, I would like to make you a proposition. What we are doing here is highly confidential and cutting edge. But it is also an experience we have all shared in. I would like to offer you fifty thousand dollars to participate."

"Will you tell me what's going on?"

"Sorry, no."

"Then I can't agree."

The entire room exhaled.

"Charlie." Gabriella waited until he was staring at her to ask, "Will you please do this for me?"

The fact that Charlie even hesitated had the skinny man on the back wall repeating the words like a mantra. "Oh wow, oh wow, oh wow."

3

Gabriella directed Charlie into the west-facing chamber. She asked him to slip off his shoes and lie down on a narrow hospital bed. The room contained the one bed, a chair, and a portable table jammed with electronic gear. The windows facing the lobby were one-way glass. Charlie stared at the mirrors and disliked how the eight other people could observe him unseen. Actually, it was only six, because Gabriella remained in the room with him, and the handsome guy had moved into the adjoining room, one clearly designed as a monitoring station. He was now seated behind a curved metal desk containing a vast array of electronic equipment. Charlie's bed was positioned so he could look through the side partition and watch the man gear up his equipment.

"I can close the drapes if you wish," Gabriella said.

"Is it important that they watch?"

"I don't know."

"You don't know?"

"Perhaps. Yes, perhaps it is important. That is, if you . . ." Gabriella sighed. "I hate this."

"Why can't you talk to me?" When she responded with another sigh, he lowered his voice and asked, "Is it Byron?"

"No." There was no hesitation to her response.

The guy in the next room slipped on a headset, then leaned forward and tapped on the glass. When Gabriella looked over, he pointed to his earphones and shook his head.

Gabriella turned her back to the side room and went on, "Before I came to meet with you, I set up a series of parameters."

The guy in the next room was clearly not happy with being unable to hear what Gabriella was saying. He tapped on the window again. Louder this time.

Charlie liked how she focused on him and ignored the other guy. He asked, "These parameters have to do with me?"

"Partly." She lifted a strap. "This waist belt is not necessary. But I would like to use it with you because it has been a part of the process from the beginning. If it makes you uncomfortable, we can dispose of it."

"First tell me again that we are safe up here."

"The elevators are locked down. The exit doors are electronically sealed and solid steel. We are safe, Charlie."

He drew his arms in close to his body. "Either I trust you or I don't."

Once the words were out, Charlie almost wished he had not said them. Then she smiled, and all his concerns just faded to grey.

The handsome guy stripped off his headset, stormed out of the chamber, opened their door, and snapped, "If you don't hit the switch, how am I supposed to monitor the process?"

Gabriella was too busy cinching the belt around Charlie's waist to look over. And Charlie was too busy smelling the closeness of her.

The guy didn't like that either. He slapped a switch by the doorway and said, "Why don't we try and keep this on a professional level."

She waited until the door sighed shut to ask, "Are all men such children?"

"You're the pretty lady. I should be asking you."

She studied him. "Are you the least bit nervous?"

"Not really. No."

"What we just went through, that does not leave you unsettled?"

Charlie was not used to discussing his internal world with others. But there was something about this woman that invited confidences. "A professional learns to deal with the adrenaline rush. It comes, it goes. Your performance level can't suffer. Not and survive."

She released a long breath, so close Charlie could taste its flavor. "I always considered myself a professional. Now I am not so sure."

The handsome man's voice boomed from the loudspeaker overhead. "Can we please get on with it?"

"We must establish a level of calm first." She looked at the window then. "Isn't that one of the parameters we agreed upon?"

The guy simply said, "Rolling."

Gabriella looked down at Charlie strapped to the narrow bed. "I am glad it was you I came to meet tonight, Charlie Hazard."

She rolled the end of his bed around so that he could no longer see the side window and the guy beyond. She then dimmed the room's lights, returned to his side, and used the bed's controls to elevate his head slightly. "Are you comfortable?"

"I might fall asleep."

"That is what we want. Not that you sleep, but that you are in a restful state." She rolled the table over and lifted a group of cables. "We like to monitor the EKG and heart rate of our subjects. But if you prefer, we can make an exception in your case."

"I don't mind."

"Thank you."

She had substituted a white lab coat for her dark jacket. Her hair was bundled so tightly it accentuated the astonishing curve to her eyes. Charlie knew he shouldn't use her closeness to stare. But every time he looked away, his eyes were dragged back.

Her voice maintained its gentle tone, probably to help him relax.

But the result was an intimacy that not even all the unseen observers could break. "The parameters go far beyond you directly, Charlie. That is one reason why I do not want to explain. This is all very new to us as well, you see. Can you open your shirt, please?"

The belt across his waist made the motions clumsy. "Are you a scientist?"

"My background is in experimental psychology. Before this, I only worked with rats. Some days I wish I had never . . ." She stopped in the process of peeling the back off a monitor pad and stared at the scar tissue lacing his chest and upper abdomen.

"It's okay."

She used a square of sandpaper to lightly abrade the skin of his chest, applied the pad, then connected it to another thin wire. "I'm sorry. What was I saying?"

"Your research is very new."

"Actually, we have been working at this project for almost two years now. It is the *results* that are new." She checked the monitor pads and wires with professional swiftness, then lifted a syringe. "I want to give you something that will aid you in resting fully."

"Will you tell me what's in your injection?"

She had clearly expected the question. "I have written down the solution." She showed him a folded sheet of paper. "I would like to ask you to please let me put this in your pocket, and that you not read what I have written here until we are done. Will you do that for me, please?"

"Yes. All right."

She slipped the paper into his shirt, then applied a tourniquet to his right arm. She lifted the syringe and spouted a little stream toward the ceiling. Then she stopped and looked at him.

All the looks she had given him before were now rolled into one tight bundle. That was how it felt to Charlie. She stared at him with an intensity that he felt in his bones.

She whispered, "Thank you for trusting me, Charlie Hazard."

"It was a slow night until you showed up."

She inserted the syringe and pressed the plunger.

Gabriella said, "I'm going to walk you through a series of hypnotic suggestions."

"Whatever you say."

"Do you pray or practice any form of meditation, Charlie?"

"Not really." He watched her unwrap the cord from a set of headphones. "Is that what this is all about?"

"Your questions need to wait, please."

"All right."

"Thank you, Charlie." Gabriella fitted him with padded headphones that covered his entire ears. She then rose to her feet and swept the curtains over the mirror windows and those over the night beyond the building, sealing them into a fresh-smelling cocoon of concrete and glass. The only people who could observe them now were in the side alcove. He heard a door open and close several times, and Charlie assumed the observers had joined the handsome guy. But Charlie's bed was now pointed away from them.

He watched Gabriella fit on a headset, pull the microphone closer to her lips, and say, "Can you hear me all right?"

"Fine."

She pulled the chair closer to the side of his bed. She adjusted the table so that she could observe the monitors, but they remained out of his line of sight. She said, "I want you to slip your arms inside the waist belt."

"All right."

Gabriella crossed her legs and held a clipboard in her lap. But she did not appear to be reading from it. "This is not a safety issue. It is actually part of the experience. You will understand when we conclude the process."

Part of his mind was connecting the dots, hearing her carefully chosen words. *Experience* and *process*. Not experiment. Not risk. Not threat.

But the largest part of his attention remained focused upon the beautiful woman seated close enough to touch, talking to him through earphones that heightened the spice of her accent. It felt as though Gabriella's voice was licking his brain.

Charlie decided it had to be the injection.

Gabriella said, "Close your eyes, please."

"Can you tell me what is going to happen?"

"No. Part of the experience is having no expectations whatsoever." She was responding from rote. Her voice adapted a steady monotone now. The scientist. "I am going to count down from eight to one. When I arrive at one, you will be floating in a state of pure alert relaxation. I am beginning now. Eight. Seven. Six. You are beginning to float upon a calm, warm sea. Five. You are leaving behind any stresses and concerns you might have brought in with you. Four. You are perfectly safe. Three. You are completely relaxed, and you remain utterly alert. Two. Your mind is refreshed and entirely engaged, and your body is totally relaxed. One. You float in a state of total repose. Can you hear me, Charlie?"

"Yes."

"You will remain relaxed and calm and completely safe throughout this experience. You will remember everything that happens with absolute clarity. You will hear all that I say and do what I ask. You will remain in complete control at all times. If you feel any sense of discomfort, you will immediately return to full awake state. Do you understand me, Charlie?"

"Yes."

"All right. I am going to start the process now. Are you ready, Charlie?"

"Yes."

"The process is very simple. I am going to play a sound into one ear. This sound is one halftone above middle C on the musical scale. This tone will be embedded in the sound of the rushing wind, which will help you maintain your relaxed state. There is no other sound or tone or message embedded in the process. Do you understand me, Charlie?"

"Yes."

"Here is the sound."

For Charlie it was like the room began breathing with him. Calm and steady and very slow. Far off in the distance, a simple, steady tone hummed in his right ear.

"Can you hear the tone, Charlie?"

"Yes."

"All right. Now I am going to play a second tone into your left ear. This second tone is precisely 1.8 percent of the tonal scale above the first tone. There is no other noise or message embedded in the wind. Here is the second tone. Please tell me what you hear, Charlie."

"A wave."

"Very good. When the sounds are this close together, the brain does not hear two tones, but one sound that vibrates in a steady wave. The pattern of this wave is determined by the tonal difference between the two sounds. This means I can make the tone vibrate faster or slower by altering the distance between the two sounds. Do you understand, Charlie?"

"Yes."

"Excellent. Now listen carefully. Remain utterly alert. I am going to tighten the distance between the two tones. This will heighten the vibration frequency you hear. You will feel yourself being lifted up mentally. This is one of the remarkable phenomena we have learned about the brain, that it is possible to heighten brain activity and slow the physical state, all at the same time. You will allow this to happen, but only so long as you remain entirely comfortable. Remember, Charlie, you are in total control. You may stop this at any time. Do you understand?"

"Yes."

"Are you ready to proceed?"

"Yes."

"I am beginning to alter the tonal frequency now. All right. Tell me what you feel."

"Higher."

"Very good. Your heart rate has slowed by thirty-six percent from what it was at normal rest. Your breathing has been cut by half. This is entirely normal. Now listen carefully and I will explain what is happening. The brain frequencies are vibrating according to a pattern that reflects the initial stage of what we refer to as higher awareness. We call this the Base Level. Now I am going to insert *additional* tonal frequencies. These new sounds are calibrated in precisely the same manner as the first. They act in harmony within the mental process, heightening the pattern's influence upon the brain and your mental state. There is no other subliminal message. These tonal frequencies will act in tandem."

Charlie heard the wind undergo a dramatic change, as though accelerating from a breeze to a hurricane. He felt a surge of power, calm as a desert dawn, yet somehow filled with the majesty of what was about to arrive.

"I am now increasing the frequencies you are hearing, Charlie. I am altering the level now."

The pattern he was hearing shifted very slightly. He felt his entire being resonate in response.

"Your breathing has now dropped by another twenty percent. Your heart rate is now thirty-seven percent of what it was when we began. Charlie, you remain in complete control. You are utterly alert, and you will remember everything that happens. If you feel any discomfort whatsoever, you will return instantly to full consciousness. We call this Level One. I am now going to alter the frequency again. Are you ready, Charlie?"

"Yes."

"This is Level Two. From this point on, speech becomes somewhat difficult. Remember, Charlie, you remain in complete control. You may exit the process at any time by simply opening your eyes.

"All right. I am going to alter the frequency again. I am lifting the tonal frequency now. This is Level Three.

"All right, Charlie. I am going to tighten the tonal frequencies. I am altering it now. This is Level Four.

"I am heightening the tonal frequencies again. I am altering it now. This is Level Five . . . Level Six . . . Level Seven . . . Level Eight. One more level and we are done. I am heightening the tonal frequency now. Level Nine. We have arrived at our destination. Your heart is now beating at a steady thirty-one beats per minute. Your breathing is down to nineteen percent of where it was upon our beginning this process.

"Listen carefully, Charlie. Your body remains in a state of complete rest. Your mind is utterly alert. You are in total control of your situation. You may stop this process at any time by simply opening your eyes. Now I am going to ask you to do something, Charlie. You should only do this if you feel utterly safe.

"I want you to rise up.

"I will count from nine to fifteen. I will make no alteration of the tonal frequency. You are in complete control of this process. You will only do this if you feel utterly safe.

"I am beginning to count now. Nine. Ten. You are lifting up. Rising up. You will hear my voice with utter clarity. Eleven. You are in complete control of this process. Twelve. Thirteen. Fourteen. Fifteen.

"All right, Charlie. When I say *now*, I want you to open your *other* eyes.

"Open them now."

4

Charlie awoke to the sound of tapping.

He opened his eyes and was instantly assaulted by full daylight. The sun hit his brain like a hammer. He shielded his eyes and groaned.

The tapping grew louder.

Charlie dry-scrubbed his face with both hands. He risked a second glance and discovered he was in the front passenger seat of another brand-new Range Rover. Only this one was steel-grey, whereas the one Gabriella had driven earlier was green. The seat had been tilted fully back, which had brought his face square into the rising sun.

The tapping sounded like it was chiseling into his brain. He realized a figure was standing by the side window, tapping on the glass with a coin.

Charlie could not figure out how to make the seat work. His hands fumbled about the door and finally found the lever.

Julio opened the door and said, "You slept here all night?"

Charlie groaned, "Where am I?"

"I guess that's an affirmative." Julio gripped Charlie's weaving arm and helped him rise from the car. "Steady, dude."

Charlie blinked and staggered and would have gone down except for Julio's firm grip. The young man was grinning hugely. Charlie asked, "How did I get here?"

"You're asking me?" Julio clearly liked that a lot. "Man, what tricks did that pretty woman lay on your bones?"

Charlie looked down and saw he was wearing his clothes from the night before. His pockets felt heavy. He reached inside and came up with a set of keys, a cell phone, and a charger. "These aren't mine."

"What, the lady drugs you, does the dirty, hands you a brand-new eighty-thousand-dollar car and a phone, then leaves you in the parking lot?" Julio laughed out loud. "I got to get me one of those."

The previous night swam in and out of mental focus. Then he recalled the slip of paper Gabriella had put in his pocket. He fished around again. The handwritten page read, "100cc purified saline solution."

Charlie asked the already hot day, "She injected me with salt water?"

Julio laughed again. "GBH, more like."

Charlie slipped the paper back into his pocket. "Coffee."

"This way, old man." Julio slipped a ring of keys from the pocket of his baggy jeans and unlocked the community center's front doors.

Charlie asked, "Where'd you get those?"

"I been working here a couple of weeks now." Julio settled Charlie into a chair and propped open the doors. "Minimum wage, no great shakes. But hey, I was coming here for free, right?"

Charlie shut his eyes to questions that could definitely wait. The breeze puffing through the open doorway was laced with salt from an onshore wind. He must have drifted off, because the next thing he knew, Julio set a steaming mug on the table in front of him and asked, "You all right?"

"I have no idea." As Charlie took his first sip, he noticed the wound on Julio's cheek. A purpling rose encircled a cut that had only recently stopped bleeding. "What happened to you?"

The kid went from sophisticated surfer to sullen teen. "Everything's cool."

"Julio. Tell me what happened."

"My aunt's taken up with a new guy. He and I, we don't get along so good."

"Can you live with your parents?"

"Not unless I get arrested. Again." He spoke with the studied calm of a guy who'd learned to tamp everything down deep. "Pop's doing eight to ten at Raiford. My mom's been gone a long time."

The kid moved away. Charlie drifted. Awake, but not really there. Circling around the previous evening like a tongue feeling out a sore tooth. Not certain he wanted to press down hard.

The phone in his pocket rang just as Irma entered through the rear doors. She took one look at Julio's face and said to Charlie, "I need your help moving this kid somewhere safe."

"Give me a second." Charlie pulled out the phone that wasn't his and said, "This is Hazard."

Gabriella asked, "Are you all right, Charlie?"

He rose to his feet, then needed a second to stop the world from spinning. "A little unsteady."

"That is to be expected. You have had a psychic shock. I'm sorry we left you in the car. But you were so deep asleep we couldn't make you respond."

"You weren't concerned about safety?"

"No."

He drifted through the community center doors and let the salt air wash over him. "Making the trip without backup, leaving me here exposed, that didn't worry you?"

"Charlie, there are things you will not fully understand at this point. An associate ascended while we were on the road. They saw the attack, but when they called to warn us, my phone did not respond, probably because it had already happened."

"Ascended," Charlie repeated.

"That is our word for what you experienced. My associate then witnessed something more, my driving you back and your sleeping in the parking lot. They sensed this was important. Why, we don't know. But you needed to wake up where you now are." Her words came in a tighter rush. "Please do not ask questions. My answers will only make sense from inside the process. And fully explaining that will require time we don't have."

He thought about the previous evening and decided he had no choice but to extend the trust further still. "Afterward, do all the participants feel like they're not completely connected to the world?"

"Most do, yes." Gabriella gave it a beat, then added, "Actually, you are the first person who has entered the experience so unprepared."

"All you shot in my vein was saline solution?"

"The power of suggestion in such circumstances is well documented. If a person thinks they are receiving a drug, the hypnotic effect is heightened."

"Why didn't you tell me what was going on?"

"Two reasons. First, I did not want my hopes to influence your base experience."

"Your hopes?"

"Why should that surprise you? Of course I hoped your experience would match my expectations. And second, it was part of the boundaries we established before I drove to Satellite Beach and met you. I needed to convince my associates that the threat was real. Your returning with me was vital."

As she spoke, the night returned to Charlie in vivid clarity. Gabriella had permitted him to remain in the state she called Level Fifteen for less than thirty seconds. Just long enough to open his *other* eyes and find himself looking down at his own body.

His vision had been vague, like a dream sequence, yet far sharper. Charlie had hovered by the outer windows, up near the ceiling. He had observed himself lying in the narrow hospital bed. He had seen how she had taped the heart monitor so that it rested on normal skin, off his chest scars. Gabriella had been intently focused upon the computer screen. She waited for a long moment, shooting glances at his body and then returning her gaze to the screen.

Then she told him to enter the chamber behind his bed.

She spoke the instructions in the same natural calm that she had said everything else. And he did precisely as she asked.

He had no sensation of passing through walls. One moment he was in the chamber above his bed, then she spoke, and instantly he was next door. The change was so swift it was almost as though he had moved *before* she spoke. As though he knew what she was going to say. Which, of course, was impossible.

Almost as unachievable as moving through solid walls. Without his body.

Gabriella then spoke into his disembodied brain.

At this point, Charlie had been hovering up near the ceiling of the other chamber. Through the observation window, he saw her lips move. He heard her voice speak to the body now lying in a slightly elevated position, such that all he could see was the top of his head.

His head.

Gabriella said, "Look for a number written on the page beside the computer keyboard."

She gave him a moment, then told him to return to his body. He heard the words spoken through the earphones even though he was looking through a glass pane at the bed holding his body, hovering above seven people clustered behind the monitor station. The experience seemed almost logical.

Charlie returned to the room and drifted down and in and heard her count him back down through the levels. He actually felt the vibrations gradually shift through the sequence in reverse, drawing him back to Base Level. Her final instructions had been for him to wake up, listen to what she had to say, and then walk to the car, where he would fall into a deep sleep. He would sleep all night, and when he woke up he would remember everything.

Now Charlie walked over and leaned against the Range Rover's front fender. The breeze and the morning light helped anchor him to reality. "What I saw of the monitoring room was a little unfocused, like a half-finished dream."

"Your vision clarifies with practice. We need to leave that for later. Do you remember the final point we discussed last night?"

"Yes." When they left the chamber, Charlie had crossed the foyer under his own steam, but Gabriella had kept a hand on his arm just the same.

The handsome guy's name was Brett. Charlie remembered that now, how Brett had come forward and ordered Charlie to tell them what the number was. Pushing at him with his voice. Gabriella had called Brett by his name and told him to back off. He had simply demanded again, "Did you read the number?"

Charlie's tongue had felt too thick for his mouth as he replied, "Nine-one-eight-eight."

The others had smiled, and the geek had traded a high five with the Brazilian. Only Brett and Byron had not looked pleased.

"Charlie?"

He remembered how Gabriella had then pulled him away from the group. She had asked one of the Tibetan women to follow them in a second vehicle. When they were alone in the elevator Gabriella had spoken to him. She had used a tone he had not heard before, soft and urgent and perhaps a little frightened.

Charlie recalled, "You said the protocols demanded that I proceed through the process knowing nothing at all."

"Very good, Charlie. Do you understand the term *protocol*?"

"Probably not the way you mean it." Charlie's boss used the term a lot. Before meeting with new clients, Major General Curtis Strang ordered his team to hold to proper protocol. What he meant was, his staff needed to be careful not to offend the power players.

Gabriella said, "In order to have a successful experiment, you must first define the boundaries. A scientist begins her research by establishing a controlled environment. Strict limitations are set on the stimuli you introduce. You develop a method for measuring both the stimuli and the subject's response. All of these taken together are the experiment's protocol."

"Last night you said I wasn't in an experiment."

"No, Charlie, I'm sorry, but you're wrong. What I said was, your experience in the lab was not part of our trials. You were not participating as a test subject. But what brought you to us was indeed a part of our experiment. And for that I had to establish protocols. Otherwise the others would not allow me to introduce an outsider. Especially one with, well . . ."

"My dark side."

"Are you so very dark, Charlie?"

"My wife thought so."

"You are married, then."

"I was. She died. Three years ago."

"I'm so sorry, Charlie. Very, very sorry." She hesitated, then said, "Every answer you give me only brings up more questions."

That was exactly what Charlie was thinking. But all he said was, "So the protocol requires me to be completely out of the loop."

"For now, yes. It is only temporary."

"Until when?"

"You have a juncture arriving."

"Excuse me?"

"Did I use the wrong word? A big choice. We all do. Different choices that may or may not bring us together again. But I hope you decide to join us, Charlie. I think we may need you very soon."

"Are you in trouble, Gabriella?"

"Your turning comes very soon. Right or left. You must choose between the safety of your current life and the adventure of the complete unknown."

Charlie almost told her that his life contained more than enough dangers already, then let it drop. "Are you a fortune-teller too?"

"I told you, Charlie. I am an experimental psychologist. How I know is only important if you decide to help us."

"So what do I do, come back to the hospital?"

"We have left the lab and will never return. That was the objective behind the protocols, Charlie. That was why I had to be so careful about what I said. The others accepted our need to depart, despite all the wonderful elements that surrounded us. But only if last night you came with me and refused payment and then took part in the process and succeeded in reading the number." She paused, then added, "So far, only about ten percent of all subjects are successful at what you have accomplished, no matter how we prepare them. And none on their first trial run."

"Why so few?"

"It is a good question, Charlie. You may ask me that if we ever meet again. Right now, what you must understand is that my team faces our own juncture. In order for them to accept the danger I have seen, it was vital that you accomplished the impossible. Everything had to happen precisely as I had laid out to my team, before I drove down and met you and brought you back to our lab. Because you were successful, the others have agreed that the *rest* of what I said was also true."

"That you're in danger."

"That we had to leave the lab."

"My doing the impossible was a sign."

"A vital indicator of direction, yes." She hesitated a moment, and Charlie had the impression there was much more she wanted to say. Instead, she told him, "If you choose not to join us, that is all you will ever know. One of my team will contact you in thirty-six hours. Do not try to contact me in the meantime. If you decide not to assist us, throw away the phone. It is safer for both of us if you do not use it again."

"What about the car?"

"You will need it very soon."

"Say again?"

"Take this as your final bit of evidence that what I say is very real. We are in danger. Soon we will need your protection. Good-bye, Charlie Hazard. I am so very glad we met. And so sorry if this is indeed our farewell." She was silent a long moment, then whispered, "Unless you choose to become my dark knight."

5

T his is it." Julio pointed through the front windshield. "Third house on the left."

Irma leaned forward and inserted herself between the two of them. "Drive on past the house."

Charlie continued on to the end of the street, turned around, and parked so that the Range Rover was partially blocked by a towering oleander but granted them a clear view of the front door. "Does your aunt work?"

"Not in years. Easier to live off her men."

"What about this latest boyfriend? He work somewhere?"

"Sure. Off the back of his bike."

Charlie nodded to show the kid he understood. The state's crack and crystal meth trades were both controlled by biker gangs. "Does he cook in the house?"

"Not anymore."

Irma glared at the silent house. "I asked friends on the local force to stop by, they did it again yesterday. Which I'm guessing is why the new boyfriend gave Julio the black eye."

Charlie went back to examining the house, a run-down single-story ranch. Local developers had thrown up thousands of them during the sixties, when Kennedy's rush to the moon had fueled the region's growth. Charlie pointed at the three Harley choppers parked in the drive, glinting like metal soldiers. "Who owns the other bikes?"

"His buddies come and go all the time. I mighta seen them before." Julio's standard tough-guy pose was gone. In its place was just a frightened kid. "Maybe we should come back later."

"No. Now is fine." But Charlie remained exactly where he was. The central bike's right side was deeply scarred, like it had been slammed at high speed into the asphalt. The front wheel guard and saddle were pitted with tiny holes. Just as Charlie would have expected after being hit by a shotgun blast. He thought it over and decided it changed nothing.

He turned to Julio and asked, "You remember what I told you?"

"Sure, sure."

"Look at me, Julio."

"Maybe this isn't a good idea."

"Julio."

The kid tore his gaze away from the silent house. "What?"

"This is my job. It's the only thing I'm good at. I guard people for a living. It's why Irma asked me to come with you, because she knows that no one will hurt you. Do you believe me?"

Julio blinked rapidly and did not speak.

"Focus on what I said. You don't introduce me. You don't look my way. As far as you're concerned, I'm invisible. Irma, give us three minutes to clear the front room."

"Roger that."

Charlie reached for his door. "Okay, Julio. Let's roll."

He walked around to Julio's side of the car and linked in as tight as sweat to the kid's right side. Julio was so frightened he probably didn't even realize he was talking. "My aunt, she's made me her ward on

42

account of how the state pays her a stipend. The social workers used to come around and check things out, but that stopped last fall when I turned seventeen."

Charlie was dressed in castoffs from the community center's goodwill hamper. He needed the people inside to assume he was just another of Julio's crowd. He wore ripped sneakers and stained surfer shorts and an aloha shirt with the pocket ripped out. He covered his face with wrap-around shades and a frayed cap advertising a bar that had died years ago. "Does your aunt try to take care of you?"

"Sure thing, man. When she's awake and straight." The closer they got to the house, the harder Julio had to fight against the tremors. "Which is, like, never these days."

"Okay. Up the stairs and across the porch and through the door and straight to your room. You don't look at them, no matter what they say. You don't speak. In and out." Charlie mounted the stairs and opened the door.

The smell hit him before he was across the entrance, a sweetish funk from old sweat and garbage and dope. The guys were Hispanic and tattooed and big. They all wore jeans and biker vests and boots. The man sprawled on the sofa's far end wore a walking cast on his left leg, and his face and shoulder were patched with bandages that looked overly white against the room's dull interior. The three men sat in front of a chattering television. The largest guy snarled something at Julio. Charlie was a half step behind the kid, his hand on the small of Julio's back, and felt him stiffen at the guy's angry words. Charlie pressed him forward.

From the living room came a roar of anger, Charlie assumed from being dissed in front of his buddies. Fear pinched Julio's face even tighter.

Charlie kept his voice level. "This your room?"

Julio nodded.

"Okay. Pack everything you need because you are *not* coming back."

The voice from the front room shouted once more. There came

the sound of boots thumping down the hall. Julio jammed books and a laptop and clothes into his backpack, his hands turning clumsy with terror. "Oh man."

"Stay cool." Charlie tossed the sunglasses into the garbage can. He moved to the bedroom doorway and crouched slightly, shoulders hunched, cap down low. Just a frightened oversized kid wishing he was somewhere else. Hands hidden down by his sides, like they were in his pockets.

The guy stepped into the doorway and snarled words Charlie didn't need to understand. Up close he was hair and muscle and stink. A hand the size of a bear's paw swiped at where Charlie's face had just been. Only Charlie was moving now.

He gripped the guy's wrist at the pressure point and swept his hand in the direction it had been going. Charlie accelerated the swing until the man's forearm collided with the doorjamb. He trapped the arm there by applying his thumb to the nerve center inside the elbow. A simple jab. He had practiced the motion a hundred thousand times.

The guy's eyes widened to where Charlie could see his pinpoint pupils. He was in low-altitude orbit, no question. Charlie hammered his rib cage just above the heart. Three quick one-hand punches, his fist only traveling back and forth about ten inches. *Boom boom boom.*

The guy started falling while still coming to terms with the fact that the kid in Julio's doorway was neither a kid nor prey. Charlie clipped him once behind the ear and saw the light of battle vanish from his eyes.

From the living room came Irma's shrill, "Freeze! Stay right—"

There was a grinding crash as the man in the cast picked Irma up and tossed her through the screen door. Charlie was moving fast now. The injured biker took one moment longer than necessary to admire his handiwork, granting Charlie time to accelerate like a rocket. Straight toward where he stood.

The biker reached behind him. Charlie knew the motion. He was going for the gun at the small of his back.

Only Charlie was faster.

The biker had survived more than his share of bar fights. The gun was firing long before he brought it fully around. He was clearly used to people flinching away from the sound of cordite flaming and bullets flying. The pistol punched three holes in the wall to Charlie's left, and then Charlie was inside the guy's arm.

Charlie gripped the wrist and not the weapon. He dug his thumb into the point where the sinews met the muscles, and twisted. Hard.

The guy howled as his wrist was dislocated. Even then, he did not go down. He reached for Charlie's eyes with his free hand, but that was only a feint, because what he really intended was to hammer Charlie's nose with his forehead. Standard prison ops. But Charlie had shifted to his right, pulling on the damaged wrist. With the attacker off balance, he chopped his windpipe.

Then Charlie felt the earth tremble. Or saw the shadows change. He kept pulling his attacker by the hand, around to where his tattooed body became Charlie's shield. The television that had been aimed at Charlie now landed on the biker's head.

The third man froze with the shock of accidentally nailing his own buddy. That one second was enough for Charlie to sweep his legs out from under him. His skull thunked hard on the table where the trio's boots had just been resting.

Irma rammed back through the shattered door, a Walther held down low by her thigh. She surveyed the pair and said, "Cops are inbound."

"You okay?" Charlie asked.

"Everything except my pride. Sorry I wasn't there for you, sport."

"You slowed him down. Without that . . ." Charlie shrugged away the what-ifs. "You have cuffs?"

She dug in her pocket and came up with plastic ties. "Everything for the happy home."

Charlie helped her secure the two men in the living room. Both were still down for the count.

The man lying prone in the hallway was gradually coming around. Charlie secured his wrists, then called to Julio, "Hurry up in there."

"Two minutes, bro."

Charlie grabbed the boyfriend's hair and thunked him softly against the hall floor. Again. When the guy drew him into focus, Charlie said, "I was in the Range Rover last night."

"I don't know what you're talking about," the guy said.

"Tell me who was behind the attack and I'll tell you where to find the bike."

The gaze hardened. "We'll find the bike. And then we'll find you."

Charlie rose to his feet. "Deliver a message to the people pulling your strings. Tell them I'm coming. And when I find them, I'm going to take them out."

6

Charlie left while Irma was still dealing with the cops, and drove Julio back to the community center. Julio stared silently out the window, too spooked by all that had just gone down to play the sullen teen. Charlie's entire perspective regarding Julio had undergone a dramatic change. He now saw a kid doing his dead-level best to stay straight. No home life to speak of, the whole world against him, and surfing was the only thing he could claim as his own.

Charlie asked, "Where are you bunking?"

"Irma said the community center's caretaker cottage is empty. I can use that for a while."

Charlie knew the place, a fifties-era cottage on the parking lot's far end. As far as he was concerned, the place held all the charm of a juvie center. He turned down a side street and replied, "Let's see if we can't find you a better place to chill."

He drove the Land Rover down streets he had known since childhood. He was repeatedly struck by lightning images—Gabriella driving

47

them south, the attack, meeting her team, the procedure, waking up that morning, his final conversation with her. He tasted the salt-laced breeze through his open window and heard Gabriella utter the words again. *My dark knight.* There was no reason why he would shiver from the memory of her soft voice. He was a professional guardian. He had protected people in some of the world's most dangerous conflicts. He was certain he could handle whatever Gabriella's situation would toss his way. But no matter how often he repeated the words, he could not bring himself to accept that this was just another job.

Charlie pulled into his drive and said, "I want to show you something."

Julio followed him around the garage and up the side stairs, looking confused, uncertain. Charlie unlocked the door and said, "My old man and I never got along. So when I came back from the Army, I tore out what probably had once been a maid's apartment and turned this into a place I could call home. Then I ended up getting married, and I moved with my wife back to her home in LA. I don't think I've spent more than a couple of weeks total up here."

The single room was sixty-five feet long and forty wide. The cathedral ceiling was laced with heavy beams that were pegged into the walnut side-panels. The floor was heart of pine, the furniture sparse, the rear wall a tall glass triangle. A kitchenette fitted the corner where the stairs opened. A trio of sliding doors hid a pantry, closet, and bath.

Charlie saw how Julio stared at the room, his shoulders hunched slightly, and asked, "How'd you like to move in?"

The kid blinked hard. "You mean it?"

"I wouldn't say it if I didn't."

"I won't be any trouble. I swear."

Charlie wanted to say something about how impressed he was, how he didn't know if he would have had the strength to emerge intact from the kid's hellish home life. But Julio was already struggling to hold on to control. So he just cuffed the kid's shoulder and said, "I'm sure of that."

Then the telephone rang, startling them both.

Charlie walked over to where the old-fashioned apparatus was screwed into the wall beside the pantry door. "This is Hazard."

The voice was male and flinty from thirty-five years of battlefield command. "You and I need to discuss a new prospect."

Charlie came to full alert, the only way to handle this particular caller. "I'm officially on leave for another three weeks, General Strang."

"Negative on that, mister. I am inbound for Melbourne airport, wheels down in forty minutes. Be planeside or you're history."

Charlie took his time hanging up the phone. When he turned around, Julio asked, "You okay?"

"That was my boss. I may be going away for a while. Here." He reached into his pocket and pulled out some cash. "Buy what you need."

Julio raised his hands and backed away. "No, look. I got the job now, I can—"

"Julio. Look at me. Take the money."

Reluctantly he accepted the bills. "This is too much."

Charlie felt better than he had for a long time. "Welcome to your new home."

7

Charlie separated all the top brass he had ever known into two piles, bureaucrats and battlefield commanders. The military produced far more administrators than warrior leaders. When it came to the backroom maneuvers required for the highest promotions, even the finest field officers tended to be ground into dust. Major General Curtis Strang was one such casualty.

Charlie had worked for the general for just under three years, long enough to know the man bore bitter grudges against the Washington infighting that had cost him his career. Curtis Strang hid his sentiments behind the cavernous features of a long-term fitness fanatic. He was sixty-one and still competed every year in what some considered the most grueling athletic contest on earth, the Hawaii Ironman. Charlie's standard response to any call from the general was to tighten down to a sniper's intensity. Today, however, was different. Perhaps it was the result of having spent the night in the front seat of someone else's car. But probably not.

Charlie treated himself to a ninety-second shower and another cup of coffee. He dressed in what passed for a corporate uniform—blue blazer, white shirt, rep tie, black slacks, and loafers. He pulled out the packed suitcase he kept on the closet shelf for just such emergencies. He unlocked the floor safe and took out a Desert Eagle .45 caliber from Colt. The Desert Eagle was the gun of choice for most specialist operatives, a massive weapon that carried the firepower of a miniature cannon and weighed so much that if the bullets missed he could still beat his assailant senseless.

Charlie returned to the garage, a separate building divided from the house by a towering stand of bamboo. He heard Julio scratching around upstairs and called up to say he was leaving. Julio appeared at the top of the stairs, his face mottled from what Charlie thought were probably tears. Charlie pretended not to notice, bid his new tenant farewell, and entered the garage feeling remarkably good about this totally strange day.

He settled into his father's last car—a memento to an engineer who had lavished far more care and attention on his machines than on his only child. The beautifully restored '59 Corvette was too small for Charlie. But the car was his final connection to a man he had never really known.

For the first time ever, the car refused to start.

Time after time, Charlie turned the key. His father's pride and passion had always performed perfectly. No doubt one reason why his father had preferred machines to human beings.

Then Charlie recalled what Gabriella had said about him needing the Range Rover.

He did not so much walk to the Range Rover as float. Ditto for the drive to the Melbourne. He left the Range Rover in the small lot next to the entrance for private aviation. The guard checked his name against his list and passed him through, but the general's plane was nowhere in sight. The concrete pavement was a superheated mirror. Charlie set the suitcase by his feet and settled into the routine every soldier came to know and hate. He waited.

When Charlie had entered the Army at twenty-one, to his utter astonishment he found a home. After basic came officer training, and from there he went straight to Rangers, the Army's specialist school. Specialist was the American military's term for attack dogs.

Six years later, a thoroughly burned-out Charlie exited the military and entered straight into the arms of his new wife. He did his best to put the military life completely behind him. He buried the memories with his uniform. He attended no gatherings. He kept in contact with just one of his old buddies. He took a job selling insurance in Ventura. He wore a starched shirt and a tie. He pretended the flashbacks and the nightmares and the sweats did not happen. He ignored how the boiling cauldron in his brain kept threatening to blow, no matter how hard he fought to keep the lid clamped down tight.

After his wife died in a traffic accident, Charlie found himself wondering if he had somehow caused her to go off the road. If maybe she had just grown tired of life with a man who only pretended to play at normality. He tried to tell himself that such suspicions were nothing more than survivor's guilt. Even so, the whispers never fully went away.

The murmurs remained a fault line between himself and ever feeling close to another woman. Charlie had never mentioned the silent undertones to anyone. But as he waited for the general's arrival, he could not stop himself from hoping that in exchange for him protecting Gabriella from her own dark forces, she might find a way to free Charlie from his.

The Gulfstream III whined over to where Charlie waited. General Curtis Strang did not actually own a jet. He enjoyed his little toys, but they did not hold him. In that way, the general was still very much Army. The military taught people in vicious clarity the transient nature of possessions, and of life.

The general rented his transport from NetJets, the world's largest owner of commercial aircraft. NetJets offered its clients what the industry called partial ownership. In truth, NetJets was in the business of supplying taxis. Luxurious, incredibly expensive, fast, ego-stroking taxis. But taxis just the same.

The jet did not power down. The door opened and the stairs unfolded. The copilot saluted Charlie's approach. As soon as he slipped through the door, the copilot retracted the steps and sealed the door and moved back into his seat. The jet was already spinning around and taking aim at the runway before Charlie buckled himself into his seat. The pilots had obviously flown the general before.

The general closed the file he was reading and said, "I left eleven messages on your cell, Hazard. When I reach out for my people, I expect to connect. Day or night. No excuses, no lag time."

"Sorry, sir. My phone was broken last night."

"Then you should have replaced it. In our business, seconds are valuable, minutes irreplaceable."

Four months after his wife's death, Charlie had gone to work for the general. Within days it felt as though he had known no other life. "Understood, General."

Strang reopened the file and adjusted his reading glasses. "Moving on. What can you tell me about Harbor Petroleum?"

"Doesn't ring a bell."

"You've never had contact with the group?"

"Not that I recall."

"What about Weldon Hawkins, their senior vice president of human resources?"

"Never heard of him."

"That's interesting, soldier. Since he knows you."

Charlie thought hard. "I'm coming up blank, General."

Strang flipped the page, but Charlie had the impression the general was not reading. "It's interesting that a company of their size would put their VP of personnel in charge of corporate security. I asked his assistant about that. She said Harbor Petroleum specialized in drilling for oil in high-risk areas. Security was an essential part of their business plan." He turned another page. "What about Reese Clawson? When did you last meet the woman?"

"Never, sir. At least, not by that name."

"I find that remarkable as well. She knew everything about you, Hazard. We might as well have been examining the same file." Strang removed his glasses and took aim at Charlie. His eyes held all the warmth and color of glacial ice. "The woman you claim never to have met told me point-blank that either I came with you or I did not come at all."

The attack of 9/11 had caused a huge transition in the American struggle against terrorism. Public awareness was heightened like never before, and many hidden trends were accelerated.

Curtis Strang's last military assignment had been second in command of American forces assigned to NATO's bases in Italy. Liaising with local military, Strang was granted rare access to European tactics in maintaining high-profile security. He knew several well-financed American groups had begun offering high-level security as a component of their operations. The largest by far were USG, Blackwater, DynCorp, Falcon, and KBR. Strang resigned his commission and opted to specialize. He targeted the highest-risk individuals in the most dangerous of circumstances. He worked on either side of the law. When questioned by the FBI and the DEA over granting protection to certain clients, Strang and his legal team always responded that they didn't consider it their business to know why the people were under threat. Their job was to keep the body breathing.

The Gulfstream flew Charlie and Strang south of Orlando and Tampa, across the Gulf of Mexico, and into an approach for Galveston. The skies were clear, the air still, the waters calm. Charlie watched tankers headed for offshore oil depots while smoke from the refineries of Houston and Galveston rose like veils knitted between heaven and earth.

The plane landed and pulled up in front of two black SUVs with tinted windows. A trio of dark-suited men and one woman stood braced against the jet's backwash. As the copilot opened the jet's door and lowered the stairs, Charlie studied the security detail through his window. These first impressions were crucial. Typically, the local security staff considered Charlie a threat. He didn't care. His one concern was whether they would try to undermine his mission. If so, they had to be disposed of, and quickly. The others were given a chance to prove themselves. Few measured up.

One glance was enough to know this crew was different.

The men were tall and trim. They were fanned out around the cars. None of them watched the jet. Instead, they scanned the horizon. Their eyes remained hidden behind shades, but Charlie could see their heads move slightly as they split the scene into tight gradients.

No question. These guys were pros.

The woman called, "General Strang?"

"Affirmative."

"Reese Clawson. Glad you could join us." She was blonde in the manner of a pure-blood Scandinavian, with golden skin and pale blue eyes and lips that Charlie could only describe as both full and inviting. She wore her hair short with little trails in front of her ears like white-gold sideburns. Diamond stud earrings and a gold Rolex were her only jewelry. She was tall and trim, yet feminine enough to have Strang's gaze drifting slowly south. She smirked in the manner of a woman who took such looks as part of the terrain. She offered Charlie her hand. "Mr. Hazard, this is a real pleasure."

"Have we met?"

"Glenda Gleeson is a friend."

"Then you move in high circles." Glenda Gleeson was a Hollywood star of the highest order, one of only three women able to command fifteen million dollars per film. She was also a UN Goodwill Ambassador, a title first granted to Audrey Hepburn. These ambassadors made high-profile junkets to regions where public attention and government funds were desperately needed. When Glenda visited Darfur, Charlie had been in charge of her security. Somewhere near the disputed border between Sudan and Chad, the star's entourage had come under attack. According to the media blitz that followed, Glenda was rescued by UN security forces. In Charlie's world, success meant remaining utterly unseen.

Reese said, "I knew Glenda before fame struck. We were friends in college."

"Rutgers, right?"

"Actually, I was down the road at Princeton."

Strang inserted himself back into the conversation. "Smart as well as beautiful. What say we continue this discussion out of the heat?"

"Certainly, General. Perhaps you and Mr. Hazard would care to join me in the first vehicle."

Charlie knew his boss well. Curtis Strang did not like sharing the limelight. In fact, any employee who threatened his position as the corporate face was soon eliminated. Strang hired his men to remain invisible, both on the job and in making the deal. He assigned duties in strict military fashion, and he was tasked with going in first and establishing the corporate beachhead. He glad-handed, made the right noises, won the deal, negotiated the contract, and headed back for his waiting jet. Bang and gone.

Charlie said, "If you don't mind, I'll travel with the second unit."

But the woman was already walking over and opening the first SUV's rear door. "I insist you ride in the back with me, Mr. Hazard. And I am the one who signs the checks."

8

arbor Petroleum is the nation's largest privately owned extraction and refinery corporation. Turnover stands at just under eight billion per annum. We specialize in high-risk regions. We operate fields in Algeria, Libya, Azerbaijan, and Mongolia. Our refineries are in Nigeria, China, and Kazakhstan."

Charlie sat beside Reese in the rear seat. He was positioned behind the general, who was clearly displeased to be treated as the second guest. Strang sat ramrod straight, eyes never diverting from the front windshield, body radiating resentment.

"We are the only American oil company still operating in Venezuela," Reese continued. "We also maintain joint ventures with the governments of Burma and Russia and Georgia. We are currently exploring new fields in the disputed waters off the coast of Turkish Cyprus and in the Chechen hills."

Charlie had the impression that Reese was enjoying Strang's ire. She occasionally gave a brief smile in the general's direction. Then she turned back to Charlie and continued talking.

But not before she gave him the look.

Her eyes were the color of dawn through a winter fire, more blue than grey, and sparked with a feral wit. Her right hand rested on the seat between them. Her fingers caressed the leather, the motions bringing her fingers close enough to touch Charlie's trousers. Every now and then she would stop talking and touch her tongue to her lips, as though she wanted to taste a certain word, as though another thought was crowding into her mouth. When she did, she gripped the soft leather seat, clawing it with her nails. Watching Charlie with those hot-cold eyes as she did.

Charlie had known since his Army days that certain women were drawn to the scent of hidden danger. But they were not normally women in limos, with security details of their own, sent to ferry the hired help back for a corporate meet and greet.

His attention was caught by the driver lifting his shirtsleeve and speaking into a mic attached to his watch band. "Beta One to CC. Inbound at one."

Instantly the woman's hand gyrations might have been in another state. Specialist military assault squads often sectioned themselves into Alpha and Beta teams. Such teams referred to headquarters as CC, which stood for combat controller.

Sending a cluster of former military pros to a Texas airport with a lone woman, no matter how fine the package, was a curious thing.

Harbor Petroleum's headquarters was a block off the main port, rimmed by smokestacks and oil-sized pipelines and holding tanks. The water washing against the breakwater was scummy and the color of dirty copper. The building was a solid cube of black glass and gleamed like an opal set beside a sludge pit. High overhead, the company's initials were framed by a pair of oil rigs that spouted umbrellas of gold.

As soon as Charlie opened his door, the air stank with sulfur. But the general had regained his good humor. He rose from the SUV, took a deep breath, and declared, "Smells like money to me."

The man waiting for them by the corporate entrance was a bulldog, built close to the ground and solid as a concrete block. "General Strang, I'm Weldon Hawkins. Welcome to Harbor Petroleum." He turned his attention to Charlie. "You must be Hazard."

"Affirmative, sir." Charlie suspected Hawkins was a former Marine. Or rather, no longer in that branch's active service. Marines liked to say they never stopped being one. Hawkins was hard as nails and merciless as the Texas heat. Handshake to match.

"Why don't we seek shelter." Hawkins marched them through a vast marble-clad foyer, up a central staircase, and into a conference room. A young man stood at a civilian's semblance of attention by a fully stocked bar. "Anything you gentlemen care for in the way of supplies?"

"We're good to go, sir."

Hawkins said to the young man, "You're dismissed."

The young man touched a keypad and the bar disappeared behind a mother-of-pearl shoji screen. Charlie noted the security had vanished.

Hawkins said, "What say we dispense with the niceties, gentlemen."

Strang settled into a chair. "I've got nothing but the highest respect for a man who values his seconds."

"We're facing obstacles and multiple threats. Two of our frontline execs in Bogotá have recently been kidnapped and are being held for ransom. We can't afford another such incident. We maintain the highest degree of professionalism in our ranks because we pay the best wages and we take our people's safety very seriously."

Strang said, "We maintain what I feel is the best hunter-seeker team in the business. I'd be happy to offer their services."

"Thank you, General. But that matter is already being taken care of. What we want to discuss with you is how we can ensure this never happens again."

Charlie said, "Your people seem professional."

"They're overstretched. What's more, we don't want to maintain a full cadre of our own. You read me?"

Strang said, "Maintaining an in-house fighting force is not your business."

"Right the first time." Hawkins crossed his arms. "You've got ninety seconds, General. Impress me."

This was what Strang lived for. "Our risk assessment detail will be inbound in seventy-two hours. We'll scope your frontline positions. Three roving units will be shoring up your weakest points forty-eight hours later. We'll work with your local security details and bring them up to speed. At that point—call it two weeks from today—you and I will meet again. I will give you a full report. This will include all the points where we feel you need a semi-permanent squad in place." Strang glanced over. "You have anything to add, Hazard?"

Charlie said, "We'll immediately set up four units on short-term travel details. It's probably not required. But such a high-profile move will assure your frontline personnel that you've brought the risk under control."

Hawkins glanced at Reese. The pair shared a nod. Hawkins said, "It's good to hear our word about you is on target, General. Here are our terms. We know your job is to sell your company, and we have no problem with that. Somebody has to run the head office. But we want to know that the man you leave behind will maintain these high standards."

"All of my risk assessment teams are the best in the business."

"We've done our own research and we've settled on the man we want running the show. First day to last." Hawkins used his chin to point across the table. "Either your man Hazard is top gun, or there's no deal."

Strang frowned with his entire being. "We try not to tie down any—"

"That was a take-it-or-leave-it offer, General." Hawkins rose to his feet. "I'll leave my associate to iron out the details."

Strang gave the air a moment to settle, then said, "I didn't catch the gentleman's corporate title."

Reese replied, "Weldon Hawkins is whatever he wants to be."

When Reese offered to take them on a tour of headquarters, Charlie excused himself and slipped outside. The visible security detail had dropped to one man seated behind the wheel of a lone SUV. The massive vehicle was parked where it could slip forward and block access to the main doors. Charlie walked over to the rocky breakwater and pulled out his phone. He dialed the number from memory and said, "Glenda Gleeson, please. This is Charlie Hazard."

"Oh, Mr. Hazard, it's so good to hear from you."

Charlie searched his memory and came up with Gleeson's PA. "Rachel?"

"Glenda was just saying the other day how much she missed you. She's going to be so happy to hear you called. Unfortunately, she's on location for a shoot and will be gone all day. She's on the cover of the next *Vogue* and they're behind schedule—"

"Rachel, Glenda said if I ever needed her, I could reach out. Day or night."

The woman did not remain chief aide to one of Hollywood's hottest stars without knowing how to distill dire need from ego. "Mr. Hazard, Glenda will want to know if this is a genuine emergency."

"Every second counts."

"Please remain on the line, Mr. Hazard."

Charlie endured the heat and the stench. The oily water lapped at the rocks by his feet. Finally he heard a series of clicks. Then a voice that fueled a generation of male lust said, "Charlie? Is it really you?"

"How's it going, Glenda?"

"You bad, bad boy. I throw myself at your feet, and you walk away. Then I don't hear anything for months. How dare you keep me waiting."

"Oh. Like you were pining for this call."

"You should see the tearstains on my pillow."

Charlie smiled. "Liar."

"Rachel said it was an emergency."

"What can you tell me about Reese Clawson?"

There was a fractional silence, then a very different woman said carefully, "Reese is a fine person."

He sensed that she was not surprised by his call. "This is me asking, Glenda."

She breathed hard. "I don't *know* anything."

"She claims you were friends."

"We rented a house together with six other students for two years. Reese was an extremely smart kid. Ambitious. Very political. She campaigned for several politicians. Did her honors thesis on her first national convention. Then she basically dropped out of sight."

When Glenda stopped, Charlie supplied, "She was recruited."

"That's what I heard."

"CIA?"

"Something highly secretive. She loved it, I can tell you that much. She adored being part of something clandestine. Everything changed the summer between her junior and senior year. Reese went off for training. When she came back, she moved into a house on the other side of town. I saw her a couple of times after that. But she never spoke again about what she did. She resigned from all political activities. From that summer on, all I ever saw was the mask. We drifted apart. End of story."

Charlie said, "She says you told her about me."

"That is both true and not true. The first time I'd heard from her in eight years was four days ago."

"So she asked about me, instead of the other way around."

"Oh, believe you me, she wanted to know *everything* about you. She made me walk through the trouble in Chad twice."

"It went down on the Sudanese side of the border."

"Not according to the papers. Are you in trouble, Charlie?"

"You know me, Glenda."

"Meaning you're not able to talk."

"Roger that." He hesitated, then asked, "Do you happen to know Gabriella McLaren?"

"Interesting name. Doesn't ring any bells."

"McLaren is her married name. Gabriella is Italian. From Milan."

"Maybe she's known professionally by her maiden name."

"I have no idea what that might be."

"It's not much to go on, Charlie. I'll have Rachel check, but I'm doubtful. Is she tied into this?"

Because it was Glenda asking, he replied, "There's no logical reason to think so. But my gut says affirmative."

"Should I be jealous?"

He smiled at the waters. "Absolutely."

"Will you call me later and tell me what's going on?"

"Most definitely."

He heard her smile. "Liar."

9

Charlie's second phone call was answered by a man who snarled, "What?"

"This is Hazard."

"Think I don't know that?"

Remy Lacoste was a Cajun who lived as far back in bayou country as he could get and still maintain a satellite feed to the outside world. Remy had lost use of his legs in Anbar Province. Charlie had not known him in-country. He had learned of the man much later, through people he trusted with his life. He turned to Remy whenever his in-house feeds were too slow or he was after something that needed to stay below the general's radar.

Charlie said, "I need data."

"Aw, Eltee. Here I was thinking you'd called to chat about the weather."

Remy had started calling him that the second time Charlie phoned. Eltee was military slang for a favored lieutenant. As in, an officer his troops actually liked. Only seventeen men still alive had known Charlie by that name.

"Harbor Petroleum," Charlie said. "Where do they recruit their security detail? I'm guessing Delta, but I need confirmation. If they've got a contact still in ops, I need his or her name. Who's responsible for hiring in-house. Any reason you can find for them maintaining this level of specialist in-house military ops."

"They your competition?"

"Clients. I need a rough and dirty in half an hour."

"I'm busy."

"I'll pay."

"Thirty minutes it is."

"Give me a full briefing in twenty-four hours. I especially want to know if anyone's been fired recently. Where they are, details of their dismissal, whether they're hungry. You read me?"

"Five by five. You need an in-house source."

"I also need any background you can dig up on Reese Clawson." He spelled the name. "And a guy named Weldon Hawkins. He's definitely ex-military."

"Hang tight, let's scope out the corporate files, see what they say about your pair." There was the sound of keys struck at high velocity. "Whoa. The woman come with the job?"

Charlie recalled the hand clawing the seat between them. "Do they ever?"

"A man can dream, right? Okay, I breached their firewalls and have access. Clawson is a low-level veep of one shade or another. Title could mean anything. Other than that, she doesn't have a file."

"You can't access it?"

"Puh-leese. I mean there's no file on the woman. Whatever data they have on her, it's . . . Hold on."

"What's the matter?"

"I'm being tracked."

"The company caught you looking?"

"This is no company techie. This is a serious attack squad." The man's voice took on the tense fury of incoming fire. "I'll get back to you through a Shanghai shadow line. When you see a Chinese phone number flash on your screen, answer the call. Remy out."

When the others finally emerged from the headquarters, Charlie was already in the SUV's front passenger seat. The general clambered in beside Reese and gave her the professionally smooth line the entire way back to the airport. Charlie said nothing and kept his gaze front and center. When they arrived planeside, he marched himself straight over to the base of the stairs, a good thirty yards from the two vehicles. He waited at parade rest while the general offered his final words for why Strang Security was Reese's company's absolute best choice. She waited until Strang turned toward the jet to offer Charlie a smile and a two-fingered wave.

The general's good humor vanished between the cars and the jet. All Charlie got for his troubles was a flinty, "Inside, mister."

Charlie followed the general up the stairs.

Strang examined the heat-stricken tarmac outside his window while the copilot stowed the stairs and sealed the plane. When the cockpit door clicked shut, the general said, "You like working with my crew, Hazard?"

"Affirmative, sir."

"We've had some good times, you and I. You're solid material. But you're a midlevel officer. You might grow into senior grade. But you're not there yet." Strang aimed a gun barrel of a finger at Charlie's forehead. "You go off on your own, and you'll most likely wind up getting yourself and your men killed."

"General—"

"You shut that hole and listen, mister. I know what you're thinking. You drop the old man, you go back to Harbor and offer yourself as the kingmaker. But here's what you're not remembering. I'm the one who can best assess the overall situation. I have the larger picture in mind. No matter how good you are on the ground, right now you're not up to the task of running the show."

Charlie settled back and waited.

"You have a great future with us. Your leadership is solid. Stay with me and there's a good chance you'll one day take my place. I won't last forever. Right now I want to appeal to your loyalty to your crew and your allegiance to our company. Think about the guys on your left and your right. You don't want to run out on my leadership and risk feeding them to the blender. You follow my tracer on that?"

Charlie did not respond.

"So here's what you're going to do. You're going to take twenty-four hours and scope out what you want. More money, more shore leave, you work it out. Then you report back to me and I'll see what kind of force package we can build for you. Now, you tell me how that sounds."

Charlie replied, "General, this whole thing does not add up."

Strang suspected him of creating a diversion. Charlie knew it the instant the general leaned back and crossed his arms. He was the only man Charlie had ever met who had the ability to frown with his entire body.

Strang said, "Explain."

Charlie relayed his conversation with Glenda Gleeson.

Strang was shaking his head before Charlie finished. He responded, "She's a star. What star tells the truth about anything? The woman is paid a fortune to make an audience believe her lies."

"She owes me her life. She has no reason to lie about Clawson."

"No reason that you know of."

"I think she was telling the truth, General."

"Say she did. All we know is Reese Clawson was formerly CIA."

"Glenda didn't say that. She said Reese came back from her summer internship and went clandestine. What intel branch sends potential agents to summer school for clandestine ops?"

"I don't follow."

"My last five years in the military, I trained covert operatives on field techniques, remember? I made it my business to understand where they were coming from, how they were recruited, what training they received. Every American intel group does their first specialty training once college is over and done. The last thing they want is to risk having a trainee return to school and start blabbing."

For the first time, Strang seemed to give Charlie's argument his full attention. He knew Charlie's background, how his in-country tour had been abruptly ended by a homemade phosphorus grenade. The same grenade that started his time as professional trainer of America's front liners against terrorism.

Charlie said, "There's something else. Did you notice the in-house security?"

"I found them very capable."

"They were more than that, sir. I'm fairly certain they all come from specialist ops. These guys were sleek, cool, alert. Five bodies with one head."

"Don't tell me you're worried about a little in-house competition."

"No, General."

"We simply insert a clause in the contract that states all corporate security must answer to you as long as you are in-house."

"Sir, we're not talking about Blackwater sending a crew beyond the Green Zone. When was the last time we found assault teams working within an American headquarters? The answer is never."

Strang mulled that over. Corporate security was, at best, retired cops coasting to a well-padded retirement. At worst, they were muscle-bound dunces who had failed the police examinations and spent their free time lifting weights and gobbling steroids. Not once in all his time with the general had Charlie ever suggested the in-house help was worth a second look.

Strang said, "You heard them say it. They've had kidnappings."

"Two. In *Colombia*. This is *Texas*. Why do they need us, General? I know they said they didn't want to build their own team. But they've already got one. Those men could train and staff and do so with in-house knowledge."

Strang wanted to argue. Charlie saw it. When nothing came to mind, the general ground the words with his molars. "Find out what's going on. That's your first duty. Once we've got the contract in our pocket."

Charlie said slowly, "I don't know if I'm ready to sign on for this job, General."

"That is not an option, Hazard. This could be the largest contract we've ever handled. You know my policy. If Strang rises, he takes his men with him."

"Sir, the first duty of any up-country officer is to know his enemy and his terrain. Right now I don't—"

"Say I start a new division. You come in as my first and only veep. Think of what I'm saying. Private jets. Serious money. Percentage of the spoils."

"I appreciate it, sir. But I've got to tell you, this job has the smell of a killing field."

Strang's gaze tightened. "You're refusing a direct order?"

"All I'm saying at this point is, I need to determine just what we're up against before I can sign on."

"If their security is half as good as you say, they'll know the instant you start sniffing around. That could well cost us the contract."

"Sir, that's a risk I think we must take."

"I'm sorry to hear that." The general's voice sounded like a cement mixer working through a fresh load of gravel. "The other day I fielded a call from a detective with the Los Angeles homicide division. He'd been assigned a cold case, one involving the woman who used to be your wife."

Charlie was punched back in his seat. His breath released like he'd taken a hit at gut level. Which he had. Two of them, in fact.

The first was having his late wife become a pawn in the general's game plan.

The second was seeing every tie he'd ever had to the man being completely severed.

"You might want to reconsider what it means to walk away and not have Strang watching your back." The general's eyes glinted with the simple pleasure of a warrior delivering a blind-side attack. "You've seen the carrot and you've seen the stick. Now you tell me which one you intend to go after."

Charlie sat there a moment longer, getting over the shock. Then he rose and walked to the cockpit. He slipped inside, shut the door, and asked the pilot, "What's our closest airport?"

The pilot pointed to where the gulf's azure waters gave way to Florida green. "Fort Myers is ten minutes out and counting."

"Radio ahead and request a landing slot," Charlie said. "I'm done here."

10

Reese Clawson kept an office on the third floor of Harbor
Petroleum's headquarters. Her name was on the door. Her
view was over the parking lot. She had a desk, an inbox, a
computer she had never turned on, and a telephone she did not use.
She locked the door and began the routine she always followed after
being away, be it for a month or for lunch. She opened her purse
and took out what appeared to be an iPhone. She swept the desk, the
floor, the walls. Satisfied, she stowed away the bug detector and seated
herself behind the desk.

Her purse was a slim shoulder rig, right down to the gold designer
label. Which meant most security stations spent their time inspecting
her and not the purse's contents. There was no existing terrorist profile
for a blonde in Valentino carrying a Ferragamo bag. If x-rayed, the
contents showed just the standard female equipment. Compact, two
phones, jeweled perfume holder, tablet. As Reese rarely showed up at
Harbor Petroleum for more than a day at a time, everyone assumed she
was some top executive's live-in pet. The women on her floor avoided

meeting her eyes as she passed. Such things used to hurt a lot more than they did nowadays. Reese had developed calluses down where they never showed.

She turned on her real phone, coded into the built-in scrambler, and listened to the series of pings confirming that the line was now secure. Instantly her phone rang. "Clawson."

"I've been phoning you for *hours*."

"I'm here now, Patel."

"Somebody is *tracking* you."

Patel Singh was the best techie Reese had ever worked with. But his verbal gyrations left her tired. "Strang's in-house people?"

"Of *course* not. You think I'd be panicked over a company *clone*?"

"Patel."

"What."

"Lose the histrionics."

"Well, he *rattled* me."

Reese tended to sigh a lot when dealing with this man. "What do you have?"

"Somebody ran through the Harbor firewall like it was *smoke*. I mean it took him less than a *minute*."

At a knock on her door, Reese said, "Hold one." She hit the switch on the desk's underside, and the door's electronic lock clicked. Weldon Hawkins and their chief of security entered. Reese waited until the door was locked once more, then said to her phone, "But you checked and there's nothing on me for them to find, right, Patel?"

Weldon slid into the seat opposite her. Trace, the security chief, took up station by the door. Weldon said, "Can Patel wait?"

Reese replied, "There's been a breach."

Trace came to full alert. "Of the Combine's security, or here?"

"We're not sure." She hit the phone's speaker button and set it on the desk. "Go ahead, Patel. We're all listening."

"I've gone all through Harbor Petroleum's system. Their file on you is empty. That's not the *point*."

Weldon nodded agreement. "The breach has to be tied to Strang's visit. Patel, who was the hacker?"

"That's the *next* problem. I can't *find* him. I lost him in Kuala Lumpur. The guy almost trapped *me*. His cutout was the Malay intelligence agency's personnel system. I heard the alarm bells in *California*."

"That all?"

"I *wish*. When your man Hazard left headquarters, he made two calls. One was to Glenda Gleeson. The *star*. The other was to a number in *Alaska*. A number that doesn't exist *anywhere*."

Trace said, "So Hazard walks outside, calls the source you used to confirm what we know about him. Then he contacts an outsider, somebody not on Strang's payroll. And we get breached."

Reese nodded agreement. "Patel, I'll get back to you." She cut the connection.

Weldon said, "Your cover's blown."

"Shredded, more like." She recalled the way Charlie Hazard had watched her play with the seat between them and said, "I thought I had the guy hooked."

"Maybe you can convince Hazard to ignore the evidence."

"Doubtful. If he already has an outside tracker hunting us, something alerted him to our hidden agenda."

Weldon shrugged. "So we up the ante. Offer him more money and anything else that might—"

The phone rang. Not her purse phone. The one on her desk. The one through the company switchboard.

Weldon said, "Answer it."

Reese did so. "Clawson."

The operator said, "Mr. Hawkins has an urgent call. I was told he might be with you."

Reese said to her boss, "It's for you."

"Put it on the speaker."

Reese punched the speaker button and said, "Go ahead."

There were a series of clicks, then a voice demanded, "Am I through?"

"This is Weldon Hawkins."

"Strang here. I wanted to thank you for the meet."

"Do we have a deal?"

"Absolutely. But it doesn't include Hazard."

"Those weren't my terms, General."

"Now, you listen up. You know as well as I do, these Ranger types are all cowboys. That's why we have them. They'll scale whatever wall stands between them and their target. But sooner or later the civilized polish wears off and you're left with nothing but extreme risk. I hired Hazard to be an asset. He's just crossed the line and become a liability. So he's been deleted from my portfolio. I'll bring in my best men and do the job right. That's all you need to know."

Weldon hesitated a fraction, then said, "Clawson will be in touch next week. We'll let you know our decision."

"Roger that. Strang out."

Weldon hit the button and said, "Toss Strang enough crumbs to make sure he doesn't squawk."

Trace, still stationed by the door, said, "Hazard was Ranger?"

Reese did not need to check Charlie Hazard's file to verify. "He did a month-long tour in Iraq. Less. His first trip up-country, he took a hit. When he got out of rehab he spent three years at Fort Benning and another two at FLETC."

Trace looked worried. "Nobody said anything about the guy being Ranger."

Weldon said, "What's the issue here?"

"For one thing, it was a total waste of time, sending some no-brain bikers up against him."

"We had an hour's notice," Reese replied. "We did the best we could. All they had to do was slow them down. They failed. We're dealing with it. End of story."

"Not if he connects us to the attack."

"We had a firewall. Several. There's no way he can uncover our involvement."

"But you want me to take him out, right?"

"Absolutely," Weldon replied. "He's walked away from the offer. We can't leave him out there to cause us trouble."

"We don't know that he will," Reese said.

"We've been through all that. There's no other reason for Gabriella's team to have brought him in."

Reese looked from one man to the other. Sometimes she felt their male aggression led from one absurdly belligerent action to another. But this time she sensed they were genuinely worried. "Hazard is just one man. And we still don't have confirmation that he's agreed to help Gabriella out. Why are we getting so worked up?"

"Because he's Ranger," Trace replied.

Weldon asked the security chief, "Can you still do the job?"

"You find Hazard for me. Fast as you can. We want to strike before he gets any confirmation we're involved." Trace frowned at the heat beyond the window and added, "I'll need my entire team."

11

Charlie rented a car at the Fort Myers airport and followed the state map to Lake City, a charmless low-rent sprawl about sixty miles inland from Tampa. From there he headed another twenty miles east, along a road so flat it looked ironed. The scenery was pure Florida wilderness, scrub pine and brush and cattle and humidity. He pulled into a tiny lakeside community at sunset, rented a motel room, and ate a solitary meal in the town's only diner. The mattress was ancient and the springs noisy, so Charlie pulled the covers onto the floor and slept soundly.

He awoke in the dark hour before dawn and was the diner's first client. He then drove to his destination, parked on the street, walked around the house, and settled onto the lakeside dock.

The home of Colonel Donovan Field was unpretentious in the extreme. The colonel had never much cared for what other people considered elements of the good life. He had lived for duty, service, loyalty, patriotism. The more these components became unpopular, the less the colonel had to say about anything.

Donovan Field had run the Federal Law Enforcement Training Center, known as FLETC among the intelligence trade. All field agents with DEA, CIA, and State, as well as every Homeland division except the FBI, trained there. Many city antiterrorism divisions also sent their detectives. Defense intel, which constituted more than sixty percent of the nation's total intel budget, used FLETC for advanced training.

Twenty minutes after Charlie arrived, he heard a screen door slam. The last time he had seen the colonel was at his own wedding, when Donovan had given his secretary away. Charlie recalled that day as the colonel tottered across the lawn to where he sat on the lakeside dock. Donovan had needed to lean heavily upon the bride's arm. That day, as now, his legs had seemed impossibly frail for carrying such a massive upper body. The colonel had been badly wounded in the first Iraq war. He did not speak about it. Charlie knew a number of other old warriors who treated their injuries in the same careless manner. The world was not perfect, their silence said. Deal with it.

A truly ancient terrier panted at the colonel's feet. Donovan limped over and offered Charlie his hand. "How are you, son?"

"Fine, sir." Charlie watched the terrier slump onto the dock and stare at the water. "I don't remember a dog."

"My sister-in-law passed away last year. I agreed to give him a home. The old boy has arthritis, a bad heart, cataracts, and no sense of smell. He's been exactly the same way for twelve years. Probably will outlive us both." The colonel settled onto the bench beside Charlie, bent over stiffly, and scratched the terrier between his ears. "I heard through the network you lost your wife."

Charlie gave the colonel the raw truth. "About nine months before she died."

"I'm sorry, son. Is that why you're here?"

"No." He stretched out his legs and watched the morning mist drift over the water. "Nice place."

"Libby thought so. But she's gone, and I find it lonely here by my-self." Donovan grunted and settled back on the bench. "Are you ready to tell me why we're having this conversation at dawn on the end of my dock?"

Donovan had several qualities rare in officers and men. One of them was the ability to set the world aside and listen. He sat and stared out over the water as Charlie described the meeting with Gabriella, the highway attack, the experience at the hospital, the telephone con-versation, the trip with Strang, the meeting at Harbor Petroleum, the ultimatum. Charlie finished with, "If you can make sense out of that, sir, you're better off than I am."

The dog growled from his position at the colonel's feet and gave the empty waters a hoarse bark. The colonel slipped his foot out of the shoe and stroked the pup's side. For the first time, Charlie saw the stubs where the colonel's toes should have been.

Donovan said, "Sounds to me like you're facing your very own breakout."

The words took Charlie straight back. The colonel had often started his toughest conversations that way. A breakout was military speak for an event that shattered all existing parameters, such as when the enemy introduced utterly new tactics, or the Pentagon sliced budgets in half and demanded the same operative capacity. The colonel had been known throughout the country's intel divisions for being the best there was at preparing agents for breakout events.

Donovan continued, "What you need to decide is whether you're ready and able to grow beyond your current mind-set."

"Absolutely."

"Don't respond too hastily. Growth means change. Change of this kind can bring gut-wrenching challenges."

A grey-winged crane swept over Charlie's head. The morning was so quiet he could hear the air filter through its wings. The crane flapped twice and came in for a landing in the reeds to their left.

Charlie said, "After the accident when my wife died, I spent six weeks lost in a fog of painkillers. Finally the doctors stopped offering refills and I switched to booze. I hated both, but it was easier than facing what I had inside, which was nothing at all."

The crane moved with impossible grace for such an ungainly beast. It lifted one leg like a ballerina caught in the amber of dawn, settling it down so carefully the water was not disturbed. It took another step, shifting through the reeds, hunting.

Charlie went on, "I started attending AA at a church down the block from my empty apartment. I went back to my job with the insurance company. I got out of bed and I put on my tie and I drove to the office and I came home and I watched whatever sport was on television. I joined a gym. I knew I was coasting, but I told myself this was the best a guy like me could ever ask for. And a lot better than I deserved."

The colonel might have waved the words aside as not worthy, or he might have been swatting a fly. At his feet the dog kept up his hoarse panting.

"Then General Strang showed up and offered me a job. Afterward it felt like I had returned to the only thing I would ever be good at. There's never been any real satisfaction to the work, not then and not now. More like, everybody's got to do something to fill the void. I might as well do this. Then Gabriella showed up, zapped me with those harmonics, zinged me out of my body . . ." Charlie shook his head. "I can't believe I actually said those words. But ever since waking up that next morning in the passenger seat of a stranger's car, I've carried the feeling that everything has changed. If I want. If I'm ready."

The crane struck the water and emerged with a fish flapping silver in the daylight. The bird lifted its head and swallowed. The fish shivered hard enough to be visible as it slid down the crane's gullet. The bird froze once more, quiet as the reeds, quiet as the water.

"The luckiest of us reach a moment when we wake up one day and discover what we want to do with our lives." Donovan's foot continued to rub the dog's scruffy chest. "I wish I could say it's all downhill from there, but I can't. What I can say is, if you don't take hold of that chance when it comes, you'll regret it for the rest of your life."

Charlie tasted the truth, retreated, then forced himself to ask, "What if I don't have what it takes anymore?"

Donovan looked at Charlie for the first time. "The life well lived is a search for identity, priorities, peace, wholeness. I'm not saying you'll ever find them. But having the courage to even speak the words puts you ahead of the crowd. Then one day, the fortunate few discover something they can give their total allegiance to. They identify a purpose that creates harmony from all the impossible elements and all the past pains. Even speaking that desire aloud is terrifying. What if you're wrong? What if you get halfway down that road and find you've been fooled by life again? What about everything you're giving up? The risks are huge. Of course you're scared."

Donovan grunted as he bent over and covered his stub of a foot with his shoe. "Too many people coast through life, Charlie. They keep waiting for that perfect solution to all their problems. Until their calling arrives risk-free and tied in a lovely blue ribbon, they have their safe little excuse for not moving at all. They never grow beyond the delusion that life should deliver dreams on comfortable terms."

He grunted again as he hoisted himself to his feet. The dog rose with him and panted off the dock. "Don't make that mistake, son. You can't attach a dollar value to truth. If you run from a lifetime chance just because the price is high, you'll drown in shadows or cynicism or both. You grab hold with both hands. And you get ready for the fight of your life."

12

I f Reese did not actually work here, she would have considered the Reserve the scariest place on earth. Forget Kabul at midnight. Skip the Kurdish borderlands between Iraq and Syria. Knowing what she did, she would rather march through Tehran wearing nothing but an American flag than take on the Reserve.

But since this was her own personal enclave, Reese's secret name for the Reserve was Power Center.

"The founders had three models in mind when they designed the Reserve. The first was a high-tech retreat center called Jason's, where each summer the nation's top fifty physicists are brought together and given a problem the Department of Defense cannot solve. Jason's was originally run by the Stanford Research Institute, but when the California university system started its leftist drift, the project was taken over by the Mitre Group out of Washington. The name originated from the myth of Jason and the Argonauts, in which the Golden Fleece offers total protection from the gods of destruction."

Reese was midway through the part of her job that she most detested. Once each quarter, every corporate member of the Combine could send their new reps on a tour of Reese's world.

The Reserve was the headquarters for a group that did not exist. But it had to have a name, so some bright individual had come up with the idea of calling it the Combine. Each corporate member appointed three senior executives who attended the Combine meetings and acted as point men. These executives were the only ones who could visit the Reserve. Just three. New corporate members often complained this was not much in return for a joining fee of fifty million dollars and annual dues of another five. But all such comments died away the first time they sought the Reserve's help.

Reese went on, "The second model used in structuring the Reserve was STRATFOR, where twenty futurologists make initial design concepts for so-called impossible tasks. Stealth technology was a direct result of their work. The third model was DARPA, the Defense Advanced Research Projects Agency, which made its name with advances in anti–submarine warfare known as MADs, for Magnetic Anomaly Detectors."

Every three months, Reese did this little go-round for new Combine execs. Weldon flatly refused to have anything to do with them. The trouble with most corporate power guys was, they couldn't keep up. They were all cloned from the same gene pool—conservative, old, stodgy. They resented change because change threatened the company's bottom line and their own grip on power. Their talk centered on risk management and hedging bets. Given the chance, they would lock the future in a cage.

Thankfully, Reese was almost done with this ordeal. They had dined in the residence and attended their first power talk in the main conference center. They had met the current team of live-in brains, brought together from a variety of fields. Four of the execs had slept right through the brains' summary of future trends. Reese had brought them outside for a breath of fresh air before the final act. They were fully alert now, waiting for what Reese secretly called the big bang.

The Reserve's nine acres dominated the largest plateau on the La Jolla cliffs. A hundred meters below them was the house that had cost a certain talk show host thirty million dollars. The Reserve's sculpted gardens contained four large buildings and fifteen elegant two-bedroom bungalows, all designed in a bizarre mixture of Spanish hacienda and Southern California bling. The structures reminded Reese of ritzy bordellos lining the Mexican Riviera.

"If you gentlemen will please take your seats." Because they were here for the first time, Reese added, "You may find it more comfortable to restrict yourselves to one company per table."

This next act was definitely not something they would want to share with members of other corporate teams.

Reese gestured to the security agent hovering in the background. He set the briefcase chained to his wrist on her table and handed her the key. Reese pretended not to see the execs share a smirk, clearly thinking this was just unnecessary theatrics. She unlocked the briefcase and passed out the files.

These updates were specifically tailored to each member company. They contained confidential reports from their biggest competitors, news about bids they were in the process of losing, products that could well wipe away all green from their bottom lines. There were a couple of gasps, a few soft moans.

"Thank you for your time, gentlemen." Reese stowed away her professional smile as she left the group. She followed the covered path away from the cliff edge and the glistening Pacific, entered the carriage house, and shared a smirk with the security guy unlocking the steel door. The Combine's newest members would not need to worry about falling asleep any time soon.

Two hours from now, the corporate jets would whine their way into the San Diego municipal airport and Weldon Hawkins would supervise the Combine's quarterly meeting. Reese's job was done. She could return her attention to other matters. Which was a good thing, because they had a problem. A big one.

She took the circular stairs into the Vault. There was a glass-walled elevator, but this was only used by Weldon and the few top Combine officials who were permitted to ever set eyes on where the Reserve's real work was done. The Vault's staff disliked being caged by the elevator. It wasn't the walls. It was the speed. Even if the elevator had descended like a bullet, it would still be too slow for Reese's crew. They all took the stairs. Unless they were *really* flying. Then they slid down the steel banister, which was very dangerous because the stairs deposited them at the top of a four-tier arena. One wired techie had flown down the ninety-three-foot spiral railing, flipped over the waist-high glass barrier, and done a headfirst dive into the first tier of flat-screens. That had happened the month before Reese's arrival. The crew loved to regale newcomers with the Vault's secret lore.

The Vault was modeled after a Defense war room. That was hardly a surprise, since it had been built by the same group that had refitted the Pentagon's own underground chamber. The Vault was 130 feet wide and 100 feet high. The front wall was dominated by massive flat-screens, while the rear wall stretched out like a concrete fan. The shape directed the crew's attention forward, surrounding them with a constant reminder to *take aim*.

Four semicircular tiers rose like arena seating from the flat-screen array. Each contained seven tech stations. Each tech station possessed five thirty-inch flat-screens. At first glance, the streaming electronic arrays were overwhelming. It usually took a new techie about a month to find their feet.

Reese demanded, "Where's Patel?"

"In Playpen One."

Reese walked around the outer rim. She passed her office with its glass wall overlooking the main arena and stopped before the next chamber. The chamber was the size of an executive conference room and contained a miniature version of the arena's data display. The Vault contained three such chambers. The techies called them playpens because they were assigned to temporary teams and tasks. Normally being assigned to a task force meant the gloves were taken off. The techies could do whatever they needed to do, ask for whatever support they felt they required. Just so long as they delivered.

All the rear offices had walls of glass. At the flip of a switch, the glass walls turned opaque and a current scrambled all internal sounds. Reese tapped on the grey glass and waited for the electronic buzzer to unlock the door. She pushed through and said, "What do you have?"

Patel whined, "We lost Hazard. The man is *gone*."

"That is unacceptable."

Patel Singh was Reese's favorite techie. The Vault crew was supposed to be leaderless, a cluster of independent operatives who answered directly to either Reese or Weldon, depending on the task at hand. But there was a problem with this approach. Most of the Vault crew's interpersonal skills were just terrible. Many preferred to skulk in the electronic shadows and let somebody else do the talking. Like now.

"Charlie Hazard left the plane in Fort Myers," Patel said. "It's taking *forever* to locate him."

Reese slipped into a chair now vacated by a woman who clung to the side wall. "Hazard argued with Strang. He either quit or was fired."

"He rented a car from Alamo." The front wall held another bank of flat-screens. The top segment flashed up a map of the Florida peninsula. "There are *eleven* different routes he could have taken across the state."

"You've got a watch on his home?"

"Of *course*. Surveillance is 24-7." The bottom half of the screen now displayed a live-stream video of a sixties ranch-style home. "The trip should only have taken him three hours, four tops. Hazard has not gone home."

Reese pointed at legs protruding from beneath a car in the garage. "Who's that?"

"Julio Lopez. He's *nobody*."

"Patel."

"What."

"The guy is on our screen. He's at Hazard's house."

"He's not at the house. He's in the garage," Patel said. "He was working on the yard for a while. Now he's got his head stuck in some old car."

"That happens to be a vintage Stingray."

"Whatever." Like most techies, Patel held the past in supreme disdain. "It's *so* last week."

"We don't know anything about Hazard. We don't even know where he is. Why don't we have audio feed?"

Patel gave her a withering look and clicked his mouse. Instantly the playpen was filled with the clamor of Hispanic hip-hop. On the screen the kid's feet danced where they stuck out from the car.

"Turn it off."

Patel hit the switch. "The kid is *nowhere*."

"I want a watch put on him. Full background feed. The works."

"It's a waste of time."

"Do it. Now tell me where Hazard has gone."

"Well, I do have *something*." On the map, all the cross-state lines vanished but one. "This is not the most direct route. But it *does* take him through Lakeside Estates. We've spent all *night* running down all of his previous known associates. Hazard's last posting was FLETC, which stands for—"

"I know FLETC. Give me the connection."

"Colonel Donovan Field, former commandant of FLETC, retired to Lakeside Estates." One of Patel's silent minions typed into her keyboard. The Florida map was replaced by a photo of a grizzled warrior. "Donovan Field is your basic gung-ho fanatic. Three Purple Hearts. Two Bronze Stars with clusters, *and* a Silver Star. He personally recruited Hazard."

"What do our Pentagon allies say about this Field?"

"That he is not a player."

Reese grimaced. The Pentagon had its own code. "Not a player" meant someone who treated military suppliers as outsiders. These were people who put patriotism above their future careers and above corporate profits. For Charlie Hazard to refuse their offer, leave Strang, and go straight to a man described by the Combine's military allies as not a player was the worst possible news.

"I have to check this out." Reese rose from her chair. "In the meantime, extend your scope on Hazard. And move back into the arena. Bring the entire crew up to speed, in case we need them."

Even the limpets clinging to the walls disliked that news, but they let Patel complain for them. "We can *handle* this guy."

But it wasn't just the guy anymore. "Do it. I want a full workup on Julio Lopez in an hour."

13

Donovan was cleaning up after a breakfast so late it might as well have been lunch when the dog at his feet barked. Which was a curious thing, since the mutt was mostly deaf. "What's the matter, boy?"

The dog was staring in the general direction of the front door. He barked again, then gave a long growl. It was the most noise the dog had made since coming to live with Donovan.

"You're not hurting, are you, boy?" Donovan was bending over to stroke the dog when the doorbell rang.

The dog growled and lay flat. Terriers were originally bred as ratters. Pound for pound, they were some of the most ferocious animals on the planet. The old dog was crouching into his position for meeting a foe. Low to the ground, protecting his vulnerable underbelly, ready to spring and strike.

Donovan used the rear passage to slip into the bedroom. He was too stiff to crouch, so he carried a towel with him, rubbing his hands like they were stained. "Right with you."

He didn't know if the words carried. Just like he wasn't sure whether there was a second person acting as a spotter at the rear of the house. He veered around the bed, still wiping his hands. He used his body to block the rear window and took the pistol from his bedside table. There had been a couple of robberies recently. The lakeside community's only police protection came through the county sheriff. But Donovan doubted the thieves would ring his doorbell.

"Coming!"

In the windowless side hallway, Donovan slipped the Smith & Wesson into the band of his trousers. He pulled out his shirttail to hide the bulge and flipped the towel over his shoulder.

He opened the door and blinked at the figure standing on his front stoop. "Vic Reames, as I live and breathe."

"Hello, Don. I hope I'm not interrupting."

"Man, you're a sight for sore eyes. Come on in."

"I was at Patrick's and had to go to a meeting in Tampa. Thought I'd take the roundabout route and stop by."

As Donovan led his guest into the living room, the dog tottered through the kitchen doorway and growled. "Don't mind that old boy."

"I didn't know you had a dog."

"Minding him for a friend. He's got gas something awful. How about a drink?"

"Too early in the day for me. How you keeping, Colonel?"

"Seen better days. Can I brew up a fresh pot?"

"Thank you, Don. No time. I need to hit the road before long." He fiddled with his hat. "Actually, I need to ask about an officer who served under you. Charlie Hazard."

Donovan paused in the process of easing into his Barcalounger. "Now, that's interesting."

"What is?"

"Charlie was here when I got up this morning. First time I've seen him in . . . what, must be going on five years."

"Mind if I ask why he was here?"

"He's been working for Curtis Strang. You remember him?"

"That's actually why we stopped by today."

"We?"

"I've got a pair of colleagues waiting in the car."

"Why on earth didn't you invite them in?"

"Can't. We're due in Tampa." The man wore the civilian clothes of a military lifer, bought off the rack, ill fitting, totally charmless. "We're thinking about offering Strang some of our consulting work."

"Iraq?"

"Farther north. Hazard's name came up. He works as one of Strang's chief risk assessors."

"Worked."

"Excuse me?"

"Strang offered Charlie the chance of a lifetime. Charlie got spooked and turned him down. Strang fired him. Charlie came here wanting my advice."

"Mind if I ask what you told him?"

"Not at all. I said fools were born every day, but losers are molded through a lifetime of mistakes. I told him to crawl back to Strang on his hands and knees. Sure you won't take that coffee?"

Reese stood in the kitchen of her Reserve studio. The northernmost building contained studio flats for all the Vault crew. Perks like this kept the turnover down to an absolute minimum. Her crew worked four days on, three off. When on duty they supposedly worked twelve-hour shifts, but the truth was that they were constantly on call. The hours would have been the same at any cutting-edge Silicon Valley firm. But the Reserve's perks were a thousand times better. These studios were a perfect example.

A wall of glass and a narrow balcony kept the campus-sized studio from becoming claustrophobic. There was just enough space for a bed and a chair and a narrow desk and a corner kitchenette and another chair and a dining table for one. The furnishings were all Danish modern, light wood and clean lines, right down to the wall-mounted light fixtures. The minuscule bathroom was done in pale granite. The units were serviced daily.

Reese could have taken her meal in the main facility. The Reserve's employees had their own dining hall located one floor below their employers' refectory. The food was the same, except the employees were served buffet-style. But Reese grew tired of the rich fare. She preferred to make her own meals and have a little time to herself.

Just as she finished washing up the salad bowl, her phone rang. She checked the phone's readout and said, "Talk to me."

Patel replied sulkily, "Vic Reames is reporting in."

"Five minutes." Reese left the studio and descended the stairs and entered the California heat. The afternoon was scented by frangipani and wisteria. Both plants bloomed year round in the perfect San Diego climate. She took the path that bordered the cliffside by habit. Her first year in the Reserve, she had been thrilled by such moments, when the sun blistered the pristine air and the Pacific shone like a burnished sapphire. A faint ocean breeze carried the flavors of sea salt and eucalyptus. Nowadays Reese scarcely gave the scenery a glance.

The Combine's corporate bosses had arrived, so the security staff was on full alert. As she walked the perimeter pathway, she also passed two strangers in corporate-security jackets. She entered the carriage house and took the stairs down to the arena. Patel ignored her as she slipped into the chair next to his. He bristled with resentment over being required to share his crew's unfinished task with the full Vault crew. Her statement that this problem might have grown beyond the capacity of his little group, and the need to prepare for any future eventuality, meant nothing. Patel wanted bragging rights for having vanquished another foe.

The pettiness of these people never ceased to amaze her.

Patel handed her the phone without speaking. Reese directed her sigh at the receiver. "What do you have?"

Major Vic Reames was a member of the Pentagon's top procurement team. He was nineteen months from retirement. He was slated to take up a senior sales position with the Combine's primary defense contractor. Which made him almost hyper-eager to please. "Hazard went to see him."

"When?"

"Early this morning."

"The colonel didn't suspect you might have an ulterior motive?"

"I gave him the company line as ordered. He lapped it up. Donovan Field is suffering from a severe case of the lonelies. The old boy almost begged me to stay. Otherwise it was a total waste of time."

"Let me be the judge."

Reames gave her the blow-by-blow, right down to the growling blind dog. "The colonel gave Hazard the only logical answer. Apologize to Strang. Crawl on his belly. Find the answers to his questions from inside the assignment your group offered Strang's company."

"You didn't get the impression the colonel might be hiding something?"

Reames laughed. "The old guy would have repeated his story a third time if it meant getting me to stay awhile longer. He's every reason why I am not looking forward to retirement."

"You'll be taken care of." Reese hung up and sat staring at nothing. There was no reason for her gut to be churning. None at all. She realized Patel was watching her. "What?"

"You look so *worried*."

She stretched. She needed a day off and knew it was not going to happen. "Do you have the workup on the kid at Hazard's place—what's his name?"

"Julio Lopez." Patel slipped the wireless keyboard into his lap. The screen closest to Reese flashed with a police mug shot. "Rising star on the amateur surfer circuit and a professional loser. He has two juvie convictions, the last was when he was fourteen. For the past three years he's stayed clean, at least as far as the authorities are concerned.

His father is a convicted felon. Mother is off the map. Julio lives with his aunt, who was arrested this week on her second meth charge. I spoke to the public defender assigned to her case. The aunt claims some bikers had basically forced her to go along. She'll turn state's evidence and get off with a slap on the wrist."

"What is the kid's connection to Hazard?"

"Skimpy at best. He hangs out at that community center where the Italian doctor contacted Hazard."

One of the women formerly attached to Patel's team announced, "We have movement."

"Where?"

"The colonel's house."

"Put it on the main board."

That stopped traffic throughout the Vault. Shifting any action to the front screens meant an elevation to high alert.

An alert status meant the events or people or both were a direct threat to the Combine.

Patel whined, "What are you *doing*?"

Reese ignored him and asked the woman, "Can you get a better resolution?"

"Working on it."

The screen flashed through red and green and purple as the computer sought to draw clearer focus from a camera that the team who had traveled in with Major Reames had fastened to a telephone pole across the street from the colonel's house. There was another camera around the back of the house and a third by the lakeside dock. The team had also attached homing devices to the colonel's car and boat.

The colonel stood in his doorway. He was dressed in a bathrobe and pajama bottoms and an Army T-shirt so washed it was more grey than green. He held the door open. Reese saw his mouth move.

"Why don't we have audio?"

The speakers crackled and she heard, "Think maybe you could get a move on there?"

The camera's view widened to show a man standing by the open rear doors of a delivery van. "You order the pizza with anchovies?"

"At my age? Are you nuts?"

"I've got six boxes here and every one of them . . . Okay. Spinach and extra cheese, right?"

"Yeah, that's mine. Oh, hang on, my wallet's in the back. Let yourself in and shut the door, I don't want mosquitoes . . ." The door slammed.

The system was not capable of catching the delivery man's muttered curse.

Patel asked, "What's so dangerous about *pizza*?"

As in, why was this on the main board and not back in the playpen under Patel's control. The answer was, Reese didn't know. But she knew her boss. Something about this deal had Weldon seriously worried. And Reese's boss did not worry easily.

She watched the delivery guy slip back through the front door and trudge around his van. The guy might have been limping, she couldn't tell. When the van drove away, she said, "Okay, take it off the main board. But stay on the colonel."

14

How much do I owe you for the pizza?"

"Come on, Colonel. You don't owe me nothing." Earl unzipped his nylon jacket. "How'd I do?"

"You did great. But you've got to let me pay—"

"The box is empty, Colonel. You didn't say nothing about being hungry."

Donovan slipped out of his bathrobe. "Laura won't miss you?"

"She's out playing bridge for the day. I left her a note. Told her I'd gone fishing, wouldn't be back until after dark. If they were biting, it might be an overnight thing. Won't be the first time."

"I don't want her angry with me."

"That makes two of us." Earl slipped on the bathrobe and house shoes. "Where are you headed?"

"East. Make yourself at home. The fridge is stocked."

The bathrobe was too short on Earl's lanky form. "You know, when I heard your voice asking about a pizza, I almost forgot everything you told me."

"I'm glad you remembered."

"This old brain putters and clanks, but it still gets me around. You in trouble?"

"I don't know."

"But you think you're under surveillance."

"I'm sure of it. Whatever you do, don't answer the phone."

"I remember that much." Earl had spent eleven years in Defense intel as a technician, then become Donovan's personal aide at FLETC.

They had discussed the prospect soon after Donovan retired. Two old codgers sitting on a lakeside dock, drinking beer and pretending like they still mattered. Donovan knew that was what Earl had thought at the time, and his buddy had probably been right. Even so, the deal was made. If one or the other called and ordered a spinach pizza to be delivered in half an hour or less, the other was to play delivery boy and get there fast.

Donovan said, "That guff about the anchovies."

"Pretty good, huh."

Donovan stepped from the hallway into the living room. He reached for the door, then stopped. "It might be best if you stayed in bed as much as you can."

"Thirty years in the military, I think I can handle a little extra sack time."

"Keep the dog locked in the kitchen and don't worry about any messes. If he growls, it probably means he's hungry or thirsty. You'll need to nose him toward his bowls."

"The wife's cell phone is on the passenger seat." His oldest friend gave Donovan a two-fingered salute. "Good hunting, Colonel."

ıļı·

Charlie spent the journey home reviewing the colonel's advice and reliving the experience in Gabriella's penthouse lab. He had heard of out-of-body experiences, even talked to a few soldiers who claimed to have watched themselves in near-death situations. But doing it himself, and having it be so calm, so *controlled*, left Charlie feeling intensely vulnerable. He was no stranger to fear. But this was different. No matter how unsettled the memory of this experience left him, his yearning to do it again was far stronger. The conflicting emotions left him feeling at war inside himself. Which was why, when he pulled up in front of his house, he had trouble focusing on what he saw.

"Julio?"

The kid was standing on a stepladder, half hidden in a palm tree. "Man, where'd you get that lame ride?"

"It's a rental." Charlie walked around a massive pile of yard debris. "What are you doing?"

"Watching your back, man. Least I could do, after your moves back at my aunt's house and then giving me this cool place to hang." The kid dropped to the ground and did a little duck and weave. His gloved hands held long-handled shears that he now used like a samurai sword. "Dude, the way you handled those bikers, that was ice."

"You don't owe me a thing."

"Yeah, whatever. Hey, check this out."

Charlie followed the kid around the side of the house. Soon as his rear garden came into view, he froze.

"Last two years, I earned my walk-around change doing lawn care. Pretty good, huh."

Charlie's rear garden was rimmed by a windbreak of Chinese cane and bougainvillea. He had always meant to trim the shrubs, which tended to rise up and overwhelm if they weren't watched. Now the bushes were all boxed into neat shoulder-high squares. The grass was trimmed, and mulch had been laid around all his flowers. Julio had even raked the sandpits surrounding his fighting pole and the workout area.

Julio was trying hard to hide his nervousness, waiting for Charlie's reaction, doing his duck and jive, swinging the shears.

Charlie said, "This is the best it's ever looked."

The kid beamed. "For real?"

"I've always meant to do it but never did. Even if I had, I couldn't have done a job this good."

Julio beamed, started to punch Charlie's shoulder, then thought better of it. "The best is yet to come, bro."

⊹｜｜｜⊹

Reese stood on the carpeted rear ring by the Vault's stairwell. She was connected to Trace by her headset. Through her earpiece she heard the jet's soft rumble and the man tapping his heavy gold ring on the table.

She asked, "Are you getting this?"

"Five by five," Trace confirmed. His face was on the arena's top right panel. His features were turned slightly orange by the in-flight transmission. "How recent is this?"

"It's live, right, Patel?"

"Real-time feed," Patel confirmed. He heard Trace the same as she did.

Trace and the Vault's crew watched Julio shout something lost to the roar of the Stingray's motor.

"Smooth ride," Trace said.

The kid juiced the engine again, then cut it off and slipped from the car. They heard him tell Charlie, "Back before he got busted, my old man used to let me work in his garage. He was magic with cars, man."

Charlie replied, "I tried to take it yesterday, but the thing wouldn't start."

"What I figured, since you left the keys in the ignition."

"I can't get over what you've done here." Charlie put his arm around the kid's shoulders. "This was my dad's all-time favorite ride."

"It's a sweet machine, bro. Pure cherry."

Charlie steered Julio into the house. "Let's grab a bite. You work up an appetite?"

Reese asked Trace, "When do you arrive?"

"Hold one." He was gone and back in ten seconds. "Pilot says we're inbound at twenty and closing."

"Once you're on the ground, how long will you need to ready your team?"

"Depends on what you want."

"I want Hazard gone."

"I know that." She could hear Trace tapping the ring in time to his words. "What I need to know is, how much noise can I make?"

Reese lowered her voice. "The less the better. But speed is the most important factor."

"We could slip in tonight, do the job, fire the house. They'll know it was deliberately set, but not why."

"No. No waiting. We've got to assume he's on to us."

"Then it's liable to get very noisy."

"Weldon will *hate* that."

"You take out a Ranger, especially one who knows you're coming, it's bound to wake the neighbors. What about the kid?"

The sound of his ring tapping the table felt like a drill to her brain. "What is the word you guys use for that kind of stuff?"

"Collateral damage."

"Just do the job."

⫶⫶⫶

Charlie was just finishing his sandwich when the phone rang. "This is Hazard."

A voice distorted by tension and cell phone static said, "Foxtrot to Eltee. Foxtrot to Eltee."

Charlie turned to stare out the home's rear window. To the left of his practice pit rose a massive live oak, a Florida tree that never lost its leaves. It was one of the world's slowest growing. It was also one of the hardest. During the Revolutionary War, planks of live oak were used to construct the ship that came to be known as "Old Ironsides," due to how cannonballs fired by British guns bounced off its gunnels.

Charlie had time to review this and the wind sifting through the tree's silver leaves, all in the space of about three heartbeats. His adrenaline rush was that strong. "Reading you five by five."

"Zenith. Repeat Zenith."

The power punch grew stronger still. "Roger that."

"Give me your RP in the one-niner-two grid."

Charlie did not need more than half a second to respond, "Java Surf at A1A."

"Hold one." There was a tense silence. "GPS says I'm inbound in eighteen. Foxtrot out."

Charlie hung up the phone. He stood gripping the receiver. Staring at the sunlit tree. He debated whether he should go back to the main house and pack a case, then decided there wasn't time.

"Charlie?"

He turned around. "Pack your things. Bring whatever's important. We leave in ninety seconds."

Reese demanded, "What did I just hear?"

Patel was scrambling. "No idea."

"Bring Trace back up. And somebody get me a source for that call." When Trace's frown appeared on the front screen, she said, "Play it for him."

"Here we go," Patel said and reran the telephone call.

The conversation lasted a grand total of fourteen seconds. Reese timed it. "Do we have a fix on the source?"

Patel's team member replied, "Cell phone. Area code is for Lake City."

Trace asked, "Where is that, exactly?"

"Southwest of Orlando," Reese replied. "Hazard has a contact near there. Colonel Donovan Field. He stopped by and saw him earlier today."

"Field is Ranger?"

"FLETC. Retired."

The techie seated next to Patel, Kimmie, said, "I have something. The nearest pizza house is 28.6 miles from Donovan Field's home."

Trace said, "Long way to go to deliver a ten-dollar pizza."

"There's something else." Kimmie tapped the keys. "This is a play-back of the original call Donovan Field made."

The sound of a phone ringing came over the line, then, "Hello?"

Patel muttered, "Sounds like the call woke the guy up."

They listened to Donovan Field order a spinach pizza and give his address, and the guy on the other end gradually come alert, confirm, and hang up.

"No business name," Reese said. "No price. No checking the address."

Kimmie said, "The number belongs to one Earl Hammond. The van's license plate matches."

Patel said, "Could be a side business."

Kimmie added, "The cell phone that just called Hazard is listed under the name of Laurel Hammond."

"Track the phone. Now." She turned to Trace's image and said, "What can you tell me about that call to Hazard?"

Trace was frowning. "It's military code."

"Well, just, duh." She snapped her fingers. "Come on. I need to know what just happened!"

"Eltee was a nickname you heard once in a while. Short for lieu-tenant. It meant an officer that the men on his team fully respected. Most officers weren't liked well enough to get tagged."

"Who was Foxtrot?"

"Could mean anything. Ditto for Zenith. Every division in the field develops its own lingo. Means they can be on the same wavelength as a dozen other squads and identify what is specifically meant for them."

"What about RP?"

Trace nodded. "Sure, that's standard chopper speak. Means rendez-vous point. He asked for a meeting place in the 192 grid."

Patel read off his screen, "Highway 192 runs from below Orlando straight to Melbourne, the city below Satellite Beach. It dead-ends beachside at Highway A1A."

Reese said to them all, "He knows."

Trace replied, "Gee, you think?"

She was going to snap at him but was saved from needing to apologize later by Patel saying, "Check out the main board." The earlier image of the pizza delivery van pulling up in front of Donovan Field's home flashed on the lower screens. "Earl Hammond retired in 2005 from thirty-five years in the military. Rank of master sergeant. A string of medals."

Trace said, "Probably a hard striper."

"What?"

"Means an NCO who earned his rank in combat."

Reese mulled that over a fraction of a second, then rolled her finger at Patel. Go.

"His last posting was as chief aide to Colonel Donovan Field."

She told her team, "Run the delivery sequence."

They watched the two men argue, then the man carried the pizza box inside and the door shut. Three minutes later, the door reopened and the guy returned to the van. Hat down, sunglasses on, jacket lapel up.

Reese said, "He's limping."

"So?" Trace said.

Kimmie read off her monitor, "Colonel Field lost part of his foot outside Kuwait City. Earl Hammond carried the colonel to safety and won a Bronze Star for his trouble."

Reese said, "Field knows we're watching. He waited to contact Hazard until we wouldn't have time to scramble." She had to report this to her boss. Weldon Hawkins hated being interrupted when the Combine gathered. But this couldn't wait. She asked Trace, "Can you still take him?"

The guy was still watching the screen, still frowning. "Tell Hawkins we don't have any choice but to light up the whole city."

15

Charlie drove them to the municipal airport in silence. He dropped off the rental and tossed Julio's backpack into the rear hold of Gabriella's Range Rover, which was still parked in the private aviation lot. Julio slid into the passenger seat and gave the side window his best sullen glare. Charlie knew Julio's life had been filled with adults who did things he couldn't understand. Sullen was probably his best defense.

Charlie told him, "That phone call I received was from the colonel I served under after I did my stint with the Rangers."

Slowly, gradually, the kid emerged from his funk. "You were one of them?"

"Four years, but less than four weeks of that was frontline duty. We were stationed in Anbar Province. The first two weeks, we had a couple of close calls but nothing serious. A few night firefights . . ." Charlie stopped.

"What is it, bro?"

"I've never talked about this before." Not even when the nightmares woke him screaming and Sylvie was so spooked she made him sleep in the living room. He shook off that batch of bad times and went on, "I was wounded before my first month was up. I spent about a thousand years in rehab. Then I was assigned as a trainer at the Ranger school. Three years later, I moved over to serve the colonel in charge of a place called FLETC. It trains field agents."

"You mean, like, Homeland Security?"

Charlie nodded. "My call sign was Eltee, a tag my NCO gave me. The colonel was Foxtrot. That's what I just heard on the phone. 'Foxtrot to Eltee.' Nobody has spoken those words to me in years."

Julio was clearly lost. "So what did the dude say?"

"That we're about to meet incoming fire. And we've got to hurry. Or we die."

Charlie stayed in the car, the motor running, the nose pointed toward the world. He watched in the rearview mirror as Irma Steeg emerged from her apartment building. The kid walked alongside her, talking a mile a minute. Irma opened the Range Rover's passenger door and Julio slipped into the rear seat, saying, "I'm telling you, Charlie's place is a trip."

She asked, "This for real, you're giving Julio an apartment?"

"That was the plan. But it looks like that may not be an option, at least in the short term." Charlie had the car moving before Irma shut her door. "I need you to take a ride. I don't have time to sit here and explain."

"All I've got holding me here is a cup of coffee that went cold an hour ago." Irma turned and said to Julio, "Only reason I haven't offered you a room is, I've got a tiny one-bedroom condo."

Julio said, "I've been to your place, Irma. I've seen bigger closets."

Charlie headed south on A1A and related the colonel's call. "Zenith is field comm for 'our perimeter is breached.' It means we've got enemy combatants coming at us and we're cut off from base."

Irma said, "You think this retired guy is going to tell you something that will put you back on the road?"

"No idea. But Donovan Field is a man who never spooks."

"So you're concerned that if somebody's after you and the colonel, and they can't find you, they might ask Julio."

"It's probably crazy."

"No, no. If they put your place under surveillance and see the kid hanging around, it's only natural." She said to Julio, "We'll work something out."

"I knew Charlie's place was too good to be true."

"The place is still yours. Soon as things cool down," Charlie said. He asked Irma, "You don't mind me bringing you in?"

Irma patted Julio's shoulder. "It's what friends do, right? We watch each other's backs."

⑂

The barrier island that began at the Canaveral Space Center and ended at Sebastian Inlet was connected to the mainland by five causeways. Each causeway was the natural extension of a major east-west highway. Highway 192 was the farthest south and joined the beachfront highway at the Indiatlantic Boardwalk. The juncture was marked by a square containing six shops. Four were aimed at the tourist trade—a Starbucks, a taco hut, a restaurant selling pizza by the slice, and a frozen yogurt shop. Tucked around the back was another coffeehouse, a locals-only establishment and easily missed. As Charlie circled the lot, he worried that Donovan would not think to ask a local, or if he did, the locals might not tell him where Java Surf was located.

Then he spotted the young man he had last seen on the hospital's top floor. Charlie rolled down his window. "Brett?"

Irma said, "I thought you said his name was Donovan."

Julio asked, "This dude was a Ranger?"

Brett was as handsome as ever, only far more worried. He slipped into the rear seat beside Julio and said, "Drive."

"I'm waiting for somebody."

"Not anymore." He jerked as Irma swiveled and pulled the pistol from her pocket. "What are you *doing*?"

Irma said, "I'm introducing you to my friend, Mr. Beretta."

"Put that away."

"He's not the problem, Irma."

"You sure? He looks like trouble to me."

Charlie drove the Range Rover slowly down the length of the boardwalk. "What are you doing here, Brett?"

"Delivering this."

When his hand went toward his pocket, Irma aimed her gun again. "Hold it right there."

"Are you *insane*?"

"I'm a cop who's stayed alive on the job for twenty-five years. Drop your hand." Irma reached into his jacket and came out with an envelope. "This what you were after?"

"I'm a scientist."

"We're all just so impressed. Really."

"Brett," Charlie said. "I asked—"

"Gabriella said to meet you here. She said there would be three of you." Brett made a swatting motion in the air between him and Irma. "She didn't say anything about *guns*."

Charlie parked by the curb but kept the motor running. "Put away the weapon, Irma." He said to Julio, "Keep a tight watch."

The kid's eyes were globular. "No problem, bro."

Brett wiped his face with a shaky hand. "This whole thing is nuts."

"Where is Gabriella, Brett?"

"She's gone."

"What's happened?"

"First I need to know if you're with us."

This time Charlie did not need to think it over. "Absolutely. I'm in. Now tell me what I've signed up for."

Brett chewed on his cheek for a second, then said to Irma, "Go ahead. Open the envelope."

As she did so, her eyes grew to match Julio's. "This is a travel agent's confirmation for three tickets to Zurich, Charlie. No names. They're good as cash."

Julio leaned over. "Zurich, like in Europe?"

Brett said, "There's a number at the bottom of the page. When you get to the airport, call it. You'll be given further instructions."

Irma looked from one to the other. "These are for us?"

"Gabriella said there would be three people traveling. Hazard, you're not one of them. She said your team must be drawn from outside standard security parameters. Does that make any sense to you?"

"Yes." Charlie knew she meant that anyone brought in from the security industry could be compromised. "So one of these tickets isn't for me?"

"No, you're going to meet her in New York." Brett clearly hated this duty. He asked the pair, "Can I assume you two have passports?"

"Backpack," Julio said. "I've just moved house."

Irma said, "I'll need to run by my condo."

Brett looked at his watch. "We've got to hurry. The plane leaves Melbourne in less than three hours."

Charlie said to Irma, "I didn't mean to drag you guys into this. You can turn this down, it's fine."

"I wouldn't mind knowing a little more about what we're signing up for here," she said.

"I have no idea," he replied.

Brett said, "All your questions will have to wait."

"Works for me." To Charlie's surprise, Irma actually grinned. "I've got to tell you, retirement is so totally the pits. I've applied for a job answering the phone for the local cops."

"All I've got on the books is a history exam," Julio said. "You think maybe I could get a note for my teacher?"

Charlie rose from the car and opened Irma's door. "Soon as I see Donovan I'll meet you at the airport."

As Irma slipped behind the wheel, Brett rolled down his window and said, "Gabriella has a very specific message for you."

Charlie said, "Looks to me like she's got you spooked."

"A woman I thought I knew tells me to stand in this parking lot, in a specific spot she described down to a stain on the pavement. She tells me you will be driving her Range Rover, and you'd be with two passengers, both of whom are to become part of this." Brett handed Charlie the third ticket voucher. "This is for your flight to New York. You have precisely forty-one minutes."

Along with the ticket was an envelope addressed to him in a woman's flowery script. "To do what?"

"How should I know? But Gabriella said to tell you that if you are anywhere you know or are known forty-one minutes from now, you are a dead man."

16

Charlie stood behind a cluster of palms that encircled the beachfront park's showers and restrooms. He held to the stillness that came naturally after years of training, melding with shadows to where the eyes of any watchers would slip over and continue searching. Or so he hoped.

Truth be told, he felt giddy. The past two days had held enough surprises to push him miles beyond any realm that had a nodding acquaintance with such mundane things as normality. Or logic. There was no logical way that a woman he did not know could beckon and Charlie Hazard would come running. Not to mention how two acquaintances would sign up for the madness as well, without even knowing why.

He was so involved in his internal musings he almost missed the grizzled head that poked from the window of an ancient van and spoke to a passerby.

Charlie sprinted across the lot and wrenched open the passenger door. He heard Donovan say, "That's all right, ma'am. I've got what I need now." The van pulled away before Charlie had his door shut. Donovan said, "Good to see you, son. You doing okay?"

"Curious."

"Long as you're not bleeding, we're ahead of the game." Donovan pulled up to the stoplight. "Where to?"

"I need to stop by my house."

"Risky."

"It's got to be done. Take a right." When the van was heading north, Charlie asked, "Where's your dog?"

"With a pal. You ever heard the name Vic Reames?"

"Should I?"

"He's an Army major approaching retirement and desperate for a fat payoff from our corporate suppliers. The word is, Vic has become part of what is as close to a cabal as we've ever had in the military–industrial complex."

"Does the cabal have a name?"

"The Combine. Does that ring a bell?"

"Sorry, no."

"No reason it should. The Combine may be just a myth, but I don't think so. Too many rumors from too many different sources. We've been trying to get a handle on them for years."

"Who is 'we'?"

Donovan shot him a look. "There's a good reason we don't share overall strategy with our frontline warriors, son."

"I read you."

"About ten years ago we started hearing tales about a group of major companies that had joined together. Most are American, but not all. They share two things in common. First, they are global entities. Second, they are utterly without scruples. Their motto, if they had one, would be 'Whatever it takes.'"

The van they were in was at least twenty years old. The carpet at Charlie's feet was worn down to the metal floorboard, and the interior smelled of hot oil. Charlie opened his window and let the salt breeze wash over him. "Is Harbor Petroleum part of this group?"

"No idea. But given what you told me and what's happened since, I'd say they are fronting for the Combine."

"What about Strang?"

"So far as I know, Curtis Strang operated below the Combine's radar until they hit on you yesterday. All I know for certain is, an hour and a half after you left, Vic Reames popped up in my doorway. He was oozing charm, all concerned about me and my retirement and my dog."

"And me."

"Vic Reames panted like the Combine's trained pup, and he asked about you. I played the lonely old codger, which bought me enough time to sneak away. But he's on to me and they're on to you. Sure you have to go to your house?"

Charlie glanced at his watch. "I've got a few minutes left."

"Says who?"

"A friend. Get in the left lane and turn at the next light."

"That woman you told me about, the one who can foretell the future?"

"Her name is Gabriella. As for reading the future, it's the only thing that makes any sense." Charlie described his recent conversation with Brett, then offered Donovan the third ticket voucher.

Donovan was shaking his head long before Charlie was finished. "I'm not going anywhere, son. I'm too old and I'm not well and I've got a dog that won't eat unless I hold the food to his mouth."

"What's the matter with your health, Colonel?"

"That's not the issue at hand. You need to focus if you want to stay alive. This Gabriella lady said you could go by your house?"

"I've got another nine minutes. I need to get a look at whoever's painted a target on my back. Turn right and pull up."

Charlie dropped from the van while it was still rolling. He loped across a yard, leapt over a humming air conditioner, skirted behind a doghouse, and was over the rear fence just as a dog's chain clinked.

He froze, waiting for the dog to settle once more. Another house, another fence, and he walked through the cane growth surrounding his backyard. He passed his fighting pole, a polished tree trunk sprouting two-foot branches at various angles. His feet crunched across the sand of the exercise pit. He fished his keys from his pocket and let himself in.

⫼

"Trace, where are you?"

"A1A, just passing the Ramada."

"Hazard has just entered his house."

"I thought you said he was at some café."

"That was *then*. Speed *up*." Reese shook her head. The security chief had her talking like Patel. "How long?"

Over the loudspeaker came the sound of squealing tires. "Ninety seconds."

The sound of six men breathing hard filled the Vault. The entire crew gawked at the front screens, which showed the view of cameras fitted to the helmets of Trace and his number two. Reese resisted the urge to snap at her crew, tell them to get back to work. The scene was too powerful. She found herself breathing in time to the men.

Someone to her left muttered, "Is this amazing or what."

The vehicles carrying Trace and his team screeched to a halt. Trace asked, "Target is still contained?"

Patel said, "The cameras on the front and back of his house are quiet."

But Trace could not hear Patel or anyone else. Any time they sent in a team, they worked according to standard combat rules. In-house chatter could distract, and any distraction could be deadly. Contact between intel and ops was held to one person on each end. If the security chief went down, Reese would switch to Trace's number two. Otherwise, this was as intimate as Reese ever cared to be with the man.

Reese said, "I confirm, Hazard is still inside the house."

Trace said, "Team Two, deploy."

"Team Two moving out."

The two cameras split and flew.

"Patel, widen our view."

The techie erased the streaming data from all the front screens and blew up the view so that each camera filled half the floor-to-ceiling array. The house appeared to the left and the right. The cameras jounced as the men flew across the lawn. On the back of each midnight uniform were the letters FBI. It was a useful cover for moving in daylight. Hopefully a nosy neighbor would think twice before calling the cops.

The views crouched lower to the ground. Four sets of black boots thundered past each team leader.

"Team Two in position."

Trace said, "On my mark. Ready, go."

The crew watched as the home was assaulted from both sides. Reese felt as much as saw a figure drop into the chair next to hers. She glanced over. Weldon was as fascinated by the action as she was. She turned her attention back to the screen. Not long now.

"Come in, Center."

"Go."

"Uh, the house is empty."

Patel said, "That is *impossible*."

Reese lifted the mike. "You're sure?"

"Roger that."

Patel's voice rose to full whine. "I am *constantly* monitoring our views of the exterior! The man has *not* left."

Trace obviously heard him over Reese's mike, because the loudspeakers to either side of the array huffed, "And I'm telling you, squirt, the dude is gone."

Weldon jammed his chair against the desk behind him and rose to his feet. "Just gets worse and worse."

Trace said, "We have neighbors watching."

The right-hand screens drifted through an empty living room.

A hand moved forward and swept back the drapes. Through a sun-splashed window they saw a pair of old people standing on the front porch directly across the street. The man held a phone to his ear.

Reese said, "Stand down, withdraw, await orders."

"Roger that. Team leader out."

Weldon called to her from the stairwell, "Damage control. My office. Fifteen minutes."

17

Charlie crept from his rooftop aerie, where the dormer windows paralleled the chimney on the house next door. The giant live oak that dominated the view out the garage apartment's rear window had one limb that extended almost to his bedroom balcony. The limb was so stable he could walk it without using his hands. Firing on this team would have been an invitation to be blown into kitty litter. So Charlie remained crouched behind the chimney until they fully deployed, then used Gabriella's cell phone, called his neighbors across the street, and asked them to go outside and tell him if his house was on fire. It was all he could think of at the moment.

He watched as the group of men filed out. Each bore the standard FBI patch on the front and back of their SWAT-style uniforms. One of them tossed the neighbors a quick salute and hustled over. The man exchanged a few words with Charlie's concerned neighbors, then retreated to the two SUVs and drove away. Just another day in vacation land.

Charlie eased back through the neighborhood, slipped into the van, and told Donovan, "Two teams in standard Delta deploy. One of them I recognize from my meeting at Harbor Petroleum."

Donovan eased the van into gear. "Back to the airport?"

"Right. Sure you won't come with us?"

"Not a chance. What's more, you don't want me."

Charlie started to mention how that was the one anomaly to everything Gabriella had said. Then it hit him that the ticket might not have been meant for Donovan at all.

Donovan was saying, "I've got friends who are as worried about these Combine folks as I am. You get into a sticky situation, you get me word, I'll see what I can do."

Charlie asked, "Could you make a side trip before going back home?"

"Probably. You got a plan, son?"

"Maybe."

Before Charlie finished explaining, the colonel was already nodding. "That could work."

"You think he'll come?"

The colonel pulled up in front of the airport terminal. "I think he's been waiting all his life for your phone call."

18

Weldon Hawkins said, "For the past nineteen months, part of our brain trust has been focused on a new issue. Many facets, a multitude of scenarios, but all derived from one base concept. Anticipate the paradigm shift."

Five of them were gathered in one of the alcoves off the conference center's top floor. The ground floor held a half dozen meeting rooms. The middle floor contained the banquet hall and a state-of-the-art spa modeled after ancient Roman baths. The top floor was referred to as the Club. The Club held bars, a cinema, a billiard parlor, a smoking room, a library, and lovely courtesans of both sexes. Its alcoves were framed in oiled paneling and Isfahan carpets and windows sealed behind heavy drapes. They were places meant for secrets and strategy. When the Combine gathered, the entire center was swept daily for bugs.

Weldon stood by a fireplace acquired from a Medici palace. Reese was seated in a straight-backed chair she had pulled in from the library.

The three gentlemen facing them were sprawled on leather settees, their jackets opened, their hands holding cigars and snifters of vintage brandy.

Weldon continued, "Our brief here at the Reserve is direct enough. We are to follow corporate and economic and political and legal trends. We are to anticipate the moves of national and international govern-mental bodies. Where possible, we are ordered to turn future trends to our members' benefit. We are to use whatever means necessary to determine your competitors' strategies. And we are to use all the powers at our disposal to further your aims."

The trio seated between Reese and Weldon were members of an intricately interlocked series of corporate boardrooms. Closest to Reese sat Edgar Ross, former US treasury secretary and now CEO of the nation's second-largest investment bank. He nodded thoughtfully as Weldon continued, "An examination of possible paradigm shifts is a natural component of our mandate. The modern marketplace is too high velocity and too intensely competitive for our members to worry about something that may or may not arrive. That's our job."

Next to Ross sat the Swiss chairman and CEO of a pharmaceutical empire that stretched around the globe. He also owned two extremely private Swiss banks. His accent was thick but polished. "Are we quite done here?"

"Not yet. A paradigm shift is defined as an event so monumental it takes humankind to a completely new level of existence. In technol-ogy, one paradigm shift came with the invention of the microchip. In medicine it was the discovery of antibiotics. Part of our think tank here is drawn from groups like the Heritage Foundation and the Brookings Institution, where they have been trained as futurists. They take raw data and search beyond the standard event horizon."

Next to the Swiss sat an Italian telecommunications mogul. He was glossy and slick, and he eyed Reese with the glittering gaze of a well-fed panther. His focus did not shift as he asked Weldon, "You have found something?"

"Until this week, I would have answered you with *perhaps. Perhaps* we have an issue that *might* be a real threat."

"And now?"

"For several years now, a number of respected academics have been predicting that the time is ripe for a *cultural* paradigm shift," Weldon replied. "For companies ready for this transition, such a change could catapult them into world dominance. For those left behind or caught unawares, it would mean oblivion and collapse."

The Swiss magnate said, "Get on with it."

"One concept arose that troubled us most of all," Weldon said. "What happened if the next paradigm shift eradicated the global corporate culture?"

The Italian laughed out loud.

"That was our initial response as well. Since the days of Phoenician traders, the world has been ruled by profit and greed. We accused our futurists of watching too many *Star Trek* reruns. But then we found ourselves unable to let it go. We lost sleep over it, every one of us. Because the more we thought about it, the more valid this concept became."

Weldon walked over to the window and drew the heavy drapes, blocking out the sparkling night. "The modern corporate culture is built upon certain assumptions. They have been around so long we forget that there was ever once a different system. Today we control the consumer. We dominate their world. We define their fantasies. We promise them fulfillment through our products. We tell them who they want to be. We define success. When they get there, we tell them how to dress and what to drive and how they'll measure their self-worth. We tell them which pills will make them well, lose weight, stay active. What music defines their life. What entertainment—"

"What did you find?" Edgar Ross demanded.

"Our team decided the greatest risk to our current system would be the simplest. And that is, what might cause the culture to stop listening to us?"

The trio ceased fidgeting.

"And the answer was, it would only happen if they discovered something that was more powerful, more compelling, than anything we had to offer them. Something we could neither market nor package. Something over which we had no control."

"You mean, another drug."

"No. Something far worse. Something without any negative side effects at all."

"Impossible," the Italian mogul declared. He was no longer watching Reese.

Reese spoke for the first time. "Think about the internet."

The Swiss gentleman waved her words aside. "We don't control the medium, but we do control the flow."

"Not all of it," the banker mused. "Not by a long shot."

Weldon said, "We asked what would happen to our situation if we were faced with a new item of such overwhelming allure that everything in the commercial process paled in comparison. Then, almost as soon as we framed the question, we discovered a team working on precisely such a concept. And they were making astonishing progress."

"Buy them out."

"Unfortunately, what they are proposing cannot be patented or controlled. Once the consumer learns of its existence, we may well lose them entirely."

"So crush them. That's what you do, yes? Operate outside the boundaries."

"We can't find them," Weldon said. "We thought we had everything under control. We drew in their financier, and without his knowing we found a way to monitor the team. But somehow they discovered they were being watched. And they vanished. What's more, they have brought in a security specialist. A former Army Ranger who trained CIA agents in counterterrorism tactics."

The room had ceased to breathe.

"We sent in our best force. All of them. He escaped."

"They know," the Swiss magnate said. "About us, and about you hunting them."

"We can only assume this is the case."

"This is terrible."

"I agree."

"Where are they?"

"We are fairly certain it's somewhere in Western Europe. But we can't be sure of even that. All we know is, some of their members flew to Zurich. Border controls being what they are these days, we lost them there. There is one possibility for finding them. Just one." Weldon focused on the two European gentlemen. "For that, we need your help."

19

Charlie's air taxi had departed Melbourne supposedly for Tampa. But immediately after takeoff it had swung north of Orlando, then descended into the rich horse country of Ocala. They made what the pilot said was an unscheduled landing on a private strip shared by a dozen mansions, all of which had airplane-sized garages fronting the strip. As Charlie descended the air taxi's stairs, a needle-sized Lear was already powering up. He boarded and the pilot shut the jet's door, telling Charlie they were headed for New York.

Charlie spent the journey north flattening Gabriella's letter on the burled-walnut table. The letter said simply, *I need you, Charlie. Please come.*

He had nothing against a woman who did not mince her words.

The jet landed at Teterboro and Charlie took a taxi into Manhattan. Remy Lacoste phoned as the taxi was crossing the Hudson River. He said in greeting, "Only reasons I'm calling is one, I said I would, and two, I want my money."

"Are they still on your tail?"

"You've brought me some serious heat. I want a lot of money, bro."

"I'm off the grid myself, Remy. Strang fired me. There isn't a lot of money to pass on."

Remy gave that a beat. "So you're taking on the Combine."

"First time I heard that name was this morning."

"You'll soon be wishing you missed that conversation. I know I do."

"Give me what you've got."

"I been tracking rumors for years. The Combine is basically your corporate bogeyman. There's nothing written, and most people who know anything for certain are too scared to talk. What I heard, they were originally founded in the early eighties to counteract the surging might of the Japanese keiretsu, or family of companies. There aren't any Chinese or Japanese companies in the group. Otherwise it's pretty much borderless. A majority of the companies might be headquartered in America, but that's basically just an address. Their loyalty is to money. Their goals are simple in the extreme. Maximize global profit and power. Vanquish all opposition. Anybody who stands in their way gets toasted."

"Why no Chinese?"

"The Chinese government and companies are so tight they're basically one and the same. The Combine doesn't include any company whose interests are tied to a national government. Sometimes they've got to take the gloves off and obliterate government opposition."

"You got anything on the two names I gave you?"

"Typical Combine personnel. Reese Clawson was probably taken straight from university, on account of how her personal records basically vanish at age twenty-one. She might as well have emigrated to Mars. Weldon Hawkins was CIA, then went to work for Raytheon. At age forty-one, he basically vanished too. Must've joined Clawson on the red planet."

"You have an address for the Combine?"

"What, you're thinking maybe you'll drop by, see if they're hiring?"

"And a phone number and website."

"Man, you are seriously twisted."

The cab pulled down a leafy side street and halted in front of a red-brick neighborhood church, the address Brett had written on the envelope. Charlie handed the driver a bill, slipped from the cab, and said, "It'd be good to have an idea how many security agents I'm up against."

"Let me see if I've got this straight. You can't pay what you owe me, you've brought me some serious heat, and you want more?"

"If you could track the movements of either Hawkins or Clawson, that might help as well."

"In your dreams, bro."

"I appreciate everything you've done, Remy."

"Wait, here's something on the house. You find the Combine on your tail, you *run*."

The church stood between Second and Third Avenues, five blocks from Central Park's north end. Charlie had left the East Side glitz about ten blocks earlier. The buildings here were modest brownstones, the pedestrians a Manhattan mix of young up-and-comers and Harlem's more international flavor.

The church was red brick and stone, very much in keeping with the neighborhood—comfortable, a little stodgy, fronted by wide steps and a few stunted trees. As Charlie pushed through the doors, the leather strips swished softly over the stone floor. He had always liked how Catholic churches smelled, the old incense a silent welcome for drifters like him. He scouted the sanctuary but did not see Gabriella. He settled into an empty pew. He did not need to reread the letter. He was as certain he had the right place as he was that she would show.

Ten minutes later, Gabriella emerged from the confessional booth. There was obviously some silent pecking order, because instantly another parishioner rose from a front pew and slipped inside, closing the door behind her. Gabriella wore a shawl of mantilla lace over her hair. Charlie watched her settle into a pew about five up from his own and wondered if this was some genetic oddity, how certain women could take anything, even a strip of coffee-colored lace, and turn it into a fashion statement.

Then the priest's door opened. A spare man with wispy hair poked his head out. He searched the sanctuary until he found Gabriella. He stared at her so intently, several parishioners turned to follow his gaze.

The priest slipped back into his booth and shut the door. The parishioners kept staring at Gabriella. She remained bowed over her hands, giving no sign she was the least bit aware of the attention. Charlie made no move to join her. She had not looked in his direction, but he was certain she knew he was there.

Ten more minutes passed before Gabriella joined him. Her first words were, "Someday I hope I find a way to say how much it means that you are here."

Charlie gave her sad countenance a brief examination. "Will you tell me what's going on?"

"Soon." Gabriella checked her watch. "We have a few more minutes. Do you mind if we stay here?"

"Not at all." He motioned toward the confessional. "Something you said sure rattled that priest."

"I told him what was happening today. I asked him if Galileo sought absolution before he wrote up his discoveries."

"Is the church threatening you, Gabriella?"

"I hope and pray not." She shuddered. "Will you tell me what has happened to you since we were last together?"

Charlie recounted the events leading up to his flights north. "Do you know who the Combine is?"

"Not the name. Not even why they are after us."

"How many are you?"

"Nine, counting you." She glanced at him, looking anxious now. "You are with us, yes?"

"That's why I'm here."

"Our goal seemed so simple initially. We sought to replicate certain experiences in a measurable and clearly defined manner."

"Religious experiences."

"That was the problem that started me down this path, Charlie. So many people today feel that *religion* is an empty word. The question for me was, how could I combine recent scientific developments with this constant human hunger for something beyond the physical." She cast him a sad smile. "Who would ever have thought we would generate such a huge . . . I'm sorry, I can't think of the word."

"Firestorm."

"Yes. That. We knew there would be opposition, but we expected it from the scientific community. But not this. Never this." She was silent a moment, then murmured, "The two default structures for mankind's perception of the world are religion and science. Since the Reformation, these two have grown farther and farther apart. Nowadays, the catchword among most scientists is *exclusive*. Either you are scientific or you are religious, but you cannot seriously be both. But this is all beginning to change. Prohibiting an appeal to the supernatural, in my opinion, cripples modern science. Quantum physics is entering a phase where these two structures are no longer so clearly divided. To progress, the new operative word must become *totality*."

Charlie said, "Okeydokey."

But Gabriella was too involved in her internal vista to realize she had lost him. "I am a psychologist. My discipline has been under attack since Freud began his studies. The criticism is always the same. How do you quantify unseen experiences so that they can be measured? Did I say that correctly, 'quantify'?"

"Your English is better than mine."

"Thank you. Yes. The problem with all nonphysical states is the same. Some psychologists, called behaviorists, have responded by claiming that all human action is based upon external stimuli, and this can be defined and controlled and measured and predicted. I have spent nine years in behaviorism and I know it to be a lie. But their *methods* are valid. Over time I met others from different disciplines who shared my desire to measure identifiable components of the human psyche."

Her voice had risen such that glances were cast their way by other parishioners. The priest left the confessional and stared at her once more. Gabriella noticed none of it. Charlie did not mind the attention, or the fact that he did not understand a lot of what she was saying. He was content to sit and draw a fraction closer to this amazing woman.

"We sought one specific issue. One definable experience. Something we could instigate, measure, and set within established parameters."

"The experience you led me through."

"I came across research done back in the seventies and eighties. The man, an American, was a radio engineer. He conducted the first-ever experiments using sound to stimulate particular brain-wave patterns. What you experienced, separating human consciousness from the physical body, was for him just a secondary phenomenon. The man has since died, and his work was left unfinished. We decided to apply new developments in quantum mechanics and something called chaos theory to a more highly refined experimental structure.

"That is where Brett came in. He is a biologist specializing in brain chemistry, which means he has also done considerable research into the electro-impulses that create thought, memory, and emotion. Brett helped us re-form the radio engineer's work around recent discoveries in brain-wave patterns. Our aim was to separate consciousness from the physical form in a controlled environment. If our work proved valid, it would mean redefining the entire structure of scientific thought and the human experience."

"You're talking about the soul, aren't you."

"Perhaps. Are you religious, Charlie?"

"Not really."

"Then I urge you to be very careful with names. Too often people use names as a shield. They say the words and pretend that is all they need, as though attaching a label grants them the power of wisdom." She glanced at her watch. "You must have questions of your own."

"So many I don't know where to start."

Her smile was as sad as her eyes. "Then we have more in common than you think." She rose to her feet. "We must go, Charlie. It is time."

They took a taxi to the other end of Central Park. The day was nice and Charlie would have preferred to walk. But Gabriella had emerged from the church wearing the day like a shroud. So Charlie remained silent and followed her lead. He asked, "Do you want to tell me what's going to happen?"

Her response was another shudder. "Not yet. Would you please just keep me company?"

"Sure. Does that mean we're not facing any threat here?"

"No physical danger. I'm sorry, Charlie. It is very hard for me to talk about this."

"It's no problem."

"I just need your strength."

"I'm here for you." Charlie gave that a beat, then added, "If there's any chance they're tracking us, you need to get rid of your phone."

"All of my team have thrown them away, Charlie. We have been made aware of this risk."

They did not speak again until they pulled up in front of a hotel. The Ritz-Carlton was too large to be classed as a boutique hotel. But its interior held that intimate feel.

Gabriella released his hand as they slipped from the taxi and entered the hotel. She marched to the reception desk and announced, "My husband checked in earlier. I wonder if he remembered to leave me a key."

"Your name, ma'am?"

"Gabriella McLaren."

"May I see some ID?"

"Of course."

Charlie remained planted by the entrance as Gabriella accepted the plastic key. She politely refused the receptionist's offer to show her upstairs, then turned to Charlie and said, "Come with me."

"Yes, ma'am." Charlie Hazard, willing servant. He followed her to the elevator, where Gabriella pushed the penthouse button. The entire ride, she stared at the elevator doors and panted softly through slightly parted lips.

She let them into a massive suite overlooking Central Park. Charlie gave the rooms a quick sweep, then joined her at the living room windows. The park was laced with springtime green and rimmed by New York bling. "Must be nice."

"We need to sit here." She indicated the space between the sofa and the window.

"On the floor?"

"We are safe here."

"You've seen this in one of your . . ."

"I have, yes." She tucked her skirt in about her knees, reached into her purse, and came out with a palm-sized video camera. "I'm very glad you are here, Charlie. Can you operate this?"

"I need to keep my hands free."

"I told you. We are in no danger."

The camera's operation was clear enough. He looked through the monitor. The camera focused swiftly, the viewfinder crystal clear. He zoomed in on a beautiful woman wearing a grim and tragic mask. He set the camera in his lap. "Can you tell me what's happening?"

She was silent so long he thought she was not going to respond. Then she said, "Everything is so new. Three weeks ago, we designed a series of trials around the instructions to determine what risk we faced. I discovered something that forced me to realize how much I was willing to ignore, how our safety in the Vero hospital was just a myth."

Charlie had no idea what she was talking about. But he could hear the strain in her voice, see the fear in her eyes. He disliked his position, behind soft furniture that would offer them no protection from gunfire. He was also unable to see what might come through that door. If he raised his head he'd be instantly silhouetted by the window behind him. It was a sucker's spot. A beginner's hideaway.

Gabriella was saying, "Each time I go hunting risk, I am given specific images. Usually this is matched by a snapshot sensation. Sometimes the emotion is clearer than the image. My last trial, the accompanying sensation left me numb. I wish I could be that way now."

Charlie stopped fidgeting. "What was it that shocked you, Gabriella?"

"You will see soon enough. If I talk about this, I will . . ." Her face went taut as a mask. She bit her lip, struggled, and forced herself to steady. "Right now I want to tell you what happened after. Usually we close a search for risk by asking, 'Where do we go next?' This time, instead of finding safety, I found myself looking at *another* danger. I saw a room as big as a cave. No windows. Four tiers of computer stations rising like an arena. The stations and the people face a wall of huge flat-panel displays. The sensation was of raw power and a frigid coldness."

"You're talking about the Combine?"

"I do not need to name this thing to know it is a bringer of death." She spoke with the steady conviction of a scientist dictating results. Every word carefully spaced. "A woman with white-blonde hair stood on the top tier. She spoke to a slender man, possibly Indian, I'm not certain."

Charlie knew she described a standard war room. The screens were the war room's eyes on the world. Incoming data streamed constantly. The analysts were arrayed according to task and seniority. The top tier was reserved for people with the power to send peons like Charlie to their death. "Did you see what was on the screens?"

"You were being hunted by a team of men in blue SWAT suits. I did not see you, but I knew it was you they were after. The men ran across a lawn toward a one-story house. I was so frightened, but I did not understand why."

A private group able to afford its own intel war room and a mercenary attack force drawn from Delta . . . Gabriella had every right to be scared.

Charlie started to tell her this had already happened when he heard the sound of a plastic key being inserted into the door.

Their location was all wrong. He should never have allowed himself to be trapped back there. Armed with nothing but a camera to record their demise.

Then he heard laughter.

A woman, probably quite young, said, "Oh, cool. A suite. Wow. What a view."

An older man said, "Yeah, from where I'm standing the view is fabulous."

"Oh, you." The young woman's voice had the hard-edged quality of too much too soon. "Where's the champagne?"

"Go check in the other room."

Charlie thought he recognized the man's voice. The one time he had heard it before had been in a penthouse lab.

The man followed the woman across the carpet, entered the bedroom, and said, "Here, let me open the bottle."

At the sound of glasses clinking, Gabriella took hold of Charlie's hand. Her grip was so tight, her entire body trembled with the force she applied to his fingers.

The woman in the other room said, "What's in the box?"

"Open it and see."

There was a rustle of paper, then, "Wow. My favorite blue."

"I know."

At the sound of a passionate kiss, Gabriella released Charlie's hand and reached for her purse. "I'm going to *end* this."

He was about to reach over and keep her from using what he assumed was a pistol. But her hand emerged holding papers.

"Bring the camera." Gabriella rose from her crouch, crossed the room, opened the doors, and said, "Hello, Byron."

The woman jerked out of Byron's embrace and demanded, "Who are *you?*"

"I'm his wife."

The young woman slapped the man cowering in the bed beside her. "You told me you were *divorced.*"

"He is," Gabriella said, and dropped the papers in his lap. "Just as soon as he signs both copies."

20

They rode in silence back to Gabriella's hotel. Her attention remained fixed upon the side window. Charlie doubted she saw anything at all. The taxi driver was a slender, dark-skinned man whose last name had seventeen letters. His license was displayed on the scratched plastic window between the front and rear seats. At every stoplight he stared into his rearview mirror, looking first at Gabriella, then over to Charlie, then back to Gabriella again. He probably assumed Gabriella's sorrow was Charlie's fault.

The taxi let them out at the Millennium Times Square. The lobby was a vast marble and granite tomb. Gabriella's room was on the fifty-ninth floor. To Charlie, the room looked like a suede-lined cell. The small window overlooked a neighboring building. The lighting was muted and the décor too dark.

Charlie said, "We shouldn't stay here any longer than we need to."

"I registered under Speciale, my maiden name, using an old passport." She spoke in a careful monotone, holding on to control by will alone. "We are safe here until tomorrow morning."

Mentally he repeated her name. Gabriella Speciale. It suited her perfectly. "You saw this?"

"Yes." Gabriella lay down on the bed and covered her eyes. Her face twisted up tightly, then relaxed. "I'm sorry you had to witness that, Charlie."

"You never have to apologize to me. Especially for something that was totally not your fault."

"I've known about this side of Byron for some time. He liked to show me off. Other than that, he treated me well. He treats all his investments well. Among his banker cronies, Byron was known as a white-knight investor. Even so, I suspected that he was incapable of committing himself fully to anything. He is like a lot of very rich men, I suppose, who treat life as a personal playground and rules as something that only applies to mere mortals. His other ladies, Byron saw like a fine meal. He had his hors d'oeuvres, his main courses, and his desserts. Many, many desserts."

"The guy," Charlie said, "is a loon."

She might not have heard him. "Byron made a polite attempt to hide his desserts from me. And I politely pretended not to see. Or hear, when people told me what they had observed, the kindness dripping from their mouths and their eyes like poisoned honey."

She went silent and remained in that same position as he ordered them up a meal and sat staring out the window at the city. He met the room-service waiter at the door, signed the bill, and locked and bolted the door. Gabriella joined him at the table but ate very little.

She continued to check her watch, until Charlie asked, "Something the matter?"

Gabriella sat up straighter and said, "I have a problem. I am scheduled to make an ascent. But I can't. Not tonight."

"That's what you call these experiences, an ascent?"

"We wanted a term without baggage. Ascent works well for many reasons." She waved that aside. Charlie had the impression she was slightly disappointed, as though he had asked the wrong question. "I cannot possibly attain the state of calm required for an ascent. Stress skews the results. Sometimes it . . . is not pleasant."

He filled in the first blank. "But you need to find out what comes next."

"We always work in teams of two. One ascends, the other acts as the compass. There are set directives, which the team works out together in advance. The last question we have been asking since this crisis started is, 'When should the next ascent take place?' Sometimes there is no answer. This time it was very clear, very precise."

"You want me to do this."

"If you will." Gabriella glanced at her watch. "The ascent should begin in seventy-three minutes."

"Do you think I can?"

She spoke very carefully. "There is no reason I know of why it should not work."

"That you know of."

She looked directly at him for the first time since entering the room. "Everything about you is an anomaly. All our other successful ascenders are brought up through stages. They remain at Base Level through several sessions, until they are fully comfortable with the concept. Gradually they are taken higher. Some ascend—a minority. Most of those who do never manage to move more than a few inches from their bodies. You are the first, the very first, to ever arrive and ascend and travel on the first go. You are certain you have never done anything like this before?"

"No." He listened to the echo of those words in his brain. *Anomaly. Ascender. Travel.* "I never have."

"That is such an astonishment. Most people are terrified of ascending. They say it is like approaching death voluntarily. The body is left behind. At some core level of the psyche, far beyond what we are able to consciously control, the ascender must face that most primal of fears. This is why we are so careful to introduce the transition in stages. It is also why we laid out the protocol for meeting you as we did. If we brought you in and followed the agreed-upon protocol, and you ascended and moved to the next room and read the note, then my associates agreed to leave the hospital and their beautiful new lab. Because they knew it was impossible for you to accomplish all this."

"Why don't you go ahead and start getting things ready?"

"Will you stay and protect us, Charlie? Even if things become dangerous?"

Charlie started to ask what she knew about the threats they would face. But her fractured gaze halted him, at least for now. All he said was, "That's my job."

21

Reese had always loved New York. The twenty-four-hour rhythm matched her own psyche far better than the more laid-back Southern California vibe. New York's avaricious edge was sheathed in an extremely elegant bling. Like a carbon steel sword kept in a scabbard of silk and emeralds. She crossed the hotel lobby and smiled in anticipation of unsheathing her own hidden blade.

Reese entered the Plaza Hotel's main restaurant, her stride stretching the fabric of her dress to its limit. She wore a silk sheath of midnight blue, so dark as to appear black under certain lighting. Not that any male in the Plaza's main restaurant was particularly concerned about the color. The poisonous looks shot her way by matronly diners only added to the night's pleasure.

The Plaza had recently undergone a complete renovation that cost over two hundred million dollars. The main restaurant shouted money in typical New York fashion, as in, too much is never enough.

When she had tracked down Byron McLaren in the hotel bar an

hour and a half ago, the man had appeared positively stricken. But now he rose from the table and greeted her with a kiss and a smile and the words, "My day has just gotten a billion percent better."

The maître d' leaned over close enough for Reese to smell his hair gel as he bowed her into her chair. Byron beamed with pride of temporary ownership as he announced, "Let's pick up where we left off. The lady will have a glass of your finest champagne."

"Very good, sir."

"Matter of fact, bring her a whole bottle."

"One glass is fine," Reese said. "But thanks just the same."

Now that he had recovered from whatever had rocked his world, Byron McLaren was actually quite handsome, in a preppy sort of way. Reese knew a lot of girls went for that boy-who-never-grows-up look. But she was not one of them.

Of course, Byron's real magnet was the fact that he was extremely rich.

He had let that one slip within the first ninety seconds of Reese sliding into the seat next to his that afternoon. At the time, however, the man had seemed to be reading off somebody else's script. Reese had let him assume she found him attractive, or at least liked the look of his wallet, which had gradually brought the man back to life. He swiftly began what was no doubt his standard windup, regretting how he couldn't fly her up to this great little bistro outside Boston, as delivery of his new Gulfstream was two months late. Something about the factory only having one set of the special gold fittings he had ordered, and they'd given them to the sultan of Brunei, can you imagine?

Byron gave her a full-frontal inspection and said, "I've got a weekend booked at a resort on Tortuga, and I was just sitting here wondering who I could find—"

"Actually, Byron." Reese leaned forward and gave him a smile strong enough to draw glances from other tables. "This meeting is not entirely pleasure."

She gave him a minute. Byron recovered well, which was good, because there was a lot of ground left to cover. He said, "So your coming on to me in the bar, that wasn't a chance thing."

She scratched a fingernail down the back of his wrist, enjoying the subtle shift of control. "No, Byron. It wasn't."

"What, you're looking for venture capital, is that it?"

"Not at all."

"I swear, you people. New York is like a hive for desperate fund seekers." He showed a lot of affected movement when he was nervous, unnecessary motions that took up a great deal of space. Like an actor who suffered from an inferiority itch whenever the spotlight moved away. Byron shot his cuffs, lifted his hands and smoothed his hair, then flung his right arm over the banquet. "My, if this doesn't just cap off a *perfect* day."

"Byron, did you hear what I said?"

"I'll give it to you straight and save us both a lot of trouble. I do all my finance work through Citi. I invest where they say. And I *never* let chance encounters develop into funding."

"Actually, Byron, the part about Citi handling all your money is not true." She always preferred to hold such confrontations in public. Meeting her prey in the spotlight of their choosing reduced the power of their scenes. They feared embarrassment heaped upon whatever horror she had to bring. Which in Byron's case was quite a lot. "How much do you actually know about your wife's research?"

"Gabriella? She doesn't have a thing to do with my investment capital."

"I'm not here about your portfolio. I already told you that. Please answer the question."

Talking about his wife clearly heightened the man's unease. That was unexpected. "I financed her project."

"Byron, I want you to try real hard and move past the money issue. I asked you about her *research*."

"I know enough. And this isn't amusing any longer."

When he attempted to lift his arm to signal the waiter, Reese froze him with three little words. "Bank of Geneva."

The sensation really was exquisite. Grabbing a man by a most sensitive body part—the wallet. And wrenching with delicate precision.

Reese drew a folded sheet of paper from her purse. "These are your accounts, Byron. All five of them. Surely you recognize the numbers."

"B-but this is . . ."

"Completely confidential. I know." Moments like this were what kept her in the game. She was offered jobs all the time, usually by Combine members. This was what held her. The rare moment when the Combine's power was truly hers to wield. "Now here, see at the bottom of the page, this series of zeros? These were your account balances exactly an hour ago."

Byron's skin went waxy as the blood drained away.

Eighty-seven million dollars. Secreted away and supposedly safe in a tight little Swiss bank on the shores of Lake Geneva.

Gone.

She anchored the page with her cell phone. "You can call and check this out, Byron. We've got time."

Wordlessly, Byron slipped from the booth and stormed from the restaurant. Or tried to. Reese had the distinct impression that something had already disarmed and wounded the man. Whatever he had been through that afternoon had marked him deeply. She was debating whether she should call in and have Patel try to discover what that might have been, in case it affected their own situation. But Byron chose that moment to return to the table.

He slumped into his seat and took a heavy slug from his glass. Spent a few moments staring at nothing. Drank again. Reese realized the man had had some work done on his face, and by someone extremely good. She saw the faint trace of scar tissue along his hairline, accented by the man's evident strain.

Byron asked, "Who are you?"

"That's not important. Right now you need to focus on just two items. First, I obviously represent some extremely powerful interests. Second, what these people have taken away, they can give back."

His voice had aged a thousand years. "You'll restore my money?"

"Every cent," she lied. "Just give us what we want, and we'll vanish. Poof. We've never even met. Your life goes back to fun and games and all the Swiss gold one bad boy can spend. And you can spend a lot, can't you, Byron?"

"You're not from the IRS?"

"No, Byron. Now that's enough of your questions. Tell me about your wife's work."

"I don't get it. Gabriella's research isn't worth this." He struck the accounts sheet with a trembling hand.

"Your wife represents a threat. That threat must be eliminated. As soon as that happens, your accounts will be restored."

"Gabriella is a *psychologist*. Before she started on this project, she worked with *rats*."

"Listen very carefully, Byron. You recall how the Vero Beach hospital's fund-raising chairman approached you and said you could have the medical school's teaching unit named after you for a ridiculously low sum. Not to mention how he let you have the top-floor research unit basically for free. That was our doing." She let that sink in. "I'm sharing this with you because I want you to understand just how vital we consider Gabriella's work to be. Now I want you to *focus*. Good. Tell me about her project."

"They're after quantifying certain experiences that the world considers totally off-the-wall. They call them ascents. Their aim is to make them measurable events. Create an environment where the events can be both repeated and computed."

Reese let him ramble on. Actually, they knew far more than he ever would. And further information was not what was required. But there was nothing to be gained by revealing this to a newly broken man.

Byron did not so much finish as run out of steam. Perspiration was not normally served as part of the Plaza's first course, but Byron used his napkin like a towel, wiping himself from hairline to neck. It was too soon for the man to enter meltdown.

"So you've assumed all this was just another quasi-spiritual sham. You figured, hey, give the girl her toys, play the hero, get a nice write-off, maybe score with some of the cute researchers. What's wrong with a little harmless fun, right?" She moved in tight. "But they've made some fundamental progress into areas we can't permit, for reasons of national security and our own corporate interests. Areas such as tele-portation." Reese straightened. "Here comes the headwaiter, Byron. You need anything?"

Byron had left polite etiquette behind a long time ago. He snarled at the waiter, "Go away."

This being New York, the maître d' simply bowed and said, "Very good, sir."

When they were alone, Reese said, "Their work is in the early stages. We think it can still be halted in time. But we're not certain. We need to move fast."

Byron again applied the napkin to his forehead. "This is nuts."

Reese moved in closer, using her looks to calm and stabilize her victim. To any observer she was simply another cute young blonde nestling up to a guy having a stroke. "Soon after they arrived at what was an absolutely perfect Vero research center, Gabriella came up with this incredible stunt of bringing in Charlie Hazard. Don't look so surprised, Byron. I told you we had surveillance in place. They tested Hazard according to these impossible protocols of hers, and then that same night everybody pulled out. A state-of-the-art facility designed specifically for her work, paid for by her loving but not-so-loyal hus-band. Somehow your wife became aware of our interest, and did so at a level beyond either the physical state or time. You see why we're so worried here, Byron? Your wife and her team have been successful at spatial and temporal shifts. She can go anywhere, see anything. No secret will ever be safe again."

Reese stopped because Byron was no longer listening. His eyes stared into the distance, far beyond their table. She asked, "What is it, Byron?"

"This explains something she's done."

She saw him reaching for his soaked napkin and handed over her own. "We're certain your wife and her team have left the country. We need—"

"Gabriella hasn't."

"What?"

"Or that man. Hazard. They haven't left." His waxy coloring returned. "I saw them."

"You're telling me Gabriella is *here*? In New York?"

"This afternoon. They were in my suite."

While she recovered from that bombshell, Reese's phone started ringing. Weldon Hawkins was listening in and now felt it necessary to intervene. Reese cut the connection and stowed the phone in her purse. "Go on."

"I couldn't figure out how she knew where to find me. I didn't tell anybody where I was staying. But she popped up out of the blue. With that man."

"Gabriella appeared in your suite with Charlie Hazard." Light dawned, and Byron's current state suddenly made sense. "She caught you with another woman, didn't she. And it must have been earlier today, before you hit on me in the bar. My, but you're a busy little boy."

"She had the divorce papers already written up. It was either sign or they'd go public with the video that man Hazard was shooting."

Reese gathered up her purse and rose from her chair. "We've got to assume they've already left town. We want you to find out where she's moved her team."

"You'll give me back my money?"

"I already covered that."

"Can I have that in writing?"

Reese was glad for a reason to laugh. "Get real, Byron. And get us that location."

143

Reese waited until she had settled into the limo's backseat to turn on her phone. It rang instantly.

Weldon said, "Teleportation?"

"Hang on a second."

The limo driver settled in behind the wheel and asked, "Where to next, Ms. Clawson?"

"Just head uptown." She lifted the phone. "So what would you prefer to call it?"

"All we know for certain is, the user's awareness is no longer tied to their physical state."

"This goes well beyond precognition, Weldon. You just heard Byron confirm what we heard on our monitoring system. Charlie Hazard arrived in their lab, and in his first experience he shifted to another room and read a sign they didn't even print until he was under. What's worse, Gabriella saw all of this before it actually happened. She knew where to find him, she knew he would go for it, she knew he would read the sign, she knew we were watching."

Weldon knew all this as well as she did. He liked to test his assumptions with such discussions. He also had a tendency to cough his words when nervous. Little verbal barks, like the beast in him was barely under control. "I've just ordered your crew to search the local hotels."

"Seeing as how Hazard and the woman have stayed one step ahead of us this far, I kind of doubt they'll make a mistake now."

"You're saying we shouldn't bother?"

"Of course not. Tell them to check the bus and train stations. Limos, taxis, the works."

"Are you returning tonight?"

"Tomorrow. We need to be certain they've actually left town."

Weldon hung up. No farewell, no acknowledgment of a job well handled. Reese started to detach her lapel mike, then decided Patel

144

needed to be a part of her final phone call. She asked the driver, "Where does a girl go for the hottest nighttime action in town?"

The driver grinned into his rearview mirror. This was clearly a question he liked. "Lady, this is New York. You got to be more specific than that. You want jazz hot, club hot, R & B hot, down-and-dirty salsa hot—what you like?"

"I'm in the mood for spicy." She kicked off her shoes. "Salsa sounds perfect."

The driver was Hispanic and proud of it. His grin grew broader. "I got just the joint."

"Great." She pulled a miniature earpiece from her pocket, fitted it into place, then spoke into her lapel mike. "Patel, you there?"

"Of *course* I'm here. Where *else* would I be?"

"Find General Strang and patch him through to my phone. We've got some serious business to discuss."

22

Charlie moved the desk and chair over so that Gabriella could sit next to the bed. He stood behind her as she walked him through the entire ascent, making corrections on her worksheets as she spoke. He studied the curve to the back of her neck and knew he should be paying more careful attention. But her words fell on him like a gentle wash, soft as summer rain.

She arranged the pages in proper order and tamped them into place. "Are you ready, Charlie?"

"Sure thing."

"Do you understand what you will accomplish in this ascent?"

"Whatever you tell me to do."

She gave that a significant pause. "Make yourself comfortable on the bed, please." She arranged her equipment on the desk and fitted the headphones on his head. "How is the volume?"

"Perfect." He could smell her perfume. Along with a smoldering trace of the day.

"Are you the least bit frightened, Charlie?"

"No."

"Most people find the second and third ascents the hardest. Particularly just before leaving the body. We call it *uncoupling*. After the third ascent, sometimes the fourth, either they have begun to find a sense of familiarity or they stop. It is not a conscious choice. Fear simply overrides their ability to ascend."

"Where are the rest of your team?"

"On their way to Italy, by way of Switzerland. My family used to rent a villa in Brunate, a small village in the mountains above the Lake of Como. There is no record of this anywhere, to my knowledge. We should be safe there. At least until we can establish a more permanent situation."

He liked how she never hesitated before answering his questions. "I've never heard of the place."

"Como is just south of the Swiss border, in the foothills of the Alps. My aunt's family, my mother's sister, had inherited a quarter share of a family villa through her husband's . . . Never mind, Charlie. It is a very complicated connection. Very Italian. But the villa itself is beautiful, almost six hundred years old—not the largest villa in the village by any means, but still very nice. I called the family and they said it was empty for the season. Just as I saw during my last ascent."

Charlie saw the shadows pass before her face again and knew she was thinking of what else had come out of that particular session. She almost managed to hide the crack in her voice as she said, "I have a theory as to why you are not afraid. Would you like to hear it?"

"Absolutely."

"Identity for most people is constantly shifting. People are this way with one person, another way with the next. They are happy, sad, up, down, backwards, forwards. Much of their internal state is dependent upon the things going on around them." She hesitated, as though suddenly uncertain she should be saying these things. "Recent studies suggest that people who fight in wars fit an entirely different psychological profile."

"The standard term," Charlie said, "is combat veteran."

"Yes. Thank you. These studies suggest one reason so many combat veterans have difficulty adjusting to civilian life is that they lose this ability to shift identities. This flexibility of character has been cauterized. They are frozen in the rigidity required to survive battle. They are precisely who they are. All the time." She stopped once more. "Was I wrong to tell you this, Charlie?"

"Not at all."

"I don't want to make you think that I do not consider you well adjusted."

"You're describing a very real problem in my world, Gabriella. A lot of guys just plain can't come back. I'm glad scientists are taking a look at it. What you're saying makes a lot of sense."

"I have been thinking a great deal about this since meeting you. Why does the warrior become so inflexible? The answer is, of course, survival. This intensity, this focused power, carries the warrior through threats that arrive from every point on the compass. This character inflexibility is a natural side effect. I wonder if perhaps your core personality, this solidity of purpose, makes it easier for you to ascend. For you, the seasoned warrior, ascending becomes the next danger zone you choose to enter."

He gave that some thought. "I think maybe there's another reason why I'm not afraid."

"Yes?"

"I've almost died twice. Once in combat, once in a car accident."

"This also carries a great deal of validity, Charlie. There is documented evidence that near-death experiences leave many subjects with less fear of the end." She nodded slowly. "Perhaps we should focus upon this in our selection of new test cases."

He could feel the heat of her body beside the bed. "I'm very sorry about today, Gabriella."

148

"We must focus on you now, Charlie."

"I just wanted you to know."

She settled a hand on his shoulder and left it there for a time, soft as whispered gratitude. Her other hand became busy with the controls. A rush of sound filled his ears. She said, "You are entering Base Level now."

This time Charlie was much more aware of the actual process. Like before, his focus gradually turned away from Gabriella's voice and her presence, taking an increasingly tight aim at his internal state. Yet at one level he remained acutely aware of her at all times. The fact that his focus could be so utterly divided and yet remain so sharp was only of mild interest, a thought that came and went in the sweep of counting upward.

Then he ascended.

The word fit the experience with exquisite precision. He *rose away* from normal awareness.

He had never considered the concept of awareness in those terms before. Normal awareness meant self, then body, then environment. It was all about analysis and search and defined concepts of danger. Normal awareness meant maintaining an island of security and safety.

Charlie literally felt his awareness draw away from all these things. The elastic moment was strong as a physical sensation. He *turned away*.

He had expected a wrenching of some sort. Every journey he had experienced started with a sensation of departure. Until now.

There was an instant of transition as natural as the tiny breath his body took. The body he was now looking down upon.

He remained poised slightly above the bed and the lovely woman who observed the body lying there. He watched as Gabriella lifted the pages. He saw the slight tremor to her hands. Then the message formed inside him in tandem to her speaking.

Gabriella said, "Identify what risk we currently face. You will focus exclusively upon the next danger at hand. You will remain in complete safety and complete control at all times. Go now."

Before the *now*, Charlie was already gone.

He knew a tornado effect. The sense of gathering force was that great. His senses were honed as he traveled, focusing with such intensity he could fracture a laser.

He came to rest in the back of a limo. Outside the limo's windows was a nighttime cityscape. Though he recognized no landmarks, Charlie knew with absolute certainty he was still in New York.

Across from him sat the woman he had last seen at Harbor Petroleum. Reese Clawson was blonde and alluring and draped in a cloak woven from sexuality and dread. The combination of menace and manipulated desire tore at Charlie's psyche. He had noticed it before, but with nothing like the pure intensity he felt now.

Reese said into her cell phone, "I appreciate your willingness to help us out, General Strang."

The man's voice on the other end of the phone came through as clearly as if Charlie held the phone to his own nonexistent ear. "I've got two reasons. First, Hazard is off the reservation. Second, I want your business."

The blonde woman pulled her skirt up a trifle, as though offering a tantalizing pose to the man on the other end of the phone. "I will be equally frank. Our background search has turned up nothing usable on Hazard. He is almost absurdly clean."

"I figured that was the issue as soon as your man placed this call."

"We need a lever, General. We need it now."

"First let's talk terms."

"You deliver and so do I."

"Same deal?"

"The same contract as before, only with Hazard erased."

"In that case, I'm happy to tell you that Charlie Hazard has an Achilles' heel."

Reese smiled. "Men always do."

·ılı·

Charlie's next transition was equally smooth and as powerful as the first. He had attended military training seminars where experienced field officers described entering new combat terrain and watching their new troops give in to sensory overload. The new scene offered that same level of bombardment.

He stood at the back of an intel war room. He had visited the Pentagon's underground chamber once, acting as aide to Colonel Donovan Field, who had been invited by a general who had once served under him. The setup was unmistakable. Arena-like banks of seats rose in four curved rows from a wall of giant flat-screens. Over the loudspeakers, Reese was talking to Curtis Strang.

Strang was saying, "Hazard was in the process of divorcing his wife."

A slender man stood by a console to Charlie's left. He had olive skin and an aggrieved air as he cried, "That is *not* part of any official record!"

On one screen, Reese winced and cupped her hand over the phone's mouthpiece. "Ease up on the volume, Patel."

"We have searched *everywhere*. Charlie Hazard was married until his wife died in the car accident. He *never—*"

"All right." Reese replaced the phone to her ear and said, "We show no evidence of that, General."

"I don't care what your records state. Forget your own data. If there was written evidence, you wouldn't be calling me. I know Hazard was divorcing his wife because he told me a month or so after he joined my team. She was having an affair."

The olive-skinned man bounded to his feet. "All *right*!"

Reese winced again. "Patel, chill."

Strang said, "Excuse me?"

"Go ahead, General. You were saying?"

"Hazard wanted Sylvie to file the papers. He called it the honor-able out."

Patel said into his mike, "I have the police records here in front of me. Sylvie Hazard died in a car accident. Charlie was in the car and was injured."

Reese said, "Sorry, General. I don't see how this helps us. The lady is dead."

"Hazard claimed he was asleep when the car went off the road. The police found him unconscious, saved by his seat belt and air bags. It appears that his wife, who was driving, was not wearing her belt and was thrown from the car, hit a tree, DOA. The authorities had some questions about Hazard's possible involvement. But they didn't know about the wife's affair. At the time, it was to my advantage for them not to find out. The prosecution decided they didn't have a case."

"You know this how?"

"I have an ally inside the LAPD."

"Can you get him to change his mind?"

"It will cost you. He's put in his twenty. He's looking for a cushy corporate security job."

"I can make that happen."

"He drinks."

"I said I can make it happen. But your pal has to issue the warrant tonight."

"And the service contract with your group—"

"Will be expressed to you tomorrow. We need an international arrest warrant, and we need it now. Not some local alert. We're pretty certain Hazard has left the country, or is about to do so."

"I'm on it. Strang out."

Reese hung up. "Patel?"

"Almost there." His fingers began a tap dance on the keys. "Is your console on?"

"Hang on. Okay."

"Here we go."

On the arena's top left screen, Charlie watched as his face appeared on an international fugitive warrant. The charge was murder. Beneath his picture, words appeared in a multitude of languages. *Considered armed and extremely dangerous.*

"Looks good," Reese said. "Be ready to put this out the instant the police act."

23

There ain't no fish round these parts. Ain't been none since them deadbeats moved in." Donovan's guide was a lean strip of leather, dyed by years of sun to a coppery black. The guide's eyes were a blue as washed of color as the sky. "But you ain't no fisherman, are you?"

Donovan eased his aching foot. "No."

"Soon as I laid eyes on you, I said, this man don't know one end of a pole from t'other. What are you, some kinda investigator?"

"No."

"You better not be no cop, I'm telling you that right straight. That's an ornery bunch up there. They don't take no truck to cops coming round."

"I'm Army. Retired. I'm looking for a friend. You been out here before?"

"When I was a boy, sure. Them shoals used to be a fine place for bonefish and snook. And mussels. Not no more." The guide spit over the side. "I hear tell there's some vets living down there. That who you're after, some head case who never got over his taste of war?"

"Yes." Donovan recognized the guide's battered headgear as a Marine field cap. "You were in 'Nam?"

"Mekong. Two tours. I don't have no truck with them head cases, I tell you that straight up."

Donovan was feeling his age, and it definitely wasn't just the heat, which was Florida fierce. He had not slept well the previous night, stuck in some Miami highway motel. He had grown used to his little routines. Taking care of the dog, meals at certain times, his pills . . .

His pills. Donovan checked his watch. He should have taken his daily dose of heart medicine four hours ago. No wonder he was feeling low. Be just his luck to get out here in the middle of nowhere and suffer another heart attack.

The air was so still and the water so calm they might as well have been slicing their way across a blue-green mirror. The sun was blisteringly hot. Donovan tilted his cap, trying to protect more of his face.

The guide must have noticed Donovan's discomfort because he opened the starboard locker and pulled out a stained windbreaker. "Put this on and fold up the collar. It'll protect your neck."

"Appreciate it." The jacket was ancient cotton poplin and smelled of oil and other people's sweat.

"Better?"

"A lot."

Between Marathon Key and Key West were sixty miles of well-traveled emptiness. The highway bridges traversed one barren coral rock after another. Traffic gradually congealed in the approach to that odd American mecca, Key West, the city at the edge of nowhere. All tourist eyes strained forward, yearning for that first glimpse of the last island. They totally ignored the same boring vista they had traversed since leaving Miami six hours earlier. Donovan had never been to the Keys before and had no intention of ever returning.

The guide's craft was a twenty-six-foot flat-bottomed skiff with a ninety-horse Mercury kicker, made for trolling the Florida Flats, which was what the locals called this region of shoals and emerald islands. Donovan knew this because the guide had told him.

From behind the boat's console, the guide said, "A buddy brought this lady out here, musta been four months back. Came looking for her little girl. The daughter'd taken off with this rough sort. The lady tracked her daughter down to this place we're headed. My friend had heard the same tales as me and didn't want to go. The lady paid him double. Only thing my buddy got for his troubles was a bullet through his bow. As they turned back the lady screamed and screamed the girl's name. Like to've broke my buddy's heart."

Donovan asked, "Where are we?"

"Near 'bout there."

"I'm supposed to be a professional tracker." Donovan peered around. Every direction looked exactly the same. Still water, small green islands with storm-twisted pines, birds standing in inch-deep shoals. "I couldn't find my way back with a Sat Nav and a chopper."

The guide displayed teeth as brilliant as his eyes. "What'd you do for the Army?"

"Rangers."

"So you're some kinda tough nut."

He slipped a hand inside his shoe and massaged where his toes had been. "Not anymore."

"Yeah, growing old is nasty business. I swear, some days I'm tempted . . ."

The guide might have stopped talking or it could have been that Donovan simply stopped hearing. They rounded another island, and suddenly there in front of them was a floating metropolis.

Hundreds and hundreds of boats. Thousands. All kinds of craft, every conceivable shape and rig, even an old paddle wheeler. The thing had to be two hundred feet long, with a shadow of the word *Casino* still visible on its side.

All wrecks.

The sailboats had no masts. Many of the yachts were missing their entire superstructure, like they'd been shaved down. Most windows were broken out and the portholes covered with duct tape and plastic sheeting. The boats' sides were stained, the waterlines fouled. The upper decks were filled with junk—wood-burning stoves, generators, lawn chairs, bicycles, solar panels, portable AC units, fishing gear. Clotheslines dangled from the stumps of masts. Anchor chains wore garlands of seaweed.

"What *is* this place?"

"Where you said you wanted to go. Hobo Harbor."

"Right, sure." Never in his wildest dreams had Donovan expected to find a floating city of derelict boats.

The guide cut his motor and shifted to the trolling station in the bow. He slipped the electric motor over the side and started forward. "Sixteen years back, a couple of big blows washed some yachts up by Mud Flats Key. The insurance fellers came down, took their pictures, and left. The owners got their checks and went off to buy new toys. Some homeless showed up one day and took to living there. One by one, more of them wrecks started showing up, usually moving in at night. There was some break-ins back in Marathon Key, and the police ran 'em off. Next thing anybody knew, they showed up here. One of them islands over there has an old freshwater spring." The motor made a soft purr as they moved forward. "My buddy said it'd grown. But I didn't never expect this."

Up ahead a trio of dogs started barking.

"Heads up, Ranger man. Move behind the wheel. If we catch incoming fire, you hit the gas and power us outta here."

"Roger that."

A few heads popped into view. Bearded men, mostly. Then a cluster of sun-blasted youngsters emerged from the tangle of green on the island to Donovan's left. Some of them wore clothes.

Sounds carried far over the still waters. Donovan heard the sharp ratchet of a rifle being cocked.

So did his guide. He cut the trolling motor and froze.

Donovan rose to his feet and called, "I'm looking for Benny Calfo!"
All movement around the boats halted.

A voice called out of the afternoon sun, "Who's asking for Calfo?"

"Charlie Hazard sent me!"

"Who're you?"

"The name is Donovan Field. Benny Calfo doesn't know me. Charlie said to tell him Eltee is calling in a debt."

The tableau remained locked in silence and stifling heat. Then an inflatable dinghy wound its way through the morass of ruined hulks.

Donovan asked softly, "What was the girl's name?"

The guide jerked. "Eh, what's that?"

"The girl your buddy brought the lady to find. Her name."

The guide blinked once. Twice. "Sarah. Sarah Long."

The dinghy's motor died. A bald man with no more flesh to his head than a skull said, "I heard of you, Colonel. Mind showing me that gimp foot of yours?"

Donovan slipped off his shoe and sighed with pure pleasure.

"Doubt there's a fed alive who'd chop his own toes off." He looked at the guide. "Can you navigate home after dark?"

"Been trolling these waters since 'fore you were born."

"We won't be too long. Come on, Colonel. Hop aboard."

Benny Calfo was too muscular to be skeletal. He simply possessed no spare flesh whatsoever. His neck and arms and chest above his tattered T-shirt were heavily tattooed. He wore an ear stud and three turquoise rings with faces that fit into a single wall when he made a fist. The rings were chipped and scarred.

Calfo lived with a woman who flitted in and out of sight. His home was an old harbor tug, steel-shanked and solid as a house. He served Donovan a jelly jar of tea in the windowless wheelhouse, the flies and mosquitoes kept out by rusty screens and duct tape.

Donovan had never been one for mincing words. He settled into the copilot's chair and said, "There was another guide who came through here about four months back. Had a very distraught mom looking for her little girl."

"Sure. Sarah. Forgot her last name."

"Long."

"That's the one. Sarah Long. Nice girl. She kept company with a bad man."

"Hearing you say that in a place like this, it'd have me worried. No offense."

"Sarah and her bad man left here about three weeks after her mother showed up, caterwauling and giving the children fits. Last I heard, Sarah was dealing high-stakes blackjack in a casino up Natchez way." Calfo had an easy smile that came nowhere near his eyes. "So how is old Eltee? Sat on any grenades lately?"

"All I know to tell you is, he's in trouble and he's asking for your help."

"Meaning if I don't go, it isn't any of my business."

Donovan sipped his tea and stared out the screen at the floating city.

"Where exactly is it Eltee needs me?"

Donovan fished the flight coupon out of his pocket and passed it over.

"Never been to Zurich." He flashed an empty grin. "There's no name on this, Colonel. Good as cash. Dangerous thing to be passing over in a place like this."

"Show the coupon and your passport at any airport." Donovan felt his heart lurch and jammed his fist onto his chest.

"Something wrong?"

"Forgot my heart medicine."

"What are you on?"

"Rythmol."

"Shouldn't be a problem." He raised his voice. "Kerry."

A shadow inserted itself into the doorway.

"Paddle over to the pharmacy and see if they've got a couple doses of Rythmol. Get some baby aspirin while you're at it, calm this man down."

When the dinghy pulled away, Donovan asked, "Pharmacy?"

"I worked out a deal with the stores in Marathon and Key West soon after I showed up. They supply us with all their outdated wares. There hasn't been a break-in at any of those places since."

"You're playing cop?"

Calfo had an assassin's easy grin. "The folks around here have bad associations with that word. My official title is chief. It's sort of elected. I make sure nobody cooks meth or steals from other boats or gets too crazy or does anything else that could bring in the feds. Otherwise, long as the strong don't hurt the weak, especially the kids, I leave things pretty much alone."

"Can you come?"

"This is for real, Hazard needs me and you don't know what for?"

"I've had just a taste of the danger Charlie's facing. A taste is all I ever need. This is as real as it gets."

A crazy glint burned in Calfo's gaze. Like the evil genie was just begging to come out and play. "Soon as my lady gets back, she and I will have a word."

24

Charlie slept on a pallet at the foot of Gabriella's bed. He had been in such circumstances many times before. But a woman's soft breaths had seldom been so alluring.

He woke Gabriella an hour before dawn. They took a room service breakfast and settled the hotel bill in cash. Charlie walked them across Times Square to the Marriott Marquis, where they joined a queue of sleepy tourists waiting for transport to Niagara Falls. Despite the hour, Charlie saw a few elderly couples holding hands and exchanging quiet smiles. As the bus sifted through half-empty Manhattan streets, the morning fog condensed into a misty rain. By the time they reached the northbound interstate, the rain was heavy and the light leaden. Gabriella watched the clogged lanes heading through the tollbooths toward Manhattan and did not speak.

Two hours outside New York, they stopped for coffee. Charlie used the rest stop's phone to contact a buddy on the NetJets admin staff. After he'd arranged enough of the general's flights, the guys on commission had started counting Charlie among their closest pals. Once the pleasantries were over, Charlie asked for two deadheads into Europe. Just as he had seen himself do in the final portion of the previous evening's ascent.

His buddy on the other end of the line replied with the words Charlie had already heard once before. "Hold one."

Gabriella leaned against the wall next to the phone. "Deadhead?"

Charlie cupped the phone. "When a plane is flying empty, sometimes they let friends or good customers travel free. These passengers aren't on any register. It's called deadheading."

His contact asked, "Who's that you're talking to there, buddy?"

"A friend."

"She nice, this friend?"

"You wouldn't believe me. You got anything?"

He replied as Charlie knew he would. "We've got an empty G-4 outbound today from T-town for a pickup in Milan."

"Two passengers, no paperwork, no record. The general does *not* need to know about this one."

"You dog. Be planeside by fifteen hundred."

"I owe you."

"Give me her number and we're even."

Charlie met Gabriella's gaze. "I don't owe you that much."

They left the bus at Niagara Falls and walked the Friendship Bridge into Canada. Charlie flagged a taxi and asked to be taken to the Toronto municipal airport. Gabriella remained not merely quiet but removed. Charlie took her silence as a compliment, a sign that she felt no need to offer him anything more than what came naturally.

They had time for a quick lunch at the pilots' café and were in the air by four. They were joined on board by a silver-haired gentleman who had his work spread across the table before the plane doors were shut. He neither spoke nor looked their way. The plane offered the same luxurious surroundings Charlie had known whenever flying with General Strang, only without the service. The pilots offered the three deadheads a perfunctory greeting and went on with the business of flying.

When they were over a cloudless north Atlantic, Gabriella said, "I have a problem."

They were seated across from one another at the rear of the jet. The executive worked at the table closest to the cockpit. Charlie rose from his seat, slipped around the table, and slid into the leather chair next to hers. "Fire away."

"Three problems, actually."

The airplane's noise formed a sweet cocoon that invited him to slip into her space. "Okay."

"One is Brett. He is my partner for ascending. He is becoming, well . . ."

"He's pressuring you."

"It is my fault. Six months ago, I discovered Byron with another woman. It was the first time I actually witnessed anything. I told you how I had always suspected, or maybe even known. What really happened that day was I came face-to-face with all the lies I had been telling myself, and how much I wanted to walk away and pretend it had never happened, even then." She shrugged. "Brett found me weeping. I needed a friend. He was very kind. We met a few times. He took me for lunches, once to the opera. Then I realized he was after being more than just a friend. I tried to tell him that what he wanted was impossible. But he refuses to listen. Sometimes he can be . . . dominating."

Charlie crossed his arms and pretended to give that serious thought. What he was thinking was, one good punch and the guy would fold like a cardboard cutout.

She must have seen a hint of it in his eyes, because she said, "I don't want you doing something masculine and stupid. Brett is a noted biochemist. He is responsible for much of our research into the brain's activities during ascent. His assistance is critical."

"I've set up security for some pretty awful people. I haven't clipped one yet." Charlie didn't see any need to add that there was always a first time.

"I need to find a new partner for my ascents. I have been thinking that if you and I work together, we might establish a greater range."

"Count me in."

"Really?" Gabriella actually looked relieved. As though he would ever have turned her down.

"My job is your safety. Seems to me this is a natural fit."

She relaxed by degrees. "Thank you, Charlie."

"What's problem number two?"

"Money. Up until now, Byron paid for everything."

Charlie knew a moment's dismay at the prospect that she was actually going to discuss paying him.

But what she said was, "Before we were married, Byron made me sign a contract—I'm sorry, I can't remember what it was called."

"A prenup."

"I am supposed to receive two million dollars. But I can only assume Byron will fight me on that. Yesterday morning before you arrived, I cleared out our joint account. It held just over sixty thousand dollars. Much of that will go to rent the villa in Brunate. But life in Italy is very expensive, especially for a team of scientists who are not used to the cost of living in Europe."

Charlie warned, "Any contact you make with Byron could tip him off to where we are."

"I am aware of that. I know he has accounts in Switzerland. I had thought perhaps I could use an ascent to discover where they are and how to access them." She shook her head. "Something is holding me back. Perhaps I am just being silly."

"If you are at all concerned about making a move like that, you shouldn't do it."

"Do you really think so?"

"You're operating in uncharted territory. Any good soldier will tell you safety depends on listening to your gut."

She touched his arm just above the elbow. It was a simple gesture, three fingers resting upon the fabric of his shirt. Yet it contained a sense of quiet intimacy, as though she had moved one step closer to trust. "You are a very wise man."

He saw no need to break the flow by countering with the truth. "Now the third problem."

"I don't know if it is a problem at all. We have been very careful to delineate our ascents. Did I say that correctly, 'delineate'?"

"Fine by me."

"Until yesterday, I was the only one able to utilize what I call this forward focus. Now you. We have always been very careful to chart our course before we start each ascent. I like working within these tight confines. It keeps me anchored. Milo and Jorge are the only other two of our team who can regularly ascend. But neither do so easily, and their orientation is not always clear."

It was only when she began twisting her fingers together that Charlie realized it. "Something is scaring you."

"Yes, perhaps. When I established these protocols, I had no idea we would succeed in such an amazing manner."

Charlie moved back a trace. He disliked doing so. But he needed to separate himself enough to focus upon whatever was worrying her.

"Now I wonder if my protocols are actually limiting us, holding us back from seeing a true totality. Keeping us from what we might discover. Blinding us to what we should perhaps have as our goal." Her eyes held a distant sheen, steel behind dark waters. "Does that make sense, Charlie?"

"I'm not sure."

She realized what she was doing with her hands and forced them down onto the table. Gripping the burled-walnut edge so tightly her knuckles went white. "I keep having these slight impressions, usually at the end of an ascent. It leaves me unsettled. And very scared."

Charlie nodded slowly. "I know the answer to that one."

"Yes?"

"The only time to move into the danger zone is when you're ready. You scout, you prep, you focus as tightly as you can. And one thing more. You never, ever go alone."

They landed in Milan Malpensa Airport an hour before dawn. Charlie and Gabriella followed the executive from the plane, pausing long enough to thank the pilots and receive a weary nod in response. They descended the jet's stairwell into a cold and rain-swept morning. The lone customs officer stamped their passports without ever really waking up from his doze.

They took a taxi to Milan's central station and bought tickets for the next express train heading north. The train station was as big as a factory and hewed from a granite yellowed by streetlights and rain. The terminal somehow looked larger inside than out. Charlie thought the place could probably swallow Grand Central Station. Gabriella led him to a café filled with other sleepy travelers and fed him a large coffee and a brioche and an orange juice.

The juice was squeezed by hand and the brioche was the best Charlie had ever had. The coffee was from another universe. There was all the coffee he had drunk up to that point, and then there was this. He lingered over it as long as he could and knew he would never forget this moment. A railside café lit with the tepid glow of a forties film noir, rain falling in sheets where the station opened to the dawn, a woman watching his face and finding something there that was worth a smile. Just the two of them, sheltered amidst the company of strangers. As alive as Charlie had ever been.

The trip to Como lasted less than an hour. But the short span of time was deceptive. In fifty-three minutes they left behind the world of plains and cities and highways, and entered the Alpine foothills. Only the rain was the same.

The taxi took them from Como's central station through a truly ancient city. Just as they entered the traffic crawling around the lake's shoreline, the morning sun emerged. In a single instant, the world was transformed yet again. Even the taxi driver seemed captivated by the change, for he reached over and turned off his chattering radio, then rolled down his window. The breeze carried an Alpine bite, and Charlie started to ask if Gabriella minded the chill. But when he looked over, he saw a woman who was happy for the first time since she had first entered the Satellite Beach community center. To Charlie, that event seemed like a hundred centuries ago.

Gabriella fumbled around an unfamiliar car door, searching for the window controls, not finding them because she refused to take her eyes off the scene. So Charlie reached across and rolled down the rain-speckled glass.

"Thank you, Charlie."

"No problem."

"It is like the best moments of my childhood have come alive again." She took a deep breath. Then she fumbled again, refusing to turn her face away from the wind and the sun and the lake. She found Charlie's hand and gripped it with both of hers.

The traffic seemed caught in the same wonder as Gabriella. Charlie could have walked faster. Pedestrians were frozen in a tableau of too-brilliant light. Every face Charlie could see was turned to stare at the sun-dappled water.

The taxi driver caught Charlie's gaze in the rearview mirror and said something. Gabriella translated, "It has rained for forty-five days straight, the wettest spring in recorded history."

One moment before, the waters had been as grey as molten lead and the world washed to monochrome dullness. Now everything sang a symphony of color. The lake was a shimmering song of blues and golds. Lakefront gardens were a chorus of every flower and every shade. Homes and buildings glistened. Windows winked a burnished welcome. People smiled. Children laughed and scampered. It was the

Italy of dreams and infinite joy. As long as a beautiful woman kept hold of his hand.

The road to Brunate began well enough, but as it rose above the city it narrowed to an asphalt track. This being Italy, the road's condition did not mean that traffic slowed. In fact, their driver used the hairpin curves as a challenge to his masculinity. Gabriella did not seem the least bit disturbed by how the driver attacked curves and blind corners, so Charlie kept quiet.

He took his mind off the road and the rise and the ledgeless drop by examining the world beyond the treetops. The lake was so vast, its opposite end faded into the mist of another approaching storm. Mountains paraded ahead of the tempest's leading edge, granite waves capped by icy froth. Farther away, clouds draped trailing veils down from heaven, fragile ribbons of poetry and rain. Charlie counted a dozen rainbows.

When they halted before an ancient gatehouse, Gabriella released his hand and said, "Welcome to my world, Charlie Hazard."

Irma Steeg approached the taxi and grinned a hello. "If I ever get to where the Italian coffee doesn't give me enough of a kick, I'll take up driving these mountain roads."

Charlie stared out the gatehouse at the lake and the sky and the vista of emerald and blue and gold. "Nice welcome."

"Take a good look, because it's not supposed to last. This is the first sunlight we've seen since we got here." She offered Gabriella her hand. "Irma Steeg."

"I am Gabriella. You are a policewoman and Charlie's friend."

"Right on both counts." She had a cop's grin, twisting her features in unaccustomed directions.

"Let me get the bags, then you can show me around," Charlie said.

Gabriella said, "Go, Charlie. I can take care of this."

"Listen to the lady, Charlie." Irma snagged his arm. "Welcome to the ten-cent tour."

"Where is Julio?"

"Sacked out. The kid is doing nights. I've got to tell you, he's been totally stand-up."

Charlie forced his head clear of jet-lag cobwebs laced with a certain woman's scent. He did a slow 360 of the surroundings and declared, "This place is superb."

"You took the words right out of my mouth."

The villa backed up to a granite cliff that rose to a summit three hundred feet overhead. The rock face was certainly scalable, but not without ropes and a harness. Any such assault would be totally visible to a watcher down below. The gardens had been built into a series of elongated steps that tumbled in weed-infested profusion to a tall stone outer wall. The wall was topped by rusty steel bars shaped like spear points. An ancient gatehouse marked the only entry.

The villa's ground floor was simply an extension of the cliff, built of hand-hewed granite with tall curved windows that were heavily barred. The upper three floors were shaped like a chalet, with blond-wood balconies and heavy oak shutters protecting all windows and doors. The entry portal was fifteen feet high and peaked. The door was blackened by age and studded with iron bars. The ground-floor window frames were a full two feet thick.

Irma declared, "This place could stop an army."

Charlie figured a team of specialists could affect a full-frontal attack in about ninety seconds if they were willing to make enough noise. The sunlight dimmed a trace, filtered now through the tight squint of a pro laying down lines of fire. He did another 360, working out how he was going to protect seven scientists from attack. With a retired cop and an amateur surfer as his only backup.

Irma noticed the change. "What's wrong?"

Charlie shook his head. He could almost hear Donovan Field tell him to do his duty with the weapons at hand. "I need a couple of hours' sack time. Then we should bring everyone together and lay things out."

He climbed the stairs and entered the villa, seeing everything through the scope of incoming fire. Back in full-alert mode. Doing the only thing he was good at. Taking serious heat.

BOOK 2

25

Illegal activity in Milan was dominated by an uneasy alliance between the local mob and Ukrainians. The Italian Mafiosi did not think much of their Eastern European allies. They considered them too soft in the brain from working with women. The newcomers had long since learned to smile and pretend not to hear what was said about them. Sometimes it was good to be underestimated.

The young man who entered the mob's café outside Milan wore a silk suit cut in lines straight as a stovepipe. It exaggerated his narrow build. Even so, he swaggered a bit, like his shoulders were so heavy that shifting their weight caused his upper body to punch forward. He had obviously seen some of the muscle walk that way and thought it was cool. One of the men at the corner table said quietly, "*Sbandato.*" Punk.

Two gentlemen were seated at a partner's desk by the grimy windows. The elder gentleman was known as the Prince because of his immaculate dress and manners. He was old and wizened and dressed in a black Savile Row suit and starched white shirt and black tie, an outfit drawn from the fifties. His dark eyes were fathomless, in the reptilian manner of one who had survived the Soviet years by simply doing whatever was required, no matter how lethal or terrifying.

He asked, "And who is this?"

The man who had brought him in replied, "Monti's uncle handles the clubs in Como. They also run our security operation in that region."

"Monti, forgive me. My Italian. What kind of name is this?"

The young man's swallow was audible from across the room. He replied, "My given name is Montefiori, capo."

One of the men seated at the bar by the side wall laughed. The old man glanced over. "There is nothing wrong with our guest's name."

"Sorry, Prince."

"Montefiori. Hill of flowers. It is a name from beyond time. Before even the Romans, your name existed. Don't shorten it, lad. You disrespect your heritage."

"Sorry, capo."

"Tell your uncle we see too little of him. Very well. I am listening."

"We heard from a client we've done business with a couple of times before." Montefiori named a certain telecommunications magnate. "They seek information about a group coming from America. But most of the group are not American."

"Terrorists?"

"I heard they were scientists."

"There is a reward?"

"Quarter of a million euros. The money is for information. They say, 'Do not strike.'" He hesitated.

"Speak, Montefiori. You are among friends."

"Capo, I thought, if they pay so much just for information, how much more do they pay if we deliver up the people?"

The room was intent now. "Capture them ourselves, you mean. Hold them for an appropriate ransom."

"Yes, capo. And maybe see if we can discover what they have that's so big. See if we can sell that as well."

The Prince exchanged a look with the man seated next to him. The pockmarked gentleman was built like a concrete slab. He nodded once. The Prince turned back to Montefiori and asked, "Does this mean you know where the scientists are located?"

"Maybe. My uncle and I, we run a cleaning operation on the side, capo."

"Did I authorize this?"

The young man paled. "No, capo. But, well . . ."

The man who had brought the young man in said, "Monti passed it by me."

"Montefiori."

"Yes, capo. Montefiori heard how we had these older women on our hands. We couldn't use them in the houses or the clubs."

"So you passed them on to our young friend, who sent them out as cleaners."

"And cooks, yes, capo."

"And if they happen to find an interesting item in one of these houses?"

Montefiori swallowed again. "Sometimes I sell the information. Sometimes me and my boys, we go in. But we always pass on your share, capo."

The Prince glanced at the other man seated in his booth. The pockmarked man nodded once. "He pays."

"Was this your uncle's idea, lad?"

"No, capo. But he gave me his permission."

"An enterprising young man who wastes nothing. I am impressed." The Prince studied him a moment, then said, "You understand, Montefiori, much depends on our taking such a step in a discreet manner. And only if the group is truly who your contact is seeking."

"The group arrived here a couple of days ago. They've rented a villa that's very isolated. I brought the cleaner here with me, capo. I thought maybe you would want to ask her yourself."

The Prince nodded once. A grave approval. "Bring her in."

The woman was clearly Slavic, with broad peasant features and hands swollen from a life of hard labor. She clunked in, her black leather tie-up shoes scraping the polished floor.

"Montefiori, be so good as to give the lady your chair. Sit, sit, madame."

She settled into the chair offered her and muttered, "My Italian no good."

The Prince shifted to fluent Russian. "I would be so very grateful if you would kindly share with us everything you know."

The woman responded in terse clips. Finally the Prince switched back to Italian and said, "She confirms all we have heard from Montefiori. They are indeed scientists. Some are American. Also two Asian ladies. There is one Italian woman who has only arrived this morning, apparently quite beautiful. They are all involved in some elaborate scientific procedure. They have filled most of the villa's upstairs rooms with their equipment." He turned back to the woman and continued in Russian. "A few questions further. When are we most likely to find them all at home together?"

"They never leave."

"What, never?"

"They stay, they work, they meet for meals, they argue, they return to their work."

"And what, pray tell, is this vital work of theirs?"

"I do not see. I cannot enter the upper rooms when they work. But there are many computers and wiring everywhere, and—"

"Yes, yes, thank you, madame. You have already said as much. Tell me, do you see any sign of explosives, guns, or drugs?"

"None. Some medicines, yes, but nothing else."

The Prince translated for the others, then asked, "Are there guards?"

"A woman and a young boy. Another man arrived with the beautiful woman."

"No professional security at all?"

"The woman and the boy act as guards, as I said. This one man who arrived today, he is different. Some do not like him."

The Prince said, "Tell me of this man."

"He is quiet, watchful. When he speaks, they all listen."

"The beautiful lady is his woman?"

"I cannot say."

The Prince translated again, then added, "So they have one guard who may be a professional, or he may simply have come for a lovely Italian woman. I think we should definitely—"

He was interrupted by the cleaner. When the woman finished speaking, the Prince translated, "She says she wants her daughter. In exchange for the information."

Montefiori said, "Her daughter dances at our biggest club. This woman pesters me constantly with her pleas."

"Would the daughter be missed?"

"She has started doping heavily."

"A pity. Very well. Give this woman what she wants. But—"

The woman wailed so convulsively she toppled from her chair.

"Help her up. Shah, my dear lady, calm yourself. You must do one thing more for us. Montefiori, make certain this happens. Bring the daughter into your personal care. My dear woman, you must stay at the villa until after this is all over and done, do you understand? There can be no surprise at your vanishing, no alarm raised. And when it is over, no concern can fall upon you and thus upon us. Are we clear on this?"

The woman made as to reach out for the Prince's hand but was kept in the chair by the man who had brought Montefiori.

"Excellent." He waved the woman away. "Montefiori, please accept my sincere compliments. When you arrived, we all wondered if this would prove to be a waste of time. Instead, we find you are indeed . . ." He turned to his associate and said, "How should we put it?"

The heavyset man replied, "*Con una marcia in più.*" The expression meant he saw Montefiori as having potential.

The young man's chest puffed out far enough to strain his suit. "Thank you very much, capo."

"See this goes well and you shall be rewarded." The Prince beamed at the room. "I have a very good feeling about this. Very good indeed."

26

"Our job is to make your job possible."

Charlie had said the words a hundred times. More. They were his standard opening line when dealing with new clients. Gabriella's scientists were seated around the table in the center of the kitchen, a vast chamber thirty feet long and twenty-five wide. The walls were granite. The floor was polished flagstone. The beamed ceiling was twenty feet high. The lone kitchen window was six feet wide, with panes so old the glass had run.

Sunlight formed a dappled design over the vast iron stove and the copper-rimmed vent and the stone sink and the walk-in fireplace. It was a good room, meant for laughter and family meals and perhaps even a few mountain melodies sung in the regional dialect. Not the frowns and the confusion and the fear that presently encircled the scarred table.

Gabriella's team had their set stations, like chess pieces upon a half-finished game. Brett was at the opposite end of the table from

179

where Charlie stood. He had the sunlight at his back. His silhouette showed the hunched shoulders and stiff posture of a very angry young man. Or jealous. He snapped, "I don't know about the others, but I'm not satisfied. I want to know what is happening. I want to know how we're supposed to get on with our work. What's the point of our being here at all?"

"You'll have to cover those issues with your teammates. My one job is to keep you safe. If we are successful, you should be able to ignore us."

"I'm still trying to figure out whether there's any real danger."

Charlie waited. He might as well let the guy go ahead and finish that thought.

Brett glared at Gabriella and said, "As in, why you brought this guy here at all."

Gabriella stared at her hands on the table. Charlie gave her a minute longer to respond, then addressed the whole group. "There are just three rules you need to keep in mind at all times."

Brett snorted. "Here we go."

"Point one: leaving the compound. Everybody needs to be accompanied by one of my team. And you need to make a record in the book that we will put by the front door. You time out, you detail your destination, and you time in. Point two: stay alert. If you notice anything out of the ordinary, tell me or one of my team. Don't assume you are safe anywhere except inside this house. Don't talk to strangers. Don't worry about bothering us with details you think probably aren't important. That's why I'm here. And point three: if any of you still have cell phones, destroy them. We'll work out a safe method of communication, probably via an internet cutout."

"Sounds to me like you're setting yourself in the spotlight," Brett said. "Creating danger where there isn't any."

"We'll know soon enough. In the meantime, my job is to give you as much freedom as possible while keeping you safe at all times."

The two Tibetan ladies, Dor Jen and Daisy, were seated by the cooker. They had their chairs drawn close to one another. Their heads turned in unison, like they were drawn back and forth between Brett and Charlie by the same thread.

Dor Jen asked Charlie, "Do we truly face a threat?"

Brett snorted again.

"I can't say for certain yet. I hope not."

Elizabeth, the pharmacologist, sat opposite the two Tibetans. She carried an aura of inapproachability. The chairs to either side of her were empty. "That's the party line. Now give us the reality check."

Charlie lifted his cup off the end of the table and sipped cold coffee. He debated replying. He would have preferred to wait until he had a better feel for Gabriella's team. But they were all watching him now. And building trust depended upon giving them total honesty.

He replied, "You want my opinion? Fine. I think you're busy running in useless circles. Right now you're completely focused on a possible danger. Your argument is over me. What this means is you've already handed your enemies their first victory."

The two techies, Milo and Jorge, were seated across the central table from one another. Jorge, the Brazilian, was on Charlie's left. He was a tall man who held himself with a hunter's stillness. Milo was smaller, with curly black hair and a lean, expressive face. He smiled at his colleague, who nodded once. A quick gesture, meant only for his pal. But Charlie caught it. And so did Brett. Charlie knew because the silhouette of the man's body frown grew tighter.

Charlie went on, "To understand your enemy, you have to determine their motive. Their principle aim has nothing to do with you personally. They want to *shut you down*."

Jorge's voice was surprisingly deep. "The man has got a point."

Brett said, "If this enemy exists at all."

But they weren't listening to Brett anymore. Not even the Tibetan ladies glanced his way.

Charlie said, "You need to stop running in place like trapped hamsters and get off that wheel. You're scientists. You're on to something big. They're not after you because of what you've done. They want to stop you because of what you represent. What you might do in the future."

Milo had a teenager's grin, so big it dominated his face. "All right. This is good."

"There's only one way to win. And that's to let us take care—"

"This is totally insane." Brett's chair crashed over. "I can't believe you're listening to this drivel."

Charlie waited while Brett stormed from the room. He gave it another beat, just to make sure no one else chose to follow him. Everyone else stayed where they were, focused intently upon Charlie.

He glanced over to where Irma and Julio were leaning against the wall by the window, almost lost to the shadows. That was fairly astonishing. Charlie had not said anything to them about placement. But somehow they had sensed that there needed to be a subtle separation between the inner circle and the hired help.

Gabriella said to the group, "Charlie has protected some extremely important people in very dangerous places."

"Yeah?" Every word Elizabeth spoke carried a combative edge. "Like who?"

Milo was still grinning. "Try Glenda Gleeson."

"The star?"

"I found the story online. Gleeson took her own security for the UN Goodwill Ambassador gig. She claims this guy saved her life in Darfur."

Charlie asked, "How important is Brett to your work?"

Gabriella replied to the table by her hands. "Very."

"Brett has focused on the bioelectrical impulses inside the brain," Elizabeth said. "He's interested in how quantum principles might apply to mental states."

"That means what, exactly?"

Gabriella replied, "Brett is applying chaos theory to my brain-wave observations. There are real-world situations where you can't predict a certain outcome because of so many different variables. Weather is a perfect example. You can't state exactly when a hurricane will strike.

But chaos theory uses uncertainty formula to calculate the *probability* of a certain outcome."

Milo said, "Up to now, all work on replicating brain functionality was restricted to one wave pattern at a time. Otherwise there are simply too many variables. Too much vibratory noise. But the brain never uses just one pattern. That's why it has been so difficult to replicate a mental or emotional state. Brett theorized that if we could replicate a *series* of patterns, we could magnify the power of influence over the subject's mental state. And elevate them more readily."

Charlie saw Irma and Julio exchange astonished glances, and said, "Amazing."

But Elizabeth snorted. "You're all missing the point."

Gabriella said, "Excuse me?"

"Brett is here because he wants to be a star," Elizabeth said. "If he came back with the first genuine proof that mental activity is a quantum state and not restricted by Einstein's concept of time, you know what would happen?"

Jorge nodded slowly. "They would place his name in lights."

Milo echoed his friend. "His very own slot as a talking head on TV. Maybe even a Nobel."

Gabriella said, "I never thought of that."

"Hey, don't let it bother you. We've all got our blind spots." Elizabeth glared at Charlie. "You never answered my question. How real is the threat?"

Charlie nodded acceptance that the woman would not let him go. "Since meeting you at the Vero hospital, I've been chased by two Delta squads disguised in FBI assault uniforms. They attacked my house in force. They were backed by real-time intel. After my first contact with Gabriella, the group I formerly worked for was offered a security contract worth tens of millions of dollars by a member of your opposition."

A round-eyed Milo asked, "Does the group have a name?"

"I've heard them called the Combine. They may bring almost

unlimited resources and connections." Charlie gave that a beat, then finished, "They are real, they are serious, and they are on to you."

Gabriella said, "But there's no way they can know where we are."

Charlie did not respond. His silence spooked the entire table. But he was not going to lie.

Elizabeth asked, "How long do we have?"

"They will want to infiltrate before you have a chance to establish a stronger network of safety."

"How long?"

"My guess is twenty-four hours. Forty-eight max."

When he started to leave the kitchen, Gabriella said, "No guns."

That stopped him. "I'm not sure that's workable."

"No guns," she repeated, using as hard a tone as he had ever heard from her. "The images about this have been extremely vivid. Inflicting death has no part in our project."

Charlie started to object. But for once, he faced a unified front. Every scientist watched him with the same grave determination. He said to Gabriella, "You and I need to go check out the future."

27

First Charlie had to go see a guy about a job.

The villa held sixteen bedrooms on the top two floors. Since there were only seven scientists, they all slept on the floor holding the kitchen and the parlor. The upstairs bedrooms were used for monitoring ascents. Almost half the bedrooms, including the extra ones along the servants' corridor, remained empty.

Brett had naturally taken the largest for himself. The room even had two sets of tall French doors with balconies looking north and east. As Charlie hoped, Brett was seated at his desk. Not packing. Not doing anything.

Charlie did not go hard. He did not push. He took the same tone of voice he'd used a hundred times before. Brett was just another soldier Charlie wanted to re-up. The last thing he could show such a guy was how desperately he was needed.

Charlie said, "I'd appreciate it if you did something for me."

Brett sneered. "What, now you're trying to get on my good side?"

"I'm not sure you have one. And if you did, I'm not sure it'd be worth trying to find."

Brett turned his face back to the grey day beyond his window. "Whatever."

"Make a list of the top people in your field."

"What?"

"Biochemistry related to the brain, right? Focus on the ones who are between jobs. Make a check mark by those you feel are most qualified to take your place."

Brett was watching him now. The fact sank in. "You're replacing me?"

"I just want to be ready when you cut and run. That's what you're sitting here planning to do, right? Leave your teammates at a crucial point and bolt. Show them just how trustworthy you really are." Charlie stared down at him for a moment, his gaze saying what any officer knew how to communicate without words, which was, *There's more where that came from.*

When Brett remained silent, Charlie let himself out.

Either it worked or it didn't.

The main room they used for ascents was located next to the techies' chamber, so the monitoring equipment could be wired in and the events recorded. The upstairs rooms were somewhat cramped, with narrow windows and a ceiling that leaned inward to match the roof's slope. Gabriella clearly had not slept well and still carried traces of that shattered look. When she asked if he would make the ascent for them, Charlie readily agreed.

Gabriella settled the headphones onto his ears and asked, "Can you hear me?"

"Five by five."

"Shall I close the drapes?"

"No need." The day had grown darker still. Charlie shifted his weight to fit around a lump in the old mattress. The room smelled of dust and disuse. He had slept almost six hours. Even so, jet lag hovered in the background like a distant fog. "Gabriella, I need to ask about your family."

Her hands froze on the keyboard. "What about them?"

"Where are they?"

"My mother is an anesthesiologist in Milan. My sister lives in Greece. She is a physiotherapist. Her husband runs one of the big luxury hotels."

"Can you get your mother to go visit your sister?"

Her eyes widened. "You think she is in danger?"

"If they can't find you, they might use her to get to you."

"Mama loves to spend time with the grandchildren. If I ask, she will go."

"Ask her today."

"All right."

"This is important, Gabriella."

"I said I would do it." She started typing again. The rushing wind filled Charlie's ears. "You are entering Base Level now . . ."

Charlie was on the move before she even finished counting.

He could hear her go through the drill—find the next danger, identify the route to safety, stay safe and in control at all times. He registered the words, but in truth he was already gone. Like he shut his eyes and in one instant he was *out there*.

The sense of being pulled through a massive vortex of power was constant. The images he received were brilliant flashes, photographic stills etched into his brain with multiple lasers.

When it was over, Charlie flew back into the chamber and inside his body with the same sense of catapulting force.

He gasped and sat up.

"Charlie?"

He swung his legs to the floor and sat there a second. Letting his heart rate settle. Filtering through the images. Setting them into careful order.

"Is everything—"

"They're coming. Tonight."

"What?"

He was already up and moving for the door. "Tell everybody to stay indoors. Call your mother. Do it now."

"Who is coming, Charlie?"

He opened the door and forced himself to slow down to a more acceptable pace. "The enemy doesn't always need a name."

28

They met in the parking lot of an abandoned warehouse owned by Montefiori's uncle. The group from Milan drove a black Mercedes S500. Montefiori's uncle considered such cars a waste of money and an invitation for trouble. Montefiori's three men sat in an Alfa Romeo sedan. Rain obliterated the night.

Vicenzo, the chief of the Milan crew, rose to stand beside the passenger door and called, "Are we going or not?"

The rain was falling so hard Montefiori had difficulty seeing beyond the car's headlights. So he walked over to the Mercedes and wiped a space on the front windshield and peered inside. He straightened and said, "There are five of you."

Vicenzo said, "What do you know, the boy can count. The village schools up here can't be as bad as they say."

"The Prince said he was sending two men."

"Two, five, we're here and that's it."

But that wasn't it at all. Five men from Milan meant Montefiori's group was outnumbered. After the deal was done, the Milan crew would take credit for their success. Negotiations would go through Milan. The lion's share of the booty would stay there.

And now Montefiori was no longer boss.

He stepped away from the Mercedes. "The deal is off."

Vicenzo was a bull of a man with a violent rep. "We're going. Now."

"Sorry. I had specific orders from the Prince."

Vicenzo slipped a silenced pistol from the pocket of his raincoat. "I'm giving the orders now."

Montefiori yelled, "Carlo!"

There was a satisfactory click, one loud enough to be heard over the rain hammering the car roof.

Vicenzo froze in the act of taking aim.

"I respectfully ask that you drop your weapon," Montefiori said. "Carlo, if he raises the gun, kill them all."

The night's silence was a most effective response.

When the pistol dropped into the puddle, Montefiori said, "Get back in your car. Please give the Prince my sincere apologies. But it is not professional to change tactics without informing your allies."

"Wait." Vicenzo started to reach into his coat but halted when Montefiori's own fist suddenly sprouted a gun. "I am reaching for my phone!"

"Slowly." Montefiori raised his voice. "You in the car, keep your hands where we can see them. You might get me. But my friend has a nightscope and flash suppressor and will take you all."

Vicenzo answered his phone, spoke softly, then said, "The capo wants a word."

"Put the phone on the car's hood and back away." He did so, and Montefiori moved forward, picked up the phone, and said, "It did not have to be this way."

The Prince demanded, "What is happening?"

"I am deeply sorry, capo. But Vicenzo came with five men. He claims to be boss here. All due respect, capo, but we cannot proceed in this fashion."

"No, no, wait. First, please accept my sincerest apologies. I will deal with Vicenzo."

"All due respect, capo, but you are in Milan and I am here in the rain with your five men."

"Tell me what you want."

"You will speak with my uncle. He will call me and confirm. You will promise him that we will handle all dealings with the Americans. We will receive payment. You will take one-third. We will part as allies."

"I agree to all of this."

"And Vicenzo will tell me in front of his men that he operates only on my orders."

The Prince said, "Give Vicenzo the phone."

29

Charlie checked his watch and rose from his bed. He still had almost two hours to go, but he wasn't sleeping anyway. He decided to put the time to better use than lying there and staring at the ceiling.

He kept the lights off. His room was in the servants' quarters on the lowest floor. The walls were raw granite. The windows were set in frames three feet thick, the shutters operated by a system of rope pulleys. Gabriella had offered him a room upstairs with the scientists, but he had no interest in adding fuel to Brett's fire. He liked how Irma and Julio had already gravitated to the lower level, shared only with the taciturn woman from some Soviet satellite state who cleaned and skulked in equal measure. Charlie yearned to be closer to Gabriella. But taking a bedroom along the upstairs hall would not change that.

With the shutters closed, the room was far darker than the night outside. Charlie touched each item of furniture, placing it in his brain. He began with stretches and calisthenics, then moved to a series of katas. His motions were restricted to fit the space he had, which was not much. He did not shut his eyes because he could not see anyway. By the time the hour was done, he was breathing hard. He was also far more easy about doing battle in the dead of night.

Charlie slipped on his clothes and knocked on Irma's door. She answered instantly, already dressed. "I hate going in unarmed."

She had said the exact same thing before going to bed. Charlie replied, "There's still time for a coffee."

"Do I look like I need caffeine?" She fell into step beside him. "Thirty years on the force and I never went into action without a piece."

"No guns."

"How many are coming at us?"

Charlie unlocked the front door, checked the night, saw nothing but rain. He stepped aside for her to exit, shut and locked the door behind them, and replied, "More than us."

Irma gave a tight hiss but said nothing more. Charlie liked that. A lot. There was nothing wrong with warriors mouthing off before combat. Long as they knew when to shut up and follow orders.

Over the course of the day, Charlie had identified eight hideaways inside the grounds. They ranged from a fissure in the granite cliff to a walnut tree whose two middle branches joined and formed a platform broad enough for six men. But the last he had found was by far the best.

The kitchen had two ancient fireplaces. The main one could burn man-sized logs. The second one stood in the corner between the stone sink and the front window and had once been used for baking bread. At least, that was what Gabriella had told him. Charlie's interest had not been in the fireplace but rather the chimney, which bulged out from the villa's front wall, forming a narrow crevice to the right of the main entrance. Charlie was certain it had been intended to hold an unseen guard. The inhabitant could observe both the gates and the front door, but the stone chimney and the upper-floor balcony shielded the guard from view. And the flue would keep the guard warm all night long.

Charlie tipped his hat to the long-dead architect and said to Irma, "I want you to take up station in there."

"How can you be sure they'll come tonight?"

"They're coming."

"You and the lady did that dream sequence thingy again?"

"They call it ascending."

"Whatever. You're sure it works?"

"I'm sure."

"You shouldn't spread us out like this."

"Put your feet on those stones—see how they protrude from the wall like steps?"

She remained where she was. "I should be down in the gatehouse with Julio."

"Irma."

"What."

"Your training was all about cleaning up messes. My job is making sure the messes don't happen."

She reluctantly accepted his hand and climbed the stone steps. She fit in the alcove like it was made for her. "I feel naked without my piece."

"You heard the lady. No guns. Reach behind you. I left you a crowbar."

She whined, "Julio is completely isolated."

"Exactly. Think of him as our tethered goat."

Charlie entered the trees between the house and the front gates and climbed the one he had selected that afternoon. The rain slowed him, but not much. He perched on a branch and watched the street. Time passed with the same ease as the rain. The night was utterly still. He could see his breath but could not feel the chill. His inner fires were burning hot now. He was exactly where he should be. Doing the only job he had ever been good at. As alive as any man could possibly become.

⫿⫿⫿

Twenty minutes later, Charlie drifted back to stand beneath the chimney alcove. He was so juiced he drifted above the puddles and the gravel, touching nothing. When he was within range, Irma hissed, "I really should be down there with Julio."

"Irma, listen to me. You are our last line of defense. Whatever happens, nobody gets through that front door. You read me?"

She released her defiance with a lingering sigh. "Whatever you say, chief."

"Good." He called softly, "Two cars. Nine men. I say again, nine."

She stiffened. "They're *here*?"

"Shh. I wasn't talking to you."

"Who else is . . ." In the light off the front porch, Charlie saw her stiffen and track a silent wraith who plucked himself from the night and drifted down toward the gate. "What was *that*?"

"Our secret weapon. Stay alert. They're coming."

30

Julio didn't mind the duty. When Irma had first asked him about playing night watchman, he had made out like it was pure garbage detail. As in, *I came six thousand miles for this?* But the truth was, he was kind of pleased. Not a lot. But some.

The night was raw for May. The wind blew straight off the huge mountains Julio had only seen once since their arrival. But he could smell them, which was a real kick. He stuck his head out the gatehouse door, the rain falling in a solid sheet off the eaves, and took a big breath. The fragrance of glacier ice as old as history was unmistakable.

The manor gates were rusted open. Which really didn't matter since the wall was no great shakes, maybe fifteen feet high and so crumbly Julio could have scaled it in about three heartbeats. He had pointed that out to Irma on day one. But she had shrugged and said if he didn't want the job she'd go find somebody else. Just Irma giving him cop-speak, on account of how there wasn't anybody else, and they both knew it.

It was his third night on duty, each one colder than the last. The villa's little stone gatehouse was down by the road. There was no heater and the door wouldn't shut properly. The wind howled through a crack in the side window. As usual, Irma had sent him off with a thermos of hot coffee and some serious cookies in a box advertising a Como pastry shop.

Truth was, Julio was totally cool with the whole gig. Midnight to seven, he was on duty. After Irma relieved him, he went up the hill and entered a kitchen that smelled like the Italian corner of heaven—fresh-ground coffee and newly baked bread and those little chickadees from all over the globe sitting there in their sleepy-time outfits and singing his name. *Good morning, Julio. Are you tired, Julio? Here, take the first cup of coffee, you need it more than me, Julio.* He just loved being the center of attention.

But the biggest surprise of all was how much Julio actually enjoyed taking orders from Charlie and Irma both. Before this gig, the one refrain he'd heard from every coach or teacher he'd ever had was, *Julio has trouble with authority.* But here he was, third man on the totem pole, just digging the scene.

Until this week, he had never been farther from Satellite Beach than the regional surf-offs at North Carolina's Outer Banks. The other kids called him an animal in the water, fighting for blood and every point and every scrap of wave. He'd always figured surfing was his one and only ticket out of town.

Back when he was little, his dad had started him out on a little thruster, small as a boogie board, the two of them laughing and screaming and sharing waves. Sharing *life.* Then his dad got sent up and his mom got sick, and by the time Julio turned thirteen, surfing was the only thing that cleared his head of the pain and rage and bone-deep loneliness. The only thing that kept him clean. The only thing he was good at. From starting horn to final buzzer, every heat, Julio was exactly what they all said.

An animal.

Only now, standing here at the edge of night, Julio could see just how much he'd lost in the process. Watching the rain fall in a sheet solid as a midnight wave, he confessed what his heart had known for a long time already. He'd lost hold of the fun.

Talk about ready to leave that world behind, man, he would have *paid* for this gig. In blood.

That was as far as Julio got on that internal ride. Because right then a human bear stepped out of the rain and shoved him back through the open gatehouse door.

Julio flew through the air, his outstretched arms tearing everything off the side counter. His heart rate zinged from a midnight shuffle to Ferrari redline as he flew. He bounced off the rear wall and fell in a heap on the floor.

The guy wore a black overcoat that turned his massive frame into a square. He growled something that might have been Italian.

Julio had years of experience dealing with hard men. He smiled politely. Kept his hands visible. Stayed planted on the stone floor. Very still. "Sorry, dog. No hablas Eye-taliano."

The man stepped into the gatehouse, compressing the air. The wind moaned about the open doorway. The man said in English, "You scream. Make noise. I help." The bear reached into his pocket and came out with a Taser. "Dog."

"Hey, you want me to sing, no problem."

The man took aim. "Too late, dog."

At that moment a phantom menace appeared in the doorway behind the man. Julio assumed it was a phantom because it moved too fast to be human.

The bear of a man had just enough time for his eyes to widen as the phantom took hold of his neck. Then he went over backward. Hard.

As in, this phantom tossed a guy weighing maybe three hundred pounds so high over his head that the guy crashed into the *top* of the gatehouse door frame.

The bear landed facedown, half in and half out of the gatehouse. His arms and legs twitched and he gave off a soft *ack*. The phantom shifted over to stand on top of him. He cocked his free arm up high, like a bird's wing. The hand drifted down and back, striking the guy's neck and then returning to the same bird-wing position, faster than Julio could blink. The man gave a final choking groan and went still.

Start to finish, it all took less than about one second.

Julio scrambled to his feet and realized he still needed to breathe.

The phantom was black on black—jeans, knit top, gloves, black stripes on his rain-slicked face. He watched Julio claw for breath. "You gonna croak on me?"

Julio shook his head and kept wheezing.

The phantom grinned. "That was pretty cool, you giving the guy lip. I liked that."

That was enough to steady him. "Who *are* you?"

"Later." He held up the bear's Taser. "You know how to use this?"

"Point and shoot, right?"

"Pretty much. The wires don't reach more than about ten feet and the aim is no better than a derringer. You need to use it, you get *real* close."

"Wait. There's more of them?"

"Nine minus this guy." He set the Taser on the counter by the door. "You use it, pop the probes loose with a flick of your wrist. Give it ninety seconds to fully recharge."

"What about you?"

The phantom grinned. "Do I look like I need that thing? Give me a hand, let's move this guy indoors."

Julio helped drag the man fully inside the gatehouse and flip him over so he lay on his back. The phantom slipped a metal tube from his pocket. "Use this to fasten his hands and his ankles. He starts moving around, seal his lips. Warn him you'll do the same to the nostrils if he lets out a peep. He'll behave. Believe me."

Julio inspected the tube. He was expecting some high-tech military secret weapon. Instead he read, "Super Glue?"

"You use what you got, bro."

Then the phantom stepped through the door, into the rain. And was gone.

No sound. No real movement like any human would make. The phantom just flowed out and joined the night.

Julio got to work. Or tried to. His hands were dancing to the same tune as his heart, quick little shudders that wracked him so hard he basically risked supergluing himself to the dude. He wound up putting so much of the stuff on the guy's hands they looked like they were coated in Pancake House syrup. Julio slapped the palms together, held them a second, then dropped them and decided, this dude was *never* gonna get free.

"You're not done yet?"

Julio's feet actually left the earth. Just levitated up about six feet.

If the phantom noticed he gave no sign. He just dumped another inert body on the stone floor and said, "You better speed things up. Otherwise our assembly line'll get all out of whack."

"How am I supposed to glue his legs?"

"You look like a smart kid. You figure it out."

The phantom vanished again. Julio was watching closely this time. The rain seemed to split like a curtain, then shut again.

The phantom was back while Julio worked on the second guy's hands. He deposited yet another body down beside the last one. "There's still more out there."

Julio said, "In that case, we need more glue."

"You serious?" He bent over for a closer look. Julio caught a whiff of the guy. If danger had a scent, it smelled like him. The phantom said, "These dudes won't be scratching themselves for about a year."

"Too much?"

He slapped two more tubes down on the counter. "Ain't my way to criticize a recruit, not when he's getting the job done."

Then the night was punctured by the coughs of silenced weapons. Hard slaps of sound, quick flashes of close-quarters lightning. A shout. Another. The phantom was already moving before Julio sorted out the noise. "Somebody's started singing my tune."

31

Charlie let the first attackers filter through the front gate. They were quiet enough for thugs trained in raw violence. They held to the shadows on the side away from the gatehouse and moved up the main drive, aiming for the front door. Charlie doubted Julio saw them at all.

There was a space after the first four invaders. Charlie noted how the two teams did not move in tight cohesion. The point of infiltration was vital, particularly when entering unknown terrain. This group had just made a mistake. One was all Charlie needed.

The second team of five men entered. He watched the last man approach the gatehouse, only to confront their secret weapon.

Charlie knew his almost-invisible friend would handle the second team. He slipped in behind the last man in the first group and made a standard triple strike. First punch to the left kidney, the unexpected blow delivering enough pain to stun the assailant. Second to the spine at heart level, breaking off the air needed to call out. Third to the carotid artery. Three strikes in one fluid action, just under a second from start to finish. Charlie lifted the man's legs free of the earth, pulled him into the shadows, and slammed him into a tree. Hard. Charlie followed this with a final chop to the nerve center where the jaw met the neck.

Charlie silently lowered the unconscious man to the ground and made a quick search. He tossed the thug's silenced pistol into the darkness. Ditto for the knife. Then Charlie hit pay dirt, a collapsible baton. Primo quality, so light he figured it for titanium and carbon steel.

As he headed back toward the gravel path leading to the villa, a voice ahead and to the right hissed, "Paolo?"

Charlie moved in at a slight crouch, his body angled as though he were headed in parallel to the path. Charlie's first instructor had called it a hyena's walk, how the animal never attacked straight on but rather loped in at an angle. The beast could change direction more swiftly and also masked precisely where the attack would happen. Ahead of him the trio clustered close enough to whisper.

Better and better.

One of the men finally spotted Charlie's shadow. Charlie knew because he hissed and turned and raised his pistol, all in one professional motion.

But by then it was too late.

Charlie flicked the baton out like a metal whip and lashed at the pistol hand, then backhanded the second man's eyes. He then stabbed the baton into the shooter's face, breaking the man's nose. He swung the baton up high enough for it to lift over the second man's face and attacked the third thug's eyes. But this man was fast enough to block the baton with his arm. He grunted with pain as it struck his wrist. The baton made a whirring sound through the air and smacked flesh and bone with sounds so swift, it was impossible to associate them with the damage Charlie knew he was inflicting.

All three men were shouting now, and two of them were trying to draw weapons clear of each other.

Charlie fell to the ground, covering the second man's dropped pistol with his body. He went to work on their legs. There were two things most baton wielders did not realize. Cops were the worst—they often took a baseball-style windup like they were going to hit the bad guys out of the park. Which was fine, as long as there was just one assailant who was going to go down and stay down. In a situation like this, the important thing to realize was how the baton, even with the slightest twitch, delivered *pain*. The person being struck often had no idea how hard he had been struck and whether he had received serious damage.

The other thing most people did not realize was, once the baton was locked into full extension, it made an excellent stabbing weapon.

Charlie whacked an ankle and thought he heard a bone break, but he couldn't be certain, what with the three men screaming and cursing overhead. He caught a glimpse of metal in the light and flicked the weapon upward, snapping the assailant on the chin and causing him to drop his pistol into the mud. Charlie rolled away.

The entire attack took less than five seconds.

He kept rolling until he was off the gravel and in the trees. Behind him the howls were more pain than rage, which was very good. The night became filled with the explosive coughs of silenced weapons and tight bursts of flame. The shots were all wide, since Charlie was no-where near where he had rolled into the shadows. As he raced through the trees he saw that two of the shooters were down on their knees. He scouted the rain-swept shadows but could not find the third man.

Charlie kept to a crouch as he filtered back through the trees paralleling the path, keeping clear of the direction of shots, searching with each flame burst for the missing assailant.

He sensed the attack before it came.

He dropped and rolled just as the night erupted.

A silenced weapon was not silent, particularly in the dead of a rainy night. The gun whuffed and the flash illuminated a bullish man with both hands holding the weapon in a professional grip. As Charlie scrambled for the shelter of the closest tree, the attacker crouched and took aim.

Which was when Charlie slipped in the mud.

Charlie kept scrambling, but the rain-wet earth gave him no purchase. The trees might as well have been on the other side of the moon.

It had to come sometime. The final opponent. The fraction of breath he would not live long enough to draw.

Then Charlie heard a meaty thud. The shooter cried in agony. A shot drilled the wet earth over to his right. Then another thud, and this time the man only grunted.

Charlie turned and watched Irma chop the man a final time with her crowbar. The thug fell hard. She stood over him, the rain plastering her hair to her skull. "I guess this one didn't get the memo about no guns."

Benny Calfo emerged from the trees. He surveyed the man at Irma's feet and said, "You got three guys in some serious hurt down the path. There are nine attackers, right?"

"Roger that. Nine."

Irma said, "And you are precisely who?"

"Hazard knows. Don't you, Eltee." To Charlie he went on, "We're missing two attackers."

Charlie said, "Julio is isolated."

"I'm on it." He vanished.

Irma's crowbar clanked on the gravel. "Am I seeing things?"

"You heard him, there are two assailants still unaccounted for. Go guard the front door." Charlie bent over the inert form. "I'll get these guys strapped before they come around."

32

Nothing like a little gunfire to wake a guy up.

Julio used a carbon blade he'd taken off one of the dudes and sliced their trousers from ankle to crotch. He slathered the back of the clamped palms with more Super Glue, ditto to the inside of their knees. It took some serious grunting to scrunch the inert body into a crouch, but once the glue hit the glue, the dude was set. Knee to back of hand, palms together, then to the other knee.

He was admiring his handiwork when he heard the crunch of gravel.

One thing Julio knew instantly, the phantom hadn't made that noise. That dude made *no* sound. Julio couldn't tell for certain, not with the rain crashing down, but he thought maybe it was more than one guy.

Julio was dressed in his warmest sweats, which were black and baggy. The only thing his clothes had in common with the fancy suits on the floor was, they were dark. The gatehouse lighting was very dim, a single bulb suspended from the high ceiling. Julio reached for two of the Tasers he had taken off the guys and dropped onto the stone floor.

He cradled his hands between his knees so that his shape conformed to the glued-up attackers. He was last in line and half hidden in the shadows at the back of the gatehouse. He figured he had about thirty seconds before the guys realized he didn't belong.

He watched through slitted eyes as two guys craned into the doorway. One was a heavy brute maxed on pasta, the other was a young snake. Hooded eyes and calm and deadly. The snake hissed a question Julio didn't need to understand.

Then the snake saw him. And raised the silenced pistol in his hand. Which was when the phantom struck.

Both of the thugs stiffened and gasped. Julio assumed the phantom had slammed them with a one-two to the kidneys. Not enough to put down a pair of pros. But it opened their eyes up to saucer size and sent the snake's shot winging through the gatehouse window.

The thugs responded as a team. The heavyset man turned and hefted his own silenced pistol. The snake fell to the stone floor, rolling to bring his firing arm around.

Julio used the inert body between him and the action to steady his aim. He fired the Taser.

And missed the snake by about six miles.

He had never fired a Taser before. Even at ten or eleven feet, the aim was lousy. The trigger popped and the darts flew, the slender wires spinning and shimmering in the dim glow. The darts missed the snake's gun shoulder by about a foot.

And sank into the other thug's right leg.

The Taser crackled with the release of energy. The thug gave a strangled cry. And toppled straight onto the snake's firing arm.

Julio took aim with the second Taser and fired.

Before the darts zinged across the room, he was already thinking, *Way, way wrong*. There was no way he could hit the snake. Not with the other dude covering him like an electrified rug.

This time the darts hit the heavy thug in the chest. He gave a little cough and went completely still.

The snake was one strong dude. He tossed the thug at the phantom like he was heaving a basketball. The phantom dodged the body, then saw the gun coming up and slipped back into the night.

Before the first shot was fired, Julio was already up and moving. The snake's gun coughed three times, firing at shadows and rain, before Julio hammered him just above his right ear. He didn't realize he still held the Taser until the snake's skull was covered with plastic shards.

Julio gripped the snake's neck and gun hand. He heard another couple of pops and felt ceiling plaster rattle down on his head. He felt his grip slipping off the rain-slick wrist. The snake's breath smelled of mint and death. Then the phantom reappeared and chopped the snake where the pulse throbbed in his neck artery. Again. The strikes were as fast as Julio's panting terror. The snake's eyes lost focus. The phantom took hold of the snake's hair and hammered the man's skull on stone. The snake went slack.

The two of them stayed exactly as they were for a second. Julio could hear himself grunting with the effort it took to breathe.

The phantom went over and checked on the other thug. "Man, this is one well-fried turkey."

Julio rolled over. Stared at the ceiling. Fought for breath. And saw only the snake's raging eyes.

"What's your name?"

"Julio."

"I'm Benny Calfo. Where'd Eltee find you?"

"Who?"

"Eltee. Hazard. Where'd he pick you up?"

Julio pushed himself up to where he could get a grip on the window-sill and pull himself to his feet. "Satellite Beach community center."

"That a fact." Overbright teeth shone from the blackened face. "Well, you did good back there. I owe you."

"Are there more?"

"Eltee and some lady took care of the rest."

"Her name is Irma."

"The way she swings that crowbar, she's got the makings of a pro." Benny kicked the pistols away from the bodies, gripped the inert thug by the collar, and dragged him farther inside. "Why don't you stitch these boys up, I'll go bring you the rest."

"What are we supposed to do with them?"

But the phantom was already gone.

Dawn was less than an hour away. Julio figured they had this particular corner of the rain-swept world to themselves. The only sound he heard was rain hammering the car roof. "You want to run this one by me again?"

"Follow me into town." If Charlie minded repeating his instructions, he gave no sign. "When we get to where we're going, we're going to cram both teams into this Mercedes here. Then I'm going to ram it into the front of a bar."

Julio looked at Irma. "This make sense to you?"

Irma must have stopped questioning Charlie entirely. "Did this come in one of those little extraterrestrial jaunts of yours?"

"I told you. They're called ascents."

"Whatever. Did it?"

"Right down to how it's just me and Julio making this trip."

"What am I supposed to do while this goes down? Take a bubble bath? Fix my nails?"

"Go and rest."

"I've never run out on a bust in my entire life."

"You're not running out on anybody."

"And just where exactly has that shadow of yours gotten to?"

"Benny will be on watch the rest of the night. And the rest of your questions about him will need to wait." When she looked ready to give him more lip, he said, "Irma, you and I have a major day coming up. Go get some sleep."

"This is more from the same ascent?"

"Yes."

"What about you?"

"I've never needed much sleep. If I get a couple of hours I'll be fine."

"You're kidding."

"No. This discussion can wait too." He turned to Julio. "Ready?"

Julio's ride was sweet, an Alfa Romeo sedan with a beast of an engine. The descent, even in the rain, left Julio certain that given half a chance, this car would purely bolt.

They entered a completely empty Como. Charlie drove with the confidence of a man on rails. They wound their way into the old city, ignoring a bunch of signs that Julio was pretty certain warned all cars to turn around and make tracks in the opposite direction. Charlie stopped at one end of an empty cobblestone plaza. Julio reversed his car and backed it to where the two trunks almost touched.

Charlie walked back and said, "Pop the trunk."

The work had them both puffing hard, extricating four human pretzels from the Alfa and cramming them into the other car. The last guy they shifted was the snake. As they were stuffing him into the driver's seat, he huffed a breath and opened his eyes. Charlie gave the guy the same bird-wing attack as the phantom had used. His hand just seemed to float down and back. A swift little hummingbird wing of motion. The snake went still.

"Dude, you have *got* to show me that move."

"Sure thing."

"For real?"

"You're one of the team, Julio. Whatever you want to learn, I'll teach. As much as you can handle."

Julio stood in the rain and watched as Charlie used the last of the Super Glue to plaster the snake's right shoe to the accelerator and his hands to the wheel. It gave Julio another chance to inspect the snake. He was younger than the other men, and perhaps a trace more refined in appearance. Very slender. Reptilian cold even when unconscious. Julio shivered and forced his eyes away.

Charlie tested the snake's foot and hands, then shook the rain from his eyes and said, "Go get ready to scoot."

"No problem, *ese*." Julio fired up the Alfa, then rose from the car and watched as Charlie used the crowbar he had taken from Irma to anchor down the Merc's accelerator. The engine gave a discreet howl. Charlie lifted his head into the rain, sighted down the hood, made a slight adjustment to the wheel, then reached in and slapped the car into drive.

The cobblestones were too wet for the Mercedes to actually burn rubber. But the car managed to build up a pretty solid head of steam as it careened down the narrow lane.

The car hit the glass front of someplace called the Bar Azzurra head-on. There was the rending screech of metal being torn from its stanchions. Glass exploded like a car-sized bomb had just gone off.

Charlie walked back with ease, as if bestowing chaos and mayhem on an ancient Italian city was something he did at least once a week. "Let's go get warm and dry."

They left the city and started up the steep road to Brunate. Julio opened his window and thought maybe he heard a distant siren, but he was enjoying the climb and Charlie was clearly not the least bit worried about the cops. Julio left the window open a notch and pushed the engine as hard as the rain and the night and the hairpin curves allowed.

They pulled through the villa's rusted gates and followed the gravel drive around to the stables built in solid to the cliff face. Charlie opened a set of double doors and waited while Julio drove the car in and turned off the engine. He shut the stable doors, and together they walked through a grey dawn and let themselves into the house.

In the downstairs hallway, Charlie stopped. Julio stood with his back to his bedroom door and listened to water drip off his clothes.

Charlie said, "Irma and I need to leave in a couple of hours. We'll be gone for a while."

Julio stifled a yawn. "You want me to stand watch?"

"No. Get some rest. If anybody on the team asks what happened, it'd probably be best if you wait until we're back so they hear the whole deal at once."

"I got no problem with that."

"You were totally stand-up back there."

"Just did my job, bro."

"Benny says you saved his life."

"Yeah, well, only because he kept me breathing through the first round."

Charlie offered his hand. "Anywhere, anytime. You hear what I'm saying?"

As Julio showered and slipped into sleep, he was still grinning like a fool.

33

Alessandro Gavi slipped into his customary pew on the left side of the church. Many considered him handsome in a spare and meticulous fashion. He dressed well, he had his hair cut every ten days, he was seldom seen without a tie. He exercised regularly, ate sparingly, and remained within two kilos of his teenage weight, even in his late fifties. Alessandro knew many considered his daily attendance of morning mass simply another precise habit. Certainly he gave no indication of extreme devotion. The reason he attended daily mass was quite simple. He had a long and intimate knowledge of evil. As far as he was concerned, such experiences required an act of balancing. Of consciously making room for the good and the just and the divine. Otherwise, he risked drowning in the sea of shadows and ghosts.

When he emerged from the church, Alessandro was pleased to discover that the constant rain had paused, at least momentarily. But the sky smoldered beneath the same heavy grey blanket that had dominated northern Italy for the wettest spring in three hundred years.

He spotted the watcher as he crossed the church's forecourt and entered the main piazza. Alessandro's first impression was that the man who observed him was an assassin. But an assassin would not stand in plain view, his hands open and at his sides. As one professional might greet another, signaling there was no danger.

The closer Alessandro came, the more certain he grew of the man's occupation. He was handsome enough to draw stares from passersby. This individual scanned his surroundings constantly. He was taller than Alessandro, and the body beneath his knit shirt and slacks was warrior hard. His features were severe. Hints of old scars peeped from the shirt's collar and his left sleeve.

Alessandro stopped in front of the man and waited.

The man spoke to him in American-accented English. "Turn on your phone."

"Pardon me?"

"You have a call coming in. It's important. Switch on your phone."

Alessandro drew out his phone, hit the switch. The instant he had a signal, it rang. He lifted the phone to his ear. "Hello?"

"Alessandro? Tell me you haven't already heard the news from someone else."

"Edoardo?"

"Who else? Tell me I'm the first."

"Have you been trying to contact me?"

"How could I, when I only heard it for myself five minutes ago? First I called around to make sure it was real, this story. And even though I have now had it confirmed by two people I trust, I still don't believe it."

It was not uncommon for Alessandro to receive phone calls upon leaving the church. This was, after all, Italy, where empty chatter was considered a vital weapon against the vacuum of silence. But to receive a phone call from Edoardo was a singular event.

Edoardo was an ally from the bad old days. He had been the head of the anti-Mafia police in Catania. He was also that rarest of breeds, an honest policeman who had survived. He and Alessandro had become natural allies in that other great battle, the one against corrupt officials in Rome. Three months after Alessandro had arrived in Como, Edoardo had been reassigned to the Guardia di Finanza in Milan. They had not spoken in four months. Longer.

"Alessandro, are you there?"

He forced his lungs to take a breath. "What do you have to tell me that is so urgent?"

As Alessandro absorbed Edoardo's news, the American remained as still as the statues cresting the central fountain. An immovable force, one so potent the very air about him was compressed. He watched Alessandro with a predator's patience as Edoardo regaled him with how a Mercedes S500 had been discovered that morning, parked in the front room of the Bar Azzurra. Inside were crammed nine men. Five of them were tied to the prostitution ring that dominated northern Italy. The other four were all members of an elite corporate security group based in Como. All but one had their palms glued together, and then the outside of their hands glued to the inside of their knees, forcing them to adopt a most uncomfortable position. Their pant legs had been sliced open at the thigh to make this possible. The ninth man had his hands glued to the steering wheel and his shoe glued to the pedal. The men were all moaning pitifully over being trapped like this, apparently for hours, crammed tightly inside the car.

Edoardo howled with the simple pleasure of being the first to inform his friend of the event.

Alessandro made noises he did not actually hear himself, then hung up. He asked the American, "This was your doing?"

"Yes."

Alessandro studied the man a bit longer. "Do I have anything to fear from you?"

"Not now, not ever."

"In that case, perhaps you should join me for breakfast."

They walked to the largest of the cafés fronting the square. The waiter saw Alessandro coming and lifted the "Reserved" sign off his customary table. It was a small favor, but one that meant a great deal, for his was one of the few outdoor tables set far enough beneath the awning that not even the strongest gusts could propel rain onto his morning paper.

Alessandro gestured for the American to be seated. "What will you have?"

"Whatever you take is fine by me." When the waiter departed, the American continued, "I'm sorry about the bar's entrance. We needed to make sure they were arrested."

Alessandro nodded as though that made perfect sense. "We."

"I serve as security agent for a group of scientists. They've taken over a villa in Brunate."

"You are a professional bodyguard."

"Currently, yes. Normally my work involves risk assessment and running security teams."

"So how many other security agents have you brought into my country?"

"Not enough." The man turned and signaled to a grim-faced woman seated at the table closest to the building. Alessandro was very good at noticing professionals, which this woman certainly was. Yet he had missed her. That only heightened his sense of being confounded by this man.

The woman carried a battered canvas case as she walked over and seated herself. "No tails."

"My name is Charlie Hazard. This is Irma Steeg. Irma, show the man your badge."

Alessandro read it. "An Orlando policewoman. Here in Como."

"That is a gold shield," the woman said. "Senior detective. Homicide. Retired."

Alessandro asked Charlie, "How did you know about the phone call I was about to receive?"

He replied, "You have two sets of questions. One pertains to the incident last night. The other is about how we have come to contact you. I would advise you to keep them separate."

Alessandro paused while the waiter set down two breakfasts of brioche, spremuta, and cappuccino. It was the sort of advice he would have himself given to a new bailiff. "Signora, will you perhaps take breakfast?"

"I'm good, thanks."

He nodded to the waiter, who departed. Alessandro asked once more, "How many are in your team?"

"Irma, myself, and a kid."

Irma said, "Julio is no kid."

"He's eighteen and untrained."

"Actually, he's seventeen, and he did just fine last night."

Alessandro raised his hand. "I have difficulty believing that the three of you and a group of scientists took out nine armed assailants. If indeed you were attacked."

"The attack was real," Charlie replied. "And the scientists didn't help. They don't even know about it yet."

Irma said, "I still feel like we should have gotten them together and told them."

"Not a chance. You want to wake up a bunch of civilians, tell them, 'Last night we took out a professional hit team, you go ahead and have your cornflakes, we're making a run into town'?"

"They're as safe as your shadow can make them."

Alessandro saw Charlie shoot Irma a warning glance, but all he said was, "That will do nothing to reassure the team. They need to hear about this from us."

Alessandro rattled his cup. "Wait, please, enough. Return to my question. You three have taken out nine assailants."

Irma said, "Charlie here is very good at what he does. He's ex-Ranger. Do you know what that is, Ranger?"

Charlie said, "We had the element of surprise on our side. We won't next time."

Alessandro asked, "How can you be certain they will return?"

"These guys won't. But others will. And the next group will be a lot worse than these punks."

"Half the men you captured have a history of violence and prostitution. The others do corporate security." Alessandro had to admit that made for some very intriguing questions. "Such attackers would carry a serious level of threat."

"They're punks. The next attackers will be people like me." Charlie reached for the detective's battered case and slipped it over by Alessandro's feet. "In there are nine silenced pistols, seven carbon knives, and four switchblades. We're keeping the Tasers and the batons."

"Please, that last word, I don't know it."

"Batons. Retractable hand-to-hand weapons."

Irma said, "Primo quality. Titanium with carbon grips."

Alessandro motioned to the waiter and waved his finger at their empty cups. "Italy's crooks always get the best toys."

Charlie said, "The Tasers were all jacked up to illegal settings."

"They were after causing maximum pain and probably permanent damage," Irma said. "These were not nice boys."

"So what do you want from me, absolution?" Alessandro pointed at the church across the square. "Please. Go. All are welcome."

The pair just sat and watched him. Waiting.

Alessandro sighed. "All right. Now we shall move on to the second set of questions. Just exactly who is this group you are protecting, and why did these attackers have such a powerful interest in them? And how did you know to tell me to turn on my phone?"

Charlie became even grimmer than before.

Irma leaned back and cocked her arm over the empty seat next to hers. She revealed a very hard smile, that of a woman who had seen as much of the world as Alessandro. Perhaps.

She said to Charlie, "Here we go, sport. You're on."

34

Charlie and Irma took the funicular back from the lake. The cog train pulled its way up the steep-sided hill, drawing them into nothingness. Midway up the mountain, they entered clouds so tightly clamped to the forest and the rocks that nothing could enter. No light, no sound. The air grew damp and wintry cold. When they arrived in Brunate, they walked an empty street. Nothing moved. No cars, no people.

Irma did not speak until the gatehouse appeared, when she called softly, "You there, sport?"

Julio's shape coalesced in the mist. "You want spooky, try standing here alone for three hours, wondering if they might've kept a couple of guys in reserve."

Irma asked, "Everything quiet at the house?"

"Totally. I went in for breakfast, they were all just hanging out. They know something went down last night. Don't ask me how. But they know."

Charlie said, "You were superb last night. There is nobody I would rather have watching my back."

Not even the day could dim Julio's pleasure. "You want to tell me who that ghost was?"

Irma said, "I already asked. The man ain't talking."

"I just wanted to wait until Julio could hear. His name is Benny Calfo. He was my NCO in Iraq."

"He was a Ranger?"

"The best." Charlie described Hobo Harbor, which pretty much explained everything they needed to know about Benny. "You won't be seeing much of the guy."

"He's still here?"

"Up in a cave above the roofline. Benny's not one for people. Or enclosed places."

"How long is he staying?"

"Long as we need his help, and not one second more." He asked Irma, "Think you could go take Julio's place? I need to address the troops and I'd like Julio to hear what I say."

"No problem. Though I doubt standing guard will do much good. I couldn't find a bad guy in this fog unless he fell in my lap."

When they entered the house, Charlie found the team bunched around the kitchen table. It was a battered affair, centuries old and scarred by hard use and eons of arguments like the one they were waiting to start with him. Outside the huge window was nothing save a dim, grey void.

Gabriella demanded, "Will you tell us what happened?"

"We were attacked," Charlie replied. "We took them out."

Brett said, "I, for one, am not satisfied with that answer."

Charlie took his time. Poured himself a cup of old coffee. Poured another for Julio. He leaned against the wall by the fireplace next to the kid. Then he gave it to them. Flat, hard, straight.

Elizabeth said, "Is this what you normally do, scare your clients into submission?"

"There is no normal. Every situation is unique. But the answer is no. Most of my clients couldn't handle the truth."

The super-still Brazilian, Jorge, asked, "So that's what you're giving us, everything?"

"You ask, I give."

Gabriella wore an old sweater the color of the stone walls and the day. "Where have you been?"

"Last night Julio and I delivered the attackers to the police. This morning Irma and I went down to meet a possible ally."

Elizabeth asked, "Was that smart, drawing attention to ourselves?"

"It all came out in my last ascent. The officer we spoke with is part of our future. Maybe."

"Who were the people that attacked us?"

"No idea. Pros. At this point, that's all we need to know." Charlie sipped coffee he did not want. "We don't think this was a hit. They didn't come to take us out."

"I'm fairly certain I heard gunfire," Elizabeth said.

"You did. But only after they were attacked. Their weapons of choice were supercharged Tasers and batons."

Milo said, "Nine men shoot up our front yard in the middle of the night. What would you call it?"

"They wanted you alive. Ransom, probably."

Milo's eyes could not have been any bigger and remained inside his skull. "This is good news?"

"It is what it is."

"So what now, we pack up and leave again?"

Gabriella said, "Charlie's last ascent did not suggest that."

Brett scowled. "Oh, so it's Charlie's ascent now."

This time Gabriella did not bend. "That's right. Your life is in his hands. Deal with it."

Brett started to respond, then noticed that Elizabeth was grinning at him. "You find this humorous?"

"I find it hilarious." She asked Charlie, "So what now?"

"Go back to work. Nothing's changed. You stop, you let them win."

"Can we do that?" Milo asked. "I mean, are we really safe?"

"This attack has been foiled. We are doing our best to establish a new ally with the local force. For the moment, that's all I can say for certain. But that is not the only issue here."

"Is that so?" Brett snorted. "We were attacked last night, but our security is not the point?"

"If anything should be clear from last night, it's that I'm going to keep you safe. That is my job and I'm good at it. Your job is to get on with your work."

Gabriella cut off Brett's response by announcing, "I must go to Milan."

Charlie knew she was waiting for an argument. Ready for it. But he didn't say what he thought, which was, *Extremely bad idea.* "I suppose you've got a really good reason for taking that particular risk."

"Of course I have reasons. Do you suppose I'm going on a whim?"

Charlie adopted his bland monotone, oil on troubled waters. "Just asking."

"I am going to work. That is what you told us to do, yes? Fine. I must meet my trial subjects. I have to do this in order to continue my research."

The Tibetan woman, Dor Jen, added softly, "It has been far too long since we last collated data. We need to formally track their progress."

"This is a vital step," Elizabeth agreed. "If we want to offer anything to the global scientific community, we have to follow their rules. Danger or not."

Charlie studied the faces around the table. Not even their evident fear erased the sense of unified need. Even Brett was in agreement. All of them ready with more arguments.

Charlie replied, "I've got an idea."

"Excellent." Gabriella stood abruptly. "Charlie, I need to speak to you."

"Shouldn't we finish up here first and decide—"

"I want to speak to you *now*."

When he got out in the hallway, the argument he expected wasn't there. Instead, Gabriella told him, "I can't ascend."

"What do you mean?"

"Exactly what I said." Gabriella's features were stretched to the limit. Lips compressed, veins on her neck as visible as tattoos. "I'm trapped inside my own skin."

Charlie led her through the double doors and into a parlor filled with lumpy furniture and the smell of beeswax. "Give me that one more time."

Gabriella entwined her hands and wrenched her fingers so hard he heard the knuckles pop. "I thought we needed to know what was going to happen next. You were gone. I asked Brett to help me."

Charlie wanted to say, *That's your problem right there.* But he didn't.

Even so, his face must have shown a trace of what he was thinking, for she said, "Brett was not the reason I couldn't ascend."

"You don't know that for certain."

"Oh really. You're the expert now?" Her sweater was oversized and slipped down one shoulder, leaving her looking even more vulnerable. "I started to ascend. But there was a barrier. Like a shield that kept me in place."

"Has this ever happened before?"

"Not to me." Her expression defined desperate. "What if it's permanent?"

He gave her hands a solid grip. "Let's go find out."

Gabriella did not want to try again, but Charlie insisted.

Not that it did any good. Five minutes into the ascent—less—she was up and tossing the headphones aside. Charlie watched her make several circuits around the room. He searched for something to say, came up flat.

When she was calmed down enough to operate, they switched places. The rushing wind filled his head. Charlie felt himself ease into the now-familiar calm. He heard Gabriella say, "I am beginning the count now."

Then it happened.

He understood what she meant. The sensation was unmistakable. He rose up in time to her count. His senses elevated. Then there came the moment of separation, rising from the physical to the *other*.

And he was stopped.

The instant he started to ascend, he struck the barrier. It was like a vise compressed him back into his body. Or a fist.

He opened his eyes. Took off the headphones. Sat up and swung his feet to the floor.

Gabriella looked at him. "Not you too."

Charlie was filled with a sense of inconsolable loss. Four ascents and he had come to accept this simply as a state of being. A part of him and his life.

He tried to rub the ache from his chest. Gabriella watched the movement of his hand and whispered, "What are we going to do?"

⑃⑂

Jorge and Milo, the two technicians, together occupied the largest of the top-floor bedrooms. Their office looked exactly as Charlie expected. Dump techies together and they'd cram the space full of wiring and flat-screens and electronic paraphernalia and a language only clan members could comprehend.

Charlie said, "So you're in communication with your previous test subjects?"

Milo said, "We were until the problems started. Initially we had two more chat rooms available to everyone. We could slip in and monitor without them noticing us. Gabriella used the chat rooms to observe who was interested in what we were doing, or wanted to sign up or just talk about the process. But they've stayed sealed since we left Vero Beach."

Charlie's inability to ascend had left him extremely disoriented. He was looking for mental handholds, searching for a way ahead. "What about your test subjects—they can still talk to each other?"

The two techies nodded in tandem. Milo said, "Back when interest started growing, Gabriella had us set up a dedicated chat room that's only available to those who managed to ascend."

Jorge spoke for the first time since Charlie had entered. "Anyone who passes on the entry codes to an outsider is banished. Not just from the chat room. From ever working with us again."

Charlie said, "So you can still contact them."

"Oh, sure," Milo said. "That is, unless they've gone off the grid. Which I doubt."

"They're there," Jorge said. "Most definitely."

"How can you be so sure?"

"I speak a little Italian. Enough to monitor their discussions. They're there, they're waiting, and they're impatient."

"Desperate," Milo agreed.

"How many test subjects are we talking about?"

"Two hundred and nineteen."

A thought began working at his brain, a tiny electronic worm, digging away. Charlie tried to listen beyond the ache of loss, tried to tell himself it was ridiculous to react to the ascent barrier like this. He violently shook his head, ordering himself to *focus*.

Milo caught the motion. "I know what you're thinking. Two hundred contacts, the bad guys are bound to be listening in. I've got two words for you. No way."

"Dedicated comm site," Jorge said. "Ultra-high-level barriers. We downloaded an encryption we designed ourselves. Only available to our test subjects."

"Okay." That was one thing Charlie could deal with. "Do you have a secure comm link to the outside world?"

Milo slid the computer mike toward him and began tapping keys. "Who are you calling?"

"Shanghai."

⑾

Remy Lacoste answered with, "You got some nerve, I'll give you that."

"They hit us last night, Remy."

"You got their ID's?"

"They carried nothing on them that could be used for identification purposes. But a local ally says the attackers were tied to regional heavies."

"You're thinking the Combine?"

"Not professional enough. My guess is their contacts over here decided to take the initiative."

"Who's handling security with you?"

"I brought two friends from the States. A homicide detective and a local. Both very stand-up."

Remy was not impressed. "Cops."

"Benny Calfo is with me."

"No fooling?" Remy coughed a laugh over the computer speakers. "I heard he was dead."

"He might be soon enough. If you don't help me out here."

"Oh, so now you're hitting me with the 'my life is in your hands' gig."

"Pretty much." Charlie turned to where Milo listened and watched. "Give him all your websites, the active one and those you've taken off-line."

Milo asked, "Just exactly who are we talking to here?"

"His name is Remy Lacoste, and he's the best there is."

Milo looked at his friend. Jorge shrugged. Milo leaned toward the mike and read off the three electronic addresses.

"Okay, Eltee, I got them."

Charlie said, "Two of the sites have been down for a few days, but my guess is the Combine still has them all on permanent surveillance. Can you ID the secret observers and trace them back without being caught?"

"This the same group that chased me when I went for the blonde?"

"Roger that."

"She's very nice, by the way. You send her my way, all debts are paid."

"Can you send me a photo?"

"Natch. Give me an e-address."

Milo read one off.

"Coming at you."

Jorge hit a few keys, and Reese Clawson's face popped onto the largest flat-screen.

Milo said, "Whoa."

"Told you," Remy said.

Jorge asked, "This woman, she is a bad guy?"

"Bad as they come," Charlie replied.

Remy added, "She's got herself quite an ops team, by the way. Real scum of the earth."

"Any ID's and background would be a big help."

"Got four now, I'll send more as they come."

Jorge set the men on the flat-screens around the blonde woman. The room went very quiet until Remy asked, "You recognize any of them, Eltee?"

"The blond guy. He was head of the security detail that met me at Harbor Petroleum, then wore the fake FBI jackets and attacked my house."

"They're all Delta except one. That particular standout is a real gem. He's the one who looks like his skin is only partly glued on. Actually got kicked out of the Foreign Legion. Must have done something truly amazing."

The four grim menaces that now surrounded the beautiful blonde woman silenced the room. Charlie heard Milo swallow hard. He settled a hand on the guy's bony shoulder.

Finally Remy said, "Okay. I've ID'd a parasite doing surveillance on all three sites."

Jorge protested, "That's not possible."

"Let me guess. University techies, right?"

Milo said, "We headed up tech support for a theoretical physics team at MIT."

Remy laughed out loud.

Charlie said, "I want you to send them a bomb. Special delivery. On my count."

"Nothing will short that team out for long. You want permanent, you need more than I've got. I might as well attack the Pentagon with a can of Raid."

"A few minutes will be enough. I just want them to go blind to the outside universe."

"That will definitely be a pleasure," Remy said. "Even though when I'm done I'll have to emigrate to Yalta."

"Hold tight." Charlie said to the pair, "Do we have a time and place for Gabriella's meeting in Milan?"

"Yes."

"Okay. Write your message to the test subjects, telling them when and where. You've got one chance to send it, so make sure you hit everybody on the first go."

Milo asked, "What about the others?"

"Who?"

"The ones who've been asking if they can sign up for the next go-round."

"You have others who want to become test subjects?"

"A ton. Our sign-up process is off-line. But some techies among the ascenders have set up a separate list where they can store the contact details for friends who want to become test subjects. They're all either Milanese or studying at the local universities."

Logic told Charlie to negate the idea. Extending the contact only heightened the risk. But he found himself hearing his own words of that morning. If they didn't move forward, the enemy had already won. "Include them too."

Their fingers flew. Two minutes, then Milo said, "Ready."

"Remy?"

"The grenade is primed, the pin is pulled, Eltee."

"Go."

"Bomb launched." A pause, then Remy said, "Kaboom."

Charlie patted Milo's shoulder. "Send your message."

35

Alessandro Gavi sat at his desk and worked through his inbox. He did not mind paperwork in the least. Long ago he had learned to assign his eyes and writing hand to one tiny corner of his brain, leaving the rest of his mental faculties free to roam. Some of his most difficult cases had been resolved while dealing with the burdens of bureaucracy. As a result, he had gained the reputation of being the only employee within the Ministry of Justice whose paperwork was always up-to-date.

Alessandro was a bailiff, an *ufficiale giudiziario*. A bailiff, in his humble opinion, was the finest position within the Italian justice system.

As any Italian with a single breath left in his body would say, the only mess in Italy worse than the police were the courts. The judicial system had been cobbled together over centuries, and each branch had developed into a modern-day fiefdom. The police were fragmented like medieval city-states, between the Carabinieri and the Polizia and the Stradale and the Guardia di Finanza and the DIA. There were plots and coups and bureaucratic sniping and corruption.

But in each province, there was only one senior bailiff. Once the judges passed on their instructions, Alessandro could do almost anything. He could call on anyone's assistance. Even the military.

The majority of his mind remained focused upon his meeting that morning with the two Americans.

Alessandro did not respond to the knock on his door. When a shadow fell upon his computer screen, he looked up. "Do you mind?"

Antonio D'Alba was a defense attorney. Alessandro knew him all too well. Antonio was a fierce combatant in court and used his considerable wiles to extend cases for years. The richer his client, the longer his cases tended to run. He fought court-ordered evictions and asset seizures tooth and nail. He had kept Alessandro in the docket for days on end, tying the bailiff up as long as his clients had funds to skim.

Out of court, Antonio was a charmer. A smiler. A stellar dresser with an eye for the women. The younger the woman, the greater Antonio's charm. Alessandro knew Antonio's wife very well. She worked with his own wife at a home where many of Alessandro's youngest charges wound up. This being Italy, Alessandro had long ago learned to disguise how he felt about philandering colleagues.

Antonio said, "I suppose you've heard."

"How could I not?" Alessandro had no need to ask what Antonio meant. The entire Justice building was abuzz.

"Interesting they would ram the car into the Bar Azzurra."

"Who did it?"

Antonio tapped the side of his nose, indicating that he knew and the information was secret. "You're a patron of the place, aren't you?"

"From time to time." Alessandro was not much of a drinker. But what professional socializing he did was there. The Bar Azzurra was owned by a former cop with the Guardia di Finanza. He had lost a leg in Catania, where he had been investigating a Justice official who was reportedly on the take. He was notorious for his hatred of corruption. As a result, his bar was a gathering point for straight cops and jurists and ministry officials.

When Alessandro had arrived at the office that morning, the bar owner had been downstairs, toasting the fates that had delivered nine thugs through his front window.

The lawyer asked, "Did you hear how they were found?"

Alessandro started to respond that of course he had heard, how could he not, when no one in the entire building spoke of anything else. Then he realized Antonio was not even listening to himself. "Is that why you stopped by?"

"Uh, no, actually . . . Alessandro, I have a question."

Alessandro put his computer in sleep mode and shut his file. "Of course. Take a seat."

"What? Oh. I . . . Thank you."

Alessandro did not offer the lawyer a chair out of courtesy. He wanted to draw Antonio closer. So he could smell the man.

"Look, I, uh, that is, I have a client. He—well, that is, his lawyers— have asked me for help with a matter."

"You're not his attorney?"

"I represent a small part of their interests, yes. But the client is very big. Sorry, I can't name them. You understand."

Alessandro waved it away, a matter of no consequence. "Of course."

"My client is searching for seven scientists. They come from America, but they originate from all over. One is Italian."

"Names?"

"Sorry, no names."

Antonio was lying. What was more, he knew that Alessandro knew. It was a typical Italian *bugia*, a lie told because the true message could not be spoken. The message was, *I can't tell you and you were wrong to ask, but I need your help, so I can't risk offending you by saying that.*

Antonio continued, "The scientists stole something of enormous importance to my client."

Alessandro asked, "Why would you be speaking with a simple magistrate in Como about this matter?"

"The American attorneys think they may be hiding here."

"In Como?"

"Somewhere in the vicinity. Perhaps."

"Forgive me. But I am still not clear what that has to do with me."

"The scientists need a large space for their experiments."

Alessandro nodded. "They could not go through normal channels to rent such a space. So you wonder if there has been any movement—"

"One of your confiscated villas, perhaps, or a warehouse."

"I will see."

"Any help you can give. Any at all."

"Of course." Alessandro rose and shook the attorney's hand and waited for the door to click shut. He turned on his computer and reopened his file, finished the report, and sent it off. He called in his two deputies and assigned them new duties. He lunched with a judge. They laughed over the antics of the Bar Azzurra's owner, who had shared his few unbroken bottles with the prosecutor after signing the official complaint.

Alessandro then returned to his desk and checked his watch. Three hours had passed since Antonio D'Alba had left his office. Long enough for there to be no logical connection between Antonio's request and his next action.

He picked up the phone and dialed a number from memory.

"Evidence."

Alessandro knew the officer who spoke. His name was Pietro, and he was extremely bent. "This is Bailiff Gavi. I need—wait, let me check. Yes, here it is. I need to speak with Officer Luca Bresco."

"He's out."

"Have him call me the instant—"

"Wait. He's just walked in."

A pause, then, "This is Bresco."

"This is Gavi. There may be a problem with some evidence you signed in."

"Again? I can't believe this is happening to me."

"My sincere apologies."

"What, I forgot to sign my name in the right spot on your six dozen forms?"

"No, no, nothing like that. But we do need to speak."

"Today?"

"Please. It is rather urgent, you see."

"Oh, all right. But only if you're here in twenty minutes." The phone was hammered down.

Alessandro rose from his desk and reached for his coat. The conversation had been for listeners. What he had requested was time alone with Luca Bresco, the one officer in the Evidence chambers whom he trusted completely.

It was time to discover what precisely lay behind the Americans and their request.

36

Charlie and Gabriella went to Milan with the two Tibetan women, the only others on their team who spoke fluent Italian. Julio traveled with them, mostly because Charlie wanted to reward the kid with a day out. When they boarded the express train, Charlie guided Gabriella into a seat separated from the other three. With the train's rumble masking his words, he sketched out an idea that had come to him while working with the techies that morning. He needed the entire train ride to explain what he had in mind to keep them safe, mostly because his plans were less than half formed. Gabriella listened with quiet intensity, her gaze holding the electric quality of a million unspoken thoughts. He finished just as they entered Milan's grimy perimeter.

Gabriella stared at him a long moment, then said simply, "Thank you, Charlie."

"It's a long way from complete."

"You have given me hope. For today, that is complete enough."

They all crammed into one SUV taxi because Charlie did not

want to split them up. As they drove along rain-swept city streets, Gabriella explained how Milan had two universities. Her father had taught philosophy at the Statale, or state university. One of her proudest memories was of her mother walking Gabriella around her late father's department, using Gabriella's new title for the first time. Her daughter, the professor. Gabriella related how beautifully painful it had been, seeing the affection her father's colleagues still held for him eleven years after he had died.

Charlie and the others were so caught up in this tale they did not notice what awaited them until Julio jerked in the taxi's front seat and said, "Dude, who set off the riot?"

The Statale's main building was fronted by that rarest of prizes in downtown Milan, a lawn. The structure itself resembled a palace turned the color of oiled bronze by the rain. A forest of umbrellas and slickers pressed across the lawn and ascended the front steps and crammed the building's doorways. It was impossible to guess the number because of the umbrellas and the poor light. But there had to be hundreds.

Dor Jen asked, "Who are they?"

"Your techies said we'd be meeting some of your former subjects and maybe a few interested new people," Charlie said.

Gabriella said, "There must be some mistake."

As Charlie opened his umbrella and sheltered Gabriella rising from the car, an Italian version of the universal geek came rushing up. He wore baggy camouflage pants, rectangular glasses, and a tattered raincoat. His sandals slapped the puddles as he ran. Two Brazilian wish bracelets jiggled on his bony wrists. He offered Gabriella a goofy grin and gibbered like he was meeting a movie star. He handed her a mini microphone and a fanny pack.

Charlie had once accompanied a mega rock star on a tour of China. The Chinese security had been so menacing, the teenage hordes had remained very subdued. But the underlying tension had remained, quietly seething and waiting for an excuse to explode.

Their entrance into the building was exactly like that, only wetter. Julio asked softly, "Bro, how you aim on protecting anybody in this?"

The answer was, Charlie couldn't. But as he scanned the crowd, the last thing he sensed was danger. Then again, he could be reading the whole thing wrong.

The building's foyer was a single mass of compressed flesh. Even so, the crowd squeezed back far enough to grant them passage. The lobby was maybe two hundred feet wide and half as long, and so quiet Charlie could hear his wet shoes squeaking over the marble tiles. When hands reached toward Gabriella, Charlie said mildly, "Don't stop. Not for anything."

The conference hall was a downward slope from the rear entrance to the podium. The passage was cramped by people crouched upon tiny foldout seats that cut the stairs' width in half. The applause and the whistles started as they appeared in the doorway and continued as they made their way to the front.

Midway down, Charlie noticed a movement behind them and said to Julio, "Go back and keep any more people from entering. We can't let them seal off the exit."

"Dude, in case you didn't notice, I don't speak the lingo."

"Do your best."

By the time they reached the front, Gabriella was flushed and could not stop smiling. She tried to tuck her hair back into place and told Charlie, "I never expected anything like this."

Her mike was still on, and the result was a burst of laughter from those who understood English.

Charlie reached over and covered the lapel mike with his palm. "Short and sweet. We don't know if we're safe, or if so, for how long."

That sobered her. "Should I tell them what has happened?"

"This is your crowd and your call. But I'd say, absolutely."

"Dor Jen, will you translate for Charlie? I want him to understand what is going on." Gabriella stepped to the center of the stage.

Charlie stood by the podium's side stairs and gave the auditorium a constant visual sweep. Dor Jen slipped up beside him and quietly interpreted as Gabriella first apologized for being out of touch, then explained about the unexpected danger they had faced, the need to flee Florida, and the uncertainty regarding precisely when they would resume testing. She spoke with the calm ease of a professional speaker, though her face remained flushed and her hands trembled slightly. She then said she needed to pose a few questions to her former test subjects, and asked for those in the audience who had successfully taken part in her experiments to raise their hands. She asked everyone else to please remain silent, and when she was done she would answer a few questions.

All the while, Charlie kept trying to get his head around what he was witnessing.

He had protected his share of stars in music and film and politics. He knew the fractious hunger that fame could produce. But this was something else entirely.

The students were young and intelligent and mostly beautiful in a scraggly student manner. They did more than listen. They breathed with her. There was something Charlie could only describe as *brightness*.

He stared out over the auditorium, back to where Julio stood by the entrance, keeping the faces crammed in the doorway from moving inside. Beyond that, Gabriella's voice resonated through unseen speakers to hundreds more. And he realized, this was it.

The reason why the enemy could not leave them alone.

Right here.

Watching this mass of students drinking in every word Gabriella spoke, Charlie knew he was staring into the face of change.

When Gabriella asked for questions, every hand in the audience shot up. A thousand voices clamored for attention. Again, there was no sense of threat. Only hunger. Raw, yearning, desperate.

But the threat was there, Charlie was certain of it. Maybe the gun wasn't aimed. Perhaps it was not even in this room. But the menace was real enough for Charlie to walk over and say, "We need to be leaving."

Obviously a good percentage of the audience understood English, because their clamor only became stronger. Gabriella stared at him. Charlie showed as much concern as he could via his eyes only, backed away, and mouthed, *Five minutes.*

When Gabriella addressed the crowd again, Dor Jen translated, "She is saying that they will begin new trials as soon as it becomes safe to bring subjects into the lab, and when they have established where the lab will be. Because time is so limited, Gabriella says only those who have been test subjects should ask questions."

A unified sigh of resignation rushed through the hall. Almost all the hands dropped. The students' regret was a palpable force.

Gabriella called on a woman. She came to her feet in a series of jerky motions. As soon as she started talking, Gabriella stiffened in alarm. She looked over at him. Then back to the woman.

Charlie said to Dor Jen, "What is she saying?"

"This woman, she has done a bad thing. Before, she studied finance here at the university. Now she works for a brokerage. When she ascended, she looked forward at what was going to happen inside the markets."

Charlie said, "Hang on a second. She was ascending without anybody's help?"

Gabriella must have been thinking the same thing, for she shot Charlie a startled look. The woman asked something, which Dor Jen translated as, "She cannot ascend anymore. She asks Gabriella how to break free."

Gabriella responded with a soothing sorrow. She started to gesture toward Charlie, then caught herself and turned the motion into an open-handed shrug.

The woman who had asked the question was crying openly now. Her fingers clutched at whatever was in reach. Her sweater. The strap of her purse. The seat back in front of her. The air before her chest.

Dor Jen translated, "How was she supposed to know she could not use it for her own gain? This was, after all, her profession. This seemed a logical step."

Gabriella looked at Charlie and said in English, "We cannot help you."

The woman responded in Italian. The crowd remained silent, totally absorbed. Dor Jen translated, "She has given all the money she made from looking ahead to charity. She will not do it again. She asks for the key. She feels that her life is a prison now."

Gabriella waited until the woman had finished, then said very softly, "*Coraggio.*"

The woman seated herself and wept into her hands.

Gabriella answered a few more questions. Charlie was about to walk over and shut things down when a young man rose and began speaking. Whatever he said now caused Dor Jen to stiffen in alarm.

The student was tall for an Italian. Charlie put his height at well over six feet. He spoke with a tenor's bell-like quality. At center stage, Gabriella appeared to stop breathing.

Dor Jen translated, "They are elevating without guidance. They ascend and they are *meeting*."

Charlie realized how shaken Gabriella had become by what the guy was saying. He walked across the stage and whispered, "Everything okay here?"

Gabriella did not bother to cup the mike. "We did not plan for this. We did not *imagine*. They have moved beyond our protocol and are writing their own experiment. And we cannot find a safe place to monitor what is happening!"

The audience seemed to gather its breath, watching the professor talk to a man she had not introduced, a stranger whose density compacted the room's illumination. Charlie looked out at the student and thought, *Those kids will be lucky to survive the night.*

He said, "Ask them how many they are."

The young man called back in English, "So far, we are seven."

"May I?" Charlie unclipped the mike from Gabriella's lapel. The cord remained attached to the battery pack in her pocket, which kept him close enough to hear her choked swallow. He asked, "Are the others here?"

In response, five others rose to their feet around the auditorium, while one hand waved wildly over Julio's head.

"Let her in," Charlie said, and waited until the young woman squeezed past the others jamming the doorway. "Do you all speak English?"

When several called back a negative, he handed the mike over to Gabriella. "Tell them they are in extreme danger."

"What?"

"This is real, Gabriella. Tell them they have to leave with us now. Tell the others not to meet together like this until we have managed to contain the threat. Ask the seven if any are married or have children." He managed a slightly easier breath when the response was a universal negative. "Thank everyone for coming. We are all leaving now."

37

The National Police occupied the newest building belonging to the Como judiciary. The structure was on the northeast side of the main avenue leading to Como's central train station. The site had been specifically chosen because of the steep hillside into which it was built. The Alpine granite that formed the building's foundation had been hollowed. The result was more of a bunker than a basement. This windowless cellar was sectioned into a series of chambers. Evidence lockers for ongoing cases occupied a small portion of the total space. The rest was given over to court-ordered confiscations.

Before arriving in Como three years earlier, Alessandro had lived and worked in Naples. During that period, it had been necessary for him to attend mass at a different church every day. He had been driven everywhere by an armored police car. But he no longer lived under the daily threat of bombings or assassins, much to the relief of his wife and son. Como, like every city, had its own share of trouble and

241

danger. But compared to Naples during the Camorristi wars, Como was a playpen for infants.

His work in Naples had centered upon a mob trial that made international headlines. Alessandro's duty was to identify the assets of all the convicted mobsters, seize them, and auction them off. But nothing in Italy was as simple as it should be. Two years before Alessandro arrived in Naples, the third bailiff in a row was gunned down while performing his duties. Alessandro's predecessor got the message. Seized houses were valued at a fraction of their actual worth, and the auctions were held in absolute secrecy, with only one bidder. Assets in seized bank accounts and safety-deposit boxes vanished. Jewelry, paintings, boats, and cars were either sold for pennies or simply declared lost and gone forever. When the public prosecutor finally turned his attention on the bailiff, Alessandro's predecessor fled to a beachfront palace in Rio.

The scandal went public, and the revelations kept mounting. The hue and cry was so overwhelming, the elephantine justice system was forced to act. They sent in Alessandro.

It was not just the local mob that was furious over Alessandro's refusal to bend under threats. His immediate superiors in Rome were irate over the loss of bribes that formerly had been filtering up their way. They became even more enraged when Alessandro fed their names and their comments to Rome's chief prosecutor.

The *Corriere della Sera*, Italy's finest newspaper, labeled Alessandro Gavi "The Guardian of Italy's Honor."

The Italian court system had learned to use the seizure of assets as a principal weapon against the Mafiosi and their lawyers. Long before the judges gave their final ruling, a prosecutor could go before the court and claim that a certain defendant was a flight risk. Over the past two decades the term had been broadened to cover an astonishing amount of territory. Before then, the courts had watched as wealthy criminals facing guilty verdicts suddenly proved to have no assets at all, while their Liechtenstein bank accounts and Swiss villas remained firmly out of reach. So prosecutors started demanding the seizure of assets at the same time arrest warrants were issued.

Everything seized by the courts, everything held against arrest warrants, everything held pending judgments—all this was part of Alessandro's underground empire. And once the cases had been tried and the appeals exhausted, Alessandro was also responsible for their sale by auction. The opportunities for illegal gain were vast.

The Como crypt covered almost three thousand square meters and was jammed full. Before Alessandro's time, there had been a constant level of attrition. Things came in the front door and things went out the back. Now much of this had stopped. Not all. Alessandro was, after all, just one man. The underground chambers nowadays held only the most valuable items. Four seized warehouses contained the rest. This being Italy, the largest warehouse was reserved for cars. At last count, Alessandro's warehouse contained twenty-six Ferraris, nineteen Maseratis, eleven Bentley Continental GTs, and a matched pair of Bugattis. The warehouse had become the favorite lunch spot for the Como police.

Alessandro knew a certain grim satisfaction every time he entered the police cellar. The Roman officials who had ordered him to Como thought they were relegating their pesky but honest bailiff to a mountain backwater. Instead, Alessandro found himself surrounded by many of the same criminals who had managed to elude justice the first time around.

Just as he was about to enter the main elevators, his mobile rang. He murmured his apologies to the other occupants and stepped out. "Hello?"

"This is Edoardo."

"Two calls in one day? Don't tell me we've been handed more thugs."

"I wish. Can you meet me at what's left of the Bar Azzurra?"

"Closed for the day, I'm afraid. The owner is currently sharing several bottles of Barolo with the chief prosecutor."

"Where can we talk that will be completely safe?"

"You sound worried, Edoardo."

"You think I would drive to Como for the waters, perhaps? For my health? Of course I'm worried."

"I am about to have a private visit with our mutual friend in Evidence."

"I will use the lights and siren and be there in half an hour."

Alessandro greeted his closest ally in Evidence with, "Where is Pietro?"

"Having coffee. He'll be gone the rest of the day." Luca Bresco spoke with the deep rolling voice of a cave troll. His skin was bone white. What he did with his spare time, no one knew. Alessandro suspected that he hunted forest mushrooms.

"It takes so long to drink a coffee?"

"It does," Luca replied, "if he is drinking with his favorite fence. Soon as I said I'd cover for him, I heard him make the call."

"Old friend, I need your help with a very important matter."

Few people besides Alessandro would detect just how pleased Luca was with that statement. "What is it this time?"

"I don't have much to go on."

"Does it involve evidence or seized assets?"

"I have no idea."

"Interesting."

"There is a box. I need it."

"Will you tell me why?"

"I do not even know what it holds."

Luca grinned. "And people think this work is boring."

"Indeed."

"You know you need it, but you don't know what it is. Has Pietro or one of the others been heard making one of their deals?"

"No. At least, that's not why I am here."

"A mystery, then."

"One piled upon another. Can you lock up for a time and come join me in the search?"

Luca sealed the basement, shut down the elevator access, then rejoined Alessandro and said, "Tell me what you know."

"Very little, in fact." He repeated the description given to him by Charlie Hazard. "I seek a box about a meter and a half long, half a meter wide, the same deep."

"Sounds like a locker."

"If so, then a very special one. The hinges and the lock shine like gold. The entire box itself is of highly polished wood, perhaps burl, and it is rimmed in silver or pewter that is intricately scrolled . . ." Alessandro stopped because Luca was shaking his head. "What?"

"It's not here."

"My contacts insist that it is."

"They are wrong. I have worked here nine years. I know all my treasures."

Alessandro could not completely hide his smile. "*Your* treasures."

"I hold them longer than most of their previous owners, they might as well be mine. At least, those not made to disappear by the robbers in uniform who work with me."

"And yet my sources claim it is here. What is more, they have told me where to find it."

"Then let us go look so you can return to these mystery people and tell them they are mistaken."

"The northernmost chamber, against the wall deepest into the cliff. Two shelves from the top."

"The north rooms hold unclaimed evidence and cold-case archives." Luca started off. He did not so much limp as rock like a boat in heavy seas. He had been an officer serving under Edoardo in Catania and had taken a bullet in his hip. Luca and Edoardo and the owner of the Bar Azzurra were the only three who had survived that ambush. "Can I ask what this is about?"

"You can. But I know nothing else for certain. Not how, not why."

"A shred of a rumor."

"One that may hold extreme importance. More than that I cannot say. Not now."

They passed through one concrete chamber after another, ignoring a vast collection of Italy's splendor all stacked like cordwood and taped with yellow document forms. The entrance to the rear room was flanked by one gold chandelier and a fireplace stolen from a bishop's palace.

Luca flipped on the lights and said, "As I told you, nothing but evidence boxes and old files."

"Is there a ladder?"

"You will make yourself filthy for nothing." Luca drew over a set of metal steps. The wheels made a noisy rattle across the stone floor. "Here. Use my gloves."

"Hold this thing steady for me."

The files lining the top shelves had been in the damp chamber long enough to become coated with mold. Alessandro began shifting boxes and coughed as dust was disturbed. Then he stopped noticing either the grime or the stench. "Well, well."

"You have something?"

"Right size, wrong color." He gripped one of the handles and tugged. "This thing weighs more than my car."

"Let me help."

"With your hip? Don't be silly." Alessandro took a two-fisted grip on the handle and managed to pull the locker forward until it stood perched on the edge of the shelf.

The locker was painted a matte black, as though someone wished for it to disappear into the shadows and be forgotten. Alessandro reached in his pocket for the penknife attached to his keychain. Using the smallest blade, he began scraping away flecks of paint. It was not the first time his prey had sought to hide treasures beneath a blanket of enamel.

He took his time, careful not to damage the underlying material, as he cleared a spot about the size of his palm. "What does that look like to you?"

"How can I say, with your head in the way?" Luca squinted as Alessandro leaned away. "As you said, silver or pewter. And burl. Amazing. Hidden here all this time."

Alessandro cocked his head. "The phone on your desk is ringing."

"So it is. One moment."

Alessandro continued his cleaning until Edoardo arrived and declared, "I race up here with lights flashing and sirens screaming, only to have you two lock me out?"

Alessandro replied, "Just the man I need. Help me lift this thing down. Take great care. The surface is coated in mold slick as soap."

"What's inside?"

"I have no idea."

Edoardo snorted. "And people wonder why Italy's justice system is in such shape."

The two of them were puffing hard by the time the locker rested on the stone floor. Alessandro's penknife had been made for him by a locksmith friend and contained special implements not normally found on the end of a policeman's keychain. Edoardo and Luca watched as he picked the lock and opened the case. The interior had remained pristine. The hinges were brass, as Alessandro had suspected, and not gold. They shone ruddy in the chamber's fluorescent lighting.

The two men leaned over his shoulder. "Are they rifles?" Luca asked.

"They are," Alessandro replied.

"I have never seen the like."

"They are very rare."

Edoardo asked, "May I?"

"Careful. Those scopes make them quite heavy."

Edoardo lifted one of the rifles from the special felt-covered hold. The nightscope was as long as the stubby barrel. "You know this weapon?"

"I do. What is more, I am probably the only person in Como who does."

Luca said, "This is very spooky."

"You don't know the half of it," Alessandro said. There were four rifles laid end to end. "These are made by a company called Wahler. The factory is located in the borderlands between Germany and Austria. It is a pneumatic rifle, accurate to two hundred meters, or so they claim. Powered by special gas canisters. I imagine if we lift the rifles out, we will find beneath that flooring both the canisters and the darts. Perhaps some pistols as well for close-quarter work."

"Who would use such a thing?"

"Oh, any number of people. Researchers tagging animals after anesthetizing them. Game parks. Wealthy sportsmen."

Edoardo settled the rifle back into the case. "Expensive?"

"On the open market, the contents of that box would probably bring half a million euros." Alessandro stared at the locker a moment longer, growing accustomed to the dual facts that Charlie Hazard had told him the truth and that he himself was going to help them. He turned to Luca and said, "I need to borrow this for a time. Without any record being made that this has left with me."

Luca gave an easy shrug. "How can I make a record of something that does not exist?"

"I will bring it back. In the meantime, I need you to find out where it came from."

"Consider it done."

Edoardo asked, "Does this have anything to do with the thugs parked inside the Bar Azzurra?"

"I think yes. Most probably there is a direct link."

"Will you tell me when you know for certain?"

"Of course."

Edoardo turned to Luca and said, "Old friend, I must ask that you leave us alone for a time. Alessandro and I must have ourselves a discussion that never took place."

Edoardo was a squat man, solid and immensely strong. He had a gaze that could probe deep as a bullet. "Tell me how you know about this rifle."

"A Camorra boss we went after was a collecting fiend. He had every rifle ever made, or so it seemed at the time. Including two of these. When they went up for auction, they were bought by Cambridge University's veterinary school."

"Is your current interest tied in any way to that old Camorra case?"

"Absolutely not."

"Will you tell me what you're working on?"

Alessandro had expected the question. And still was uncertain how to answer it. "You would not believe me."

"Tell me anyway."

So he did. The meeting outside his church. Turning on his phone. Speaking with Edoardo. Everything the Americans told him.

Edoardo mulled that over, then said, "If I did not know you as the most honest man in Italy, I would say you should have worked up a better lie."

"I admit, it sounds insane even as I tell you. Then again, we have no reasonable means to explain how the nine came to be trussed with Super Glue and parked in the bar."

Edoardo nodded slowly. "Tell me about this American. What was his name again?"

"Charlie Hazard. He is so still, you could easily ignore him. He compresses himself into a space smaller than his own body."

"Sounds to me like a professional assassin."

"He could be, and a good one, were he not so principled."

Edoardo gave him a skeptical look. "You're certain of this, are you?"

Alessandro spoke very slowly. "I have earned a doctorate in the art of lies. After all, I have been an Italian bailiff for over thirty years.

I have been lied to by the finest. I know all shades and permutations. And I am absolutely certain Hazard told me nothing but the truth."

Edoardo shut the locker and set his briefcase on top. He extracted a laptop and turned it on. "As I told you on the phone, the attackers your American faced were two squads. One was led by a punisher for a Ukrainian known as the Prince, who handles most of the Natashas in northern Italy. The other was led by this man."

"I know him."

"Of course you do. His name is Montefiori, and his uncle runs the Como club scene. The three men with him are employees of a professional bodyguard and corporate security group. We have long suspected the security firm of criminal connections. But this is the first concrete evidence we have ever obtained. Which means this case has moved far beyond a simple assault on a bar."

"I understand."

Edoardo tapped the face on the screen. "This morning, Montefiori slit his own throat. Inside the prison. After being skin-searched by pros."

As Alessandro absorbed this news, Edoardo ran his thumb over the laptop's fingerprint scanner and coded in a lengthy password. He entered a file name and said, "What I am about to show you, you have not seen. How could you, since it does not exist? We have wired the prison room used by defendants and their lawyers. We can't use anything from this surveillance in court. We can't tell a judge we're doing this. Permission has come from the absolute highest levels—verbally. Anything we learn, we never use unless it is first discovered by some other source. One that we can make known publicly." Edoardo hit the switch. "This happened earlier today."

As soon as the image appeared, Alessandro cried, "That lawyer was in my office!"

"When?"

"A little over six hours ago."

"Which means he went straight from you to the prison."

Alessandro watched as Antonio D'Alba entered the grey room and seated himself at the metal table across from a brute with a killer's face. Antonio said, "The Prince wants to know who did this."

"We were ambushed inside the wall. I don't even know how many there were. Many."

Alessandro said, "Actually, there were only—"

"Shh. Watch."

Antonio said, "Tell me where this happened."

"I can't."

"This is the Prince asking."

"The man has my highest respects. But I cannot give what I don't know. All I can say is, we were in Brunate."

"The village above Como."

"The same. You know how it can be in the mountains. It was the middle of the night and raining hard. The clouds were a blanket. We followed Montefiori's car. I could hardly see the building from inside the wall. It was a villa. There was a gatehouse. More than that I can't say."

"The Prince will be displeased."

The brute shrugged massive shoulders. "Ask Montefiori."

"I can't. He's dead."

The brute smiled. "Pity. I was looking forward to doing him myself. Slowly."

"Montefiori's men claim they knew nothing more than you. There was a woman being held in Como, a dancer. They learned of this group through her mother, who was the villa's cleaner. Both the mother and the daughter have vanished."

"Perhaps Montefiori's men know more than they are saying. I could ask them myself."

The lawyer rose to his feet. "First we have to get you out."

Edoardo stopped the video feed. "That will prove more difficult than he expects, now that we have evidence of criminal collusion.

Not to mention how one of their own has managed to kill himself while in solitary lockup."

Alessandro straightened. "Will you help me shift this case to my car?"

After they settled the crate onto a wheeled cart, Edoardo asked, "What was the name of the Orlando policewoman?"

"Irma Steeg." Alessandro spelled the name. "Senior detective, retired from Homicide."

"I'll see what I can learn."

As they passed the front barrier, Luca looked up from a dusty file and announced, "I think I know where your locker came from."

"Tell me."

"The year before I started here, there was a conviction." Luca read from a mildewed file open on his counter. "Europe's biggest importer of forbidden animals."

Edoardo grinned. "I remember that. He had clients everywhere. Even inside the president's palace."

"And the Mafia," Alessandro recalled. "They love to collect wild animals for their private zoos."

Luca read off the screen. "The court ordered all his assets seized."

"Let me guess," Alessandro said. "The records show he went to prison a pauper."

"Hardly a penny to his name." Luca tapped the page. "It says your box should contain four air rifles and two air pistols. Purpose: target shooting. Total estimated value: five hundred euros."

Edoardo said, "Someday soon, he'll be freed on parole. The lost items will suddenly be discovered. An auction will be held at midnight. Few people will bother to come. His old friends will reward his silence by restoring his possessions."

"It's a familiar tune," Luca said.

"I hate it all the more for that reason," Alessandro said. "May I also borrow the file?"

Once they had bid Luca their farewells and were safely inside the

252

elevator, Edoardo said, "Warn your Americans that the attackers will return. Of that I am utterly certain. And sooner rather than later."

"I think," Alessandro replied, "Charlie Hazard already knows."

When they had loaded the locker into Alessandro's car, Edoardo warned, "Be careful, old friend. We don't want the enemy to know of our interest until we have already left the beast's lair."

38

Charlie and the ladies took a taxi from the Statale back to Milan's main train station. Julio followed in a car owned by one of the students. Three minutes into the journey, Charlie turned around and asked, "Did anyone see the housekeeper this morning?"

"I don't . . . No. But my mind was on other things." Gabriella blinked. "Charlie, is this something we have to discuss now?"

"Maybe." He asked the two Tibetan women, "What about you?"

"No," Daisy replied.

He said to Gabriella, "Call the house. Ask around."

Two minutes later, she hung up and said, "No one has seen her since last night."

Charlie watched the windshield wipers thunk back and forth. The fact that he had not thought of this before left him feeling vulnerable. He had been too focused on what the ascents revealed, on the prescient. He had not maintained his standard hyper-alertness. Mistakes like this could get them all killed. He did not speak again until the taxi stopped before the train station.

Charlie sent Julio and the Tibetans to the café on the platform, then walked Gabriella over to where the students were clustered by an empty bus stop. "I'm winging it here, so if you think differently, just sing out, okay?"

"Do what you think is best, Charlie."

The seven students were clearly freaked to the max by being drawn into the mystery of now. But something they saw in Charlie's face was enough to calm them. Charlie asked the tall young man, "You speak English, yes?"

"I have been to two basketball camps in your country," he declared proudly. "One in Miami, the other in Chicago."

"What's your name?"

"Massimo."

"Okay, Massimo. I want you to translate exactly what I am going to say. If you don't understand something, stop me. Don't guess. Don't approximate." Charlie gave each of the students a ten-second inspection, boring in deep. "My name is Charlie Hazard. I am a former Army Ranger. Right now I am handling security for the scientists. You don't need to come any farther than here with us. I'm sorry to have dragged you away like that, but I had to get Gabriella out of there. You need to vanish. Right now. Don't go back to the university. Don't go home. Give Gabriella your names and contact details. As soon as the danger eases, she'll be in touch."

To their credit, none of them gave him lip. Instead, when Massimo finished translating, they clustered in closer. One of the students, a young woman whose rectangular glasses framed eyes of black fire, spoke in Italian. All the others nodded. Massimo translated, "We cannot come with you?"

Charlie glanced at Gabriella, but the woman simply gave him a trusting gaze. He said, "You can, if you are certain that's what you want. It may be dangerous. Last night we were attacked. We defeated them. This time."

Massimo said, "Please, excuse me. But you are certain this threat is real?"

"They sent in two hit squads, one of four men, one of five." Charlie watched their features go as grey as the rain. He was sorry to kill their smiles. But it had to be done. "If you want to take off on your own, that's fine. It would probably be safer. But you need to make yourselves scarce. You represent the threat they are trying to extinguish. You've taken the basic deal and . . ." He stopped because they were talking among themselves. He glanced at Gabriella. She raised one finger. *Wait.*

Massimo collected firm assents from the entire group, then said to Charlie, "We can help, yes?"

"I have no idea."

Gabriella addressed them in English. "This morning Charlie and I could not ascend. We were trying to determine where the next attack might come from. Neither of us could do it. So yes, we could use your help identifying the threat and the timing. But remember what happened to the woman banker. What if the reason Charlie and I cannot ascend is because of what we have been doing? There is a risk that if you get involved with us, you might find yourselves in the same state."

A shudder ran through them. Even so, when Massimo asked the others, they all agreed. He said, "We want to fight your fight."

Charlie offered the student his hand. "Welcome to the club."

Gabriella remained intently withdrawn during the journey back to Como. Her gaze was fastened upon the night beyond their window. Occasionally she made terse notes on a pad she held in her lap, then returned her attention to the stream of streetlights and rain. When they arrived back at the villa, she asked Charlie to assign the students rooms for the night, said they all should meet at noon the next day, then vanished before Charlie could ask her what was the matter.

On Sunday Alessandro phoned Charlie and made arrangements to meet him that afternoon. He then walked with his wife through the center of town, taking aim for the lakeside ferry port. The weather played the Italian temptress, promising much, giving little. Tiny slivers of daylight played among the clouds, brief glimpses into a different season, a different world. The ferries all left from piers along the Lungolago, the broad avenue rimming the lake. The street actually changed names seven times as it meandered along the city's waterfront. Alessandro had made it a point to learn such items upon his arrival, part of acclimating himself to this new posting. Carla neither knew nor cared. For her, like for most of Como's residents, the one name was more than sufficient.

Sunlight played upon the lake as the ferry departed. The passengers were all bundled against the chill and the damp, and much of the conversation was about the lost season. Carla was content to silently hold his hand and drink in the morning. Ancient villages climbed the steep slopes, eventually giving way to the emerald green of Alpine forests. And everywhere rose the lakefront palaces, Medici and Gothic and medieval and Renaissance jewels.

On the best of Sundays, Alessandro watched the shadows dissolve from Carla's features. She had been deeply stained by his work in Naples, and by her own. Until threats against their son had forced her to relocate to Rome, Carla had served as administrator in a church-sponsored orphanage. Many of her charges had been indirect victims of mob violence. That morning, Alessandro studied his wife's lovely features and felt he could assign a child's tragic story to every line.

Novara was one of the lost villages, largely ignored by tourists and thus a delight to visit. The hill was too steep for easy access, the stone cottages too somber. Most tourists preferred the glitz of Bellagio and Cernobbio, with their palatial hotels and ten-dollar coffees. They climbed a rain-slick cobblestone path up into a silence that could only be described as medieval.

Afterward they had lunch in the Imperial Hotel, a distinctly Italian fixture from the age of Victorian travelers. The lakefront dining room had once hosted the likes of Byron and Shelley and Twain.

The clouds were thicker now, the color a more uniform slate. But the atmosphere remained warm and genteel, the chamber filled with the music of Italians determined to wrest a good time from the grey day.

Carla waited until they had ordered to ask, "Are we being sent back to Naples?"

"What? Don't talk silliness."

"It is not anything of the sort. You would only bring me here to celebrate or to soften me up for very bad news. Is everything all right with our son?"

Their only child was a banker in La Spezia. "So far as I know, he is happy and well, as is his wife and our granddaughter."

"It is not my birthday or our anniversary." She planted her hands upon the starched linen. "So what is it?"

Alessandro took a long breath. "I am thinking of taking early retirement."

"Good."

"You don't want to first know the reason?"

"I don't care why. I've been waiting for this moment since we left Naples."

"Nothing is certain. Yet. But I wanted you to know that I am thinking of it. Very seriously."

"It could not be serious enough for me. Nor come too soon." She paused while the waiter poured their wine. She lifted her glass and said, "To freedom."

"I have never considered my profession to be imprisoning."

"I know." They drank. She set down her glass. "Do you want to tell me what has happened?"

"Yes." This was as clear an indication of coming change as anything that had happened, for Alessandro never spoke about his work. The shadows were already too close, the fears too great. But this time he needed her to understand. Or rather, know as much as he did.

Carla was an exceptional mother and a far better wife. Hers was a caring nature. Her heart was made for love. Her laughter was a chime strong as Alpine winds. Her eyes were dark and deep, made to swallow a man whole. As he spoke, Alessandro found himself seeing his wife anew. He talked through the entire meal. He held nothing back. He spoke of the meeting after church, the call from Edoardo, the visit of Antonio D'Alba, the discovery in the Evidence vault, everything. Carla listened with the patient intensity of a woman who had waited thirty years for this conversation.

Over coffee, he said, "Edoardo phoned last night. The American woman is indeed a retired homicide detective. Irma Steeg is held in the highest esteem by her colleagues. Which adds credence to their story. It is impossible, I know, and very hard to accept . . ."

Alessandro stopped because his wife had leaned across the table. She gripped his arm and said, "I want you to listen very carefully."

"Very well."

"You will help them. But on one condition."

"And that is?"

"They will let me do this thing. Ascend."

"You cannot be serious."

"Look at me, Alessandro. Do I appear to you like a woman who's joking? You must do whatever it takes for them to allow me to experience this. You *must*."

"I don't understand. Why ever would you wish to have such an experience?"

"I have my reasons."

Alessandro sat and stared across the table at his wife and lover. Carla's face was set in immutable lines. He had no interest in arguing with her. He changed the subject with, "Would you like to know what they have asked me to do for them?"

She replied with the clipped tones of a very determined woman. "I assume it is something that on the surface challenges your concepts of right and wrong. And the fact that you are willing to agree means that you are needing to leave your current work behind."

He shook his head. Her ability to see to his deepest core was astonishing. "Charlie Hazard says I am crucial to their future safety. Exactly how, he does not know. But this absence of knowing does not affect his certainty that it is true. He claims this impression comes from such an ascent."

"Which means they will hardly be in a position to refuse anything you ask of them."

"Very well, Carla. I will ask."

Her grip only intensified. "Soon?"

"This very afternoon."

She released both him and her building tension. She leaned back in her chair and turned to face the window. Finally she asked, "Do you know what I heard as I listened to you speak?"

"I have no idea."

"The chance to regain what our life has stolen away from me. I heard the sound of *hope*."

39

Just before noon on Sunday, Gabriella entered the kitchen. She wore jeans and a sweatshirt and no makeup, her hair gathered back in a simple band. The smudges under her eyes suggested she had not slept. In Charlie's mind she had never looked more beautiful.

Rain beat a steady pattern upon the window, and daylight held to its customary grey. The kitchen felt slightly cramped for the first time since Charlie's arrival. Gabriella took the seat at the head of the table, while Charlie leaned on the wall behind her. The scientists assumed their customary places around the table. The Italian students perched on the fireplace's massive lip or leaned on the cabinets next to Irma and Julio.

Gabriella said, "Yesterday Charlie told me of a plan he has designed to keep us safe. He left it to me to decide how much to tell you. We are a team. I want to tell you everything."

She repeated her words in Italian and kept up the same dual cadence throughout her explanation. Before she had finished speaking, Brett exclaimed, "This is insane!"

Elizabeth, the white-blonde pharmacologist, smirked across the table. "What's the matter, big boy? Afraid?"

"Elizabeth," Gabriella said.

"I was just asking—"

"You're not helping."

Elizabeth flushed. Charlie waited for the outburst, but when she spoke again it was to say, "This is a good plan."

Brett said, "It's nuts, is what it is."

Dor Jen said, "Elizabeth is right, Brett."

"Not you too."

"Yes, me." She turned to Gabriella. "Thank you for trusting us with this."

Milo was as pale as the day beyond the window. He followed the exchange with rabbit's eyes. "When do you think they'll attack?"

Charlie replied, "We have no idea. Gabriella and I have been unable to ascend."

Gabriella added, "But we are hoping our new guests can find that out for us."

Massimo said, "Please, we did not come here to be guests."

"I don't like anything about it," Brett said. "The whole thing stinks of unnecessary risk."

"Charlie kept us safe before," Jorge said quietly.

"That doesn't mean—"

"Brett," Elizabeth said. "For once in your life, do what she asks without the lip."

Gabriella gave that a beat, then went on, "The last time we were all together Charlie told us something else. If the opposition stops our research, they don't need to kill us because we are effectively dead. We need to focus on our work. On our future. Beyond this threat. On the reason we are here at all."

Elizabeth said, "Now you're talking."

"We must accept that our preliminary phase is concluded. We have achieved irrefutable success." Gabriella ticked off her fingers. "Subjects can and do ascend. A significant number of these subjects erase temporal and spatial boundaries. What is more, some subjects manage to ascend without external stimuli. And they manage to gather together."

Brett objected, "We don't have the documented evidence to substantiate any—"

"The boss is on a roll," Elizabeth said. "Let her finish."

"No. Brett is correct. We must prepare a clearer method of scientific documentation. But that is for later. What is most important is how these seven newcomers reveal something we must acknowledge. We are supposed to be in the lead on this, but these students represent the fact that we risk being left behind. We must refocus our aim. We must begin preparing the next stage of our studies. We must look beyond tomorrow."

"I like this," Jorge said. "I like it a lot."

"We must assume that Charlie will once again do his job. Fine. Then what happens after? All of you know what awaited us in Milan. It is no longer an issue of finding willing subjects. As soon as we put out word that we seek to begin phase two, we will be *invaded*. Which means that right here, right now, we must use these final moments of solitude to prepare."

Elizabeth asked, "Did you come up with anything specific during your nighttime ruminations?"

Gabriella had clearly been expecting this. "Some of you know the limbic system is the portion of the brain that regulates emotions and social bonding. Over the past several years, three noted psychiatrists have been studying the complexity of human love. They have determined that it includes the hippocampus, which is involved in the sorting and maintaining of memories, and the amygdala, which assigns intensity to emotions and regulates how emotions are held by past experiences.

"This has now broadened to include the concept of social intelligence, which shows how the brain develops physically as an individual deepens his or her understanding and usage of compassion and concern for others. There is a documented alteration of the brain's chemical and neurological functions, which mirror an individual's ability to bring peace into situations of conflict and build intergroup relations where none existed before. This study has become known as 'the movement from I to we.'"

She began rolling her empty cup around its base. "I am certain our own work dovetails with these findings. I want to use SPECT scans, which are a refined version of the PET brain-scanning systems, to develop images of the brains of various people in these periods of controlled ascent. What I expect to find is that there is a marked decline in energy within the parietal lobes, which process information about our physical orientation within space and time, while there is a heightened intensity within the prefrontal lobes, which is consistent with intense concentration. Taking this one step further, using the students here as our first test cases, we may be able to offer concrete proof of an interweaving of human lives, as well as a recognition that life and time and space all have definable boundaries that must be reconfigured to match the nonphysicality component of life."

"I am liking this," Jorge said softly, "more and more."

"I want each of you to design your ideal next goal. Your optimum objective. We will then meet and begin designing a formal structure for phase two. I want us to incorporate the best and the highest potential objectives. And then obtain them."

At Charlie's request, Gabriella sent Brett to guide the students through a mass ascent. She remained in the kitchen while Charlie reviewed the next steps with Irma and Julio. Brett and the students were back in the kitchen so fast, Charlie knew the plan had failed. Even before Massimo grimaced in apology. Even before Brett slumped into the chair. He knew.

"I'm sorry, Charlie," Massimo said. The other students filed in dejectedly and sprawled about the table. "It did not work."

Brett scowled at the two of them. "Don't look at me."

Gabriella said, "No one is blaming you, Brett."

Charlie said, "Tell me what happened."

"I followed the standard procedures we used with all subjects. I walked them through the objectives step-by-step. They said they didn't need the equipment, which was good, because we're not wired to do multiple ascents. I told them to go to Base Level. I read out the same objectives. Then I called them back. Nada."

"Massimo?"

"He counted, we went. He said go . . ." Massimo shrugged. "We were trapped."

Charlie glanced at Gabriella. "All of you?"

"Yes. None of us could move at all."

One of the two women students spoke softly from her place beside the chimney. Massimo translated, "She says to tell you, even if this is permanent, she is glad to come. As I am. But also afraid. For to ascend has become a triumph."

"Let's hope these barriers are temporary. For all our sakes." Charlie rose from the table. The day loomed like yet another storm.

Gabriella asked, "Where are you going?"

"I need to go have a word with a bailiff."

⁘

At three that afternoon, Charlie stood where Como's main piazza met the lakefront road. An approaching squall was mirrored on the lake's surface, a vivid reflection of every cloud, every ribbon of rain. Strips of grey lace draped about the mountains and the water. Rain dimpled the lake and the streets, and the Sunday strollers harvested a citywide crop of colorful umbrellas. Birds sang from emerald trees. The rain fell and fell.

When he spotted Alessandro approaching, Charlie rose from the bench and said, "I thought Italian springs were hot and beautiful. Sun every day, all the people smiling, great food, the works."

"That is a different Italy. Come, let us walk."

Alessandro led him north, along the lakefront and away from the old city. Past the Piazza de Orchi, traffic was halted and the pedestrians filled the road as well. He led Charlie over to one side, away from the market stalls fronting the lake. "Before coming to Como, I was senior bailiff in Naples. Did you know that?"

"I told you, I didn't know anything beyond the one moment of our meeting."

"I heard the words, but still . . ." He waved it aside. "During much of that period I was involved with the Camorristi trial, which resulted in the imprisonment of the region's most high-profile mob bosses. The mob in Naples, by the way, is called Camorra. Not Mafia. The trial dragged on for four years. During much of that time, outside the courtroom, Naples was trapped in a war between various mob groups that sought to fill the vacuum. The war claimed four thousand lives. Much of the violence was controlled by the men under arrest. I learned to hate during that trial, watching the men in the docket pass notes to their attorneys, smiling at me and the judges as they did so, behaving with the arrogant brutality of princes."

The street market was over a mile long. The crowd was defiant of the miserable weather, particularly the children. It reminded Charlie of a carnival. He walked alongside the bailiff, content to let Alessandro set the direction and the pace.

"After each segment of the trial finished, I confiscated as much of their wealth as I could find. I auctioned their villas. I traveled to Switzerland and Luxembourg to track down their hidden millions. I refused the offers of bribes and ignored the threats against myself and my family. When it was all over, I was reassigned to Como. It is a rather bitter irony to land here, as the region is filled with rich people who do not deserve to be rich."

"Why are you telling me this?"

Alessandro stopped and faced Charlie. "Because as bailiff, I cannot do what you ask."

"I understand."

"My vow to remain honest is the only thing I have left from all the ideals I brought into my profession. It is not enough to *appear* honest. All of Italy takes great pride in maintaining this appearance. Wherever there is even the slightest question, I must lean toward the strictest order of the law."

A trio of young children approached the nearest stall and began selecting from the rainbow assortment of sweets. The thrill of choosing from such a vast array left them breathless and shrill. They splashed the puddles with little yellow boots as they danced and pointed and called.

"And yet, I find myself wanting to help you." Alessandro watched the children with Charlie. "I am *drawn* to this."

Charlie struggled to fit the pieces together. "So you are leaving your position?"

"I see no other option. For that reason, I must know that what you have told me is the utter truth."

"I have given it to you as straight as I know how."

"I believe you." The bailiff pointed the hand holding his umbrella. "Come. There is someone I want you to meet."

As they continued along the lakefront market, the air became spiced with odors from a very different place. One whiff of the all-too-familiar scents and Charlie was transported. Away from the rain and the cold. To another continent, one far hotter and drier and deadlier.

"This section of Como's market has been taken over by Africans and Caribbeans. Gradually they extend their reach. One by one, the Italian stallholders are giving up, moving on. Their places are always taken by more from this darker clan." The music was now reggae and calypso, the chatter Jamaican and African. "They sell everything. You understand that word, everything?"

"Absolutely."

Alessandro signaled to a slender man tending a stall selling African masks. "I will ask. You will listen. I do not know if he speaks English. If he does, he may pretend not to understand. You will speak with great care."

"Roger that."

"This is Bene. He is from Bamako. Perhaps you have heard of this city?"

"Capital of Mali. I have been there. Twice."

There might have been a flicker of interest from the Malian, there and gone in a flash. Up close the man bore far deeper scars than merely the tribal markings slashed down both cheeks. His gaze was a liquid wall.

Alessandro said, "In Italian, the word *bene* means 'good' or 'okay' or 'fine.' His name is a joke. Because for Bene, very little is okay or good or fine."

He switched to Italian. The pair spoke for a time. Then Alessandro said, "Bene says that the men who attacked you were from two different groups, but they are joined together because they both traffic in women. The Russians are involved, especially with the women. The other group operates a large corporate security firm. All this I already know. But it is very interesting that word has passed to this level of the local underworld."

Charlie nodded. "The information is not common knowledge. Which means that whatever else Bene has to say is valid."

Alessandro glanced at him. "It is very good to work with a man who understands the unspoken."

He and the African spoke at length. "Bene says word has come from hunters outside Italy. They say to look for a group of scientists. The scientists travel from America, and only one of them, a beautiful woman, is Italian. The hunters will pay, and pay well. But all they want is the address where these scientists live. The hunters say do not approach, do not strike. Just supply the information and accept payment."

Charlie ran that forward. "Our first attackers must have twisted these orders around. They probably figured, get the scientists under lock and key, then up the ante."

"Bene thinks the same. As do I."

The African spoke a question, his gaze hard on Charlie.

"Bene asks, why were you in his country?"

"I think he knows."

"He asks, on which side did you fight?"

"I was working security detail for two different sets of company officials. One group wanted to do business with the government. The others thought they could cut a better deal with the rebels."

"Bene says, you do not ask which side he fought for."

"From this distance, it really doesn't matter. Does it?" Charlie saw the unspoken question in the African's eyes. "Tell Bene he can pass on the information to the hunters."

"He likes you. He thinks you are a warrior of honor. As he is himself. Pay him a hundred dollars and he will forget this discussion ever took place."

"Tell him that our address is bound to come from somewhere. He might as well collect the bounty. Ask if he will hold off until tonight."

"Bene says, for a man of honor, he will not pass on the information until dawn."

Charlie offered his hand, felt the all-too-familiar calluses of one for whom the weapon had become an extension of his limb. He spoke the only words of Bambara, the chief Malian language, that he remembered. "*Mansin marifa.*" Machine gun.

The African's smile defied the rain-swept day. Alessandro translated, "Bene always preferred the Nambu, unlike most of his compatriots, who were in love with the Kalashnikov."

Charlie said, "The scientists are staying at the Villa Calma in Brunate."

Alessandro translated, then said, "Bene wishes the honorable warrior good hunting."

40

Alessandro watched his wife follow Gabriella from the kitchen and felt adrift.

He sat at a kitchen table from his childhood. People bustled about. A group of Italian students arrived with two older nerdish men. Together they made a cold meal and tea and carried it away with them, talking about things that made absolutely no sense to Alessandro. Then two Asian women entered, followed by a man as striking as a model. He was the only person who did not treat Alessandro with courtesy. In fact, Alessandro had the impression the young man sought not to see anything or anyone.

Charlie sat across from him. Between them was a pot of fresh-brewed coffee and farm bread and crumbly cheese and mountain salami and olives. Charlie had set a bottle of wine on the table, but when the others did not drink, Alessandro decided to leave it alone. With them were the Orlando detective and a young man they introduced as Julio. The young Hispanic clearly idolized Charlie. Alessandro had the impression

Irma Steeg felt just as strongly, but she had a detective's hard-earned ability to hide almost everything.

A blonde woman entered and grabbed a plate and joined them. She was very attractive, though not in the same league as Gabriella. Charlie introduced her as Dr. Elizabeth Sayer. Another beautiful scientist, this one with the coldest eyes Alessandro had ever seen, as though she went through life poised to attack anyone who might offer her a compliment or kind word.

Charlie said to Elizabeth, "First thing tomorrow, I'd like you to go into Como with Julio and help him buy some clothes."

Even at this, the woman bridled. "What am I now, the resident personal shopper?"

"You're available, and you have both the moxie and the good taste required to point him in the right direction."

"What about—"

"Gabriella and I are going to be busy preparing for the next assault."

Elizabeth's brittle exterior cracked momentarily. "They're coming?"

"Almost certainly."

"When?"

"I hope we'll know by this evening. But I think very soon."

Julio said, "My sweats are good enough for clothes, man."

"Not for what I have in mind. I need a spotter."

Irma gave Charlie a look sharpened by old combat. "Smart."

Charlie went on, "I need you to dress like a regular Italian stud."

"I don't need a lady to tell me what to wear." He turned to Elizabeth. "No offense."

"Hey, *ese*, whatever rocks your boat."

Charlie said, "This is not about buying things that suit your tastes. I need a certain look." He addressed Elizabeth now. "We're after a total remake. Greys and blacks and navy blues are best. Discreet and classic. Two pairs of expensive sunglasses, one set with pale lenses since it's raining so much, then another pair with dark lenses. I need him to be able to fit into a crowd of locals and disappear in plain sight."

The threat of attack had left her pliable. "I can do that."

"I know you can." He said to Julio, "Your goal is to meld into the scene, just another Italian stud hanging around the local café, spending your days eyeing the ladies."

Julio beamed. "Bro, this is a job I was born for."

Elizabeth asked, "What about money?"

"I've liberated some of Gabriella's cash." He passed the roll to Elizabeth, along with a slip of paper. "We also need a set of handheld radios with some extra electronics. Gabriella wrote out the Italian names for you. It's too late to get it all done today, but it'd be good if you can be ready to roll at first light."

She hesitated, then asked, "Will we be safe?"

"I hope to know that before you move out." Charlie looked up as the tallest of the Italian students reappeared in the doorway. "Can you join us for a couple of minutes?"

"Of course, Charlie. We are still waiting for Milo and Jorge to finish wiring the room so we can all be guided through an ascent with the electronics. They think perhaps if we are all listening to the vibratory patterns and all receive instructions to search for danger, we can accomplish something more. Milo says they need at least another two hours, perhaps more."

"Have a seat. Alessandro, I'd like you to meet Massimo. He's sort of leader by default of what I guess you could call our accelerated ascenders."

The student's chest puffed slightly at the words.

Alessandro asked, "That means what, exactly?"

"Gabriella's initial study had two hundred test subjects drawn from the Statale student body. Massimo and his team have managed to keep ascending, even without the external stimulus. And they've done some things that have the scientists reeling."

Alessandro nodded as though he understood, then asked, "Does it hurt, this ascent?"

Massimo replied, "No pain. Only joy."

Charlie said to him, "I need you people to understand completely the risk—"

Massimo raised his hand. "Please, Charlie. There is no need to say it all again. We know. We accept. Of course, we hope it does not happen. But we accept."

Alessandro asked, "Accept what?"

"Since the attack, Gabriella and I have found ourselves unable to ascend again."

"This is bad?"

Massimo had the natural exuberance of a man who was born to sing. Yet answering this question left him somber. "We could not ascend today. It is a small death."

In that instant, Alessandro realized why he was seated there at all. It was not for a simple country meal. Charlie wanted him to understand that he was part of the team. That nothing was hidden. Alessandro understood that it was not the man's way to speak empty words. Charlie wanted to *show*.

He asked Charlie, "It has also been hard for you, not ascending?"

"Worse than I could have imagined." Charlie leaned back in his chair. "Every time I went was nicer. Even with what we were doing."

"Which was?"

"Trying to stay one step ahead of the hunters." Charlie looked at him but appeared to survey a realm beyond Alessandro's imagination. "I don't know if each time became more intense or if I just got to the point where I could realize what was happening."

"Both, I think," Massimo said. "We speak of this change. With the pleasures of this world, the more you take, the less joy you find. With this, it is the exact opposite."

Alessandro's phone began buzzing in his pocket. He pulled it out, saw who was calling, and said, "I need to take this in private."

Charlie led him into an empty bedroom and shut the door.

Alessandro said, "Edoardo?"

"I have something for you. It arrived through normal channels two days ago. I only noticed it now because I thought I recognized the name. What was the American called who works with those scientists?"

"Irma Steeg."

"Not the woman detective. The man. The soldier."

"Charlie Hazard."

"Yes, it's him, all right."

"Tell me."

"I am holding an international warrant for his arrest. The charge is murder. He is considered a flight risk and extremely dangerous."

"I do not believe it."

"I'm only telling you what I have here. But I confess, I do not care much for this either. Shall I tell you why?"

"Please."

"The warrant comes from Los Angeles. I phoned the homicide bureau. The death took place almost five years ago. The man I spoke with did not know the case, but he had a look on his computer. He informed me that the warrant is dated four days ago. The victim was Charlie Hazard's wife. The detective assumed there must have been a discovery of new evidence."

"Perhaps. But the timing is remarkable, wouldn't you say?"

"If you want my opinion, I'd say this smells worse than the Naples sewers. I personally do not intend to act upon it."

"Thank you, Edoardo. Please let me know if anything further arises."

Gabriella led Carla Gavi into the upstairs chamber the group used for testing. She watched as the bailiff's wife took in the bare plank flooring, the rough-hewn table, the lone wooden chair, the single bed.

Carla said, "Other than the electronics, this looks almost monastic."

"We have not been here long."

"Would you change things if you stayed?"

"A bit. Fresh paint, new bed with an adjustable headrest, definitely a nicer chair for the observer."

"What should I do?"

"Sit here on the bed. We must speak before you begin. You need to understand, more than half the subjects who participate do not ever ascend."

"Perhaps they do not need to do so as desperately as I."

Gabriella found the bailiff's wife immensely disconcerting. Usually by this point the subjects were showing initial symptoms of extreme anxiety—accelerated pulse, visible tensing, dilated pupils, compressed lips, clenched jaw and neck. They had started injecting the saline solution to counteract the fear-related stress with the suggestion of an externally generated calm. Yet all the anxiety Carla had shown downstairs was now gone. In its place was a serenity as intense as sorrow.

Gabriella found herself drawn to this woman. She said, "Very few of our subjects manage to ascend on their first attempt."

Carla did not respond.

"Only one, in fact."

"Was it the man Hazard?"

"I . . . should not speak of other subjects."

Carla nodded, but not to what Gabriella had said. "Can they hear us?"

"No."

Carla leaned forward. "The others do not see it. But he is your warrior, yes? Your knight in this arena of danger and peril."

The shock of hearing her secrets spoken aloud by a woman she did not know left Gabriella breathless.

"My husband survived the Camorristi for over a decade. We both left Naples wounded. Not our bodies. Our souls. Do you understand?"

Gabriella nodded slowly. Once.

Carla swung around and lay upon the bed. In repose, she held the fragility of a child. Or rather, the otherworldliness of one who did not age. She said, "I think we should become friends, you and I."

Gabriella reached for the headphones and fitted them into place.

She said through the microphone, "What do you hope to gain from this?"

Carla closed her eyes. "I desperately want to find what I have lost."

Alessandro stowed his phone away, entered the kitchen, and said, "There is something I would like to show your security team."

Charlie, Irma, and Julio followed him out to where his Citroën was parked in the villa's forecourt. The day was brooding and grey, but dry. The trees dotting the villa's front garden were vague silhouettes draped in blankets of fog. Alessandro opened the rear door and flipped the blanket off the locker. "This was found in the Evidence vault."

"It looked different in my ascent." Charlie bent in closely to the spot that Alessandro had cleaned with his knife. "No. This is it. May I open it?"

"Be my guest."

He eased open the top. Studied the rifles. And smiled.

"Do you know what they are?"

"Not only that," Charlie said, "I know why we need them."

Julio leaned in closer. "What are they?"

"Air rifles."

Julio ran a hand down the polished barrel. "You mean, like, BB guns?"

"A little more sophisticated than that."

Irma said, "Are those nightscopes?"

"They're light magnifiers. As opposed to infrared. Snipers prefer them because the targets are clearer. These are excellent quality, but a couple of years out of date."

"Four, to be precise," Alessandro said. "At least, that's how long the previous owner has been locked away."

Charlie shut the locker, flipped the blanket back into place, and nodded once to Alessandro. "There is another member of my team you need to meet."

Irma made round eyes. "You're introducing an Italian cop to Benny?"

"Please, I am a bailiff."

"Whatever. I'm sure Benny is going to be real relieved to hear it."

Julio grinned. "Man, this is gonna be some kinda trip."

The stables and gardeners' hut stretched in a haphazard line between the left of the villa and the outer wall. Charlie led them back toward the rock face. There he stopped and addressed Alessandro directly. "I started a tour in Anbar Province, then got wounded."

A voice drifted down from above. "On account of how he shielded his sergeant's body with his own. Dumb move, you ask me."

Charlie went on, "When the scientists were forced to hide here, I asked a buddy from the force to come give us a hand." He pointed at a series of rocks protruding from the cliff face, rising to a ledge Alessandro had not noticed until that moment. "And he hates all cops."

Alessandro gripped the rocks and started to climb. "Then he and I have something in common."

The ledge was in line with the villa's roof and opened into a cave that was shielded from view by a broad granite protrusion. Alessandro arrived at the mouth slightly giddy from the prospect of descending.

The man who awaited them reminded Alessandro of some of the veteran anti-Mafia squad he had known in Naples. The cave dweller was lean in the manner of a warrior who had lost all taste for food. He ate to fill his belly only. His senses had room for only one thing. The flavor of cordite.

Charlie settled by the man's butane stove and motioned at Irma. "This is Irma Steeg."

"The lady cop with the major-league swing."

Irma remained poised by the cave's mouth, as far from the man and his lair as she could get and stay out of the rain. "Didn't I arrest you a while back?"

The man's grin was a mere stretching of taut features. "If you came up against me, babe, either you'd remember or you'd be dead."

"Don't call me babe, meat."

"You children play nice." Charlie motioned to Julio. "I believe you've already met the youngest member of our squad."

The man had forgotten how to make noise. He walked over and offered Julio a soul handshake and the words, "I'm still not certain that dude needed two full doses of Taser."

"Too much of a good thing ain't never enough, *ese*."

The man's grin was more genuine this time. "Yeah, I believe I've sung that tune before."

"And this is Alessandro."

"Another cop."

"Actually, good sir, I am an *ufficiale giudiziario*. In your language, I am called a bailiff."

"This means something to me?"

"We need him, Benny."

"Maybe you do, Eltee. Me, I'm feeling a double case of cop hives coming on."

Irma said, "Could have something to do with your sanitary habits."

"Enough," Charlie said. "We're here because we need to talk strategy. Everybody sit down." When they didn't move fast enough, Charlie snapped, "*Sit!*"

Benny took a seat next to Julio and said, "Hearing Eltee bark like that took me straight back to duty-ville."

Even Irma lowered herself to a rock. "We could do this easier inside."

"We are here because Benny saved our collective bacon. He could move like he did because as far as the rest of our team and the outside world are concerned, Benny Calfo does not exist." Charlie's gaze was officer hard. "Now unless you've got something constructive to say, keep it to yourself."

Irma muttered tersely about how she'd stopped being a recruit forty years ago. But something shifted deep in her gaze. Alessandro had seen it happen often enough. The strong and the independent being molded into a working team by a good officer.

Charlie told Benny, "Alessandro has just delivered us four Wahlers." This time his grin was real. "I'm thinking serious fun and games."

"With nightscopes. And a pair of matching pistols. They haven't been fired in four years. I need you and Irma to lube the works and calibrate them without firing. I counted two dozen gas canisters. But we can't be certain if they've kept full charges. And we won't be getting any replacements."

"What are we using for ammo?"

"I'm working on that. Give me your blade."

Alessandro was staring straight at Benny Calfo and still did not see the man's hand move. A knife simply appeared in Charlie's hand. Charlie began drawing in the cave's sandy floor. "This is the villa. Gatehouse. Wall. Cliff. Stables. I'm thinking they'll use at least three teams. One by the entrance, either rearguard or decoy or both. Another over the wall here, where they can fire ropes from the stable roof to the northern balconies. And a third team rappelling down from the top of the cliff."

Alessandro asked, "You *think* they'll do this?"

"That's right."

"You don't *know*?"

"I told you. I can't ascend."

"What about somebody else handling that responsibility?"

"The only other person who's been able to look forward and determine risk is Gabriella. And she's locked out like me. Ditto for those Italian students, who are possibly sacrificing their ability to ascend in their attempt to help us." Charlie shook his head. "I hate that worse than anything."

Alessandro felt the tension that had gripped his chest when he entered the cave give way entirely. Charlie Hazard was an officer. Like all good officers, he measured success by two yardsticks. Winning the objective and bringing his men back intact.

Alessandro sighed long and low. Charlie noticed. "Something the matter?"

"I want to help you."

"You already are."

"No. Not the guns. I mean, I want to help you any way I can."

Charlie leaned back. "Well then."

"Tell me what you need."

Charlie's gaze burned in the cave's dim light. "Give me a while to think on that."

"As long as you'd like." Alessandro reached in his pockets and came out with a card and pen. He scribbled, then said, "My home number and my cell phone are on the back."

Benny said, "How about you ask the dude here for some real firepower."

Irma said, "I hate to agree with Benny about anything. But he's right."

"No guns. Gabriella was firm on this. And very clear why."

Benny snorted. "All due respect to the scientist lady, Eltee. But you know what they say about an officer who takes his orders from a civilian? Dead and deserves it."

Irma said, "What if we can't protect our people any other way?"

Charlie dug the knife's tip into the sand. "Gabriella was right to say what she did. There are things at work here that go far beyond what we can see and hear. I can't say it any better than that."

Benny said, "You're talking about this electro-ghost thingy again?"

"Yes."

"Which you can't do."

"That's right."

Alessandro found Benny's grin very frightening. The warrior almost purred, "You've worked up a plan. Tell me I'm wrong."

Charlie continued to draw points of attack with the blade. "You're not wrong."

When he finished laying it out, Benny said, "It could work."

Alessandro said, "This is an excellent plan, Mr. Hazard."

"Please call me Charlie."

"In fact, Charlie, it is better than excellent. It is devious. Are you sure you are not Italian?"

"Pure American mongrel."

Irma said, "Timing is crucial."

"Wouldn't hurt us to have one of those periscope views into the future either," Benny said.

"We're doing all we can on that score." Charlie rose to his feet. "Let's get to work."

41

They descended from the cave in murky twilight. When they returned to the kitchen, Gabriella and Carla were seated at the table. Alessandro walked straight over and said something to his wife in Italian. Carla took her husband's hand and smiled. Alessandro's tension eased with a single long breath. Charlie studied the pair of them and wondered what it would be like. Binding himself so tightly to another that they breathed together.

Charlie left the others in the kitchen and walked the main passage to the floor's largest bedroom. He knocked on the door. At a sound from within, he opened it and found Brett working at his desk. The laptop was shut. In front of him was a sheet of paper. Charlie shut the door. He saw that the page had just two lines of writing. The man's total output for the afternoon. "It's a tough deal, isn't it."

"What is?"

"Committing yourself to the unknown. Very hard."

Brett turned the page over. "What do you want?"

Charlie dragged over another chair and seated himself. "I want you to guide me through another try at ascending."

"Is this a joke?"

"No, Brett. No joke."

"I heard you couldn't. You and Gabriella both."

"That's right."

"So why not take it up with her, you two are so tight."

"Gabriella is busy with the students, trying to point them away from the here and now, looking ahead to a safe tomorrow."

Brett glanced down at the overturned page. "Will there be one?"

"It might help us get there," Charlie replied, "if you and I could do this thing."

Charlie waited until he was seated on the edge of the bed and Brett was preparing the equipment to give the real reason he was there at all. "You got sideswiped, didn't you? By Gabriella."

The guy's jaw muscles were so tight, it looked as though he was sucking on a pair of walnuts. "We met at a conference. The entire group was laughing about this research project she'd proposed. Seeking to define the concept of nonphysical life in scientific terms. Take finite measurements from beyond the physical realm. They thought she was totally nuts."

"And you left a good job to help her out," Charlie guessed.

"University of California at Santa Barbara," Brett replied, staring at the paper on his table. "Assistant professor. Tenure."

"Can you go back?"

"Not if they catch wind of how I've spent my sabbatical."

"So you showed up in Milan, you got to work, you did what Gabriella asked. Then what happens—wham. A bolt from the blue."

Brett's eyes narrowed as he glanced over. "What is this, your idea of male bonding?"

"I just want you to know that I understand, and I'm sorry."

"Sorry doesn't cut it."

Charlie gave that a beat. Long enough to register his disapproval. Then he said, "My impression is, you've already made your choice. You're in for the long haul. And this prospect, along with getting hit by the lady's lightning bolt, has left you with a scary sense of no control. You can't focus. You want to, but you can't."

Brett sat there staring at him, his features set in stone. "Why are you telling me this?"

"The only way this is going to work is if we're totally reliant on each other. That's why I came up here and asked for your help. Because the barrier between you and me doesn't really matter, not in the long run. Our quarrel is over a woman who more than likely won't choose either of us. I'm sorry to be the one to tell you, but it's true. She's been burned bad and it's going to take time for her to recover. And when the healing is done, she'll probably choose a guy who's . . . well, not you and not me."

Brett turned his face to the wall.

"You want my opinion, I'd say it's time to return to the original reason you signed up. Which was, this thing has got some serious legs. It could carry you right to the stars. All of you."

Then he waited.

Brett's voice had gone hoarse. "I'm not certain I can do that. Give her up like that."

Charlie took the confession as a very good sign. "I know what you mean. All too well. But the truth is, it probably doesn't matter a whole lot whether we can or not. What we want isn't part of her equation."

Brett continued to stare at the wall.

Charlie went on, "When I was a kid, I had these books about medieval knights. I was seriously into the chivalry thing. How they would pledge their lives to a woman they honored beyond anything known in cynical times like these."

Brett might have nodded.

"Only a few queens actually deserved their act of fealty. These ladies, they remained ever removed from their knights. Even so, the knights were willing to sacrifice everything, even their lives." Charlie gave that a beat, then said, "I think about that a lot."

42

alpensa Airport predated the Second World War. Until the early eighties, most airlines except Alitalia were relegated to this dilapidated outpost. Italy's flagship carrier had a dead-solid lock on the far more modern Linate. Only when the European Union's economic watchdogs began growing teeth did Italy reluctantly abandon this farce. Now Malpensa was slated for closure. But nothing happened swiftly in Italy. For the moment, it served as the city's municipal airport. Maintenance was nonexistent.

Trace, the Combine's head of security, stood by the Gulfstream's port engine, watching their gear being unloaded from the rear hold into two windowless vans. "What a dump."

Reese stood in the shelter of one wing, staring out at a reluctant dawn. Her phone rang. The readout said it was her chief techie. Reese walked a few paces away and said, "Give me the good news."

"There *isn't* any. We tracked the attacker who overloaded our system to the Bank of Singapore. The next thing we knew, we had their *secret police* tracking *us*."

"That cannot happen."

"Weldon took care of it. But he had to go to the Combine board for help. And there's something else. We know why they sent the bomb. They used the time we were down to send out an alert. Yesterday they met with students from the Statale. That's where they did their original—"

"I know all that."

"What you *don't* know is, they took seven students back with them. The intel we've received about them is secondhand and garbled. But apparently these people are *extremely* gifted. If what we have learned so far is correct, these students have already moved beyond the team's original parameters."

The shifting dread she had carried with her across the Atlantic solidified. "This is extremely not good."

"Tell me about it. Wait. Weldon wants to have a word."

Trace walked over and said, "Heads up."

"Not now."

"We have a situation."

"Deal with it. Weldon is coming online." Reese walked farther away, clutching her umbrella more tightly against the gusting rain.

Her boss said, "You're late."

"Our flight was delayed almost four hours. Some light went off in the cockpit."

"Do I need to tell you what to do about those Italian students?"

"No, Weldon. You don't."

"Give me your update."

"We know where they are. Some African trader working the Como street market came up with the address." She gave him a chance to respond, then asked, "Is Byron McLaren in place?"

"He's just across the border in Switzerland, awaiting your word. What's more, he's become a serious pest."

"Who wouldn't be, when you're holding eighty million of his dollars."

"Byron has turned to his contacts in Washington, trying to get some leverage he can apply against us. I'm thinking it's time to introduce the guy to his last day on earth."

She watched the rain drip off the lip of her umbrella. "Actually, the man might be extremely helpful just now."

"I hope there's some serious risk involved. For him, not us."

She outlined what she had in mind.

Weldon mulled it over, then said, "Keep him alive only as long as he serves your purpose, get me?"

"Loud and clear."

"Now for some bad news. Our local allies, you know who I mean?"

"The group that owns the security business."

"Correct. They demand to be included."

"We don't need any help."

"I didn't ask if you *needed* it."

"Weldon, this situation is already beyond the pale without including strangers—"

"I couldn't agree more. But they've got ties that go right up our own food chain. I've heard from our *board* on this. They're involved."

"But why?"

Weldon sighed. It was an odd sound. Reese tried to remember if she had ever heard the man breathe his version of submission. "My guess is, because we're operating on their turf, and because the deal is big enough to have our Italian magnate become personally involved."

Though she had a dozen reasons for why they should fight it, what she really thought at that moment was, at least Weldon was being honest. "When in Rome . . ."

"Or Como. Right. Now get this done and get back here. We've got a dozen other things brewing. Weldon out."

She cut the connection and turned around to discover a pair of dark Maybach sedans pulled up between the jet and the airport exit. An elegantly dressed man stood under the shelter of a large umbrella, which was held by a massive brute of a bodyguard.

Reese walked over. "And you are?"

"My name is Dimitri. These days, I am normally referred to as the Prince." The man was ancient, but his age mattered very little. He carried about himself an air of timeless dread. "My sincere apologies for this dreadful weather, Ms. Clawson."

"Is that a Russian accent I hear?"

"My heritage is of no importance. Think of me as your personal customs officer. Entry into Italy will require me to become your escort." His smile was meaningless. "But I suspect you might already have heard that from others."

⁙

Trace and Reese shared a limo with the old mobster. Trace said from the front seat, "You're that guy, the one who blew his hand with the scientists we're after."

The Prince sipped coffee from a pewter mug. "The man who failed me decided to slit his own throat in prison rather than face me. It would be wise of you to remember that."

Reese said, "I'm still trying to figure out why you think we need you at all."

"You misunderstand, Ms. Clawson. You intend to operate in my territory. Beyond that, I have scores of my own to settle."

"You guys have got some nerve, I'll hand you that much." Trace's smile was evident in his voice. "You go against our explicit instructions. You totally fail. Now you want to leech off us—"

"Trace."

"I was just telling the Prince here how—"

"Be quiet." She turned to the Prince. Trace's attitude was making it easy for her to play good cop/bad cop. "How much do you know about these scientists?"

"My information is, they are an international group, drawn from many nations. Only one is Italian."

"Right so far."

"Perhaps this Italian has relatives we could visit."

"We've already thought of that. Her mother lives in Milan, but she has vanished. There is a sister in Greece."

"We have allies there. But I dislike the idea of bringing them in. They can be, shall we say, heavy-handed."

Trace snorted. "Like you guys know the meaning of the word *subtle*."

"Stow it, Trace." Reese kept her gaze on the Prince. "We are ordered to do this and get out. As quickly and quietly as possible. But there's a problem. They know we're coming."

"You are saying there is a spy?"

"Worse."

"None of my men have informed. I assure you of that."

"They don't need informers. They have developed a method of silent infiltration. Anywhere, anytime. Which is how they managed to take out your first team."

The Prince's eyes gleamed. "Such technology would be worth a fortune."

"Only if it can be controlled. That's why we need them alive. And why we gave explicit instructions not to move on this yourself."

He waved it away. "That is behind us now."

"Is it?" Reese slid across the seat, coming as close as she could without actually touching him. She could see he disliked it, which was why she made the move. "I need to know that you and your men will actually follow orders this time."

"I am honorable in my dealings, I assure you. Now please—"

"And your men?"

"They obey me."

She licked the words, a delicious whisper. "And when we get the prize, do we have to worry about you flying off on some private tangent or deciding you can make for yourself a better deal?"

His fretting motions stilled. "I and my men will hold to our agreement."

"Excellent." Reese returned to her side of the seat. She gave the men what she had worked out on the flight across the Atlantic. "Here's what is going to happen. Our teams are going to make multiple strikes."

Trace said, "That is seriously a serious bad idea."

"Listen carefully to what I'm saying. *They know we will attack.* They find us out before we even move. So we make a *series* of attacks. Not with feints. They will recognize a fake. We'll carry out multiple strikes—two, three, four, all in rapid succession. The Prince and his group could actually help us out here. His team leader will work independently on the how and the where. Just like you, Trace. When your crew gets into position, the team leader will then call me for the final go."

Trace swiveled around in his seat, watching her now. "Standard request for the green light."

"Just prior to penetration," she confirmed. "Like always."

"Nobody knows until the last minute which attack is real."

"They are *all* real. The question is, which team actually makes the move?" She turned to the old man. "I need to know just how well your men obey you. At the final moment, in full adrenaline rush, will they accept my command and withdraw?"

He was looking at her differently now. The complacent superiority gone. "And the purpose is?"

Trace replied for her, "To wear the opposition down."

"They're a small team," Reese said. "Seven scientists, three guards, maybe a local hire, whatever. We prepare to strike over and over. Night and day. As fast and as often as we can prep and go. When we've softened them up, we go in hard."

The Prince said, "I underestimated you, Ms. Clawson."

"Bad idea," Trace said, his features taut with the prospect of coming battle.

Reese leaned back, satisfied. "We start in eight hours, once my team is rested up. Trace, your men go first. Prince, your team follows ninety minutes later."

As Trace and the old guy got busy on their phones, Reese leaned back and closed her eyes. It was vital that the two of them bought into the plan and started moving immediately, losing themselves in the details of attack before either had time to scope out the flaw in her plan. Because there was one. A gaping maw that threatened to swallow them all.

43

Charlie began the next day the same way he had ended the last, walking the perimeter with Irma and Benny. He had given the kid the night off, knowing Benny would be a better guard dog asleep than Julio ever could be awake. Beyond that, he wanted his meager force to be as close to optimum performance as possible. He did not need an ascent to know another attack was imminent.

Irma took up station at the gatehouse. Benny retreated to his private aerie. Charlie woke up Julio, then went upstairs to find Gabriella and Dor Jen seated in the kitchen. Charlie poured himself a coffee and pulled out the seat next to Gabriella. He could feel the house stirring and sensed the quiet thread of anxiety that coursed through the day.

Gabriella announced, "Byron just emailed me. He is across the Swiss border in Lugano. A half hour from Como. He wants to meet."

"Not a chance."

"He says he wants to give me my share from the divorce settlement."

293

"He might. Then again, he might be working for them."

Gabriella showed no surprise. "Did he always, Charlie? Work for them, I mean."

"That's not the issue right now. We can debate that when the threat is behind us."

He expected her to come back with more of the same. After all, they were discussing the same guy who continued to crease her features with regret. Instead, Gabriella said, "It was good of you to speak with Brett. He is staying. Because of you."

"He had already made his mind up before I got there."

"Perhaps. Perhaps he had decided." She sipped from her mug. "Brett told me you were able to ascend."

"Sort of."

Dor Jen interrupted them. Her voice was scarcely louder than the rain tapping against the window. "Are we safe, Charlie?"

The question caught Elizabeth and Massimo just as they entered the kitchen. Their faces both bore the creases of sleep. It was a bad time to be struck by fear.

Gabriella did not need volume to sharpen the edge to her words. "Charlie will do his job. We need to focus on ours."

Charlie exchanged surprised glances with the others as Gabriella demanded of her scientists, "Have you outlined your objectives for our phase two?"

Elizabeth replied, "We're working on that."

"Work harder." She caught Charlie's look and said, "Is something the matter?"

"Not a thing."

"Will you tell me what happened when you ascended?"

"Sure thing."

From the outset, there had been a different flavor to the ascent. Charlie had sensed it as soon as he settled the headphones into place, perhaps before. Hearing Brett's voice begin the cadence—what until then he had only heard from Gabriella—heightened the shift. He realized then that the ascent wasn't just his experience, but both people. Both people *interacting*.

Brett's voice directed him to move out and determine the next risk. Only he couldn't. Instead, Charlie found himself hovering. Where, he could not say. He had moved from one state to another. He knew he was fully out of his body. But he could not see where he was.

He remained in that place, wherever he was, for a time beyond time. Hovering in a state he could neither name nor see, until Brett instructed him to return.

By the time Charlie finished relating the experience, the kitchen had filled. No one, however, joined them at the table. Gabriella's intensity created an invisible boundary that none of the others wished to penetrate. They settled on perches around the perimeter, prepared breakfasts and more coffee, all with little whispers of sound. Even Brett when he entered seemed instantly aware of the shift. The lingering vestiges of sleep were erased long before he knew what precisely was going on.

When Charlie finished, Gabriella asked, "Do you have any idea why the ascent happened as it did?"

"I'm still working on that."

"But you have an idea." Gabriella was dressed in a flannel robe over a pale grey nightdress with a matching ribbon holding her hair. But none of that mattered. She was in full scientist mode. The leader. "Will you tell me?"

"That morning after my first ascent, you described your protocol as a set of boundaries that are necessary for any successful experiment."

"It is true. Without clearly defined parameters, you cannot have verifiable data."

"But they are something more. They are *goals*. You tell me where to go, what to search out, what to watch for, when to return." He started to lift his mug, then realized it was empty. Silently Dor Jen rose from her chair, took the mug, and walked over to the coffeemaker. Charlie continued, "Remember when we were in Milan, I realized the housekeeper had vanished. I should have noticed that immediately. Instead, it was hours later, after we had left the house. I was paying too much attention to what I was finding during the ascents. I had missed factors I would otherwise have noticed. So this time I ascended but didn't go anywhere. I was *blind*. Do you understand what I'm saying?"

Brett was the one who said, "Absolutely."

"My goal is to keep you safe. It's not just a purpose for these ascents. It's my one defining issue. And this restriction when I ascend might mean that to do my job, I need to focus on the here and now. At least, that's what I think."

The kitchen was silent save for a quiet murmur as Massimo translated for the students who did not speak English.

Gabriella said, "What you describe is the ultimate risk of every experiment."

Charlie nodded his thanks as Dor Jen replaced his mug. "Sorry, I don't follow."

Elizabeth said, "Shaping parameters that limit instead of define."

"Precisely," Gabriella said. "Last night as I worked with the students on their joint ascent, I found myself totally dissatisfied with the goals I had set for the phase two trials. They were all too limiting."

Brett asked, "How did it go with the students, by the way?"

"There was no real progress," Milo answered. "We tried it three times. The ascents were blocked. They remained trapped."

Charlie said, "Explain what you mean by 'limiting.'"

"Think of what you just said. I, too, am restricted from ascending. But defining danger is not my primary task. My purpose is to create documented evidence. But evidence of what? What would happen if I took aim at something else? What if that is why I am no longer ascending? That my aim is not correct? That I am dominated by fear? That I am *terrified* of the prospect of aiming at something else?" The intensity of her words caused her entire body to shiver slightly. "So what happens but a group of students go where my parameters keep me from going."

"You don't know that," Elizabeth said. "There could be any number of reasons why you weren't at the forefront on this."

296

"My protocol should be freeing. Phase two should be designed around *discovering* limits, not *setting* them."

Jorge set his mug down on the kitchen cabinet and started applauding.

From her place across the table from Charlie, Dor Jen said softly, "You are not the only one who is terrified." Her eyes were black opals set in a slightly flattened face. "Would you lead me through the process, Charlie?"

Gabriella said quietly, "Not everybody ascends."

"The only time I tried, I could have risen and did not. It called to me and I refused. But I think maybe if you are with me, Charlie, I will feel protected enough to fly."

Elizabeth muttered, "Fly."

"No problem, but it will need to wait awhile." Charlie decided there was no better time to ask about what he had cooked up during the night. He said to Dor Jen, "I need your help with something first. Can you write me a prescription?"

"Of course. I am licensed to practice medicine in Italy. Are you ill?"

"No." Charlie outlined what he had in mind, then waited.

When he was finished, the kitchen remained utterly silent until Milo breathed, "Man, that is totally wicked."

Dor Jen nodded slowly. "I am very glad you are not my enemy, Charlie Hazard."

Until that morning, shopping would never have made the list of Julio's top ten activities.

As far as he was concerned, a mall was just another place to hang. Talk trash with the ladies. Skateboard down ramps hidden from the security joes. Waste a few hours in the food court.

Julio had always hated how the shop windows were filled with things he could never buy. And how the corridors were filled with happy-sappy people wearing easy smiles and clothes that hadn't been washed about a billion times in his aunt's old machine.

Today, though, was so totally different, Julio needed a new word to describe it.

For one thing, he had a pocket filled with money. And his job was to *spend* it.

Oh really. Like this was another chore he had to sweat over.

Not to mention the other person along on this gig.

Elizabeth was a mystery lady. Totally off the charts in the looks department, but able to freeze a guy up solid from fifty paces. Julio saw it happen while he was buying the funicular tickets and this old dude slipped in next to Elizabeth and offered his best line. She gave him two seconds of the ice glare, and the guy backpedaled so fast he almost fell over the family standing behind him.

Julio knew Elizabeth was expecting some lip from him. Ready to put him down, clear the air, and make sure he stayed well and truly tamed. But the day was too cool for hassles. So Julio played it easier than he ever had with a lady this sweet. As he stood at the window of the funicular, he did not say a word until they broke through the clouds and there before him sprawled a view of rain-swept perfection—slate-grey lake, forested slopes, lakeside villages in miniature, toy boats chugging about, the Alps capped by their shroud.

Julio told Elizabeth, "Heads up, we got Italy on display."

Up to that point, she had been totally focused on the writing pad in her lap. Sketching out what looked like words and mathematical symbols both. So intent over her work he added, "Sorry to pull you away."

"No, no, you're right, this is an amazing view."

"I meant, sorry to pull you from your work. Coming down to shop."

"Hey, I've got cabin fever too. I didn't get the chance to go to Milan, remember?"

He motioned to her writing pad. "How's your work coming?"

Elizabeth's head dropped down. "Early stages yet."

"It's got to be big, you carrying it into town."

"Gabriella gave us a real challenge. Figure out what would be my

298

ideal situation. Develop a thesis that could be woven in with everyone else's new goals. Define our next set of parameters."

"She is one smart lady." Julio lowered himself into the seat next to her. "Get everybody looking beyond the threat, remind people why you're here at all."

"It's a lot more difficult than I thought."

"Does taking things to the next level include me?"

He regretted saying it almost before it was out of his mouth. But she just gave him a light elbow to the ribs and, "Get real, *ese*."

"Think maybe you could put your goals into words a surf dog might understand?"

To his genuine pleasure, Elizabeth stowed her pad and pen back in her purse. "A small group of scientists have begun work on what they term *coalescing field theory*. They propose that human beings, at their most elemental, are a pulsating energy charge. This has created some serious heat in my field. Pharmacology is based upon the concept that human beings are essentially a series of carbon-based chemical actions and reactions. When the chemical process is interrupted, human life ends. The coalescing field theorists say this is totally incorrect. All that happens is the physical shell ceases to interact with the larger physical universe. The core human entity simply changes from one state of awareness to another. You with me?"

On any other woman, Elizabeth's white-blonde hair, pale complexion, and faint dusting of freckles would have been enough for some serious heat. Julio was totally into just having a reason to look at her full on. "Oh yeah."

"What came next was the real declaration of war. Coalescing field theorists suggested these pulsating energy fields—what they hypothesize are the essential human structure—are also not isolated. Instead, these theorists applied a development in quantum theory known as nonlocality."

For the first time, Elizabeth started showing some real animation. Her hands went into a little dance all their own, her eyes lighting up enough to defy the grey day beyond the funicular's window. "In essence, nonlocality states that at the quantum or subatomic level, the entire universe is interconnected. Any quantum entity, such as a single electron, can influence another entity, *regardless of space and time*. The effects are instantaneous and can theoretically occur over any distance. At the quantum level, the speed of light is meaningless. In fact, it is theoretically possible for the effect to result *before* the event actually takes place. Coalescing field theorists use this concept of nonlocality as the basis to insist that all human entities are interconnected."

"Yeah, that'd sure get me reaching for the guns."

She might have smiled. A tiny one. There and gone in a flash. "So what got you to sign on to this gig?"

"You mean, other than the weather?" Julio turned to the window. "I got to tell you, I could learn to love this place. If only we could have a little sun. I'm a Florida boy. I haven't been this long without sunshine since . . ."

"Since when?"

Julio wished he hadn't started down that road. "Juvie."

"You mean, juvenile detention? You were in jail?"

"Reform school. Jail is for adults. Like prison."

Hard as it was to talk about that stuff, it was still kind of nice to find them arriving at the Como station, walk out to the lakefront, and have Elizabeth keep talking to him like they were two normal people. "That's right. I heard Charlie telling Gabriella a little about you. Your father is in prison, isn't that right?"

"Raiford."

"I'm sorry, Julio."

"It's cool."

They walked on for a while, Elizabeth tracking them on a city map where Gabriella had highlighted the shopping areas. "My family is a mess too."

"But rich, right?"

"You wouldn't believe me."

"Try."

"My old man is worth half a billion dollars."

"Get out."

"For real."

"Girl, where is your limo?"

"My old man disowned me."

"For what?"

"He owns a big portion of America's largest pharmaceutical empire. When I said war, *ese*, that's exactly what I meant."

"I believe I know that tune." Julio nodded with his entire body. "You can hide a whole world of hurt in a few little words."

"Tell me about it."

That about did it for their personal history session. But the ice lady walked easy with him as they entered the pedestrian zone. And when it started to rain she even shared his umbrella. Every pair of male eyeballs scoped the two of them out.

Just *digging* it.

44

Alessandro and Edoardo stepped through the glass doors and entered the largest bank in northern Italy. The main lobby held a palace's grandeur. Alessandro paused for a moment's admiration. "Look at the floor. Polished Carrara marble. Enough to cover a football field. You could comb your hair in the reflection. That is, if you had enough hair left to comb."

Edoardo sniffed. "This is supposed to impress me?"

"And the ceiling. Those beams are covered in real gold leaf. That chandelier must weigh twenty tons."

"This place just reminds me of all the crooks who got away. I want my bank to take my money and go out and make more money. Not spend it on building a bordello."

"Your money. Ha."

Edoardo said to the two uniformed officers who had followed them inside, "Plant yourselves by the door. Await my signal." He turned back to Alessandro and said, "Remind me what we're doing in this hovel."

"We are about to frighten a very rich gentleman half to death. A man, I might add, who deserves to be frightened."

"Oh, good." Edoardo produced a rare smile. "This trip might be worthwhile after all."

Alessandro had telephoned his friend the instant he had finished speaking with Charlie that morning. The prospect of what lay ahead was too exquisite not to share. "As I always say, a man should find pleasure in his work. Ah, this must be the bank's director now."

The man approaching them wore an expression that was appropriate for having two strangers enter his bank flanked by uniformed policemen. "What is going on here?"

Alessandro and Edoardo produced their badges. Alessandro gave the man a moment to sweat over what he and his clients might have been caught doing, then said, "Our reason for visiting your very fine establishment is not based upon you or your staff."

Edoardo growled, "Not today, anyway."

"Edoardo, please. This gentleman is going out of his way to be of service. Is that not so, good sir?"

The director said stiffly, "If my bank is not under suspicion, why are those policemen guarding my front door?"

Alessandro met the man's glare with a very warm smile. "We have need of a conference room."

"I beg your pardon?"

"For a few moments only. A matter has arisen regarding a gentleman here on the premises."

"I thought you just said—"

"You. Pay attention." Edoardo required no additional volume to inject a note of menace. "We need a room for an hour."

"Less," Alessandro said.

"We'll have our meeting and we'll leave. That's all you need to know."

Alessandro sighed. "I apologize for my colleague. But we are dealing with a most critical matter. You are aware, of course, of the recent incident at the Bar Azzurra."

"None of those people were our clients."

"Naturally not. But one of their colleagues will shortly be arriving in your bank. We require a room. For a brief conference. To ensure that no illegality occurs here in the future."

The bank director clearly did not like it. But one glance in Edoardo's direction was enough for him to say, "I'll see to it."

"We are in your establishment's debt."

When the director scurried away, Edoardo demanded, "Our target is tied to the Azzurra mess?"

"Charlie thinks so. From what he told me this morning, I agree."

"So why don't we have this conversation back at headquarters?"

"Because it is possible that this gentleman is being used. Not that I am suggesting he is entirely innocent. He was definitely walking the wrong side of the street. He hid quite a large sum from the tax authorities by using numbered Swiss accounts. This has come to light. I am thinking perhaps some of our old foes may have forced him into aiding their plan to take out the scientists."

"I hate him already."

"It may help us if he happens to know that."

Edoardo hesitated, then asked, "Forgive me, old friend. But are you certain you can trust these scientists and their guards?"

Alessandro's mind flashed back to an image of earlier that morning, as his wife emerged from the Church of San Fedele. She had slipped the mantilla lace from her head and stowed it in her purse. Dipped her fingers in the holy water and crossed herself. Then paused at the doorway and turned back for one final moment of silence. Alessandro had stood and watched her in utter amazement. It was the first time Carla had accompanied him to weekday mass in nine and a half years.

He realized Edoardo was still waiting for a reply. Alessandro said simply, "With my life."

"Byron McLaren?"

"What—uh, yes?"

"How do you do? My name is Alessandro Gavi. Will you come with me, please?"

"I'm, uh, waiting for someone . . ."

"We are aware of all that, sir. Please, this way."

"But it's very important—"

"Dr. Gabriella Speciale has been unavoidably delayed. If you will just—"

"Now look here. Your bank stands to gain a great deal from my being here."

"Actually, Mr. McLaren, I am with the police."

His professional tan went waxy, like coloring applied to a corpse. "What?"

"We have a few questions." Alessandro did not need to turn around to know Edoardo was presenting the American with his most menacing glare. "Either we can cover them here, or we can place you under arrest, cuff you, and take you to police headquarters. The choice, Mr. McLaren, is yours."

When they entered the conference room, Alessandro shooed away the bank executive, shut the door, and made a process of settling Byron McLaren into a chair and then seating himself across the table. Edoardo took a leather case the size of his wallet from his pocket. He turned the miniature gadget on and swept the room. "This thing is often wrong."

"It is probably not necessary. I doubt very much the bank would wish to have any record of our even being here."

McLaren watched Edoardo slowly move about the room, waving his arm at the walls and the lights and the phone and the table. "What is he doing?"

"This is for your own safety, Mr. McLaren. We need to be certain that the bank is not monitoring our conversation."

Alessandro's calm tone did nothing to assuage the American's tension. "I want my lawyer."

"We would be most happy to accommodate you, Mr. McLaren. Although I must tell you, there is actually no requirement for us to grant you legal representation at this point."

"But I'm an American."

"And what a very fortunate man you are. But I regret to inform you that this is Italy, and your nationality changes nothing. If you wish to have your attorney present, we will need to take you to headquarters and arrange for a hearing before a magistrate, which will necessitate formally charging you with a criminal offense. We would then be required to fingerprint you and have you wait in custody until your representative can be contacted. Which we would happily do, if you insist. But the process could take days. Even weeks in some cases."

"No, no, this is insane. All I want—"

"Is to see your ex-wife. Yes, we know all about that, sir. Now then, if you will just be so kind as to answer a few questions, hopefully—"

"Did Gabriella set this up?" He managed a bit of futile rage. "Oh, cute. I suppose this is her idea of revenge."

Edoardo's English was brutally awful, his grammar almost as bad as his accent. He shut off his monitor, flipped open his jacket far enough to reveal his weapon, pulled out his badge, and slammed it down so hard McLaren blanched. "You. Signor American. Read what says."

"I-I don't speak—"

"*Read!*"

The American squinted over the badge. "Guardia di Finanza."

"Edoardo, please." Alessandro pushed the badge away. "My associate is a detective with the national anti-Mafia police force. And I am the senior bailiff of Como. What my colleague is trying to tell you, Mr. McLaren, is that senior officials of Italy's judiciary are not in the habit of playing roles for women, no matter how beautiful they might be."

Edoardo slipped the badge back in his pocket. He growled in Italian, "She's pretty, his ex?"

"Utterly stunning. According to Charlie, she filed for divorce after catching him with other women. Many times."

Edoardo slapped his cuffs on the table. "Then the man should be locked up for stupidity."

McLaren jerked away from the glinting metal braces. "No, wait. That's not . . ."

"I completely agree." Alessandro slid the cuffs farther away. "Perhaps you could tell us, Mr. McLaren, who is aware of your visit to Italy."

"What? I'm here—"

"Because the terms of your prenup require a rather substantial payment. Did I say that correctly, 'prenup'? We have already spoken with your ex-wife and are aware of these matters. But the timing, Mr. McLaren. This is what we find of such interest."

Edoardo said, "Ask him about the plane."

"My colleague is most interested in a flight that landed before dawn today at Malpensa Airport."

"I-I flew into Lugano."

"How nice for you. But you see, the plane that landed at Malpensa is what we call a ghost flight. It off-loaded ten people and a number of large crates and then departed. Yet no official record of this flight exists."

"I-I don't . . ."

"The airport's log claims that no plane arrived, no people disembarked, no cargo was unloaded. But my associate has the airport under secret surveillance. We have photographs of all those who arrived. And they were met by a most unpleasant individual. A Ukrainian gentleman who handles much of this region's illegal trade in prostitutes. This contact suggests a very high level of corruption. Not to mention what those crates might have contained."

"Drugs," Edoardo growled. "Guns."

McLaren looked within nodding distance of a heart attack. "I just came to see my *wife*."

"Your ex-wife," Alessandro corrected. "As I said, sir, the timing of your visit is quite remarkable. You see, we know all about the attack on Dr. Speciale's villa."

"That has *nothing* to do with me!"

"He's lying," Edoardo said. "Arrest him. Now."

"Let me be perfectly frank, Mr. McLaren. We could release you but keep your passport and issue strict instructions for you not to leave Como. Then let us say that in the next day or so your ex-wife is attacked a second time. The people who perpetuated the first assault were thugs associated with the gentleman who met the plane this morning."

"Killers," Edoardo said. "Assassins."

"Indeed. Now let us say that this second attack results in the death or disappearance of your lovely ex-wife or her associates. Who, as far as we can tell, are doing nothing wrong." Alessandro spread his hands. "You can see the situation we would be placed in. A woman who recently forced her husband through a humiliating divorce, being assaulted while you are in the area and on the loose."

McLaren flushed. "This is *insane*."

"Of course, sir. I quite agree. But you must see how this would look to us. A wealthy American makes contact with Italy's underworld, which acts on his orders—"

"That is *not* what is happening here!"

Edoardo did a vulture's loom over the poor man's chair. "You *know* of these people! You are . . ." He snarled to Alessandro in Italian, "Give me the word."

"My colleague is convinced you are colluding with organized crime in a distinctly illegal activity," Alessandro said. "Which is a felony under Italian law."

McLaren swiped at his face with both hands. And moaned.

"It would only be to your advantage, sir, to tell us everything you know."

The words emerged from behind his hands. "I'm being framed."

"If that proves to be the case, we will erase your name from our files. This meeting never happened. You can now understand why we wanted this conversation to take place outside of police headquarters." Alessandro pulled the mini recorder from his pocket. "Which is where, I regret to tell you, we must now move this conversation. Unless, that is, you tell us everything."

The telling took quite some time. When it was done, Edoardo spread out his photographs on the table. McLaren gave them a swift glance. "I only know one of them."

"Look longer," Edoardo demanded.

But not even the detective's growl could raise the man from his gloom. "I'm telling you, the only person I've seen is this woman here."

Alessandro asked, "Her name?"

"Reese Clawson."

"And you are claiming that she somehow managed to make a withdrawal from your Swiss accounts."

"She didn't withdraw. She cleaned me out."

"And the sum was?"

"We've been over and over this."

"Only because it is so vital."

"Eighty-seven million."

"Francs."

"Dollars." The man looked like a wax doll held too close to the flame of avarice. "It's gone. All of it."

"You will please excuse me, Mr. McLaren. But for someone to access a private Swiss account suggests a level of power that is, well, rather hard to believe."

"I checked. Believe me. I've checked and I've called and I've gotten nowhere. It's just . . ."

"Yes? Please do tell us."

"I've heard rumors for years about this group. They call themselves the Combine. They're supposed to be the top guns from different industries. People who hire and fire presidents of countries. After this happened, I started asking around. And I got a call."

"Who from?"

"A guy so far up the power ladder he breathes a different air. He told me to stop asking. He said if I didn't, I'd be gone faster than my money."

Alessandro leaned back in his chair and asked in Italian over McLaren's bowed head, "What do you think?"

"You've wrung him dry." Edoardo gave a grudging nod. "You have missed your calling. We could use you in the Guardia."

"That is high praise, coming from you. Have you ever heard of this group?"

"I'll check. But nothing comes to mind."

"It couldn't hurt to spread this around a little." Alessandro switched back to English. "Very well, Mr. McLaren. There is just one small matter left to handle."

"I've told you everything."

"And we are indeed grateful for your cooperation. So now if you will just make the transfer, you are free to go."

The American jerked upright. "*What* transfer?"

"Why, is that not clear? The one you came to Italy to make. The two million dollars you owe your wife. Please excuse me. Ex-wife." Alessandro held out his hand. "If you will please be so kind as to give me your passport, this will be returned to you once she acknowledges the funds have been received."

45

Como's clothing stores smelled of crushed flowers and oiled wood panels and money. Julio thought the prices were gun-to-the-head high. As in, three hundred dollars for a *shirt*.

Elizabeth might have been semi-poor, but she was the right lady for the day. He knew this because, when she pulled out a pair of pants by Ungaro and he caught sight of the price, then converted it from Euros into dollars and got ready to holler, Elizabeth gave him a tiny slit of the icy gaze. Julio caught the message in a flash. *Suck it up, big boy. You're playing with the major leaguers now.*

Elizabeth guided him through the purchase of two complete outfits—one in grey and the other in midnight blue—from shoes to cashmere sweaters, then made him wear the greys out of the store. Truth be told, he would have gone for a little more color and a lot less severe. But then she hiked up his shirt collar enough to hide all but the top line of his neck tattoo, smiled for real, and said, "You clean up good, *ese*."

There were worse ways to spend a rainy day.

They stopped for a stand-up meal of toasted sandwiches and fresh-squeezed orange juice and the finest cup of coffee Julio had ever tasted. As they were finishing, he said, "Can I ask a favor?"

Elizabeth instantly got that locked-and-loaded set to her features. Ready to shoot him with those ice bullets of hers, straight to the heart. But all she said was, "Sure, Julio. Ask away."

"It sounds like anybody who wants to do this thing, they work as a team. Am I right?"

"You're talking about ascending?"

"That's the deal. Will you do it with me?"

She hesitated. "Not everybody can handle it."

"Hey, I've taken off on a twenty-foot Puerto Rican rocket. I can handle anything."

"Everybody knows you've got the goods. There are other ways to help out than doing a kamikaze dive off the deep end of reality."

"No, I mean it. I want to get out there, shoot myself out of their cannon. I can't tell you why. But it calls to me." The words came faster now in the face of possible denial. "I used to feel that way about the waves. Wake up before dawn, lie there, knowing the sound I hear isn't thunder. Monster waves, just waiting to chew my bones. Waves big enough to kill. But I go out there anyway, because I feel the hunger and the power and the thrill, and I know I can handle this thing. I lost that hunger somewhere. Don't ask me how. But it's gone. Now it's back. I hear this thing calling to me. This ascent. I want to *do* it."

Elizabeth gave him a long look, then said, "Let's get out of here."

Which just about did it for their one moment of intimacy. "Sure thing."

Julio paid and they left the café and he opened the umbrella, half expecting her to draw away. But she fell into step beside him, their shoulders touching. When they reached the lakefront, she said, "I can't ascend. I tried and I failed. It felt like I was trapped inside a straitjacket."

"Man, that is tough."

She stayed silent on the road that wound around the lake. Julio figured it was her way of saying he needed to go ask somebody else. And there was no reason for him to feel as disappointed as he did.

But when they settled into the funicular for the ride back up to Brunate, she said so softly he almost missed the words, "I could feel something clenched all around me."

"What?"

"My anger. It felt like I was wrapped in red-hot barbed wire."

"Whoa."

"It was worse than awful, Julio." She looked at him, revealing the horror behind the ice. "I still have nightmares."

He read the warning written in her gaze. "That could be me."

She did not nod so much as rock. Forward and back. Once.

They stayed like that for a while. Caught in the realization that they shared a lot more than either had expected.

Finally Julio said, "I need to at least try to do this thing."

"I understand."

"Will you help me?"

"Yes. On one condition." It seemed more than the altitude made breathing hard for her. "I want to try it again. I've wanted it ever since that day."

"So let's do it, girl. Together. First me and then you."

Another slow rocking forward. "Okay."

Julio leaned back in his seat. "You know what this reminds me of? My first tow-in. The larger the wave, the more water rushes up the face. It gets to a certain size, you can't paddle over the lip. You've got to be towed in behind Jet Skis. I was surfing a coral ridge off Tres Palmas in Puerto Rico. We're talking maybe twenty-five, thirty feet. Strong offshores. Barrels so big you could park a train inside. The sound of those waves breaking was this constant *rip*, like they tore holes in the world. I could feel the sound in my chest."

Elizabeth had that look in her eyes again, letting him see down below the iced surface, down deep to where the real woman lived. "But you did it, right? You went."

"That's the rule of the jungle, baby. Go for it."

She linked up with him as they left the funicular and started toward the villa. The air was a lot colder up top, and the wind was strong enough to blow the rain under his umbrella. But Elizabeth did not seem to mind. Instead, as they made the final turn to the road leading to the villa, she said, "I'm glad we could do this today, Julio. Really, really glad."

He was still working on a halfway decent response to that little gift when he caught sight of the cars. And the men seated inside.

Four men in each car. Straight off the same block as the group that had attacked out of the night and the rain.

Julio said, "Take the bags."

"What?"

"We're being watched. Do what I say. I'm gonna slip my arm in yours. Lay on you some sappy lines. No, girl, don't look at the car. Look at me. That's good."

He wiped the rain from his face, not surprised to find his fingers were jumping to the same tune as his warbly voice. He linked his arm through hers, and the heat of that fine body steadied him enough to say, "When we get to the gatehouse, I'm going to kiss you."

"Julio—"

"Wait, now, listen to what I'm saying. You're going to slap me as hard as you can. Then you take off for the house. Alone. Here we go." He pitched his voice up a notch as they passed the car, talking trash he didn't bother to hear himself.

He felt the eyes drilling into him as he sauntered up to the villa's entrance. Swung her around. Caught Elizabeth's fear and defiance and tight anger. But she was a player. Oh yeah. She let him move in and watched him lower his face to hers. He tasted the honey of warm lips and cold, cold rain. And for a moment, one long shared heartbeat, he gave himself in to the pleasure of kissing her.

It almost made up for the English she put into her swing.

He staggered back toward the funicular, rubbing his face, amazed she hadn't taken the skin off.

He could hear the men in the car laughing.

The tension in the two cars carried a deadly force. The four men in each vehicle had been intentionally mixed together. They knew each other, but none had worked together before. Especially not on a hit. In public. In what passed for broad daylight, in this season of perpetual tempest.

Half the crew were the Prince's men. Half came from the man who controlled Como's action. These men had arrived filled with their capo's angry grief over losing his favorite nephew and heir apparent. The Prince and the uncle had appeared together with the strange blonde American woman, and together they had passed on the instructions. Attack the villa. Kill any opposition. Seize all who surrender. The more they captured alive, the higher their reward. But no one could escape.

Then came the astonishment.

They were to get in position. Work out precisely who was to do what. Climb from the two cars. Cock their guns. Then phone the American woman for the final green light.

If she said go, they had their orders.

If she said stand down, they were to return to the cars and back off.

If any of their crew started to attack the villa after being ordered to stand down, the rest of the team were to shoot him dead.

The men in the front car watched as a pretty woman with a very cold face walked past them. She was accompanied by a guy who was clearly much younger. The kid was talking a mile a minute in English. The man in the front passenger seat, the appointed leader of the two crews, cracked his window a notch. The kid was saying something about getting together later, he knew this great club, they could meet up with some friends, hit the scene. The woman said nothing. Her features were very tight, almost angry.

Then the kid leaned in and kissed her.

The men in the car laughed in unison as the woman hauled back and slapped the kid hard enough to shoot him halfway across the street.

The kid was still rubbing his face and gawking at the villa's entrance long after the woman disappeared. Then he turned and stumbled back toward the funicular station.

The leader gave it another fifteen minutes. Then he pushed open his door and said, "Call the lady. We move out."

46

Reese's phone rang just as her car approached Como's Palace Hotel. A man with heavily accented English said, "We are ready to attack."

"Wait right where you are." Reese cupped the phone and said to the driver, "Turn the car around."

"Signora, this is a one-way—"

"Take the next left. There!" She shook the fist not holding her phone. The coin she had been holding for hours rattled about inside. She muttered, "Heads, we go in. Tails, we stand down."

"Signora?"

"Nothing." Reese opened her hand and revealed the tiny sweat-slick Euro penny. Tails. She said to the phone, "Stand your men down."

"Signora, we can do this thing."

"And I am telling you to stand down. Return to your cars. Pull back two hundred meters. Wait for further instructions." Reese ended the call and mimicked, "'We can do this thing.' Why do men always turn orders into a macho challenge?"

The driver had been supplied by a lean, grey-haired Como thug who clearly thought little of the Prince and his men. "Signora?"

"Stop here a second."

The driver was a bright young man who could not understand why his passenger insisted on changing her mind every thirty seconds. Since picking her up he had driven twice around the old city and once up into the hills, only to turn around just before they reached Brunate. She had ordered her American team to attack, then she drew them back from the brink, and now she had done the same thing with the Italians.

His gaze in the rearview mirror said he was certain the lady was over the edge and falling fast. "Very sorry, signora. Up ahead is the Duomo. No car can stop here."

"Go, then. Make a circle around the city."

"Sì, signora. Another circle."

She hit the speed dial on her phone and asked Trace, "When can your team be ready to move?"

"What, again? No offense, but you're acting a little nuts."

"And you're totally missing the point. I can't explain it better than I already did."

"Look, my men are having trouble with this random attack. If they think an assault is green-lighted, they get totally amped. When you keep pulling them back at the point when the deal should be going down, they lose their edge. I can see—"

"Just get them ready and go. And when you get there, you *call for instructions*."

She cut the connection and shut her eyes. For a moment, one brief instant, she gave in to the fear that gnawed at her gut. The worry that had left her feeling helpless for the first time since she'd started working for the Combine. The concern that she dared not share with anyone. What if their opponents could see around this corner as well? What if they could see *probability* as well as action? What if they already knew the difference between the ruses and the actual attack, even if she didn't?

On the flight over, Reese had come up with only one option that might work. *Might.*

She could not know herself which attack to let loose.

Make all her actions random, even where she drove. Nobody knew when to go. Not even her. Until the very last minute.

She opened her eyes. The car's interior did not hold enough air for her to breathe. She started to roll down the window when she realized that pedestrians had stowed away their umbrellas. Then she recognized the name chiseled above the entrance they were passing. "Stop the car."

"Sì, signora. We stop."

"I'm going for a walk. Wait for me back at the hotel."

Irma waited while Charlie monitored Massimo phoning his girlfriend. When the Italian student handed the phone back to Jorge, Charlie told him, "That was as professional a job as it's ever been my pleasure to hear."

Massimo grinned. "You did not understand a single word."

"I did," Gabriella said. "You were perfect."

"But what if the enemy was not listening?"

"These are pros. They're tracking all our outgoing signals." Charlie turned to Irma. "You need something?"

"Come with me, sport." She led Charlie down the upstairs hall, and Gabriella followed. They entered the largest of the upstairs bedrooms. Irma walked them to the rear closet, hit the light switch, and said, "Ta-da!"

"Oh, man."

"Tell me this is as cool as I think it is."

Charlie stood in the closet doorway and gaped. "This is amazing."

Irma gave Gabriella a satisfied smirk. "Told you."

"If our plan works, it's because of you two. And this."

Irma shook her head. "It's your plan, sport. I'm just one of the grunts pulling duty."

"No, Irma." Gabriella rested a hand on the older woman's arm. "You have made yourself a part of this. The plan, the goals, our work. Everything. How did you find this?"

"I was going over Charlie's plan and scoping out the house. My mind kept returning to that cubbyhole by the chimney where you stuck me. I figured, hey, the guy who thought that one up had to be pretty sneaky, right? So maybe there were more."

"But how did you find *this*?" Charlie said.

"I asked Gabriella."

They were in the techies' office, the largest of the top-floor chambers. Only this room, the bedroom on the villa's opposite end, and the two chambers directly below them on the middle floor had real closets. The rest contained European clothes cupboards, tall mahogany chests with inlaid doors.

At the back of the techies' closet was a second door, only about four feet tall and eighteen inches wide. When it was shut, there was no sign that it existed. It was operated by a latch set in the closet's dusty corner. Beyond this second door was a room, five feet square, lined in raw brick and unfinished wood.

"I had forgotten all about them," Gabriella said. "We played in here as children. My uncle showed me this when I was very little."

Irma said, "Apparently at one time there was a network of tunnels that ran between the floors."

"They were all shut up many years ago," Gabriella said. "It happened when they rebuilt the walls to put in electricity and plumbing. Now there is only this and one other on the ground floor."

Charlie shut the door. Ran his hand over the seamless wall. Hit the lever. The door popped open. There was no sound. "This is *great*."

Irma did her best to hide her pleasure. "Shame about the tunnels."

"This should do us just fine." Charlie turned to the ladies. "Gabriella, it's time to gather everybody."

Irma started for the stairs. "I better go give Julio a heads-up."

∙⑂∙

Reese entered the central Como bank where Byron McLaren had arranged to meet his wife. She really had no need to be there. Patel had been trying to raise Byron on his phone for hours. But she wanted to come have a look for herself, just to make totally sure the man had indeed vanished.

The building looked like a palace. A plaque on the wall claimed it had been built by some Renaissance prince for his mistress. Reese scanned the interior, decided she wouldn't mind having somebody deed a place like that to her. The main chamber was a temple to greed. She could move in tomorrow.

Reese scouted the interior but did not see Byron. The man was well and truly off the grid. He was supposed to have called as soon as he met his ex. Reese had intended to time one of her possible strikes on the villa then, when their leader was trapped down here in the bank.

How they managed to spirit Byron away from the busiest bank on Como's busiest street raised Reese's worries to the redline and beyond.

She left the bank and started toward the old city's pedestrian zone. Beyond that were the steps leading to the Duomo's cloister. She spotted a couple of men eyeing her as she walked. They were extremely well dressed, well groomed. Late thirties, early forties, in the middle of some intense conversation, breaking it off to give her the eye. Keeping things in proper Italian order. She should definitely hang around there for a while after the job, see what kind of mess she could make of a few men's lives.

Patel phoned. "I have bad news and *worse* news."

"You're paid to handle things. So handle."

"Not this time."

"In case you haven't noticed, I'm in the middle of a big deal." When Patel responded with silence, she said, "Okay. Hit me."

"Weldon wants you to come home. Now."

She froze. "He's pulling me out?"

"We've intercepted an alert sent out by the Guardia di Finanza. That's Italian for serious police. They've issued a circular calling for you to be *arrested*. They have your *photograph*."

"This can't be happening."

"Weldon says to leave it in Trace's hands and come home."

"Trace will drive this straight into the ground."

"Weldon says—"

"Is he there in the Vault?"

"No, but—"

"You haven't found me."

Patel's whine was so practiced, she suspected he had been waiting for her to say those very words. "Weldon could *fire* me."

"Do it. Please."

"You owe me."

"I know."

"You owe me a *lot*."

"I said all right, Patel. What else is there?"

"Surveillance cameras are up and running. The villa is surrounded, including the hill above it. But we can't see as much as we should. There's a wall, and beyond the walls are so many trees it's like trying to penetrate—"

"I know about the walls and the trees." She and Trace had driven around the villa while his men had set up the cameras. "Have you seen anything?"

"A pharmaceutical company's delivery van came and went about an hour ago. And a Como market delivery van. Bread and milk and vegetables. Otherwise, nothing."

"Maybe we could appropriate the vans, use them for breaking in. Feed the names and addresses to Trace. Anything else?"

"Well, there is *one* thing. We just intercepted a cell phone call. One of the students who vanished after their visit to Milan called his girlfriend."

"I thought you said all their phones were down."

"They *were*. But we kept up the monitoring. And right after Weldon stormed through here, one of them popped onto the grid."

"Did you insert our package?" They had managed to obtain a pirate copy of Chinese software developed by their military in time for the Beijing Olympics. The software rode the signal into the phone like an electronic parasite. Once embedded, it gave the operator total control. Even when the phone was off, monitors could continue to use it as a bug.

"Of *course*."

"Can you confirm the signal originates inside the villa?" If the phone had GPS capacity, even if it was not activated, the phone could be used as a homing beacon, precise to within half a meter.

"That was the *first* thing I did. He called from the northeast corner room."

"Okay. Okay." Her mood brightened with the day. This could be the break they had been looking for. "Tell me what you heard."

"The student apologized to his girlfriend for being out of touch. He complained about rules the Hazard guy had set up, like the only place they were allowed to phone from was through the main computer. Their technicians had accessed a phone system in Hong Kong. But the problem is, they have to stand there next to the technicians to make their calls, and this student Massimo hates how they can hear—"

"Patel."

"What."

"Skip the windup."

"Well, you *asked*. Then he said that they had failed. They could not perform what they had been brought to the villa for. He was really upset, this student. He said that the professor couldn't ascend either or look—"

"He said *what?*" Her shout turned heads as far away as the Duomo.

"That the woman—he called her the professor—she couldn't ascend. And the man Hazard couldn't either. So they sent the students out, or tried to, and Massimo and the other students tried but they couldn't help. But we don't know for certain—"

She cut the connection, then shouted her rage and her triumph to the sky. Only one thing made sense. Her randomness had clouded their ability to determine the future's course.

Reese speed-dialed the phone. When Trace answered, she said, "We're going in now. Repeat, *now.*"

The guy responded with total boredom. "And I'm telling you my guys are still worn out from your last theatricals."

"This is *not a drill*. We are going in!"

"This is for real?"

"The enemy is blind. They can't follow our attack!"

The tension in his voice rose to match her own. "Where are you?"

"Three hundred meters and closing on foot."

"We'll meet you in front of the hotel. Hurry."

47

Julio said, "I counted two rides. An Alpha Romeo like the one we got parked in the stables. And a stud-ugly sedan called a Lancia thirty meters farther down the hill."

He and Irma were crouched by the window of Julio's room, in Brunate's only hotel that overlooked the road leading to their villa. The cramped little single was tucked under the eaves. They could not stand upright and see out the window.

Irma said, "Yeah, I scoped them on the way over here. Four in each car. All local. We still haven't found the Combine's team."

"Maybe they didn't show."

"Oh, they're here, all right. Charlie got a call from his pal on the local force. That guy Alessandro is totally stand-up. He and a buddy put the handle on Gabriella's ex-husband."

"Sure, the rich dude."

"Yeah, him. The guy told them the woman Charlie saw in Texas is here. Her name is Reese Clawson. Charlie's certain she wouldn't travel without her team. He says they're Delta."

The window was so narrow they could both look out only with their shoulders touching. Close enough for Julio to pick up Irma's taut eagerness. The lady was back in full cop mode. Like it was totally cool, going up against Delta.

Irma caught his sideways glance. "What."

"Nothing. Not a thing. How did you get here without them seeing you?"

"Over the stable roof, around the cliff on a ledge, through the neighbor's gardens, and out their gate. Not bad for a retired old lady." Irma was dressed in a pair of sweats made grimy by her little trek. Ten minutes ago she had popped up in Julio's doorway, grinning with wicked anticipation.

Irma went on, "Your main job is to let us know the minute they start in. You got the number for Milo's cutout in Rio?"

"Right here."

"Call us on the hotel phone. Once you report in, hold back until you're certain everybody is inside, then take up station by the gate-house." Irma slipped her backpack around front and unzipped the top. "And for your continued entertainment, we have this little darling. I assume you know how to fire a gun."

"Can't do any worse than I did with the Taser."

"Hey, an arm like yours, you miss, just haul back and hammer the guy between the eyes. The gas canister goes in here. Flip this lever once, it's primed. See the gauge here by the trigger? When it goes red, you change canisters—you've got another in the pack. Pistol holds five darts, you've got five more in the pack. They all contain Dor Jen's version of a pharmaceutical nightmare, so be sure not to scratch yourself with one of the tips. Just flip the bolt here, slip in this clip, you're locked and loaded. This baby doesn't have a safety." Irma's smile held a foretaste of peril. "We couldn't be certain all the canisters actually still hold charges. We fired two, though, and both were fine. I'd say you're good to go. The nightscope off one of the rifles is in here, but I doubt you'll need it. Charlie thinks they'll be moving soon. You're clear on your job, right?"

Julio stared out the window to the empty entrance and the gate-house. The sky was grey, the wind hard and blowing the damp air back to where he sat, hidden from view. "This waiting, man, I never knew a minute could last all day."

"You want to be a cop, first lesson you've got to learn is how to wait."

"Who said anything about me wanting to join the po-po?"

"There are worse ways to spend thirty years."

"Yeah, like what?"

"Say, hanging out at the local community center, sweeping floors, waiting for trouble to take you to lunch."

"That's a low blow, dog."

Irma chuckled, her voice so easy she might have been sipping a latte in the community center. "Everybody's idea of a good life is different. My first partner after I made detective used to say his idea of success was, at one hundred and eleven years of age, he gets shot by a jealous husband."

Julio did not nod so much as rock in his seat. "I used to think it'd be wiping out on the biggest wave ever surfed. A hundred cameras marking time."

He expected her to give the standard adult comeback. How it was such a waste. How he had to focus on the important things in life. Like a job and a salary and wearing a tie. Instead, Irma gave him a pair of breaths, then said, "And now?"

"I don't know." He kept his voice steady by strength of will. "It feels like everything is shifting inside."

"Sorry you came?"

"It's not that." His swallow was so tight he was certain she could hear it. He said what had come to him in the middle of the night. "I feel like I've been carrying this weight all my life. All this pain and anger. It never goes away."

Irma said softly, "Like it makes you who you are."

"Like it's the only thing I can count on."

"I guess it's time for a confession of my own. I've wanted to tell you this for years. That first day you walked into the center, I didn't just happen to start chatting you up. I knew you already."

"Where from?"

"I was there the day you were busted. I'd just made detective. They hadn't placed me yet. I was assigned to grade some rookie cops up for their first review. They rolled on this disturbance call. And there you were."

"Oh, man. I never saw you."

"I hung back. But I stayed through the whole deal. Carting you downtown. Printing and photographing and charging, the works. How old were you, fourteen?"

"Twelve."

"Big for your age. What were you doing over in Orlando, anyway?"

"You know. Chilling with the homies. Looking for trouble."

"You sure found it. I'd never been at a bust before where I wasn't totally involved in the action. Hanging back was weird. I couldn't take my eyes off you. You were such a handsome kid. Strong. Great eyes, I remember that. And how sad you were."

He sat and stared out the empty window at the empty street. The sun had vanished quick as it had arrived. Julio felt the wind drag cold, wet rain across his face.

Irma said, "You had a major impact on me. When my husband passed, I kept things together by going back to school. Got accredited as a CASA—court-appointed special advocate. Started working with other kids carrying their load of pain. Then I retired. And one day I was hanging around the center, and look who walks in. I mean to tell you, that gave me a serious case of the chills."

"Why didn't you tell me?"

"Didn't want to bring up your bad old days. I mean, you were doing good. Staying clean. Working your way up in the surfing world. Hanging out at a safe place."

Julio leaned back in his chair. Ready now for a little confession of his own. "You know how it's felt since I got over here? Like I've just managed to escape. Soon as I get back home, I'm one step from the next chase. I run and I run, and I can't ever escape. All my life I'm just waiting for the time to crash and burn."

"That's what your friends are for, *ese*. To make sure that doesn't happen. You should give joining the police some thought." Irma rose from her chair, gave him a one-armed hug. "I can't think of anyone I'd like more to have officially watching my back."

Julio squinted out the window at the street and the gatehouse there in the distance. He clenched his jaw, clamping down on the sudden terror. When he was certain his voice wouldn't break, he said, "Tell Charlie I won't let you down."

Irma stopped in the process of opening the door. "Julio, that is the *last* thing any of us are worried about."

48

The two carloads of Italian thugs left their positions outside the villa and met Reese's team on the road to Brunate. They were parked in a turnout meant for tourists. Four of the brutes emerged from their cars when Reese's van pulled in and stopped. Their appearance slowed traffic and dragged the tourists' attention away from the billion-dollar view.

Trace said, "What is Italian for *low profile?*"

Reese said, "Radio your second team. Tell them to proceed to target."

Trace touched his earpiece and relayed the orders. A second van roared past and continued up the hill.

The men who approached their van might have been dressed in suits. But as far as disguises went, their clothes were about as useful as shoving a bazooka in a shoulder holster. Two men took up station by Trace's door. A third approached her window. He reeked of menace. He offered her a cell phone and said, "My capo wants a word."

She accepted the phone, but before she could speak, another man shoved his way forward. This one was slightly more polished, a typical security chief. But his attitude was just as bad. He snarled, "We go no matter what the Russky says."

Reese noted the anger between the two groups with some heat of her own. "You're not together?"

The security guy made as to spit at the ground by the other man's feet. "They work for the Ukrainians, they're good with the ladies. My capo is boss in Como, not this Russky Prince. You say go, signora, we go."

The first thug had a few choice things to say about that, none of which required translating.

Trace said, "Do you *believe* this?"

Reese lifted the phone and said, "Did you catch that little exchange?"

The Prince sighed. "My sincere apologies. The man addressing you is cousin to the one who killed himself for disappointing me. There are issues. I will clear them up."

"When, next week?"

"No, no, immediately. As soon as we finish, I will call the Como boss. He will speak with this gentleman. Now to the matter at hand. I understand you wish for this attack to go ahead."

"That is correct."

"In broad daylight?"

"If that's what you call this." A damp wind blew hard through the van. Overhead, the sky wore a uniform grey. "We have a very tight window of opportunity. The crew in Brunate is blind."

"I do not understand."

"We intercepted a cell phone conversation between one of the Italian students and his girlfriend. Their ability to view forward has been lost."

"You are certain this was not a ruse?"

"It's a risk. But a small one. The odds are in our favor."

The Prince hesitated, then said, "I will speak with the Como boss."

"You have five minutes," Reese said, her gaze on the two men outside her window. She cut the connection, handed back the phone, and said, "Here's how it's going to play out. My group will attack in two teams. You are backup."

"Please, signora, I ask that you forget these Ukrainian scum and allow us to—"

"Either you go with my plan or you get in your cars and drive away. I know my people. You, I don't know. I need to be certain that we kill the guards and trap everybody else alive."

"We can do this, signora."

"So far, your record for following orders is not the best. We do it my way. You park where you can see the villa's gates. Anybody who gets past us, you stop them. I need a phone number. You get my call, you come. Are you with me so far?"

Neither of them liked it. But further protest was cut off by two cell phones ringing simultaneously. Both thugs stepped away from the car.

Trace said, "I'm loving this place more by the minute. Great weather, lovely people—"

"Stop it."

Both men put their phones away, glared at one another, then turned toward her. The Como man said, "We follow your orders, signora."

"Glad to hear it. When I phone, you move in fast. Anybody you find unconscious, you bundle into this van. When it's full, use your trunks."

"And your other van?"

"It's already headed for the top of the ridge. My second team will rappel down and attack from the roof. Now listen carefully. If anybody comes at you, you shoot to wound, you got that? Shoot to wound, not kill. If it's one of the guards, we'll take care of him later."

"Sì, signora. We understand."

"Then get into position."

When the men moved back to their cars, Trace said, "Can we go now?"

"Follow them through the village. I want to make sure they park in the right spot."

As Charlie and his team made their preparations, Gabriella could not take her eyes off him. Charlie had a rangy build, balanced stance, and certain rawboned handsomeness. His taut menace was mostly masked by his air of quiet reflection. His gaze was hard and focused and steady, no matter how slanted the world might become. He saw everything and was surprised by nothing.

Beyond that was the man's force. He held the latent power of a jaguar. Strong and supple and constantly ready to attack. The potential for violence was there beneath the surface. Not brooding or seething, however. This particular man had nothing to prove, not even to himself. He simply knew with an ancient's wisdom that he was ready for whatever came.

She had never seen Charlie in his element before. His core intensity burned so powerfully she thought she might well be scalded by a single touch to his skin. She imagined it was like this before a volcano erupted, the lava fuming far beneath the surface, the raw power ready to surge at any minute.

They were gathered as Charlie had instructed, in the largest of the top-floor chambers. The techies' equipment had all been pushed to one side. Pallets were laid out on the floor. A second set of pallets had been laid out in the room where Charlie had slept. Each was covered with a heating pad taken from the villa's winter cabinet. A fierce wind blew through the open balcony doors. Even so, the room still smelled of camphor and overheated dust.

Gabriella watched him run through the plan a final time. She realized that here was another reason why he could ascend and move with such ease. Charlie was never more focused than when facing danger.

He moved forward when everyone else would think no further than which way to flee. Which was the case right now. The room held a palpable sense of terror that infected everyone but him.

Charlie must have felt her eyes, for he approached her on cat's paws. "Everything okay?"

The urge was so strong, she had no choice but to give in. Gabriella gripped his face with hands one stage removed from claws. And kissed him. She kissed him so hard it bruised her lips. She intended to leave him so thoroughly kissed he would carry it forever, straight through the fire that awaited him.

She heard a sigh from the team gathered by the balcony doors and knew it came from Brett. But the moment remained unbroken until the phone started ringing. Gabriella released him then, clinging to him with only her eyes as Irma walked to the phone hooked into the computer, pressed a button, and answered with, "Go."

Irma listened, then said, "Roger that. Good luck, bro." She set down the phone. "Julio says the two cars are back, only now they're with a van. He says a second van identical to the one parked outside our gates went racing by about three minutes ago."

Charlie kept his gaze steady on Gabriella as he said, "The Americans have split into two teams."

Behind them, Milo exclaimed, "Who is *that*?"

Gabriella turned to find a man perched on the balcony railing.

Charlie said, "His name is Benny Calfo. Benny, meet the team."

Eyes of cobalt ice flitted across the room. "Julio got it right. The Americans have a five-man team up top, they're preparing to rappel down. Another five-man team in the second van. The locals are four and four. Looks like they've been ordered to hang back."

"Irma, give Julio a quick heads-up on the teams in reserve."

"Roger that." She picked up the phone. "Milo, you want to come dial this thing for me?"

Benny went on, "The woman you told me to look out for is with the team by the front gates."

"Okay. Help move this group into position. Then ready yourself." Charlie turned to the scientists. "Do exactly what Benny says. This is not a drill. No hesitation. No heroics."

Gabriella said with the knowledge of true conviction, "You will keep us safe."

"No." Charlie looked at her. But his focus was elsewhere. "I will end this."

49

What are we waiting for?" Reese demanded.

"Just hang tight," Trace replied.

She could have ordered him to supply a better answer. But she knew that was what he wanted her to do, so he could turn to the man behind the wheel and smirk. Telling his team she didn't belong.

Which, of course, was absolutely correct.

They had expected her to direct ops from the van. But there was no way she was going to sit this one out.

When she demanded to go in with them, Trace's team didn't like the idea. They did not say anything and they didn't look her way. But she knew. They were a unit so tight she could feel the current surging below the surface. That was why she wanted in, so she could go play with the big dogs.

The van was parked twenty meters down the hill from the gatehouse. Trace turned in his seat and said, "Go check out the grounds."

The man seated in the rear slipped from the van, loped up the street, and scaled the fifteen-foot wall like he was climbing stairs. Just put one foot above the next and disappeared.

Trace must have heard something because he touched the button on his earpiece and said, "Go. Roger that. Start your scan." He dropped his hand. "Team two is in place."

The scout loped through the villa's open gates. He stopped by Trace's window and reported, "Gatehouse is empty."

"Walking the perimeter?"

"Can't say for certain. Trees block a lot of the terrain. There's a cup of coffee in there, and it's cold."

Trace checked his watch. "Little late for lunch."

Reese realized he was waiting for her orders, but he would not turn and ask. Not in a million years. She said, "Let's do what we came to do."

50

Edoardo sat behind the wheel of an unmarked police car. "This car's color was wretched before the paint dried."

The interior smelled of cigarette ashes, old coffee, stale sweat, and tension. Alessandro's seat adjuster was broken. A hairline fracture ran down his side window. The car had done three hundred thousand kilometers. Alessandro had spent far too many hours in such cars. The smell alone took him straight back to Naples and the days when he went nowhere without his armed escort.

Edoardo had the habit of becoming morose whenever he was breaking a major case. The more severe his expression, the closer he was to bagging his prey. Today he looked positively funereal. "Are you sure they're coming?"

"I dialed the police headquarters," Alessandro replied patiently. "I spoke personally with the watch commandant. You should stay awake. You miss the most interesting events."

"They're taking too long."

"It's been twelve minutes. Not even you could cover the distance from Como to Brunate in that amount of time."

"You shouldn't have told them no siren or lights."

"Today we are merely acting as backup. We have no evidence to tie the mob to the villa up ahead of us," Alessandro replied.

They had covered this same terrain several times already. The fact that he was right only added to Edoardo's dour state. "We have the testimony of an American military officer and a retired detective."

"Please, Edoardo, we have discussed this to death. Charlie Hazard was most explicit. We must allow their teams to enter the villa. If we stop them, they will only return at another time. Our only hope is that Charlie is as good at his job as he appears."

"I did not claw my way up through the ranks to play backup."

"Nonetheless, that is our role today." Alessandro felt positively giddy. He always felt that way in the presence of danger. Only afterward, when he was safe and lying in his bed and reliving the moment—usually at three in the morning with Carla asleep beside him—did he know terror. Just now, however, he was having a wonderful time. "Isn't this fun?"

Edoardo shot him a look of sour astonishment. "Now I know why they made you leave Naples. You are insane."

"We're saving some very good people from some very bad men. What could be more fun than that?"

"We're two people against eight. One and a half, really, since you refuse to carry a gun. My SWAT team is trapped on the motorway inside a traffic jam sixty miles long and won't be here until November. So for backup we have one carload of Como's local constables." Edoardo shook his head. "They'll probably shoot us both."

"They will do just fine."

"And I am telling you this as a friend. Seek help before it's too late."

Alessandro's phone chirped. He checked the readout and said, "It is our brave lads." He had specifically ordered them not to use their radios. Italian police radios were so often tapped by the bad guys, they might as well use megaphones. "Hello?"

"We are entering Brunate now."

"We are in the unmarked car around the corner from the funicular station. Pull up behind us." He ended the call and conceded, "They do sound rather young."

Edoardo sighed and reached over. "Give me that thing." He had depleted his own phone's battery yelling at his backup. He dialed a number, and instantly the tinny sound of sirens came from the cell phone's speaker. He shouted, "How long?"

Alessandro said, "Not so loud, please. My ears."

Edoardo hung up and said, "Another hour."

"Which means two." As soon as Alessandro held the phone, it chirped again. "It's the Americans." He put it to his ear. "Hello?"

Charlie said, "Two teams are inbound. Both Americans. Two carloads of locals are also parked outside the gates. It appears they're assigned to a backup role. Can we leave them to you?"

"Of course. You are sure you would not rather have us—"

"Stick to the plan. Hazard out."

Alessandro set down his phone. Felt the most delightful shiver of nerves. "It has begun."

51

A sudden shift occurred just as Reese passed through the villa's front gates. The rain did not simply stop, nor did the clouds lessen. Instead, the season of gloom completely vanished. The change was so drastic they might as well have left one world and entered another. The sky became a huge open field so vast it shamed the remaining clouds into scuttling away. A blast of wind caused the surrounding trees to give great shuddering heaves. Sunlight turned the falling droplets into gems.

Trace muttered, "Shame it couldn't wait another ten minutes."

"This is bad?"

"Makes us easier to spot." He raised his hand. Keyed his earpiece. "Go . . . Okay. Which corner? . . . Roger that. Hold for the green light. I say again, hold position." He released the mike and told his team, "Our spotter is in place. Top floor's action is restricted to two rooms. In the room to our right somebody is playing a computer game. And a man is talking softly in the southeast corner, to your left and back against the cliff. Spotter says it sounds like the guy is counting."

Reese stiffened. "This is not good. According to what we've managed to ascertain, counting is part of how they do this ascent thing."

"So do we pull back?"

She stared at the villa, her focus so intense she could almost peel away the stones. Beyond the walls, the village was utterly silent. Not even a dog barked. "If they're not out here waiting for us, it has to mean they haven't been able to break through again."

Trace said, "A lot depends on you being right."

Reese started to snap that he was the one who didn't want any more false starts. But an argument would get them nowhere. All she wanted was to get this over and done. The thought of her face on an international arrest warrant was a hot flame pressing her forward. "I say let's do it."

Trace walked over to where his teammate held a scanner. "Show me."

The guy steadied the apparatus on one knee and took aim through the eyepiece. Trace knelt as his guy pulled a small flat-screen from the apparatus's side, connected to the machine by a flexible cable. Reese moved in close beside Trace as the guy said, "Starting with the ground floor. Infrared first." He did a slow sweep. "There. Back north room. Could be as many as six laid out on the floor, one person seated."

"I see it."

The screen was filled with a rose-colored glow near the base. A single figure rose above the cluster of light.

Trace asked, "That's the best you can do?"

"It's the stone. The walls must be two feet thick."

"Try the other."

"Switching to X-ray." The screen went blank, then was filled with a faint bluish glow. The lone figure appeared on the screen. The image zoomed in closer. "He's sitting down."

"Any others?"

"They're too close to the floor. The heat image is clearer. Switching back. I say a minimum of four, more like six. All but the one guy lying down."

A sudden gust blasted through the trees, showering them with droplets. Reese cleared her face and said, "It's how they ascend. One person directs while the others lie down and go."

"I don't understand a word you just said, and I don't care. Are we good to go or not?"

She wanted desperately to say yes and saw the same taut desire on his face. "Check out the rest of the house."

Trace turned back to the screen. "Go back to X-ray."

"Roger that. Okay. Rest of the ground floor looks empty."

"Go to the middle floor."

"Middle floor looks totally vacant."

"Top floor."

"Activity on the top floor. Two rooms occupied. We've got what looks like a woman standing in an inside doorway in the middle bedroom. She was the one playing with the computer before. And there in the back is another guy seated."

Reese said, "Where is everybody else?"

Trace said, "Switch to infrared."

"Switching now. Okay, the north room here, it's only got the lone woman. Here to the south, we've got the same deal as we saw on the ground floor. Only the glow is clearer. Walls must be thinner. Nothing on X-ray, they meld with the floor. Must be on pallets. But look, here's the heat image. Okay, I count six prone bodies."

Reese felt the steel bands about her chest ease slightly. She speed-dialed her phone.

Patel answered, "You are *so* in trouble with Weldon."

"Where is he?"

"Pacing the top tier. Talking on the phone. *Very* angry."

It could not be helped. The only response to Weldon angry was the same as to Weldon happy. Bring home the results. "Are you monitoring cell phone activity?"

"Of *course* I am."

"And?"

"Twenty minutes ago, this Massimo spoke with his girl again. She is named Consuela. Another student called her mother and said she wanted to come home. The pharmacologist, Dr. Elizabeth Sayer, called her father."

"I thought they were estranged."

"They are. Is that a problem?"

Reese pondered that, then set it aside. "Go on."

"Twenty minutes back, the conversations ended. We continue to monitor the cell phones. I can hear nothing through two of them. Through the third, Massimo's, I might hear a man counting. Or chanting words. It is very faint. The phone must be in a backpack."

She ran through everything another time. "The pharmacy van."

"What about it?"

"Anybody say anything about being sick?"

"Not on the phone. But we've accessed the Italian students' university files. One of them is diabetic."

"Okay."

"Weldon wants a word."

"Not now." She ended the call. "Nada."

Before Reese could say anything more, however, Weldon's voice burrowed through her earpiece. "You think you can deny me access by shutting off her phone?"

Reese turned her back to the villa and the team. Not that it would do any good. Weldon was speaking through the open circuit, which would connect them all once they went in. They could all hear her as she hit the mike button and snapped, "No, Weldon. Being the pro you are, I assumed you would get the message that *now is not the time.*"

Weldon breathed twice, then cut the connection. Trace grinned at her. "Bosses are such a pain."

"Okay, here's my take," Reese said. "They're still blind. They've got everybody clustered in two teams, trying to get somebody out here to find us. It's desperation on a new level."

"So we go?"

Reese did not nod so much as shiver. "Right now."

52

The four police officers who pried themselves from the car appeared scarcely removed from their teenage years. The lone woman was their senior officer. She asked, "Bailiff Gavi?"

"That would be me. Show them your badge, Edoardo, that's a good man. My colleague is with the Guardia di Finanza."

She saluted. "Officer Benedetti. The commandant says we are under your command."

Edoardo growled, "How old are you?"

"Edoardo, please. Officer Benedetti, please forgive my colleague. He is just emerging from hibernation. He will be fine as soon as the action starts and he can feast upon the bad men." Alessandro asked his friend, "How shall we do this?"

"Two teams. These officers will take the first car, we will go alone for the second." He asked the four, "Have any of you made an armed arrest?"

Only Officer Benedetti lifted her hand. "I have, sir."

Edoardo sighed.

Alessandro told the woman, "You will lead your team."

Edoardo checked his watch. "The American truly says the attack has begun?"

"Charlie Hazard is not one to exaggerate."

"We cannot wait for my men. We must move now."

"Indeed."

Edoardo's scowl was enough to bring all four young officers to attention. "Listen carefully. There are eight thugs in two cars. Some of them may be private security personnel. If any of them flash a badge, I order you to ignore it. They will all be armed and ready for combat. The critical issue is to *give them no chance*. You will approach with weapons drawn. You will watch their hands and their eyes. If any of them make a move for their weapons, you fire. You shoot to kill. But *only* if they make a move. Because the raw fact is this: if we fire, they fire. And if that happens, one or more of us will never taste wine or pasta again. Do you understand what I am saying?"

Alessandro watched one of the young men go bone pale. But they all nodded assent. He said, "Let's go."

Alessandro and his little team moved forward on foot. It was half a kilometer to the villa's entrance along an empty road. The road was steep enough to have them all puffing hard, even Edoardo. Alessandro was certain his own breathing was rough. But he could hear nothing. Not his breathing, nor his footsteps, nor the wind that lashed the trees overhead. There was nothing in his ears save the sound of his own life's blood.

Which was the moment the sun broke through.

All six of them stopped for a moment. The effect was blinding. Every surface was wet. They were surrounded by a billion brilliant mirrors.

Alessandro realized, "This is our chance!"

Edoardo squinted. "What?"

"They are as blinded by this as we are."

Edoardo hissed, "On the double, move!"

53

All the villa's downstairs windows were barred, which meant Trace's team was restricted to the front door, unless they used charges, which Reese nixed. The front door was massive. Reese clustered with two of the crew behind a huge elm as Trace and another man climbed the stairs. Trace swept the perimeter while his man picked the lock. Both teams were switched to the open frequency. Reese's head was filled with the heavy breathing of nine highly amped men.

The lock picker opened the door a fraction, then backed up and scouted the perimeter. Trace slowly opened the door. He then turned and looked straight at Reese. She gave him a thumbs-up.

Through her earpiece, she heard him say, "Green light. I say again. We are green for go. Weapons hot. Remember your orders. First team, on my one. Three, two, one."

The insertion was nothing like what she had expected. In her mind, the attack should have been full of testosterone and noise and speed. A lot of bangs, a lot of bullets, a lot of fear.

Instead, everything was silent. And slow.

The loudest sound was the screaming inside her brain.

As soon as they were all inside, Trace softly shut the front door. The entrance hall was paved in broad flagstones. Directly ahead rose the broad central staircase. To her left was a massive display case set in an alcove peaked like the front door. The glass shelves were filled with pottery and ceramics. To her right, a trio of stone steps led down to a gloomy hallway. The four men fanned out so that their backs were to the entrance. They scanned and they waited. In their left hands were spray canisters of nerve gas. One whiff and the recipient was out for ninety minutes. In their right hands were silenced pistols.

Back in the hotel Reese had heard Trace drill the men over and over. Left hand for the techies, right for everybody else. She had thought the repetition absurdly trivial. Now it was all she could do to remember which hand was which.

Trace pointed to his men. Two up the stairs. One with him down the hallway. He turned to Reese and pointed to his back. Then he pointed two fingers at his eyes. Stay behind him and watch. She nodded that she understood. Fine with her. Leading from behind suddenly held a huge amount of appeal. Trace must have understood her response, and his men as well. They all shared a final smile.

A voice in her ear whispered, "We're on the roof. No movement."

Trace whispered back, "Enter by the north and south balconies. Watch for our men coming up the stairs. Go."

Trace and his man moved down the hall in a cautious rush. At each doorway the lead guy checked with Trace, then went in high, Trace low. Reese remained plastered to the wall just beyond the action. Her heart was a frantic bird, struggling for a way to escape her chest.

At the rear of the house the hall took a sharp left turn, then ended by a final door. The door was wooden, ancient, and painted a muted color that looked grey in the dim light. Reese watched as the two men positioned themselves. Steady as a pair of human rocks. Trace pointed to the man's nerve gas, then to the floor. His crew member was to go for the people on the floor. Trace lifted his pistol. To Reese, the barrel and silencer looked six feet long.

Trace nodded. *Go.*

Then over her earphone, she heard a voice say, "What the—"

Trace's man was already committed. But she felt Trace's hand punch her back. Slamming her against the wall.

Over her earpiece she heard the sound of a sack dropping.

At the same moment, she watched as their lead man stiffened, slapped a hand to his neck, and fell. Hard.

He landed on a pallet. The pallet did not move. She realized with awful clarity that all the pallets were empty. There was nobody lying there.

Trace shouted, "Alert! The house is a kill zone! *Shoot everything!*"

Reese took a step back as Trace fired repeatedly through the open doorway. The gun's flashes illuminated a room that was empty save for the man sprawled at his feet. Trace raked the room. He slapped a fresh load into his gun, leapt through the doorway, rolled, and came up firing.

Overhead and through her earpiece Reese heard a tempest of men yelling and the crash of furniture and the quick whuffs of silenced gunfire. A man yelled that he was hit. Then another.

Trace's gun ran out. He dropped the empty case and reached for his belt.

A man separated himself from the corner. To Reese it seemed as though he had drawn himself from the shadows.

The stranger flitted across the room. The air was filled with a whirring sound.

Trace used his empty gun to block the blow. The man's baton made sparks when it struck the pistol. Trace whipped the gun down, trapping the baton on the barrel and pulling it down to where he could stomp on the weapon.

The man released it and went for Trace's neck. Trace dropped and rolled and responded with a pair of kicks that sent the man flying.

But the man came up like his body was spring-loaded. Trace swept his other arm in the air between them. Reese heard a quiet hiss and realized Trace had released the nerve gas.

The man backed up farther and came up against the desk. Suddenly the air was full of missiles. A laptop, cables, monitors, headphones. Trace deflected them in a series of blocks but lost the canister in the process. Then the man tossed the table, easy as a kid shooting a Frisbee. Trace flipped over backward and tumbled.

The man shot her one look. A killer's glance, holding her so tight her heart lost its ability to beat. Only then did she realize it was Charlie Hazard.

He did not move forward so much as stalk Trace. The men came together in a flurry of moves so fast as to meld together in the dim light. Their limbs and bodies blurred. There was no way two human beings could move that fast. They danced to the tune of huffs and blows and crashes.

Charlie seemed to toss Trace over his arm like he was flipping a towel. The move was impossibly smooth, even graceful. Yet Trace landed so hard his head cracked against the stone floor. He lay there, blinking slowly, too stunned to move.

Only then did Reese realize she was screaming. A high-pitched shriek, a release of hyper-tense steam that had to get out somehow.

Charlie paid her no mind whatsoever. He reached back into the shadows and came up with a rifle. The haft was shattered, clearly from one of Trace's bullets. The rifle dangled from his arm as he moved back over and shot Trace at point-blank range.

Reese turned and fled.

54

Perhaps it was not the most organized assault in the history of Italian police work. Mainly because by the time they scaled the final steep rise and arrived at the cars, they were all puffing so hard none of them could shout a thing.

Edoardo leaned against the second car's hood, tapped the windshield with his badge, and aimed down the length of his gun barrel.

Alessandro realized his friend was too winded to speak, so he did the honors. "Guardia di Finanza! Hands where we can see them! Remain absolutely still! You are surrounded!"

The astonishment on the faces inside the cars was almost comic. Clearly it must have seemed as though the officers had been fashioned from the impossibly brilliant sunlight.

Edoardo scrabbled at the door latch. The female officer did the same at the driver's door of the first car. Adrenaline so fueled the young officers that for those inside the cars, it might have seemed as though they all moved in tandem. All the young officers began shrieking as loud as their winded bodies permitted. They yelled for the men inside to come out, keep their hands in the open, make no sudden moves.

Alessandro found it necessary to wipe his hand over his mouth to hide his smile. It appeared as though the four young officers were shouting whatever order came first into their heads. He was fairly certain one of them yelled that this was a one-way street. Thankfully, the men inside the cars knew the drill, undoubtedly better than the young officers. All but one emerged from the cars and assumed the position against the villa's ancient walls. The remaining man made an extremely Italian suggestion to the female officer. She made sure he regretted it.

Edoardo supervised as the men were cuffed and one of the officers scampered downhill to fetch the police van. Then he turned to Alessandro and asked, "You are okay, old friend?"

"Apparently so."

"No bullet holes anywhere?"

"I believe I might have noticed such a thing."

"I'm not so sure about that, given your current mental state."

"Guns make ever so much noise. I'm sure I would have heard."

One of the thugs said, "You've no right to arrest us for sitting here enjoying the view."

Edoardo turned to rebuke the man. But before he could speak, the young woman stepped over and snarled, "Did you hear anybody address you? No you did not."

"This is harassment."

She kicked his legs farther apart. "Shut up and take a good look at the wall. It's the only view you're going to have for the next ten years."

Edoardo turned back around and lifted his eyebrows at Alessandro, who nodded agreement. The woman definitely had potential.

A shadow flitted across the road, a wraith slipping across a sunlit stage.

"Sir!"

The shadow became a youth. One Alessandro had seen before.

The young man's name was Julio, and he carried one of Alessandro's appropriated air pistols.

Alessandro said, "Everything is fine, Officer Benedetti."

Julio cast him a grin and a thumbs-up as he leapt through the gates.

"Sir, that man was armed with—"

"There was no man," Edoardo growled. "And since there was no man, there was no weapon. Are we clear on that?"

The woman looked from Edoardo to Alessandro and back again. "Absolutely, sir."

Edoardo actually smiled. "Officer Benedetti, have you ever thought of a career with the Guardia di Finanza?"

55

The villa's downstairs hallway was ten miles long.

Reese made the final turn by slamming into the front wall. She scrambled up the three stone stairs and tore at the front door. She heard crashes and yells behind her. She felt Charlie Hazard's approach like a dragon's breath on her neck.

One of Trace's men stumbled down the main stairway. He managed to hold himself upright by hugging one arm around the banister. Reese screamed at him, "Hazard is behind me! Shoot him! Shoot!"

The man's shoulder and neck and cheek were all leaking blood from tiny needle-sized wounds. He gasped and tried to speak, waving the silenced pistol in a wild sweep.

Reese clawed open the door and raced down the front stairs. She kept herself upright by taking a two-fisted grip on the sunlight.

Somehow she made it down the gravel drive. She had no idea whether someone was behind her or not. She could hear nothing but the whimper of her too-tight breaths and the thrashing tree limbs overhead. She flew through a crystal veil of sunlit rain.

The gatehouse appeared before her. Beyond that was the entrance and freedom. She had never moved so fast in her entire life. Her feet skipped over a cushion of air, not even touching the earth. Not even when she slipped on wet leaves and had to use both hands on the gravel, not even when she felt blood seeping from a wound on one wrist. She touched nothing. Saw nothing but the two stone pillars marking her escape.

A figure appeared beside the gatehouse, like the sunlight had co-alesced into a final guardian. He lifted a hand. And fired.

She felt a tiny stab just below her left collarbone. Like a bee sting. Nothing that would come close to slowing her down.

Except her legs suddenly lost the ability to carry her forward.

Reese watched the gravel path lift up and slam into her face. She kept whimpering, kept drawing in that one breath that would refuel her escape.

A young man who looked vaguely familiar leaned down close enough to smile into her face. "I'd tell you, sweet dreams. But hey, why waste my breath?"

56

Gabriella huddled with the rest of her team at the back of the cave. Before them were the long planks they had used to cross from the villa's top rear window to the cave's mouth. Gunfire erupted five different times, shattering the windows and the balcony doors she could see from her station at the front of the group.

Then nothing.

Wind howled and moaned beyond their rocky haven. Behind where Gabriella stood gripping the air pistol, someone whimpered. She wanted to tell them it was all right. Charlie was out there. They were safe. But she could not find the air to speak the words.

Outside the cave, branches shook and weaved, like the trees needed to share her fear. Her vision felt scarred by the flickering shadows.

When a scrabbling sound came through the opening, Gabriella gripped her weapon so hard she thought her bones would break. Then a voice called, "Don't shoot."

"Charlie?"

"Yes." A shape rose gradually into view. But the sunlight was strong behind him, and it was suddenly very hard to see beyond the veil shimmering before her eyes. "It's over."

⫶⫶⫶

Alessandro returned the salute from the young policewoman. Officer Benedetti was seated in the passenger seat of a blue police van. Two of her fellow officers were seated in the rear with the captured thugs. Alessandro watched the van trundle down the hill and said, "Such fine young people. Italy should be so very proud."

Edoardo grunted. "The woman's not bad."

"You certainly made her day. Were you serious about that job offer?"

"I never joke about such matters. Our lives hang in the balance." His smile was scarcely more than a squint, like he was taking aim at a memory. "Did you see her confront the driver?"

"I fear that happened around the time of my heart attack from running up that hill."

"He tried to give her lip. She almost pulled him through the window." Edoardo's eyes tightened further. "She's small and she's young and she's angry about being both. She should fit in very well with my team."

A few villagers clustered down by the funicular station, their curiosity in conflict with their innate Italian desire to have nothing whatsoever to do with the police.

Alessandro gave them a cheery little wave. "I wonder how the main event has gone."

Edoardo grunted again. "Perhaps we should go see."

"The villa does seem a bit quiet."

As they approached the main gates, Charlie appeared between the stone pillars. "Are the other officers gone?"

"Indeed so. How are your friends?"

"Safe."

"Excellent. Allow me to introduce my dear friend Edoardo di Santo. Edoardo is with the anti-Mafia force of the Guardia di Finanza. You must forgive him. He is convinced he speaks perfect English. Unfortunately, he is mistaken."

Edoardo shook Charlie's hand and said, "Poor Alessandro. He has problem in head. Very serious. So sad."

Charlie nodded as though it all made perfect sense. "There are a few more head cases up at the villa. We could sure use your help with them."

As they walked the gravel drive, Alessandro took time to study the American. Charlie had a bruise forming where his jaw met his neck. A thin line of blood ran from his left wrist to the sleeve. Alessandro could not tell whether the blood belonged to Charlie. The man held himself slightly curved as he walked, leading Alessandro to wonder if he might have cracked a rib. Edoardo noticed the wounds also, as well as the man's silent disregard for his state. He caught Alessandro's eye and nodded once. Charlie Hazard was his kind of man.

They entered the villa together and stopped in the front portico. Gabriella stood there frowning at Edoardo. "Who is this?"

"Alessandro's friend."

"He is police?"

Edoardo stated, "Guardia di Finanza, signora."

She crossed her arms. "Is this a good idea, Charlie?"

Alessandro watched how the warrior gave her room. A strong man acknowledging the lead of an equally strong woman.

Charlie said, "It's your call. But I say yes."

Edoardo did not seem to be the least bit fazed by the exchange. He crossed to the staircase, where divots had been torn from the railing. The villa's air still stank from cordite. "Interesting."

Alessandro suggested, "Perhaps this lovely villa was once attacked in the last war."

Edoardo flicked away a bit of raw wood. "No, this is much older than that. I think many centuries."

Gabriella asked Charlie, "You trust him?"

"I trust Alessandro."

"And I, signora, trust Edoardo with my life."

Gabriella stepped aside.

Charlie pointed at the ground-floor corridor. "This way."

Edoardo offered Gabriella a courtly bow and followed Charlie down the stone stairs.

The locker they had taken from the Evidence chambers was set on the first room's bed. Charlie lifted one of the guns. "This rifle got a little bent."

The stock was split in two. The lower segment was missing entirely, the upper hanging by a splinter. "What happened?"

"Bullet. Knocked it clean out of my hands. The missing stock whacked me in the chest. I didn't notice it at the time. My opponent was armed with a nerve gas canister and a silenced .45. I had a laptop."

Edoardo frowned. "Please. You shoot this man with a computer?"

"It doesn't concern us, Edoardo." Alessandro replaced the rifle and shut the case.

Charlie offered, "I'll pay for the gun."

"There is no charge. Officially, this locker has never left the vaults. In four years our gentleman comes up for parole. When he is released, he will discover that these items have been auctioned off and the proceeds given to the state. End of story."

Edoardo asked, "He is in so long for shooting animals?"

"And two game wardens. And a pair of activists who captured his work on film. Fortunately, the last of their little group managed to survive and bring their evidence back to Italy."

"Ah."

"This was not a nice man."

"Speaking of which . . ." Charlie led them out of the room and down the narrow hall. In the last chamber they found nine men and one woman stretched out on floor pallets. The room stank of gunfire and plaster. A line of chest-high holes was gouged from the walls.

Alessandro nudged the closest body. "They are alive?"

"Yes." Charlie pointed to five bulky packs leaning against the wall. "Their weapons."

Edoardo bent down and unzipped the first pack. He whistled softly. Gingerly he sifted through the contents and came up with a silver aerosol can. The nozzle was as long as a gun barrel. "This is what, please?"

"Nerve gas."

Edoardo dropped the can and zipped the bag.

Alessandro asked, "What did you use in the darts?"

"A mix of two drugs. One dose of GHB. It's a general anesthetic used by emergency rooms and day clinics for moderate to severe operations. The patients have a vague idea of what's going on, but they feel nothing and remain totally immobile. Motor function is nil. Very fast acting. Often used in date rapes."

"How long will they be like this?"

"Eight hours for the big guys. Probably ten for the woman."

"Can they hear us?"

"Doubtful. They're a little busy right now."

Edoardo asked, "This business, it comes from the other drug?"

Charlie nodded. "KeBrescone."

Alessandro said, "I believe I have heard of this."

"Animal tranquilizer. In humans it acts as a hallucinogenic. Never caught on as a party drug because it carries a high risk of very bad trips."

Edoardo laughed out loud.

"KeBrescone causes extreme but temporary psychosis. The effects normally come and go for several days. Memory is affected for much longer. Temporary amnesia often lasts for weeks."

Alessandro said, "We can't just leave them here."

"I have an idea," Charlie said.

When he finished explaining what he had in mind, Edoardo asked, "Your family, they are Italian?"

"I already asked him," Alessandro replied. "He claims not. I think perhaps Charlie is mistaken."

"This plan of yours," Edoardo said. "Machiavelli would be very pleased."

"I quite agree." Alessandro rubbed his hands together. "Very well. Let us begin."

57

The next day, Alessandro called and said that Charlie and Gabriella needed to take a drive with him. The villa remained a very subdued place, filled with shadows that no amount of cleaning and airing could fully erase. No one was sleeping well. Julio looked like he had aged ten years in the previous forty-eight hours. Even so, there was a quiet unity about their actions, a sense of the entire group having come together. Charlie was fairly certain they would all heal without lasting wounds.

Waiting for Alessandro to arrive, he and Irma visited the cave, only to discover that Benny had left in the night. She surveyed the neatly piled refuse and said, "He just took off without a word to anybody?"

"That's Benny's pattern. I'll go see him next time I'm in the States. Find some way to thank him."

Irma chewed the inside of her cheek. "I don't like not being able to make peace with the guy."

"Maybe you should come with me." Charlie heard a car roll up the drive. "I've got to go."

Irma settled onto a ledge by the cave's opening. "I think I'll stay here awhile."

When Charlie arrived in front of the villa, Alessandro inspected the welt that had darkened on his neck and said, "You did what you promised. You kept them all safe."

"It is what he does." Gabriella slipped her arm into his. "And because of Charlie's assistance, today we began ascending again. All of us."

"They are fortunate to have you, Charlie."

"Indeed we are," Gabriella said.

"Enough of this." Alessandro rubbed his hands together in anticipation. "Everybody, into the car."

As they drove away, he confessed, "I am terrible with surprises. You should see me at Christmas. My wife has to lock my presents in a vault. But today I am not receiving. I am giving. Which is even better."

They descended the hill and drove through Como and joined the highway north. They passed through Swiss customs at Chiasso and entered the system of tunnels and bridges leading to Lugano. Alessandro spoke of inconsequential matters, of the weather and a nice restaurant where they might stop for lunch and a phone call he had received that morning from his son the banker.

They continued past the city, taking a land bridge that traversed Lugano's main lake. Ahead of them, the Alps were crowned with late-season snow. The sky was burnished an impossible color.

When they exited the highway, Alessandro said, "All right, you two. Time to pretend you are excited over my big surprise."

Charlie said, "Excitement is in short supply. We're pretty exhausted."

"Nonsense. You are young. Who needs sleep?"

"I do," Gabriella said. "Years and years."

"You can sleep when you are my age."

Charlie asked, "Where are we?"

"Campione. The hotel and casino are straight ahead. A favorite watering hole for my enemies. Have you heard of this place?"

"Not that I recall."

"Its history is a distinctly Italian sort of tale. Once it was a principality, the smallest in the world, smaller even than Monaco. Back when borders were often redrawn by marriage, a bride's parents gave this tiny region away as a wedding present. Nowadays Campione is Italian on paper only. The police are Swiss, and so are most of the laws. Most, but not all. It is a muddle. My enemies love it for two reasons. First, there are no income taxes. And second, they are protected by the Swiss, who are very no-nonsense when it comes to such things as guns and violence. But they are also protected *from* the Swiss, so long as they do not break Swiss law."

Gabriella asked, "Why have you brought us here?"

"Ah. The lady is interested now. Perhaps she has guessed what my surprise might be." Alessandro turned onto a narrow lane that began climbing the steep hillside. The lane turned a very tight corner, then broadened as it passed between high stone walls. One wall followed another, each marked by a car entrance, a number, and then a smaller door for pedestrians.

Alessandro reached into the glove box and pulled out a padded envelope, which he handed to Charlie. "Open it, please. Tell me the number on the card again."

"Thirty-six."

"Excellent. Here we are. There should be a keypad in that envelope, yes? Hand it to me, please." He pointed it at the windshield and hit two buttons. In front of them, a steel gate rolled silently away, revealing a long flagstone drive.

Alessandro parked in front of a garage separated from the main house by a tiny Japanese garden and lily pond. They crossed a narrow stone bridge and entered an alpine paradise. The gardens were a profusion of flowers and butterflies. They rounded the corner to find the lake and the mountains on eternal display.

"The front door is operated by the same keypad as the main gate. You must key in the number of the house, thirty-six. Do so once for the main gate, and twice for the front door. All very high-tech, don't you agree?"

Gabriella did a slow sweep of the grand house, the gardens, the view. She slipped her arms around her middle, making herself smaller in the process. "Whose is this?"

"Did I not say? Yours, if you want it."

"I can't afford this."

Alessandro beamed as he slipped his hand into his pocket. Clearly the man had been waiting for those very words. "As a matter of fact, my dear, you most certainly can. Your ex-husband proved most amenable to my suggestion that he pay you what was promised in your prenup."

She accepted the papers, read, and grew smaller still.

"The villa belongs to the same gentleman whose rifles proved so useful. At least, I am fairly certain he is the owner. The title is actually held under a group whose name I believe translates as 'The Institute of Mysteries.' Which is most interesting, you see, because no such institute exists, not anywhere in the world. My associates have checked this out most carefully. So I have taken the liberty of having the courts issue you a license for that name."

Gabriella's hand was very shaky as she cleared her face. "What?"

"That is, if you want it. I personally found the title rather catchy. Especially given the nature of your work." Alessandro was clearly enjoying himself so much he almost sang the words. "Now then. By the power vested in me as senior bailiff of Como, which Campione officially belongs to, I am offering you the deed to this villa for a period of no less than four years. During that time, my successor will do his best to determine the villa's legal ownership. If it proves to be the man I suspect, the court has already ruled that all of his assets are the result of illegal operations and are to be auctioned off. But this may take some time. Years, I suspect. Which is why the justice system would be well served to offer you this tenancy. It is open-ended, which means you may continue to rent this place for as long as you wish. As official tenant you hold the right of first refusal if ever the villa comes up for auction. The rent is moderate for a place of this magnitude, but given my confidence that you would be an ideal tenant, I think the price is most adequate."

Charlie asked, "Your successor?"

"I have submitted my notice for retirement. To my wife's eternal relief."

Gabriella gripped Charlie's arm with the hand not wiping her face. She scanned the front of the villa, but he doubted she was able to see much of anything.

"The new Institute of Mysteries has five formal chambers and sixteen bedrooms. There is a guest house, a swimming pool, and servants' quarters behind the garage. All in all, I think it will prove a rather adequate location for your research." Alessandro pushed open the door. "Shall we go inside?"

58

Edgar Ross, former treasury chief and now director of one of America's largest banks, tried to tell himself that it was just another Hollywood lunch. And he might have succeeded, if everyone around him had not been quite so excited. Not even the jaded Hollywood crowd could hide their anticipation.

He was in Los Angeles to renegotiate his bank's revolving finance deal with one of the major studios. The line of credit was for six hundred million dollars. The deal was suitably complex. Every project had to be separately okayed. On the bank's side, Edgar was the only person who could sign off. The bank would finance a maximum of half the film's production cost. The bank's principal was paid back from the first generated revenue. Instead of interest on their loan, the bank received points in each film. So far, nine films they had financed had generated a profit. Five others had tanked. Even so, the bank's overall rate of return was twenty-one percent. The bank's executives liked to moan over the flops, but they loved this deal. The studio complained about the terms, but they wanted to up the ante to a billion and a half. The bank wanted to give them the money. The negotiations had taken three days and were like a very long and tiring dance between two partners who both lusted after each other yet pretended to be angry.

The studio had pulled out all the stops, parading both stars and clips of ongoing projects for Edgar Ross and his team. Even so, this particular lunch was totally out of the blue.

That morning, as they argued over the remaining two issues, the studio chief had made Edgar an offer. Finish the deal this morning, and they would set up lunch with Glenda Gleeson, who was starring in their next film.

Glenda Gleeson was not only one of Hollywood's biggest female draws. She *never* did promo work. It was one of her defining traits.

Edgar had been secretly in love with the woman for seven years, ever since he had watched her play a love-torn hooker in her breakout role.

Their trio of limos pulled up in front of The Ivy. The venue was another puzzler. Since it had been featured in two major films, stars avoided it like they would a lame script. The restaurant was a series of cramped, low-ceilinged rooms with varnished plank flooring. When it was full, the noise was deafening. Yet Glenda had only agreed to meet if the lunch took place in The Ivy's front room.

The Ivy, of course, had been fully booked. But what Glenda wanted, Glenda received, even if it meant crowding a table into an already cramped room.

The air was stifling. The waiters were forced to shuffle sideways and press against the seated patrons as they moved about. No one complained. Not after being told by the maître d' that they could either accept the situation and dine in the same room with the star, or move outdoors to the patio.

The noise inside the restaurant's front room was like an orchestra pit during a full tune-up.

Glenda was naturally late. Edgar sat with his back against the side wall and his belly jammed into the table. He watched as one of the studio execs shouted into his cell phone, trying to track down the absent star. Edgar watched the faces around his table begin to cloud over, and feared they had been stood up.

Then the world stopped turning.

Glenda did not merely enter the restaurant. She redefined the room.

Conversation halted because no one was listening, not even to themselves. The focus of each person was drawn completely to the woman who crossed the room.

Toward *him*. Smiling at *him*.

The studio chief shouldered the maître d' aside and insisted upon holding the back of Glenda's chair. Edgar knew he was gaping and did not care. Especially not after the star said to the studio chief, "Thank you, Jack. But if you don't mind, I'd prefer to sit next to our guest of honor."

Places at the table shifted with lightning speed. Glenda slipped into the chair next to Edgar. She pressed his hand with both of hers, looked deep into his eyes, and said, "I have been so looking forward to this."

"Have you really?"

"Oh yes. There's so much I want to talk with you about."

"Me? Really? I'm sorry. I didn't . . ." Edgar knew he was jabbering like a moonstruck teenager. But the woman's presence was simply too overpowering. He was vaguely conscious of someone ordering something for him to eat. He heard the room resume its cacophonous din. He knew the rest of the table was watching them and only pretending to talk among themselves. He did not care. He was glad the room was so loud. It meant he had the star all to himself.

Not only that, but in order for Glenda to make herself heard, she had to lean in close. So close, in fact, that her cheek brushed against his own. His chills were so intense he almost missed her saying, "I have a message for you from a friend of mine."

"What—uh, you do?"

"His name is Charlie Hazard. You don't know him." She leaned back and gave him another dose of those incredible eyes. "But he knows you, Edgar. He knows you very, very well."

"I-I'm sorry, I don't . . ."

"Let's try another name I'm *sure* you know. Weldon Hawkins."

Her words robbed the day of all color. "W-who?"

"Weldon has been trying to attack Charlie and some friends of his. And you helped them." She tapped the back of his hand with one fingernail. "You bad, bad boy."

His heart was hammering so loudly he could no longer hear the restaurant's din. "That is not—"

"I have a packet of information Charlie and his team have pulled together. Some truly amazing secrets. They've detailed several projects backed by you and your bank. Things I seriously doubt you would like the government to hear about. I couldn't help but have a look. I think you'll be impressed with Charlie's discoveries." Her face crinkled with pleasure. "In fact, I'm sure you will."

He watched the star pull an envelope from her purse, reach forward, and slip it into his jacket pocket. The entire table saw her pat the place, but only he could hear her say, "Here's the deal, Edgar. You make all the charges against Charlie Hazard go away. Permanently. You ensure the Combine never comes close to Charlie and his friends again. And don't bother telling me you don't know about the Combine, because we both know you're lying, and it's not nice to lie to a lady. You're going to do this, Edgar, because if you don't, the information in that packet is going straight to the attorney general and the IRS. And once they've seen what I've seen, I'm sure they'll be delighted to send you away for a long, long time."

Glenda turned and smiled for the room as only a star could. "Isn't this *fun*?"

⟨⎪⟩

Colonel Donovan Field was limping badly by the time he reached the reinforced gates. He knew it looked bad, this sweaty old man hobbling around the curve and climbing the empty drive. The guard behind the closed gates watched his approach from behind mirrored shades. Normally Donovan hated anything that drew attention to his old wounds. He had continued physical therapy for six months after the VA stopped paying, until he could balance himself so well no casual observer would ever have reason to ask about the absent toes. He never wanted to talk about the explosion or his injury. But the rental car's GPS had told him to park three blocks downhill. And Donovan was too stubborn to walk back and drive up and start over. Besides which, it was a beautiful day. Fantastic view. And the purpose of his visit filled him with an immense sense of anticipation. He was having too good a time to worry about a little pain.

The security guard was dressed in a typical blue jacket and black trousers. He remained as silent and immobile as an MP on parade.

Donovan stopped before the gates and said, "I'm here to see Weldon Hawkins."

"Sorry, sir. There's nobody here by that name."

"He will want to see me."

"Sir, I suggest you continue with your walk."

"Ask me my name, soldier."

"Sir, I'm not a soldier and—"

"I am Colonel Donovan Field. My walk will take me from here to the *San Diego Union*, where I will bend the ear of an old friend who now is the newspaper's senior editor. Tell that to Weldon." He opened his jacket to show he was not armed, then slipped two fingers into his pocket and drew out an unsealed envelope. "Then give him this."

The guard kept his hands by his sides. "Sir, I can't accept anything from you. Especially for a man who isn't here. Please go."

"There are two pages in this envelope. One contains a list of all the Combine members. The other describes how its Delta teams kidnapped the president of Kurdistan's middle son, laid the blame on terrorists, then went back in and rescued him, so that Harbor Petroleum would gain a monopoly on drilling rights to the country's largest fields."

372

"Sir, the drive where you are standing is private property. If you won't go I will be forced to call the police and have you removed."

"No problem." Donovan tossed the envelope through the bars, then turned and limped down the road.

He returned to his car, opened all the windows, and sat while the breeze off the Pacific cooled him down. He wondered if they were going to call his bluff, which he decided was both good and not good. Donovan had a military officer's distrust of the press. But a somewhat unpleasant lever was certainly better than none at all.

Donovan turned on the car and began the laborious process of coding the newspaper's address into the GPS. He did not own one himself and had only used the gizmos a couple of times. He was so intent on his work that he jerked when a fist rapped sharply upon his car roof.

He glanced up. "Is there such a thing as a simple route to downtown?"

The stubby man shifted so as to block out the sun. "You know who I am?"

"Weldon Hawkins."

"Are you wearing a wire?"

"Absolutely not."

He pointed at the black SUV now parked behind Donovan's rental. "Turn your car around and follow us."

The SUV drove past the house, almost to the summit, and halted before a narrow city park. Eucalyptus trees whispered a greeting and spiced the air.

Donovan walked over to the shaded table where Weldon waited and allowed one guard to pat him down, then another to wave a wand around his body. The second guard declared, "He's clean."

Weldon waited until the guards had moved away, then said, "I assume you've got an offer for me."

"What were you, CIA? DOD intel?"

Weldon merely checked his watch.

"When Charlie first told me about this project of his, I doubted his sanity. Then I saw your men hit his house and I knew at least part of it was real. But I never thought they'd really be able to observe the future and the past. Our little meeting here today has to do with that second bit, by the way. Moving backward."

"You're not making sense," Weldon snapped. "And I'm still waiting for your offer."

"You don't get it, do you. There is no deal. They've gone back and observed the Combine's last gathering, Hawkins. They read each of the files your woman laid out around the pool. They have the details of all your filthy habits. *All* the details." Donovan folded his arms. "So now *you* tell *me* what the deal is going to be."

Weldon fumed for a time, then demanded, "What happened to my team? And *where is Reese Clawson?*"

Donovan checked his own watch. "I'm still waiting."

59

She came awake in gradual stages. She had to struggle to open her eyes, which felt as though they had been glued shut. She blinked hard. But her vision refused to clear.

She vaguely recalled a series of bad dreams. Worse than bad. Catastrophic.

Her entire body hurt, like she had laid in the same position for so long her every muscle had locked solid. She realized she was curled into a fetal position, her arms wrapped around her legs.

Straightening proved as hard as opening her eyes. Harder. As she tried to raise up, she discovered that she was tied to the bed.

"Ah, signora, *finalmente*. You are awake. And not screaming. Wonderful."

She dragged a hand over her face, trying to clear her eyes. Her mouth felt gummed shut. Everything hurt.

She had no idea where she was.

"Can you speak Italian? No, we thought not. All your screams were in English. Wait, signora. You wish to rise? Here, let me help you."

A figure hovered over her bed. Hands reached over and untied the belt. "The restraints are there only because we were so worried, you see. You wanted to run away and you could not see. You cried of attack dogs and so many other awful things. I hope this is over now. You frightened me so much."

Rising to her feet proved extremely painful. Agony. But there was a good flavor to the pain, as though it meant she had finally returned from wherever she had been. Her feet touched the cold floor and she jerked them back. Where were her shoes?

"Ah, yes, the floor, it is freezing, no? And this is August. You wait until you touch the floor in January. Then you will know cold. Here are slippers. Wait, I will help you."

Her thirst was a raging force. Her throat and mouth burned with the need for water. She gripped the woman she could not actually see and pushed herself upright. Suddenly it was as important for her to stand as it was to drink.

The woman both supported and guided her. They passed through a door that groaned as it opened. They entered a hall. She saw figures silhouetted against sunlight coming through a window at the hall's far end.

Then she saw the cart. It was parked against the wall. She recognized the form on its top tray as a water pitcher. She whimpered and reached with a hand that to her fractured vision resembled a claw.

"You are thirsty, yes? Of course, signora. Here. Lean against the wall. Good. All right. Here, take this cup. No, signora. Slowly. Drink slowly. More? Of course. Wait. Here you are."

She drank three cups, drenching the front of her clothes with the liquid that she could not take in fast enough. Her throat felt swollen and raw. The woman had said she had been screaming.

"Please, signora. The nurses, they do not speak English. This is why I was placed in your room. So that I could ask, who are you?"

She held out the cup. The woman refilled it. She wanted to shape the word *nurse*. But when she tried to speak, the only sound that emerged was a tight little whine.

"Your name, signora. It is important, you see. Because you cannot be committed unless they know who you are. It is the law. But the police, they keep coming by, asking questions the doctors and the nurses cannot answer. When they found you, you had nothing with you. No identification, no money. Nothing. And you were screaming. So they brought you here."

The woman's words were a confusing jumble. They pressed at her. She felt panic rise up inside.

She did not know her own name.

She wet her fingers in the cup and wiped her eyes. Again. Gradually her vision cleared.

The woman standing before her was a hag. Her grey hair was in wild disarray, wreathing a shattered stick figure with red-rimmed eyes. The woman wore a tattered bathrobe over a stained nightdress and ancient slippers.

She looked down at herself. She was dressed in a similar nightdress, stained even worse than the woman's.

A figure shuffled past her. A young woman. Her gaze was utterly vacant. Her hands twisted in a manic dance before her face.

She looked farther down the hall. Other women limped and writhed and moaned and sang.

The window at the corridor's end was tall, the glass frosted. The sunlight turned the bars into dark shadows.

She opened her mouth and screamed as loud as her damaged throat allowed.

THE STORY CONTINUES IN

TRIAL RUN

1

When Hal Drew turned off the Pacific Coast Highway, his wife took that as the moment she'd been waiting for and reached for the real estate brochures. Again. Hal told her, "Don't get those out. It's too dark to read."

"I'll just turn on the inside light."

"Leave it off. I don't know these roads and I need to see what's going on."

Mavis Drew watched Santa Barbara slip away, the brochures clutched in her lap. "Tell me which development you liked best."

Hal waited until he was headed east out of town to say, "Remind me which one had that view of the ocean."

"Oh, you."

"It's a fair enough question." He pointed to the top brochure. "The Pacific is right there on the cover."

"So they dressed things up a little." She lifted one he didn't need to see. Again. "This is my favorite."

Mavis had begged him to make this trip. Just visit Solvang for a look-see. She'd been going on for months about how these California housing developments were going bust. She claimed they could get a steal on a home and live her dream of retiring near the ocean. Which was why they'd taken this miserable excuse for a highway from Solvang to Santa Barbara. So Mavis could have a look at the Pacific. Soon as they drove along the harbor and saw all the pretty sailboats bobbing in the blue Pacific waters, Hal knew he'd lost his wife to the California myth.

He said, "I'm thinking we're better off staying in Phoenix."

"Why does that not surprise me."

"Who do we know in California? Not a soul. It's just six hundred miles farther from the kids."

"Hal, both our children live in *Georgia*. There are *airports* in Santa Barbara. We fly to see the children now, what difference does it make?" She stared out her side window, seeing a lot more than the dark night ahead. "I loved that townhouse with the lake and the view."

"We got lakes out by where we live now."

"And the mountains. You said they were nice."

"We got mountains too." When she did not respond, Hal added, "I've put down roots. I like where we live, Mavis."

"And I'm ready for a change."

Hal drove in silence and fumed. The road heading inland was in wretched shape. Get away from the money and the robbers that lined the coast, and California treated their own state like an afterthought. The pockmarked highway stretched out before them, veined like a cadaver. Beside him, Mavis gave a dreamy sigh. Hal thought of the arguments to come and sighed as well.

Then it happened.

Mavis screamed so loud he slammed on the brakes before he even knew the reason. A souped-up Japanese car appeared out of nowhere, no lights at all. Hal almost took a bite out of the trunk. The shadowy car crawled along at something like twenty miles an hour, utterly dark.

Hal turned into the oncoming lane and hit the gas. The road ahead was black. Hal felt like he drove through an empty tunnel. The night just sealed them in.

As he started to overtake, his wife screamed a second time. Why, Hal had no idea. But he felt it too. A weird sensation, like the dark had grown claws that scraped the skin off his spine.

Hal slammed on his brakes again and pulled back behind the night crawler. He turned to his wife and started to ask her why she was making all the noise and freaking him out.

When it happened a *second* time.

A shadow roared past them. It had to be a car. No missile could fly that low. This second car was doing 120, maybe more.

And no lights.

The car ahead of them roared to life. It pulled a smoking wheelie and accelerated to warp speed and roared off after the other car. Still with no lights.

Hal stopped and pulled over to the side of the road. He needed a couple of minutes to pry his shaking foot from the brake pedal. And a while longer to stop his heart from stuttering over how they'd just been handed a tomorrow. Because his wife had screamed at an empty night.

When it happened a *third* time.

Two SUVs and a van roared past. Their lights were off as well. All three looked painted in shadows. Hal's headlights revealed that all the passengers wore night-vision goggles.

Then they were gone. And the night was empty. Black. Silent.

Hal turned to his wife and said, "I'd rather retire on Mars."

The woman who led the operation was seated in the first SUV's passenger seat. She knew the men had expected her to take the safer middle car. The lead vehicle was always the one to catch the worst incoming fire. Particularly in a situation like this, flying down the highway in the dead of night with the lights off. The agents from the local FBI office probably thought she was riding in the most vulnerable position to show she was as tough as any of them. They were wrong. The woman would have to care what they thought to make such a move.

She spoke for the first time since they had started off. "Are the police in place?"

The guy seated behind her said they were.

"They know what to do?"

"We've gone over it with them in detail."

"For your sake, I hope they follow orders," the woman said. "Call it in."

The driver picked up the radio on the seat between them and said, "The ops is a go. Repeat, go."

The woman said, "Light us up. Keep the siren off. I want to hear myself think."

They stripped off their night goggles as the driver turned on the headlights, then set the bubble on the dash and hit the switch.

The man in the rear seat said, "Sooo, they have a name for this midnight madness?"

The woman replied, "The car running hot is called tricking. The setup car is trolling. They trade back and forth."

The guy in the rear seat said, "Redline down an empty highway looking for death—this is a game?"

The driver said, "I guess if I had enough drugs in my system I wouldn't care either."

The woman said, "They do it straight. That's part of the deal. Straight or not at all. It amps the fear factor."

The guy behind her asked, "How did you find out about this anyway?"

The driver agreed. "I've been stationed out here for nineteen months, and this tricking hasn't ever surfaced on my radar."

"Radar," the woman said. "Cute."

"Is that your answer?"

The woman pointed ahead. "Here we go."

The road ahead was suddenly illuminated by police cars flipping on headlights, spotlights, flashing top lights. The two racing cars spun about, only to find the trio of followers had stretched out, running in flanking position, blocking the entire highway.

For once, the local police did exactly as ordered. The officers stepped forward, guns drawn, but they held their fire.

There were two kids in each car. Three guys, one girl. Aged nineteen to twenty-three. They were cuffed and searched and crammed into the unmarked van. The kids watched through the van's open door as two agents got into their tricked-out cars and drove away.

The woman opened the van's passenger door, then turned and said, "Thank you, gentlemen. That will be all."

"That's it?" The senior agent exchanged astonished glances with his men. "What happens to the culprits?"

"Your commanding officer did not find it necessary to ask any questions when he received the call from Washington," the woman said. "I suggest you do the same."

The agents and the police watched the van drive west, into the night-draped hills.

The unmarked van drove to a blank-faced building in the industrial zone east of the Santa Barbara airport. The building was rimmed by fencing designed to look like a sculpted garden of metal staves. The fence's razor tips were blackened to mask them from curious eyes. The infrared cameras and ground sensors and electronic attack systems were carefully hidden. The building's windows were a façade. Behind them were walls of steel sheeting.

The van's driver coded them through the unmanned entry and pulled up to the loading zone. Three security men came out. They brought the kids inside.

The kids were photographed and fingerprinted and led to individual rooms. Actually, one was led and the other three were dragged screaming and fighting. It made no difference. They were sealed into rooms fashioned like an officers' barracks, tight spaces with narrow foam mattresses and a six-by-six shower room and a small fold-down desk and a three-legged stool. The door was plastic-covered steel and had a little ledge at eye level. Two hours after they arrived, the slit was opened and a tray was passed through with food. Otherwise the kids were left alone. No one spoke to them. There was nothing to read. There was no television. There was no sound except what they made themselves.

The woman let them cook overnight. She would have preferred to make it longer, but she was in a hurry. Outside events were bearing down.

Besides which, in her tradecraft these kids were classed as disposables.

The kids were brought into another featureless room, this one with a conference table. The woman took fractional pleasure in how they moved as they were told and seated themselves where directed. She took her time and inspected them carefully.

The girl was dark haired and beautiful in the manner of a crushed rose. She exuded the scent of undiluted sex. The woman seated on the table's other side did not need to check her file to know the girl's name was Consuela Inez.

The girl said, "I want a phone call and a lawyer."

The woman took her time inspecting the three guys. Two of them aped how the girl slouched in her seat. The pair did not actually look at her, but still they mimicked her motions and her attitude. The exception was Eli Sekei, aged nineteen. He was tattooed like the others, same spiked hair, same piercings. Same sheet of juvie offenses. But he remained very alert, very self-contained.

"Hey." The girl thumped the underside of the table with her shoe. "I'm talking here. I know my rights."

The man standing in the corner of the room started to reach forward, intending to grip the girl and straighten her. The woman said, "Let it go, Jeff."

The man resumed his position. The girl swiveled her chair. "Yeah, Jeff. Back off." She faced the woman. "About that phone call."

The woman said, "Officially you no longer exist. Your cars have been wrecked and burned to a crisp. Your families have been notified of your deaths. The newspapers carried photographs. You are gone. If you don't do exactly what we say, we will make that happen. Take a good look at me, and see if you believe I mean what I say."

It was all a lie, of course. But by the time they discovered she was not telling the truth, the outside world would have lost its hold. Either that, or they would not ever have a chance to make the discovery.

The woman knew how she appeared to them. She had been beautiful once. But now she looked blasted by some furnace, melting her down to an ultra-hard core. She spoke with a rough burr that might have been sexy on someone else. On her, it was like listening to distilled hate, or purpose, or an intent that turned her eyes into pale lasers. She gave them thirty seconds, then said, "Now sit up straight and pay attention."

The two older boys were born followers. In the time it took for them to settle properly into their chairs, they had switched their allegiance from the girl to her. The woman had no idea whether this was good or bad. She made a mental note. Over time, if her project proved successful, such items might prove vital in making future selections.

She turned her attention to the girl. "This is your last and final warning."

The girl scowled and cursed but obeyed.

When the woman turned back, she saw that Eli Sekei was smiling. She resisted the temptation to smile back. She hoped he was the one she was looking for.

"My name is Reese Clawson. I need two people who are utterly without fear. Only two. Two people who are willing to explore the impossible. Two people who have nothing to lose. People who will be utterly mine. In return, I'll give you anything you want. Money, travel, sex on command. But no drugs. That's the key. Anything else, name it, and it's yours."

The girl gave her a sullen look. "So how about my freedom?"

"No problem."

Eli spoke for the first time. "After all this, you'll just let us go?"

"If you make the cut, absolutely."

"So what keeps me from going home and blowing your cover?"

"Forget that, man," the girl said. "What happens if we don't make the cut, that's what I want to know."

Reese kept her gaze on the kid seated directly across from her. "Eli Sekei, what kind of name is that, Persian?"

"Turkish."

Reese knew that already. She just wanted to know if he would respond in a decent manner. "Well, Eli. The answer is, if you were so happy being home, you wouldn't be spending your nights out tricking on the Chino highway. But that was then and this is now. What I have is so amazing, you'll never let go or do anything that would risk your chance to do it again." She hesitated, then added, "That is, assuming you survive."

It might have been just the two of them in the room. "How about slipping a television in my room? Nintendo, something. I'm going nuts in there, staring at the walls."

"Sure, Eli. I can arrange that." Reese stood and motioned to the two men standing guard. "But after next week, I doubt you'll be much interested. Not ever again."

Thomas Locke is a pseudonym for Davis Bunn, the award-winning novelist whose work has been published in twenty-five languages. He has sales in excess of seven million copies and has appeared on numerous national bestseller lists. His titles have been main or featured selections for every major US book club.

Davis serves as Writer-in-Residence at Regent's Park College, Oxford University, and has served as lecturer in Oxford's new creative writing program. In 2011 his novel *Lion of Babylon* was named a Best Book of the Year by *Library Journal*. The sequel, *Rare Earth*, won Davis his fourth Christy Award for excellence in fiction in 2013. In 2014 he was granted the Lifetime Achievement Award by the Christy board of judges.

A film based upon *Emissary*, the first novel in the Legends of the Realm series, is now in development.

Don't miss a moment
in the explosive

FAULT LINES
series!

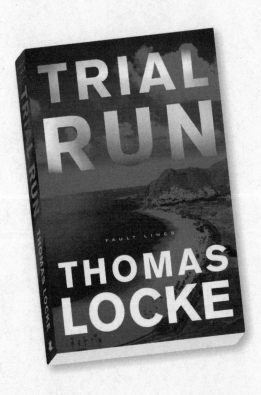

In the clash of science, government, and big business,
one thing remains clear: **what you don't know can kill you.**

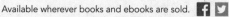

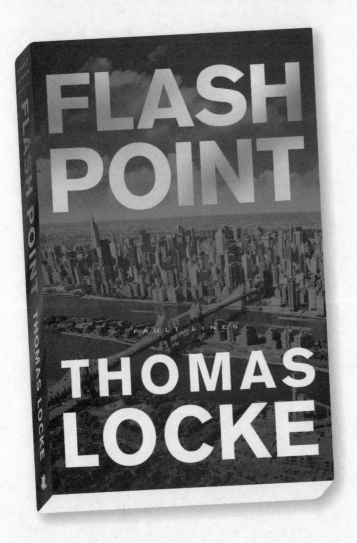